Siren Song

♪♪♪♪♪♪♪♪♪♪♪

Har Megiddo 2.0

© Ian T King 2017

Copyright © 2017 Ian T King

All rights reserved

ISBN 13: 978-1546947424
ISBN 10: 1546947426
Library of Congress Control Number:
CreateSpace Independent Publishing Platform
North Charleston, South Carolina

Acknowledgments

This work was conceived and written while the author was in the MFA in Creative Writing program at the Queens University of Charlotte, NC. The novel's final outcome was much improved by the many suggestions and criticisms that were offered by faculty and fellow students. Especial thanks are owed, in particular, to Pinckney Benedict, Naeem Murr, Jonathan Dee, and David Payne.

As always, I am indebted to Cindy Thornton, my wife of thirty-three years, for her undying love and support; and to my mother, Joyce Kuhn, who still believes, contrary to all objective evidence, that I am something truly special.

stulti sunt innumerabiles
--fools are without number

res sunt humanæ flebile ludibrium
--human affairs are a jest to be wept over

quæ te dementia cepit?
--what madness has seized you?

The people portrayed in this work are fictional. Any resemblance to persons living or dead is purely coincidental.

1

"All Quiet on the Western Front, my Captain!" Private Dixon guffawed as usual, and grinning like the inane idiot that he was.

He wished Dixon had never seen *Dead Poet's Society*, nor heard of the title of Remarque's book (unread by the unread dupe, he was sure; there was doubt he'd even read their Manual!). But, unfortunately, Dixon had seen the movie and had latched onto the title now become irritating mantra coming out of his stupid mouth.

Was it really necessary to have to listen to the dolt's irritating banter even on Christmas Day? It was bad enough to be on duty and away from his precious family — was it too much to ask for some peace and quiet for once, in compensation?

"Silent as a graveyard," Dixon prattled on. "*Hello?*" he called out. "Anybody *there?*" His voice echoed back and forth in the acoustical chamber that was the interior of the dome of the US Capitol building in Washington DC. He grinned again, like a little kid pulling off a cool practical joke. "Guess not," he concluded, when the echoing finally faded away.

"Cut the crap, Dixon, will you? How many times—"

An enormous explosion and an avalanche of falling masonry abruptly ended their conversation. The two members of the Capitol Police Force, along with four of their colleagues, died immediately on devastating impact, and before any of them had been able to consciously register what exactly had just happened.

But someone, indeed, had been there.

Or, rather, *something*. It, along with three others in close formation, had been approaching the policemen's location for several minutes, swooping undetected down the Mall on that quiet Christmas night—in that part of the city, at least. For those who might have witnessed the coming onslaught, it would have been impressive. Indeed, if they'd listened hard enough, put their imaginations to the test just a bit, before the first explosion they would surely have heard the *Ride of the Valkyries* playing in the background, the perfect orchestral accompaniment to what was about to take place.

When the Hollywood version of 12/25 comes out, I'll bet you that's how it'll be.

...

Arm in arm, like two young factory girls leaving work after their shift has ended, they were just having a good time: walking home and talking, joshing about their boyfriends, discussing women's stuff, a meandering potpourri of things like that—minding, in short, their own goddamn business.

It was dark, close to a blackout on the tree-shrouded gravel pathway. But then it seemed like someone had just thrown the circuit breaker for the universe, and everything, literally, had gone as black as coal, as if God, on second thoughts, had just declared "Let there be *no* light—*whatsoever*," and extinguishing all life as we know it in one omnipotent flick of the wrist.

Somehow, though, one got away, screaming for help.

But the other...well, she tried to scream too, but the more she tried the worse her asphyxiation became. Something smelled rank, a foul fishy stench mixed in with the fustiness of damp hessian. She struggled to take in air, her lungs heaving with the strained effort. She made the desperate gasping sounds of someone drowning, suffocating. She felt something cinch tight around her neck. She fell silent; her limbs gave way, their muscles deprived of oxygen.

She went...black.

Someone, in this case, had *definitely* been there.

...

You're not dreaming as such, you've drank too much hooch for that, but something fucking weird is going on in your sleeping brain, nonetheless. It's not the first time, that's for sure; it's actually become part of your lifestyle these days, such as it is.

You slowly sense something picking at you; you half-consciously fear the onset of withdrawal, or maybe some other new malady that's crept up on you in your spiraling descent into homelessness. Whatever, you already know it'll remain untreated—except for anything that an alcoholic pickling might do for it, that is. Or maybe, you smile to yourself in your semi-sleep, it's a pigeon searching for crumbs in your dirty facial hair—*Good luck with that!* you wish it, almost sincerely.

You feel something shake you from your slumber; something's run into the bench you're sleeping on, dislodging the torn-up cardboard sheets that are your only bedding, among the few items that you can make some anarchic claim to own. Something makes you struggle to your rickety feet and stumble forward at the oncoming figure—a distant memory of the war in Afghanistan, perhaps, or just whatever pure animal reflex you have left in you, now.

Yes, you have him! There's life in the old soldier yet.

But not much...

There's no pain at first, not even any notion that it may have happened. Just a spreading warmth in the chest coming over you, like you're shooting up and getting the first glow. It's almost pleasant against the cold of the late winter's day.

"Ahh," you softly exclaim, and the glow fades with the sudden onset of throbbing pain. You put your fingers to your chest and search for the spot. You feel your grubby shirt at first, but the sticky wetness soon becomes undeniable.

And then it hits you.

You've been...

But when you'd lain down, there'd been no one there at all — not a soul. No one ever came to the park in Russell Square on a day like that.

Never!

...

He wondered how he'd look when they found him; like the John the Savage guy in *Brave New World*, swinging like a compass needle, his feet pointing out in slow succession north, north-northeast, northeast, east-northeast, and then lazily back again? He wondered how they might react. Would they care, feel sorry? Or would they just say "Good riddance?"

Collateral damage.

How much more might there be? *Plenty* — no doubt about it.

He realized that he had become such small beer that he might not even qualify for that less-than-exalted categorization. Chances were he'd be lucky just to qualify for some sort of pauper's burial or, most likely, cremation, on second thoughts. Then he'd quickly return to the dust he'd come from, a mere speck again in the great marauding scheme of things they called human history, and that some — of his own kind — called *holy jihad*. After all had been said and done, after all the shit that had gone down, he'd done nothing more than come full pathetic circle: a nobody to a nobody — except for a brief moment in time when he'd been consequential enough to add his two cents' worth to the carnage.

But to what end?

Well, his own, that was going to be for sure. It was the least he could do, after all. Wasn't it?

But, he finally thought as he tied the sheet tightly around his neck, would it be enough?
...
When the first signs emerged, you didn't even recognize them for what they were. Surely, it was just the unusual food, the strange land with its unknown pathogens, something parasitical in the water.

Then, when your belly started to swell, you feared the worst, the absolute worst. It wasn't because you were putting on weight—at least that wasn't the *whole* story. It was someone else's growing poundage you were taking on board; an unwanted burden that meant there could then be no going home anymore, escaping from the hell you were in.

You decided that you just had to end it, somehow, despite the self-mutilation that would be necessary. But you failed. You hadn't known it then, right away, but the change in your body had triggered a transformation in your head. Virgin child had become expectant mother. The self-mutilation, you realized, would have been tantamount to murder, the suicide of the best part of you, your legacy, and a chance to do good in the world...after *everything* that had happened.

You delivered a trinity—if not quite holy, then hopeful.

And Hope did come—*deus ex machina*, a god in a helicopter.

But there was gunfire, a stand-off. Two opposing Horsemen of the Apocalypse armed with the Truth...and the power to impose it.

On those who embodied a purer truth, but they were aborted.

You were aborted, too.

In the final seconds, you remembered that Jesus died for us all. Perhaps your little ones did, too, *please God*.

You asked, like the Savior, why God had forsaken you.

But you heard…*nothing*.

…

"Off you go now, or you'll be late for school. Don't forget your lunch."

Mom considers the weather forecast: temperatures dropping like a rock by early afternoon. "You'll need your hat, scarf, and gloves, too," she instructs, a little more sternly than she intends to.

"Must I?" her young daughter whines, and sagging like she's just had all the stuffing taken out of her, like life with her mother is the absolute pits. Hearing no reprieve, she takes the said items from her mother's outstretched hands with the *appropriate* attitude, and stuffs them into her already bulging backpack. She struggles to hoist the pack onto her tiny frame, grunting with the effort. As she exits the house, she looks like she's carrying the whole world on her shoulders. It's almost funny, but not quite.

"'Bye now. Have a great day. Love you!"

"Love you, Mommy!" And she does. They both do, deeply, even if they don't always show it exactly.

Mom will wish she had, though, by later that day, when she'll be shivering by the playground and waiting anxiously, terrified, for someone to come and tell her…if she's one of them.

One of them he…

He'll not really know why he'll do it, despite the fact that he'll have been planning it in great detail for several weeks. He'll even have written a manifesto about his gripes with the world, the voices that are telling him what to do. Just minutes before setting out, his backpack packed to the gills like he's an elementary schoolkid too, he'll even post a chunk of his scribblings on Facebook. In a court of law, it'll look like he's of sound mind, capable of "malice aforethought." But he'll not be, not really; he lives half-in and half-out of the rational world we might presume we occupy most of our time, at least in our more lucid moments.

Either way, premeditative or not, the deed will be done; he'll be a nervous soldier or a programmed robot clearing out an occupied building, room by room. They'll never stand a chance. They'll fall like mown wheat, attired in bloodied hats and scarves and gloves, and excited about recess, despite the weather. Their mothers' love will not be enough to save them.

"I'm so sorry to have to tell you, but..."

Mom won't hear the rest; her knees will be already buckling, her mind instantly frenzied with utter despair. She won't be able to believe it, *it cannot be true*; just a few hours ago, everything had been perfectly fine, like it was supposed to be...just the slight concern about the weather, that's all...

A police officer will walk by. His arms will cradle three firearms and several clips of ammunition, all in plastic forensic bags. It'll be quite a stash. Even he won't have access to such as that, not even professionally.

But there you go, who needs God or jihad when the Second Amendment's on your side?

That's what Mom will wonder—for the rest of her wretched life.

Won't we all?

♠

[The Void, Star-Date: Alpha-Omega 6]

Quite a collection, isn't it?

A bit enigmatic, some of these snippets, I'll grant you, like they're random clippings from some sort of tabloid given over to a good dose of poetic license, or a shameless literary device to hopefully get you hooked right from the get-go. But there's more to them than meets the eye. Believe me, serendipitous as they may seem, they're really connected parts of a much greater puzzle. You'll see. In fact, you're right in the middle of it all!

...

It's hard to take it in my elevated position sometimes—well, truth be told, just about all the time, these days. I even wonder myself if the End of Days haven't snuck up on me somehow; perhaps I'm losing it a bit after all this time. Being the CEO of All Creation is a tough gig. My beard is long and it's a whole lot greyer than it used to be, that's for sure. Just like the American president's late second-term hair.

Enough about feeling sorry for myself, although there's more than enough spilt milk to drown me in by now. It's true what they say, the best laid plans of mice and … and all that. I had the mother of all plans once upon a time, but it's in ruins, shredded by the very beneficiaries it was meant to help. Who could have foreseen the consequences of "original sin"? It was only supposed to be a relatively minor part of the plan, to get you guys to accept some responsibility for your actions. It was never meant to get *so* out of control—honestly.

For the *love of God*, what happened? Spot the double entendre here? No? Well you should by the time we get through with this sorry tale.

Even if what you're about to learn wasn't true—the tragic consequences of the dumb hubris of those who march to war in my name—it'd still be hard to buy into even as science fiction or dystopian fantasy. But, then again, based on my omniscient experience, you'd probably believe just about any stupid thing, anyway. The old Yiddish proverb just about captures it all: *Man thinks, God laughs.* Well, it used to; it's only half right now. I did laugh a good deal the first few times around, but then it all just got too ridiculous for words. If I laugh any more these days, it's not often. Tears of laughter have morphed into those of genuine despair.

No doubt some of you might implore me to ask *WWJD*? Not sure even he'd know, the poor, wretched dupe. Would he tip over some tables this time, or turn the other cheek, love his jihadi neighbor as himself? The kid's surprised me over the years; thought he'd be a chip off the old block, but he turned out to be a socialist for the most part—a fact that seems to be entirely lost on most of you Jesus-loving, God-fearing types.

Anyway, where to start with this sorry tale? There's no beginning as such; things just sort of boot-strapped themselves into their pernicious existence, overriding my, apparently, less-than-absolute veto. But here's as good a place to start as any: a young woman in the basement of a derelict house, being held captive. A bit small beer, you think? Well, wait until you see what happens *next*, for Christ's sake...

Sorry, I'm getting ahead of myself. Take a deep breath, calm down...there, that's better.

She's writing in what's left of a child's tattered notebook she's found in the cellar, a sort of journal if you can imagine that. She doesn't know I can see her; no one does, even though some are hoping desperately that I can—it's almost an article of faith with them. She only has a few brief moments in which to undertake her task—the three times a day that they let her go to the toilet. She keeps her journal in a plastic zipper bag hidden in the cistern. They're so dumb that they never think of looking there.

But, then again, why would they? They're getting what they wanted—at least for a while.

2

[5 November 2016]

I don't even know for sure whether it's night or day down here, let alone what day it is. But I can hear what sounds like fireworks going off somewhere in the distance. I know it must be close to Guy Fawkes' Day, since they brought down me here last Saturday, October 29th. And I've been counting the breakfasts they've been bringing me since then—cereal every time, like they've profiled me, as opposed the rice-muck they deliver on all the other occasions—and I'm up to six already. I'm keeping a tally in this "journal" that they don't know about. It's the only thing that's keeping me fucking sane.

Last Saturday? What a night! Six days? Seems more like six goddamn years.

I'm in a windowless cellar, so I feel suspended almost, disoriented like I'm in a featureless goldfish bowl, a world without edges and horizons. I sleep a lot, fitfully mostly, but I don't know for how long at a time. No clocks down here. I've tried to catch a glimpse of their watches when they come, but no luck. More often than not they aren't wearing one anyway, and a good deal of the time they're down here with me they keep me blindfolded. But I do believe I'm still somewhere in Rotherham, the car ride here couldn't have taken more than forty minutes or so, at most. This cellar I'm tied up in, it's really filthy and falling apart. Looks like an abandoned house—a fairly recent foreclosure victim, no doubt. But there are thousands of them in town now, thanks to that old rat bag, Maggie Thatcher, so how will anyone find me? You all obviously must know I'm missing by now, but it'll be like looking for a needle in a fucking haystack! I don't suppose you've any clue where I am, not even Kathy Green. She got out of there so fast when it happened, and it was dark, really dark. As far as you all are concerned, I could be anywhere in the whole country by now, perhaps overseas, France or somewhere. I'm right here, right under your noses, but you can't see me. If you got close enough you'd smell me alright—just follow the curry trail and it'll lead you right to me. But why would you associate curry with me—you know I hate the stinking stuff!

Oh, god, how did this happen to me? To me! Please, God, let them find me!

Robbie, where are you?

Where were you that night? Why didn't you come?

No, I can't cry; I refuse to cry. Just one tear too many and I know I'll crack. If I start, I'll never stop. And that's just what they want. They may well take everything else from me, but they're not getting that!

Oh, Robbie...

...

I've got to get out of here!

I can hear them upstairs. Every move they make makes the floorboards creak; sometimes, when they're being particularly clumsy for some godforsaken reason, they manage to dislodge a pile of muck down on me. Some of it lands on my head—my hair's full of the fucking stuff! But no sign of getting a shower yet. I can't stand it! I've got to have a shower, even a small basin of cold water if that's all there is. And a brush, oh what I'd give for a brush. I can feel it now...gently massaging my scalp, sheening my hair...a golden wheat field, everyone used to say...but now, raking my fingers through it, all I feel are knotted strands, thick with dust and grit and grime and...who knows what other verminous stuff?

For God's sake, please let me wash my hair!!

I sometimes think about dousing my head with the cup of water they bring with my meals. I imagine it somehow self-combusting with a luscious lather of shampoo, draping my hair and head in a lava-flow of cleansing foam. But I know it is pure *fantasy. And I am so thirsty—I need every drop of the precious liquid to sustain me, moisten my cracked lips, soothe my sore throat.*

...

I've looked everywhere down here, every nook and cranny, but there's no way.

No windows, except for a small one in the wall to my right. For some ungodly reason, it's been painted over, it looks like, letting in absolutely no light whatsoever. But it's high up, beyond my reach, and there's nothing down here to stand on—not a goddamn thing. In any case, there's bars across it, and by the look of it, it could well be rusted shut, even if I could get to it. I did try throwing some bits of broken masonry at it, thinking if I could smash the glass I might be able yell loud enough that someone might hear me outside and get help. But my aim's worthless, and as you would have said, Robbie, I throw "like a girl." That was kind of cute once, but not right now. My shots kept weakly hitting the bars and bouncing harmlessly off, leaving the glass without even a fucking scratch on it. And as you might have guessed, they heard me before long. After slapping me around a bit and chewing me out, they nailed a piece of thick wood up there. So now, there's not even the illusion of daylight on the other side of it to give me hope that it might be an avenue of possible escape.

When the light's on, I keep eyeing the door at the top of the steps. I know it's locked—they make a big fucking production out of slamming the bolts on the other side into place and rattling the chain that they must have rigged up there, too. But it's weird; I just can't stop looking at that door. It's as if I believe that ultimately there's nothing they can do to stop it somehow fulfilling its purpose—to let me out, to let me go free. I know that it's pure fantasy, like Alice and her magic looking glass, but that's what pure desperation does, I suppose—makes you keep believing, yearning, hanging on. Until, I guess, the days go by and that door's still there—SHUT!

...

If only I could get a message out.

Every now and again, I adopt the lotus position I learned in my yoga class, and close my eyes and try to meditate. Well, not meditate so much, more like I try to send ESP messages to you, to anyone really, anyone who somehow can read my thoughts, my pleas, in the ether out there beyond these walls.

And sometimes, I'm sure I can hear someone, sense someone, trying to communicate back to me. There's a sort of radio static in the background and a crackly voice fading in and out. It sounds like they can't quite hear me. I keep hearing the same question: Are you here? I can't see you. Are you sure? And I insist yes, yes, I am sure. Look, look over here, I'm right here!

Perhaps I'm beginning to lose my mind already...
Oh, please, God, show me a way...please!

3

[17 May 2016]

Mo—Mohammed Khalid Hussain—shuffled along the rain-swept cobblestones, hooded head down fending off the relentless drenching as best he could.

Low steel-grey clouds blanketed the skies all the way to the horizon, shutting out whatever weak-willed warmth the wintry sun might have been able to provide had it been given the chance. Mo wondered whether the sun actually existed on the other side of such a suffocating cloud bank on days like this. But this was northern England—was it really in the same solar system as the rest of the planet? In any case, whatever light was struggling to get through the great grey shield had already passed its pallid peak several hours ago. The streetlights—what remained of them in working order, that is—were desperately trying to splutter into life announcing the arrival of yet another utterly fucking pointless evening in Rotherham, south Yorkshire. Mo squinted through the rain at the deserted street, the seventh he'd sloshed through aimlessly already that early evening. Everyone in town seemed to be indoors somewhere, warm and dry he presumed. Most were probably at a place they called home, and might well have meant it. But for him?

Home, such as it was, was no sanctuary whatsoever, no place in which to do much more than just sleep—if that's what you could call it, scrunched up in a tight fetal ball, fully clothed and under a pile of ratty blankets in order to try to fend off the numbing cold in his father's perpetually unheated and damp-ridden slum. Sleep? *Pfft!* He was usually thankful when the frail dawn came and he could get up, grab a chunk of stale bread for breakfast, and get the hell out of there before the old man roused himself with no other agenda in mind than to lecture his son about his ne'er-do-well ways. But he'd have little choice in just another few hours than to return to the very place he least wished to be, hoping to god that the old man was still down the pub, giving Mo a chance to escape the predictable, alcohol-fueled wrath of his father by feigning deep sleep when the old sot eventually stumbled in. More often than not, though, he'd rarely had such luck, his father nearly always beating him home first, such was Mo's desire to avoid almost at all costs going back to 99 Victoria Park Avenue, Rotherham.

Oh, the fucking sermonizing, the petty, mean-spirited accusations! Why wasn't he as smart as his friend, Saeed Karlal? Why didn't he get a job, any job—no matter how demeaning? Bagger at the supermarket? No way. Why didn't he buck himself up, and stop wearing his stupid hoodie? No wonder no employer would take him seriously. No wonder he had no girlfriends! Who was he trying to be, one of those gangsta-rapper niggers from America? Well, what was so bad about that? Look at those guys: street-cred by the bucket load! Fuck him, fuck the old man. What did he care what his pathetic father thought? What had he done that was so great?

Father? Since when?

Mo tried to remember his mother, her warm touch, her soothing words, but the cold rain washed them away before he could recapture their full flowering in his thoughts. He sneezed violently. He sensed a chill coming on—yet again. Another stick for his father to beat him with, no doubt. No paternal sympathy to be expected from that direction. His mother, on the other hand...

Behind him, Mo suddenly sensed the approach of a vehicle in the otherwise traffic-less street. The splattering of the rain gave way to the sound of puddles being disturbed by something weighty gliding through them. He suspected that the vehicle had probably been tailing him for some time—why else would it have been going *so* slow?—its measured approach muffled by the rain's fury. Brakes gently squeaked, and Mo felt his already sodden feet engulfed by a surge of dirty water washing up over the curb and onto the pavement. A voice from within the car, its passenger-side window wound down, gruffly accosted him.

"Going anywhere special, son?"

It was two policemen in their squad car, the one in the passenger seat looking at Mo with marked contempt, ready to give him the verbal once-over, Mo could just tell. Mo ignored the policeman's question, pretending he hadn't heard him because of the rain, coming down heavier now. He heard the car door slam behind him as he continued insolently on his way. He knew what was coming, but it still shocked him when it happened. An arm roughly wrapped itself around his throat and pulled him back in a destabilizing embrace; a hand grabbed his right arm and bent it painfully up behind his back. Mo choked, struggling for breath and wincing with pain.

"I asked you a question, you little stinking fuck!"

The police officer pushed Mo face-first against the wall of a derelict house.

"Spread 'em!" the officer commanded.

By now his colleague, the driver, had joined him. He was a hulking figure, obese almost, compared to his unusually skinny colleague.

"Frisk him, Charlie," Mo's captor said.

"Be my pleasure," a growling, almost lascivious, voice replied.

Mo heard knuckles crack in obvious anticipation of doing some real damage. He tensed from head to toe, expecting some of his bones to soon break or joints to painfully dislocate. He felt the hurt even before contact was made. He audibly whimpered, despite the pounding rain.

Two more hands, vise-like claws this time, roughly grabbed and pinched him, traversing Mo's body from top to bottom, but they found nothing untoward. Then they returned to his groin and squeezed his nuts as hard as they could, and not letting go as the driver put in his own two pennies' worth: "Want to keep these, you little fuck?" — Mo yelped in response—"Then you'd better be more respectful next time when an officer of the law asks you a polite question. Doesn't your fucking imam teach you good manners, or are they something your goddamn Mickey Mouse religion doesn't subscribe to? Or are you too busy thinking about *jee-hard*, or whatever you call it? Planning some big fucking deal, are we? *Phhhtt!*"

Mo was released and spun around again until he came face to face with a stiff, stubby forefinger jabbing into his forehead, its long nail drawing blood. Its movement synchronized with the driver's final admonition: "I-will-be-keep-ing-my-eye-out-for-you, got-it?" He shoved Mo one more time against the house wall as he finally let him go.

The policemen returned to their car and sped off, making sure to send one last surge of puddle water Mo's way. As they disappeared into the sheeting rain Mo flipped them the V-sign. "Fuck you! Pigs!" he yelled after them, although he knew they could neither hear nor see him by now. "Shit!" Mo gently touched his forehead and examined his fingers—a trace of crimson, but nothing too serious it looked like. The blood soon washed away in the rain, although it did nothing to dilute his humiliation. It took a good while longer, though, for the pain in his groin to dissipate, and he gritted his teeth as the debilitating discomfort slowly—*oh-so-slowly*—subsided. "Oh God," he finally gasped as he managed to get himself almost fully upright, capable of some form of hobbling motion.

"*Bastards!*" he cursed.

Mo stumbled off for home, staggering like a drunk, but less consumed now by the dread of encountering his inebriated father and suffering through yet another cold, lonely night in his room. Instead, his thoughts turned fleetingly to his imam, not the one at the local mosque with whom he rarely interacted, but the one he occasionally communed with in cyberspace at his friend Saeed's place. Jihad, he thought to himself, yeah, jihad, that's what we call it! And jihad's what those bastards are gonna get one of these days!

Suddenly the rain ceased and the scuttling clouds lifted and parted, just long enough to reveal a crescent moon hovering over a rain-soaked Rotherham. It reminded him of the birthmark on his left cheek that his long-dead mother had always insisted had been a truly momentous providential sign as to his inevitable future greatness, even though all the evidence that lay all around them and on into the first years of his life had all pointed in exactly the opposite direction.

"One of these days...," Mo said to the heavens, "one of these fucking days...*Inshallah*."

Mo felt his feet squish in his shoes as he set off again. They were well and truly soaked through. He wondered if there would be any hot water at home to bathe his feet in when he got there, but the house was in darkness when he arrived. His dad had spent all his change at the pub, and the meter had run out cutting off the electricity supply. Mo tried the bathroom tap. It ran warmish for a second or two, teasing him, but then it gushed like an icy mountain stream, coughing and spluttering and discharging clumps of who knew what into the sink. The plumbing shuddered and thumped as the flow suddenly came to a gear-grinding stop.

"Shit!" Mo hissed.

That night, he spent sleepless hours tormentted by the extra discomforts of frozen feet, a sore forehead, and a groin far too tender to withstand his habitual nightly bout of aggressive self-gratification.
What a night.

4

[May 2015]

John Buchanan "Jo-Buck" Brown waited patiently for the pews to empty, before being the last worshipper to exit the sanctuary of First Presbyterian church in his home town of New Haven, Nebraska. As he rose, he smoothed out his kilt and adjusted the hang of his sporran. It would most likely be a good while, he thought, before he would get to wear his beloved tartan again.

Outside, Minister McKinley had almost reached the end of the line of his departing congregation, thanking them for their kind words about his sermon and offering them his well-wishes for the upcoming week. Most of his flock didn't usually linger long after Sunday morning service, the rumblings in their stomachs that always seemed to punctuate the proceedings urging them on to brunch as soon as possible. But today, everyone was hanging back after their few seconds with the minister, coalescing into a small crowd and looking in the direction of the church door, as if they were expecting something unusual to happen there.

Jo-Buck stepped into the sunlight, and the applause started up as soon as they saw him.

"All hail the conquering hero!" a crusty male voice barked out, inflected heavily with a guttural Scottish brogue. It was Doc Haldane, ever the first to pronounce on high whenever there was an audience that might hear him. "Best o' luck ta ye, Jo-Buck Brown!" With that, he slapped Jo-Buck heartily on his back, almost sending him stumbling down the church steps.

The congregants pushed forward and soon enclosed the latest in a long line of New Havenites who'd done their patriotic duty by going off to war; in Jo-Buck's case to rid the world of the evil of radical Islamic terrorism, even if the president didn't quite like (or didn't have the guts) to put it so starkly that way. Everyone in New Haven, Nebraska, thought of themselves as straightforward types who liked to call a duck a duck if it quacked like one, and those Islamic State evil-doers were quacking loud and clear, even if it was with an Arabic accent. They hated to lose their boy—just last year he'd quarterbacked the town's high school football team to its second state championship in a row—but a patriotic call was a patriotic call, and there was nothing much higher than that. And now this morning, they'd included a special prayer for Jo-Buck in the service, giving that call, they confidently presumed, God's backing as well.

"Here, take this," the old widow Miss Brodie croaked. She pushed something into Jo-Buck's hand. "My Donny wore it throughout the War. Swore it saved his life." Jo-Buck opened his hand to reveal an old silver coin on a neck chain. "It's a 1918 half crown." She pointed with her trembling finger. "Look, there's old King George." There was a dent right in the middle of his forehead. "German sniper's bullet, Donny reckoned. A miracle." She closed Jo-Buck's fingers around the coin again, then looked up and smiled at him, although he was sure her eyes were watery with the memory of loss, and, no doubt, with the expectation of loss yet to come—after about eighty or so, it seemed, one kind of loss after another was about all you could ever hope for: teeth, looks, hair, memory, stamina…spouse, kin, friends, lovers …loved ones.

"Thank you, Miss Brodie," Jo-Buck said, hesitant to take such a treasured thing. "It's so very kind of you." But he immediately fastened the coin around his neck. A malformed monarch's profile nestled on the frilly adornment of his shirt front. He wasn't at all superstitious, but right then the idea that lightning—or a sniper's bullet—never struck the same place twice suddenly seemed like a piece of propitious folklore he might do well to invest in, especially where he was most likely going to find himself located in just a few months' time.

Miss Brodie looked at the half crown. She patted the back of Jo-Buck's hand. "Goodbye, dear," she said. "Come home safe." She shuffled off with the aid of her walker to her waiting car.

Jo-Buck felt something pull sharply on his jacket sleeve. He instinctively looked down. A cherubic face beamed at him. "Jo-Buck, Jo-Buck!" the young child insisted, clamoring for attention.

"Hey, Bobby!" Jo-Buck greeted his number one fan, crouching down to get eye-level with him. "What's all the fuss?"

"Do you have it done yet? You said you would before you left."

"Oh...well, let me see—"

"You promised!" Bobby complained, readily susceptible, as he always was, to instantly fearing betrayal at the merest playful drop of a hat. Such a short fuse seemed to run in his family, but, then again, they weren't Scottish, they were English.

Jo-Buck opened up his sporran and put his hand inside. Bobby watched him intently, as if he was trying to make sure that he wouldn't be misled somehow by a conjuror's sleight of hand. Jo-Buck was a star quarterback, after all; deceiving flicks of his wrist in order to fool his opponents were his stock-in-trade. Jo-Buck made a pretense of rummaging around inside the sporran. "Mmm," he murmured.

"But—"

"Ah, what's this?"

Bobby bounced on the balls of his feet, and clapped his hands. He let out a squeal of delight as Jo-Buck whipped out the promised prize from his sporran. Bobby snatched it out of Jo-Buck's hand before he'd even had a chance to see what it was.

"Careful—"

"Ouch!" Bobby looked at his finger; a pin-head of blood bubbled up at its tip. "Cool. A dagger!" He simulated a couple of stabs towards Jo-Buck's abdomen, but fell short of actually hitting his target.

"Hey! No," Jo-Buck cautioned, sucking his gut in. "It's not for playing with, Bobby—okay?" Bobby started to look around him, intently searching for something, all the while slashing away with the dagger. "It's a dirk, Bobby. It's just for show, that's *all*, like this." Jo-Buck displayed his own ceremonial dirk attached to his belt. "See?" he began to explain. "Look at the handle. See how pretty it is? Just for wearing, like a badge, okay?"

Bobby looked to where Jo-Buck was indicating. Then he looked at his gift, comparing the two. They were identical, except Bobby's had been shaped out of wood. "Did you *really* make this?" he asked, but he already knew the answer. Jo-Buck had a well-earned reputation as being the best whittler within at least a fifty-mile radius of New Haven.

"You betcha, I did," Jo-Buck confirmed.

Bobby gently fingered the exquisitely carved handle of his wooden dirk, the interweaving swirls of its classic Celtic design puzzling him mightily as to how it could possibly have been fashioned by mere human hands. "Wow," he breathed. *"Wow."*

Jo-Buck smiled. "Like it?" he asked. Bobby nodded. "Pretty, isn't it?" Jo-Buck continued. Bobby nodded again. It looked like the kid was getting the point at last. "So, it's just for show, all right?"

A fat bee buzzed them, tracing a figure-of-eight around their heads at great speed. They both ducked their heads, and waved their hands at it, trying to shoo it away. But the bee was persistent, perhaps provoked by their flailing arms. The figure-of-eights became tighter, closer; the bee's buzzing ratcheted up, like a sawmill going full bore.

"Aah!" Jo-Buck exclaimed. The bee was on his arm. It got him — once, twice. "Ow!" He staggered away a few paces, frantically trying to get the bee off him. He felt a slap. Bobby had just whacked him on his arm. The buzzing abruptly stopped. Calm was restored.

Jo-Buck looked at Bobby, but the boy had already turned away and was looking down at the ground between their feet. "There it is!" Bobby hissed.

The stunned insect lay on its back, just about equidistant between them. Its legs waved weakly in the air, more as a matter of impaired instinct rather than any serious attempt to gain effective traction. Before Jo-Buck could say or do anything, Bobby had pounced. He pinned the bee to the ground with a twig, and then in one clean, swift motion he decapitated it with his new prize. "Got you!" he triumphed. The bee's head stuck to the tip of his wooden dirk as he pulled it away from the execution site. He examined it closely for a second, then spat on it before casually flicking it away.

"Did it sting you?" Bobby inquired.

Jo-Buck didn't answer. He was too mesmerized by the sight of a small boy so suddenly emboldened to carry out an act of such summary justice by the mere possession of a wooden, toy dirk. He knew kids could be cruel—not many stones, indeed, he could have cast first, if invited—but the rapid, unexpected transformation in that moment caught him completely off-guard, like he was an innocent *naïf* all of a sudden. Bobby's eyes in that moment; that posture—the ape with that leg bone in its hand, canines bared: he looked just like it. He tried to remember if he'd ever done anything quite like that, like those boys in the Lord of the Flies, when he was Bobby's age...

"So what are you two gentlemen up to over here?" Minister McKinley interjected.

"Look!" Bobby demanded. "Jo-Buck gave it me. To keep."

"A dirk!" Minister McKinley exclaimed with exaggerated delight. "That's a fine, generous gift, Bobby. Have you thanked Jo-Buck for it, I wonder?"

Bobby's dereliction of duty flushed up his face, a rising tide of crimson. He turned to Jo-Buck. "Thank you," he said, sheepishly. He scampered off before any more admonishments might be forth-coming, for he surely knew from even his limited experience that whenever the minister was in earshot, irritating reprimands were soon going to follow, most directed at him.

Jo-Buck smiled. "You're welcome, Bobby," he said. How quickly the ape with a leg bone had become just an innocent little kid again.

"Ach," Minister McKinley growled, "that boy's headed for trouble, there's nae doubt it, none whatsoever, just you mark my words. He's got the curse of the Camerons alright!" He looked at Jo-Buck expectantly, as if he was waiting for confirmation of his prediction.

Jo-Buck just nodded his head, but noncommittally, neither up-and-down nor left-and-right. He looked like one of those stupid-looking, nodding dog figurines that people used to put on the ledge behind the back seats of their cars.

"So," Minister McKinley continued, palpably a wee bit peeved at Jo-Buck's lack of support, "this is it, eh? Tomorrow's the big day. What time do you set off?"

"Crack of dawn, sir. South Carolina's a long way."

"Parris Island! Are you ready for it?"

"Yes, sir, I believe I am."

"Yes, I'm sure you are, Jo-Buck. But it'll be a lot tougher than going a whole season without being sacked!"

"I know it. But I feel *called*, sir. After 9/11, I haven't been able to think of anything else but doing my duty. I have to go and do my bit. We've got to rid the world of their evil, once and for all."

Called. By God, the president, or Pat Tillman, Minister McKinley wondered? Most likely the latter, if he knew Jo-Buck as well as he thought he did. For the likes of Jo-Buck and his crowd, the notion of going from superstar footballer to military hero was too irresistible to resist. He'd wanted to ask Jo-Buck if he knew just how Tillman had died, by so-called "friendly fire," but he never had quite gotten around to it.

Minister McKinley remembered the time when he'd felt so overwhelmingly called with regard to joining the ministry. He'd been about the same age as Jo-Buck was then, and about as pathetically savvy as to what was really going on in his mind, with his hormones, with what was *really* at stake in life, and one's immature and mal-informed choices with reference to it. But, latterly, he'd begun to feel less called than stuck in a rut, compelled to soldier on by the path-dependent life choices he'd made in his innocent youth. "Indeed," he said, planning to weakly leave it at that. But this was Jo-Buck who was going off to war; he needed to say more. "God be with you, my son. The greatest marine of them all 'has your back,' you can be rest assured about that."

"Amen tae that!" a booming voice proclaimed. It was Doc Haldane, determined, it seemed, on having the last word before Jo-Buck set out on his crusade. "God speed John Buchanan Brown. And God bless America!" He grabbed Jo-Buck's hand and shook it wildly, like the great boastful showman he always was, trying to grab the center of attention even on Jo-Buck's last day among them.

"God bless America," Jo-Buck echoed, and with that he smartly about-turned and marched off, like he was full-fledged United States marine already setting out on his first combat mission.

"What a laddie!" Doc Haldane gushed. "He'll do us all proud, I know he will!" He started to hum the tune to *Onward Christian Soldiers*, his favorite hymn.

But he was hopelessly out of tune, especially on the higher notes, Minster McKinley realized. He wished the Doc would button it — for once. He didn't feel like singing at all, right then.

5   *[11 September 2016 CT (Christian Time)]*

Somewhere in Florida in the United States of America—I can't tell you where exactly; it's a national security secret, they claim (like I'm not on the "need to know" list)—I see two eyes concentrate on a pair of computer screens sitting side by side, and two steady hands—a right and a left, respectively—carefully manipulating a joystick and typing on a keyboard.

    One screen displays the image of a featureless rocky desert across which a convoy of three vehicles is making a speedy, bouncy transit; the other shows the view from above from several hundred feet or so. The fingers of the left hand dance briefly across the keyboard and a close-up of the vehicles materializes on the first screen—Toyota pickup trucks ("technicals" they're weirdly known as, for some god-known reason), mounted with heavy-caliber machine guns in their cargo beds. The trucks are partially hidden by the clouds of dusty sand thrown up in the trucks' swirling wakes. The right hand maneuvers the joystick carefully and the middle of the three vehicles zooms into ever closer view on the second screen, a winking white box bracketing it in its pixelated embrace. The truck bobs and weaves as it leapfrogs across the uneven desert floor, but it cannot escape the box's close, persistent, stalking attention.

The owner of the two hands (again, I know who he is, but...you know) smiles faintly in appreciation of his own skill and at the expectation of fulfilling his task. His thumb gently caresses the tip of the joystick. The thumb is itching with nervous anticipation, but resists the temptation to breach the strict discipline of a military drone operator. Patience, precision; patience, precision: he's waiting for exactly the right moment for maximum effect—a perfect kill, of everyone and everything, in this global war on terror.

He's almost...almost...ready—

But then he suddenly hisses: *What the...?*

The desert dust clears on the monitor's screen. The vehicles have found a partially paved road. On the second computer screen the bottom halves of dried-mud buildings flash past cartoon-like behind the vehicles, slowing down now.

Shit, he swears, unaware that I can hear him, even from here.

The keyboard clicks with activity again, and the picture on the first screen zooms out: the trucks are entering a village.

Fuck it!

I see a gaggle of children rush out now from a narrow alleyway leading to the road the trucks are on, excited, no doubt, to see Allah's brave fighters entering their midst. They jump and skip and chase in pursuit, waving their arms in the air and yelling "Allahu Akbar! Allahu Akbar!" mimicking the belief that the men in the trucks share and have taught them, that God's grace—apparently—comes out of the barrel of a gun. And there, but for the grace of God, they will no doubt go, too, someday—and much sooner than I'd like. An eye for an eye, et cetera, can only get you so far.

The trucks continue to slow down, and the view of them on the second computer screen becomes interrupted ever more frequently by buildings flashing by, as their density increases towards the village's center. The screaming boys catch up and run alongside the vehicles, melding with them into one large undifferentiated mass.

I see the drone operator checking his orders again, and speaking frantically into his headset, desperate for confirmation that he should still go ahead and execute his mission: to take out Abdal Ati, number two in Islamic State: *Highest Priority Target*.

I read his mind. He's thinking: *Nine-eleven, seven-seven; nine-eleven, seven-seven. Twin Towers burning. Onward, Christian Soldiers marching as to—*

He grimaces, his thumb squeezes, and the deed is done. "Mission Accomplished," as a former commander-in-chief once put it. (Whether it was or not, who the hell could know for sure? Was Abdal Ati *really* dead? Even if the missile was deadly accurate—and it was, as you'll soon learn—there's no telling about the so-called "intelligence." And how much intelligence do you need when you see what came next?)

The computer screens mushroom white, followed by a plume of grey turning black. The screens clear again after a few moments, but there are no signs of life anymore, just the mangled wreckage of scorched vehicles, and, a few yards to the left of them, a crude wooden nodding donkey on four wobbly wheels, miraculously—so they would all later claim—still intact and tethered by a piece of string to the severed hand of a child, my child, made in my image.

♠

"Collateral damage?" the news reporters ask the Chairman of the Joint Chiefs at his press briefing just a few hours later.

"Unfortunately, yes," he matter-of-factly says with superb military equipoise.

"*Al Jazeera* reports young children involved. Is that correct?"

"Not to my knowledge, but we're still doing post-mission analysis," the Chairman claims, his crisp uniform, his row upon row of medal ribbons, and his gold braid all meant—presumably—to signal his authority as an unalloyed truth-teller. It's obvious that his golden lie dazzles the reporters, at least for the moment—after all, he is a Guardian of the Peace, someone whose job it is to allow America's little children to sleep soundly in their cribs at night. He turns to leave: "Now, if you'll please excuse me…"

"Mr. Chairman!" the rookie reporter from CNN shouts out. He's clearly yet another wannabe Wolf Blitzer in sheep's clothing, chasing the celebrity status I might let him have for his Warholian fifteen minutes, if he's lucky. "Do you have any comment about General Gordon's alleged affair with the wife of…" But the Chairman is gone before he can reveal the starlet's name, although everyone there knows it anyway, including, of course, yours truly.

I sense the Chairman is wondering how on earth he'll ever put this scandal to rest. It's annoying the shit out of him, I can tell you. That, and the sure knowledge that when he gets hauled up in front of his next congressional committee, some smart-ass politician is going to ask pointedly "Was al-Adrum in a declared war zone, General?" And that when he necessarily dissembles in response, hemming and hawing about the semantics of "war," "conflict," and "zone," the suspicion that perhaps a "crime against humanity" has been committed will foul the air for weeks to come, mightily disrupting his sleep patterns. He's going to fulminate (at least in private) "How the fuck do they think we're supposed going to get the terrorists with one arm tied behind our backs?"

To which I can only add: "Good point. Must be a bummer."

♠

At the very moment the Chairman of the Joint Chiefs is briefing the press, I see the bereaved parents of al-Adrum bury their sons—or what remains of them after the Hellfire missile had obliterated them. It's quite a scene.

There's a swarming crowd, the women ululating and the men carrying the coffined body parts of their dismembered children high above their heads. The men transport the coffins forward, hand over hand from person to person as if they are a human conveyor belt or an upside down millipede, itself on the move and doing some sort of weird, dry land, backstroke. The coffins seesaw from side to side, threatening to discharge their loads at any moment, but they don't. At the edge of the village, the throng stops by the side of several open pits, freshly dug as if a planting for the spring is about to take place. But only loss—and, perhaps, the seeds of revenge—are being interned there.

One by one, the crude wooden coffins are lowered into the ground as the crowd gathers in self-organized, respectful formation around the graves, as if they're a flock of geese coming in to land on the water like splash-free synchronized swimmers. A turbaned cleric commands the scene now, and the crowd praises Allah and cries its children a teary farewell, despite the theological promise that their dead offspring are about to enter Paradise. And then, it is over, and the mourners and bereaved slowly melt away.

Except for a lone child, barely five or six years old. She's holding the only thing that survived the missile intact: the wooden nodding donkey on wheels, its painted stripe of a mouth grinning stupidly like a fool. A man—perhaps her father—comes back to find her. He takes the toy from her hands and looks at it, as if he's puzzling over the significance of its survival, until, perhaps in desperation rather than with unalloyed faith, he says, "It is a sign from Allah that vengeance must be had," like the guy's reading my freakin' mind.

But, just to make sure he's going to act with the impetus of faith as opposed to easily sidetracked desperation, I have him stumble on the piece of the missile that bears the name of its country of origin. He picks it up and stares at the strange writing; it's clear that he can't read it. But, soon, he's jumping up and down as if he's just been bitten on the ass. He takes off, back towards the village, yelling and screaming: "Amerika! Amerika!" I can see it from here, Uncle Sam's Stars and Stripes, still red, white, and blue as plain as you like, notwithstanding the piece of shrapnel's charred condition. His neighbors come rushing back to meet him, echoing an "Amerika, death to Amerika!" answer to his call. The reformed crowd jostles with a joy verging on insanity, now, bereavement having met its dialectical twin, the massive compensation of recompense, and eye for an eye, a tooth for tooth. Holy *Jihad!*

And so, a fragment of the missile proudly identifying its owner becomes proof positive that the jihadists have been right all along: that the Americans are engaged in a total war on Islam, Islam the one and only true religion—as if there were, indeed, any such thing.

I know that many of the elder brothers and sisters of the slain boys will leave home soon, on their way to swelling the ranks of the so-called holy warriors. The massacre at al-Adrum, undoubtedly and so predictably, will never be forgotten—I'll put any money on that you like; it's a one-way bet if ever I saw one, and I've seen a few in my time. The massacre at al-Adrum will be "a day that forever will live in infamy," as that crippled American president once said long ago about another sneaky, deadly attack; and it will be avenged, the siblings will solemnly vow, just like that imperious American voice had once vouched vengeance, too—and one day he'd gotten it in the form of a great billowing mushroom cloud towering to the heavens (a bit too close for comfort, if you ask me), and not once, but twice.

Vengeance? Wherever did they all get that idea from? It's enough to make you curse. And why just eyes and teeth, anyway? We're talking about much bigger body parts than these, aren't we?

6

[10 November 2016]

Robbie, you'll never believe this—after all is said and done—but it's the smells that get to me most.

God, they make me gag! Some sort of fishy fucking curry stink for starters, that seems to hang in the air even after they've long gone back upstairs. Then there's their truly stifling BO, like they haven't taken a bath in weeks—months even, knowing them. And God, the dried...gunk. They can't even be bothered to wipe it up. It doesn't smell, I know, but believe me theirs really does—you can really smell it. It's a smell you can actually literally see—trust me, I'm not making this up. The crusty, creamy-white stains on my dress and underwear, they feel like horrible bugs crawling up my legs, invading me, infecting me. God, I've got to get out of these shitty clothes, take a bath, but they won't let me. They say there's no running water here anymore. They bring in whatever water there is in big jerry cans, but there's very little for me, just a cup to drink with my meals, a half cup on occasion so that I can make some sort of a go at cleaning my teeth with my finger, and once a day a plastic bottle full so that I can flush the toilet—or make an attempt to, at any rate. Yuck! They just leave me here until the next time, chained to this goddamn radiator, lying in my own—and their—filth. I feel diseased, fouled... desecrated. Yes, desecrated.

Pakis! What else can you expect?

...

Robbie, where were you? We waited, but you didn't show up, and then...

...

We'd been having such a good time. The Palace was humming as usual. Some of the blokes as you can imagine were well past it by about nine, so I just danced with the girls for the most part, until closing. But when I got outside, you weren't there. I couldn't understand it. You've never been late. Billy Gubbins offered to give me a ride home, but I knew he'd be at least another half-hour as he has to shut the club up, so I said no, that you'd be there soon enough, I was sure of it...so sure.

...

I thought I heard your voice today, Robbie. In fact, for a moment, I was so sure of it I cried out to you, but the gag over my mouth muffled my effort. My heart was pounding like a drum; it felt as if it might literally burst right out of my chest. I tried again, then listened...but nothing, nothing but silence. I can't stand it that you might have been there—right up there at the top of those stairs, just on the other side of that fucking door! I cried quietly then, until I fell asleep. When one of them came down to give me something to eat, I could tell that he knew I'd been crying—my dried tears, no doubt, gave me away.

As soon as he'd removed my gag, I asked him: "Was someone else up there with you today? An English..."

He just looked at me, then a mocking smile slowly broke out across his greasy face. "Hearing things are you?" he said. "Forget it, sister; nobody'll come looking for you here. You're not going anywhere." He put down a plate of stinking curry in front of me, and turned to leave. "Bye for now, ducks," he said in a fake Yorkshire accent. He pointed at the food. "Gerr it etten. An' be quick abaht 'it!"

He sounded just like you...

...

These splash marks, they're not...It's so hot down here that the sweat's just pouring out of me—or is it a fever? I'm holding on. I mustn't break. It's the only chance I have.

I keep looking for a way, anticipating a moment when it might be possible to make an escape, when perhaps one of them forgets to bolt the door, or when he's too engrossed in his pleasure to notice that I'm about to stave his skull in... But I need a weapon

first, and I've looked and looked—I know every fucking square inch of this goddamn cellar—but there's nothing...
   ...nothing.

7

[18 March 2016]

"Welcome to the United Kingdom," the immigration officer at Heathrow airport cheerily said, as Jamal Shirani anxiously approached the official's booth, the last barrier to be breached on his return to London.

Jamal hadn't anticipated such a response to his arrival from Pakistan, especially since the line in front of the immigration officer's booth was so long and so agonizingly slow-moving. The officer had seemed palpably irritated just a few moments before by the fumbling, clueless passenger immediately ahead of Jamal, and Jamal, already nervous about re-entering Britain after such a long absence in Pakistan, expected that his reticence to disclose too much about what he had been up to there would only add fuel to the flames of the immigration officer's mounting displeasure.

He was already sweating profusely, sheets of perspiration ink-blotting his chest. He looked down at himself hoping to God that the sweaty configuration wasn't somehow betraying his secrets, like a leave-it-all-out-there Rorschach test. He thought he could make out the shape of a mushroom cloud, but tried to convince himself that the bulbous mass could just as easily be an amoeba on steroids or, indeed, nothing at all. But he decided to button up his jacket, just in case, although doing so only made him sweat even more; he felt as if he was going to melt, right there in front of the immigration officer. Folks passing close by him visibly constricted their nasal passages and audibly *phewed* at the odor he was emitting—Jamal could even smell it himself. But the immigration officer seemed remarkably unfazed as he casually took Jamal's dog-eared British passport from him.

"How long have you been away?" the immigration officer continued, and he smiled as if he at least half meant it.

Jamal opened his mouth, fully expecting his intense rehearsals as to how to respond to this thoroughly predictable question had equipped him to automatically deliver a cool, confident, and convincing response. But, despite all the preparation, he totally fluffed his lines. *What was it about him that practice could not make perfect?* "Umh…," he stumbled, "a year"—the immigration officer raised his eyebrows—"umh, a year-and-a-bit."

He'd actually been gone closer to eighteen months, but the immigration officer, after briefly looking at the exit date from London in Jamal's passport, made no comment as to Jamal's vagueness. Jamal wasn't good at lying, never had been, but now his life had taken him to a place where he'd have to become expert at it or face the consequences—most of which would be none-too-agreeable. Jamal knew he ought to look his interrogator full in the face when he answered his questions, but he just couldn't seem to do it. His eyes flitted around his immediate environs as if they couldn't decide where to settle. Jamal forced himself to focus. On the Departures Board to his left Jamal suddenly saw a flight to Guantanamo Bay flashing "Final Boarding."

"Guantanamo?" he blurted out.

"What?"

"Final...?"

The immigration officer turned to look at the Departures Board, too. "What?" he said again.

"Gua—"

"Guatemala City? What about it?"

Jamal saw Guantanamo Bay instantaneously morph into Guatemala City (via Houston). He let out a short girlish giggle of relief.

"Care to share the joke?" the immigration officer asked. His half meant smile had fully gone now; the kid was beginning to annoy him.

"Sorry, sir," Jamal quickly replied, the grin on his face disappearing twice as fast as it had made its appearance. "It's nothing—nothing at all."

The immigration officer rubbed his double chin and pursed his lips. "A year-and-a-bit, eh?" he finally said. "Care to be a bit more specific?" He flipped through the pages of Jamal's passport again—better not fucking lie to me, his officious gesture seemed to say.

"Um...fifteen months, actually."

Jamal eyed his adversary's fingers; he wondered on what page they might stop, what lie it might disclose—it was impossible to argue with the definitive declarations those imperious rubber stamps left behind. He noticed that the officer's fingertips were heavily stained, like a deep suntan, except the indelible pigmentation was a dark purple as opposed to a sun-worshipper's golden brown. The old guy must have had a lot of experience—*seen it all before*.

"And *what*, may I ask, took fifteen months to take care of?" the immigration officer sneered, opening up a page of Jamal's passport and holding it up in front of him for closer scrutiny.

Jamal had also rehearsed the answer to this predictable question over and over on the almost thirteen hour flight from Islamabad, but all he could think about in the moment of finally being asked it was the truth of what he had been mostly up to, not the seven-eighths fabrication he'd managed to concoct. Behind his interrogator's head, he saw a series of images flash by, one after the other as if they were part of a movie trailer: the high snow-capped mountains to the northwest of Peshawar; the hidden valley where the camp had been; the days of vigorous, relentless training; the long sessions on the sayings of the Prophet and the true meaning of jihad; his new friends, holy-warrior comrades all. Nanny Laila's house, let alone his grandmother herself, was hardly anywhere to be seen. But somehow his mouth did not—at least not entirely—betray him.

"I went to see...my grandmother," he stuttered. "She's been ill."

"Sounds serious—*if* you had to stay for so long. I take it she must be better now?"

"Yes...yes. Well enough, anyway."

"So, what was wrong with her?"

"Hmm, I'm not entirely sure—some kind of woman's problem. The doctor didn't really tell me all that much." Jamal half-smiled, half-grimaced, as if he didn't need to say anymore, that the immigration officer, a fellow male, would appreciate his reluctance to know too much about the alien, even slightly distasteful, maladies of women. He was right; his antagonist quickly changed the subject.

"Do anything else—travel around, while you were there? After your...*grandmother* got well enough for you to be able to leave her for a few days by herself, under someone else's care?"

"Oh...just a little. Didn't have enough money to do much. The flight over and back just about took whatever I had."

"So," the immigration officer said, looking down his nose, "where does she live, *your grandmother?*'

"Palosi...Palosi Peshawar."

Peshawar? Peshawar...yes, he knew that name. Not much innocent about Peshawar! The immigration officer swiped Jamal's passport through the scanner on his desk with such aggression that it seemed like he was trying to slice right through it. He looked up at the computer screen in front of him, concentrating fiercely.

Jamal could see the officer's eyeballs moving left to right over and over. The officer made a few keystrokes on his computer's keyboard and then began to read again, if anything, even more intently. His eyebrows arched up several times, as if something was really piquing his interest. Jamal suddenly desperately needed to go to the bathroom, but before he had the unfortunate accident, the immigration officer abruptly stopped reading, stamped Jamal's passport granting him re-admittance to the United

Kingdom, and held it out to him. As Jamal reached out to take it, his jacket sleeve rode up exposing a few inches of his forearm.

"What's that?" the immigration officer enquired. "On your arm."

Jamal quickly retrieved his passport and pulled his sleeve down again. "Oh, nothing. Just a stupid tattoo, that's all."

"No, let me see. Looks interesting."

Jamal reluctantly held out his arm and pulled up his jacket sleeve.

"*Guns N' Roses*?" the immigration officer slowly read out aloud. "Huh. Never heard of it. No, wait a minute, they're some sort of…rock group, right?"

Jamal nodded, embarrassed to admit he'd liked the blasphemous band once.

The immigration officer examined the tattoo. It was composed of a human skull wearing a black top hat, whose hatband had the group's name emblazoned on it. Behind the skull and hat, two pistols were arranged like crossbones, and the whole composition was encircled in what looked like a halo of barbed wire.

The immigration officer pulled a face. "Doubt I'd care too much for *them*. What are they? Heavy Metal? Punk?"

"Heavy Metal, I suppose," Jamal mumbled, anxious to get going.

The immigration officer tried to connect Heavy Metal and Pakistani Muslim in his head. The pistols could easily relate, he supposed; the world was awash with guns and violence, especially these days, whether one was religious or not. But the top-hatted skull—it threw him for a bit of a loop. It looked satanic. He tried to remember, did Muslims believe in Satan, too? No doubt the spooks would figure it out, he assumed.

"Well, whatever. Looks like you'll have to learn to live with it now." The immigration officer suddenly noticed a rose peeking out from behind one of the pistols. It looked misshapen, as if it was wilting for lack of water. Now he thought about it, the whole tattoo looked amateurish, almost as if a kid had drawn it. He shook his head and sighed, but compensated for his disgust with the hope that Jamal was amateurish all round. It'd make everyone's life easier if he was. "Okay, off you go," the officer gruffly continued, sending Jamal on his way with a nod of his head in the direction of Baggage Claim and Customs.

Jamal took off as quickly as he dared. It was all he could do to not start running. Even though his bladder had now stopped threatening to embarrass him, he went straight into the toilets anyway. Thankfully, they were empty. He walked into a stall and locked the door behind him. He sat down on the toilet seat and put his head in his hands. "God, that was close," he whispered to himself. "Too fucking close for comfort." He tore off a great ream of toilet paper, a good four feet long, and tried to mop up his perspiration, but the shiny, cheap stuff, thin as an onion skin, merely smeared the sweat around even more. Still, the Rorschach test had lost its incriminating shape by then. Jamal took off his jacket, grateful to be able to sigh with some measure of relief.

The immigration officer watched Jamal rush off to the lavatory. He picked up the phone on his desk and dialed. Someone picked up on the other end of the line.

"Jamal Shirani," the immigration officer said into the mouthpiece. "That's J-a-m-a-l, S-h-i-r-a-n-i, British Passport Number 09487628. He's just returned from Pakistan—*Peshawar*, more precisely. I'm filing notice right away. He'll be in Baggage Claim within a couple of minutes. Blue jeans, lightweight bomber jacket, red and green check shirt. Has a full beard now, not like in the picture we have of him on file." The immigration officer put down the phone and began filing his report on the computer, greatly annoying the next passenger waiting in line. When he finished his report, he waved his fingers beckoning the wearied traveler forward.

"Welcome home," he said, and then thought, as he flipped through the pages of the passport handed to him, *Guns N' Fucking Roses! Thought that lot despised that stuff even more than we do. Religion and Rock — I just don't get it.* He looked at the little old lady standing before him—no grisly tattoos there, and probably a Frank Sinatra fan, too, thank God. As he handed the old woman her passport back, he noticed Jamal exiting the toilets, his jacket slung over his shoulder, a bit too cockily for his taste.

"Shouldn't be long now, Shirani old son," he said to no one in particular. "Not long at all—you little fuck!"

The old woman, no more than a couple of paces away from him, stopped in her tracks. Had she heard him cuss, or was she just taking a breath? He watched her back, stooped over with arthritic age, trying to divine an answer to his question. The old gal fiddled with her hearing aid; it whistled and whined in response to her clumsy maneuvering. Then she hobbled off on her way. He bit his tongue; you couldn't be too careful about what you said these apocalyptic days. For a moment, he felt as concerned as to what the old woman might do—report him, or some such—as he did about Jamal's next step. Strangely, the stakes seemed potentially as equally ominous in their own separate ways, whether he eventually might lose his job or perhaps lose his life.

What a weird world they were all living in these days.

8

[July 2015]

Well, it had to happen one day. And it did — on Parris Island.

I was finally sacked. I went down like a sack of shit.

Not on the football field, mind you, by some lardass mastodon of a lineman packing more than a couple of spare tires around his midriff; but by my drill instructor, on the parade ground, precisely at the time I was least expecting it. He knocked me flat.

"Fucking dupe, Brown," he said. "Next time, out there in jihadi-land, you'll be fucking dead meat. Got it?"

That's when I understood it was all much more than just religious warfare or the clash of civilizations, although both of those would have been bad enough. That's when I knew it was going to be mano a mano *for the likes of me, a pure Darwinian struggle for survival when it finally came to it, red in tooth and claw. Him against me, personal in that brutally stripped-down sense, uncomplicated by the tags we attach to ourselves and the causes we choose to fight for; victory — the only sort that really mattered when push came to shove, anyway — going to the last man standing, religious affiliation, or whatever, be damned. It was going to be what we packed, not what we claimed to be, not what sacred oaths we'd resolved to uphold.*

And I vowed then, my face mashed to the ground, that I wasn't going down first when the time came, no matter what it took.

I was going to throw the winning touchdown pass, not some fucking Jihadi John.

The War on Terror would boil down to a barroom brawl, both of us too drunk to remember what it was we were supposed to be fighting for — except survival.

I was becoming a robot with a will to power.

Or, as some might say, a killing machine.

Can't say as I would wholly disagree with them, but there was a war to win, a battle to outlive, one's own ass to save.

And that's what war does to you, reduces your moral compass to the power of One. And I was fine with that, then.

9

[15 March 2015]

Ayaan Pellegrino stood alone before the entrance to the Royal Spanish College at the University of Bologna.

She had come here many times before during her university career, mostly at special moments, times when she was about to reach a significant milestone on her way to earning her bachelor's degree in chemical engineering, or when, as now, she was troubled by something, an itch concerning her sense of self that she could never seem to quite satisfy, even though she had scratched at it often enough over the years.

Gazing through the archway at the ornate porticum and loggia across the cobbled courtyard, she would try to place herself, her life, in the context of this venerable institution of higher learning. The university was the oldest in Europe, had been in existence now for over a thousand years, and she, just a twenty-year-old student, was soon to become one of its most recent batch of graduates, a mere contemporary, transient speck in a deep ocean of learning and tradition. The carved columns supporting the graceful arches across the way seemed so firmly planted in the place they had stood on since the Spanish students had had them built there in medieval times that they looked as if they had rooted themselves like ancient trees into the ground. What history had these revered stones witnessed; what secrets did they know? Any of hers perhaps, even ones she didn't know about? And the Spanish students, why had they been here setting up something as permanent as this beautiful structure before her? Had they been estranged from their homeland—been exiles? Had the founding of the college helped them to rediscover themselves, to shed their alien presence in a stranger's land?

The last rays of the westing sun blipped into extinction, cut off now by the college roof's ridgeline, suddenly plunging the enclosed courtyard into darkness. The lanterns flickered on gamely enough, but cast little real light, just enough so that you could find your way in or out. But Ayaan found them soothing; they helped her think about her life without the fear that they might shed *too* much revealing light upon it. Although she often hankered to know more about her past, about which she knew next to nothing, she also lived in trepidation that there might be things about it that she'd be better off *not* knowing. The very little she knew about her ancestry unsettled her, made her wonder about her genetic inheritance and whatever surprises it might hold in store for her—there'd been one or two remarkable ones already. She wondered, too, what her real parents and their families might have been like, what they might have taught her, how they might have brought her up—what kind of *person* she might have turned out to be, if not the one she thought she was then.

She had been just two years old when her biological family had fled a war-ravaged Somalia as refugees, but Ayaan had no memory of the circumstances of the flight from her homeland, or what more specifically had occasioned it. Nor was there any documentary evidence of any kind—a birth certificate, a passport, a diary, some letters, her parents' recorded testimony before an asylum judge, for instance—to help fill in the blanks. Ayaan's very existence was, of course, proof enough that she'd had parents, and other refugees who had shared the crowded, dilapidated boat with her family had verified that they'd seen a young couple taking care of her. But when the craft had capsized in a storm just three miles from the island of Lampedusa, Ayaan's caregivers, along with several dozen more wretched souls, disappeared beneath the waves, most never to be seen again. A few bodies from the wreck did wash up on the island sometime later, but none that could be identified as her biological parents. The circumstantial evidence, such as it was, pointed to a Somali heritage, but that was just about it—it just pointed, nothing more. There was also Ayaan's name, of course, one common enough in Somalia, and it was the one folks thought they heard her say when she was asked after her miraculous rescue, but it wasn't conclusive by any means.

Ayaan was plucked from the storm-tossed Mediterranean Sea by the crew of an Italian coast guard vessel. Fearing danger themselves and knowing they wouldn't be thanked too much for bringing *too many* refugees ashore by the local authorities, the crew might well have "overlooked" Ayaan's distress. But when one of their number saw her floating miraculously on the waves, it reminded him so much of Moses in a basket in the bulrushes that he couldn't help himself but to jump into the water and save her. The sailor claimed later that he had heard the voice of God commanding him to rescue the imperiled infant. This claim to divine intervention soon became myth, then incontrovertible *fact*. He'd seen her with his own eyes and he'd heard God with his own ears, and all God-fearing folk believed him, especially when the Pope endorsed the sailor's miraculous assertion just a few days later on Easter Sunday, a portentous day as any for God to work in his mysterious way.

Back on shore, in Lampedusa, Ayaan quickly became known as the "Miracle Baby," as if she'd been born by Immaculate Conception in the sea, a sin-free daughter of a Catholic Neptune. All of Italy, and far beyond, soon became entranced by her story, what little was known of it as opposed to so much that was concocted in a mass, media-led frenzy of religious fervor. Before long, Ayaan's increasingly legendary tale reached the ears of a childless couple living in Bologna: Piero and Pia Pellegrino. Piero was a titan of Italian industry, a shipping magnate of almost Onassian proportions. He was fabulously wealthy and equally fabulously well-connected. A fruitful combination of financial favors and the calling-in of IOUs from the folks that could move and shake such things soon resulted a few weeks later in the delivery of Ayaan to the Pellegrinos' guardianship. They foster parented her at first, but before long they legally adopted her as their own. For once, the lethargic wheels of the Italian legal system moved surprisingly quickly and it was far more accommodating—as opposed to frustrating—than any lesser Italian than Piero Pellegrino might have had any reason to expect.

Ayaan knew most of this tale; Piero, the father she soon came to love, had told her as much but only in his rather barebones, almost tight-lipped fashion, as if it really wasn't all that important, and that she didn't need to dwell on it too much—except for the miraculous part, that is, the part that made you revere an existence like that and be eternally grateful for the great good fortune that God had decided to steer your way. But, as with her pre-Italian life, she had no real memories of any of these meagre details that her father related to her. She'd had nightmares for a while after being adopted, no doubt, she later supposed, brought on by the several traumas she must have suffered during her flight to Lampedusa, and then being brought to the home of strangers speaking a language she'd never heard before. But she'd soon enough settled into the life of the spoilt only daughter of wealthy parents. By the time Ayaan was four, she was a very happy and confident little *Italian* girl, loved beyond measure and experiencing a life of seemingly boundless horizons.

But before too much longer, the itch that she had become increasingly familiar with by her twenty-first birthday first reared its ugly head: she came to recognize—along with so many derisive others who didn't know any better, or didn't care to—that she didn't quite *look* the part she'd inherited. She had a head of dark, crinkly hair that wouldn't straighten no matter how hard her mother tried, and an olive-brown complexion that was dark even for an Italian from the Mezzogiorno. Her high cheekbones did lend her a degree of sculpted beauty, to be much admired by a long line of suitors by the time she got to high school and then afterwards at university, but that dark skin tone, that wild hair, those wide, sapphire blue, dazzling eyes? To many a jealous Italian girl she looked almost Roma, and some of them let her know about their suspicion and spread the rumor as if it were practically fact. Her parents insisted, of course, that she was beautiful, and that she shouldn't listen to such evil people, but they weren't entirely convincing — after all, she didn't resemble them in the slightest, and why did her mother try so hard to straighten out her curls if they were so precious?

The questions and accusations about who she *really* was did rankle, of course, as they did now as she stood in the courtyard of the Royal Spanish College wondering where her life might go next, after graduation. But for the most part, her many triumphs and privileges had oftentimes compensated for this nagging itch that wouldn't quite go away, even when she felt on the top of the world. Private tutoring and elite private schooling had brought her outstanding academic success. And in just a few short weeks she'd be graduating at the top of her class with a degree in chemical engineering, the only female in a cohort that was otherwise all-male. She knew she had the world in the palms of her hands as a top-notch female scientist, and that, should she so choose, she could have any job she wished along with the attentions of any of the fawning, slobbering, male students who lustfully worshipped the very ground she walked on.

What was she so worried about? She knew, rationally, that the jibes about her ancestry meant rather little in the larger scheme of things. Nothing could stop her, ruin her life. Her parents kept telling her that, and they had the means to ensure such an outcome. But still…the comments about her looks …they hurt, and the fact that so many boys found them so enticing did little to dull the pain. She touched her cheek, her fingertips dancing on the skin as if they were feeling for something—a scar perhaps.

Two boys whistled from the balcony above her. "*Bellisima!*" one of them cried down to her. "*Mi vuoi sposare?*" beseeched the other.

Ayaan gave them a dismissive look, and then turned to walk away, leaving them to pathetically keep calling after her. They were so annoying, so typically Italian *macho*. But on the other hand…they did make her smile.

Maybe Roma was *trés chic* after all.

10

[16 November 2016]

It didn't take long, as you might imagine, given all the filth down here. I knew they'd be here somewhere, the filthy vermin. You know how I hate them so.

There's a hole where the sewer pipe runs through the wall. I'd been staring at it almost constantly as soon as I'd noticed it. For a good hour or more, there was nothing, and I must have dozed off. But when I woke suddenly with a start, there it was. The biggest fucking mouse you ever saw.

I was terrified, more of it almost than the scum who've kidnapped me. I was getting closer and closer to really freaking out, but the last thing I wanted to do was to attract their attention, let them know that I was terrified of mice. Just think what they would have done to torture me with them if they'd found out?

The mouse was sniffing around like they do, twitching its ugly long snout. And the way its long tail slithered back and forth across the floor made me want to throw up. I kept as still as I could, hoping like crazy that it wouldn't sense my presence, even though I knew it would.

Then it spied me. I thought I was going to die.

For a while, it just sat there, sizing me up. I kicked a piece of rubble in its direction, trying to scare it off, but it didn't move. It just sat back on its haunches and started to preen itself. It kept at it for quite some time, and it suddenly occurred to me that the beast might well be cleaner than I was. Certainly, less foul than those filthy bastards upstairs! But when I kicked another piece of trash at it, it stopped its grooming, turned around, and went back through the hole in the wall. I was so relieved, but the beast's behavior surprized me, got me thinking...

It didn't return for a couple of days, and I wondered why. I started to imagine where it might be, what it was doing. I even gave it a name, Johnny Town-Mouse, and composed stories about in my head, as if I were Beatrix Potter. By the time he reappeared, I was almost glad to see him.

He entered through the hole in the wall again and sat in the spot where he'd cleaned himself before. I spoke softly to him. "Hello, Johnny Town-Mouse," I said. I could barely believe what I was doing, that I was so calm in his presence. I was unbound this time; they'd untied me from the radiator so I could eat my so-called breakfast. I broke off a piece of the weird-looking bread thing they'd given me—roti or chapatti, I think it might be called—and held it out between my fingers towards him.

His snout twitched; he could obviously smell it. He started to move towards my hand. Just before he got to it, I dropped the food onto the floor—he was close enough. I retreated a little, unsure as to how he might react. He crept up to the bread and nibbled at it. In a couple of seconds it was gone. He looked at me, like he was Oliver Twist asking for more. I prepared another piece of roti, but held onto it this time. Johnny Town-Mouse came to me and ate it from the palm of my unshaking hand. I felt the wetness of his snout, the tickle of his teeth and tongue, then the softness of his fur as I stroked him. I couldn't believe what I was doing.

Johnny Town-Mouse came to see me every morning after that, for what seemed like a week. But then he stopped, and I wondered why. I had a plan for him, an almost last desperate hope. What had I done wrong?

...

Standing out there by the Palace doors waiting, I'd also started to wonder what I'd done wrong, that maybe I'd pissed you off or something... I know we hadn't done it in a while, but I'd told you why. The pill...it was fucking with my hormones, and you wouldn't use one, so...

I know I shouldn't have gone to the Palace without you, but there was no good reason not to show up, was there? Not after what's happened.

...

The "Impersonator," whenever he comes down here, keeps doing his fake Yorkie accent. He's quickly cottoned on that it annoys the shit out of me. He grins and pulls a stupid-looking face whenever he's about to launch into his routine. I must admit, though, he's got the dialect down pretty much spot on, more's the pity, but he could use some help with the fucking repartee. He's like a one-trick pony—well, two at best. His usual salutation—if you can call it that—is: "'Eee by gum, you're a reight good sort, a proper bobby dazzler!" Then he makes a grab for me, like he's trying to squeeze my tits. I sometimes make to slap him, but don't. The rules are different down here, not like the Palace. Bloke try to pull a trick like that there, and I'd have slapped him one—as well you know! His only other one-liner is the one he leaves me with when he goes to shut the door on me again: "Tarra then. Oops, better put wood inth'ole! Flippin 'eck, wouldn't want you flitin' down't road!"

...

That's your line, though, isn't it, "puttin' wood inth'ole"? Open doors, as well as your mantra about lights being unnecessarily left switched on—I drove you crazy, didn't I? And that's how it often started, wasn't it, you yelling at me to "shut the goddamn door," or muttering under your breath something about me having "more brass na brains" when it came to the use of electricity? I'd come back at you, though, wouldn't I, demanding to know if you thought you were my boss or something, and what about you leaving your stinking socks wherever you happened to have taken them off?

And then off we'd go, spiraling out of control...until something neither of us really wanted to happen, did.

...

Come to think of it, it was the bathroom lights that night, wasn't it? As a result, I went to the Palace and you didn't.

All this, just because of that? Well, of course, not exactly just because of that. We had bigger fish to fry, didn't we?

You'll be pleased to know, though, there's fat chance of me leaving the lights on down here or forgetting to put wood inth'ole. But when he stands up there, far enough away so that it's hard to see clearly, I'll swear I see and hear you. I know you're not here, not even anywhere close. But for some reason I keep sensing that you really are, that you have to be in some form...

My life depends on it...

11
[20 May 2016]

"And what is wrong with you that you fight not in the Cause of Allah, and for those weak, ill-treated and oppressed among men, women, and children, whose cry is: "Our Lord! Rescue us from this town whose people are oppressors; and raise for us from You one who will protect, and raise for us from You one who will help." [Noble Quran 4:75]

"Oh, come on, Saeed," Mo whined. "Let's get back to the game. I'm not interested in this shit."

Mo and Saeed had been playing "Grand Theft Auto," their favorite video game, on line again when Saeed had suddenly switched to a web page. It hosted the text of the Holy Koran. It was called "The Koran for Dummies." Mo didn't know why, but Saeed had been going to the site a fair bit recently. He wondered, implausible though it should have been, whether his best friend was getting religion all of a sudden.

"No, wait," Saeed admonished Mo. "I have to do this. My Dad'll get on my case if the imam tells him I haven't being doing my homework. It's alright for you, your old man doesn't give a flip, but mine does!"

"Well, what's so important about it all? *More* important than 'Grand Theft Auto'?"

"Take a look," Saeed said. "You might actually learn something."

Mo rolled his eyes and made a face, but if getting this over with was the price to be paid for getting back to the game, then so be it. He began to slowly read what was on the computer screen.

Saeed stopped scrolling down the webpage, and waited for Mo to catch up. "Ready?" he said impatiently after a few seconds. He knew Mo had always been a slow reader, and it still looked to him like Mo needed the remedial help he'd had in school. Saeed fiddled with the mouse anxious to get going again.

"Hang on a minute, will you?" Mo complained. "This stuff's weird, hard to follow. Why can't they write in plain English, instead of all this ancient-sounding gobbledygook? What 'town' are they talking about, anyway?"

"'What *town* are they talking about?' What does it matter? It's the overall message—the command—that matters. It's the call to jihad in aid of our oppressed Muslim brothers and sisters—that's what you're supposed to be focusing on! Please don't tell me you think it means Rotherham?"

"No...well, why not?" Mo whined, but then he warmed to his cause as he realized he might have at least half of a point to make after all, anything to rid Saeed of the idea that he, Mo, was an incurable dumbfuck. "Why *not* Rotherham?" Mo arched his eyebrows and opened his eyes wide in a sudden know-it-all's insistence that he knew he was right. He raised his chin and stuck his chest out slightly, and then out it came, one of the few aces he had ever been able to play at Saeed's intellectual expense, his friend's presumed bragging rights that he had a least a smidgen's worth more of worldly knowledge than Mo himself did. "Where do you think you are, Saeed? Look around you. Half of this shit hole of a town is full of 'weak, ill-treated' — and what is it? — 'oppressed' Muslim brothers and sisters. So, why not — why not Rotherham? *Tell me that!*"

Saeed blinked in surprise; his mouth hung open, but for a few seconds he was speechless.

"Well, I admit," he eventually managed to say, "you do have a point, but, still, the town referred to can't *literally* be Rotherham, can it? I mean, we're talking about the Koran here, and in case you didn't know it Rotherham didn't exist back then. The town has to be somewhere in the Arabian Peninsula, most likely Mecca or Medina, I'd say." Saeed sat back in his chair, thinking that his superficial knowledge of the life of the Prophet that Mo didn't possess had regained him the upper hand. But it was only a semantic victory, if that.

"Well, that's as may be, but we're not in the — whatever — peninsula, are we? We're here in our thousands in Rotherham…and — *and* — we're sure as hell oppressed! I can fucking well vouch for that." Mo touched the spot on his forehead where the police officer had poked him with his finger the night before. It had scabbed over, but a trace of dried blood—forensic evidence of his most recent humiliation—caught in his fingernail. Mo scrutinized it for a second or two before flicking it angrily away.

Saeed knew that what Mo was saying was true, even if less so for him and his relatively well-off family than for many others of their kind, including Mo. Some silent, telepathic cue told both him and Mo that their debate had been settled by an intuited, unspoken agreement about the truth of their world. Like synchronized swimmers, they both turned their attention back to the computer screen again. Mo resumed reading aloud haltingly from the same Koranic verse.

"'Rescue us from this town whose people are...are oppressors; and raise for us from You one who...who will protect, and raise for us from You one who will...help.' Hah! In this town? Fat chance of that. Every one of us whom I've seen 'raised' has gotten the hell out of town as soon as they fucking well could. Remember Danish and Latif and Taj? All of them gone like rats out of the sewer. Off to university in London and America with their scholarships, every last one of them. Can't say as I blame them, though. I'd do the same thing if I had the same—fat fucking—chance." Mo looked at Saeed, and in that momentary glance they both knew that a university scholarship for Mo was about as likely as...well, you name it.

"Ah, what's the point of reading this shit?" Mo finally said, pushing his chair back from Saeed's desk. "What good will reading the Koran do? I don't understand most of it, and even when I do, what it says seems hopeless. Let's get out of here before I lose it."

Saeed didn't want anything untoward to happen to his precious computer—like Mo smashing the screen in one of his renowned temper tantrums—so he quickly and without comment shut the device down, and put on his jacket. By then Mo was already halfway down the stairs on his way outside.

Saeed eventually caught him up by the garden gate opening onto the deserted, trash-strewn street. Mo turned right towards the disused gasworks, a great rusting hulk broodily wasting away at the end of the street on a piece of waste ground, but then suddenly did an about face, and headed towards the town center, such as it was. Saeed tagged along, a yard or so behind. They didn't speak, although neither of them knew where they were going as there really was nowhere of any consequence to go. They were both hunched over against the cold air, condensing their breaths into swirling vapor clouds as they trudged on.

From time to time, Saeed furtively looked over at his friend; he could sense that Mo was someplace else in his thoughts, a not unusual frame of mind for him to have, as he well knew. Mo had always been a closed-mouthed, brooding sort, loathe to sharing his secrets or his matters of the heart. But he didn't look mad or frustrated so much this time, somehow; the expression on his drawn face suggested deep, sober thought, as opposed to being flushed with emotional turmoil, as was the usual case. And, to top it all, at least it wasn't raining—for once; and the wind had changed direction, too, blowing untypically from the south-east.

Saeed knew he was no meteorological expert, far from it, but something in that wind told him that a change was on the way, perhaps a changing of the seasons, earlier than expected—and perhaps a little out of climatological kilter to boot.

He looked at Mo again; yes, there was definitely something "up" with him.

12

[September 2015]

The dog found me first, then the kid.

We were on stand-down for fifteen. I was sitting behind a low wall, my back leaning against it. The rest of the platoon found their own spots to take cover, well-spaced apart. It didn't pay to congregate too much, even if you hadn't seen a goddamn thing for the last four hours on patrol in this godforsaken place. I didn't know just where in the world it specifically was; all I knew was that we were somewhere in Syria, or maybe Iraq, but that was all any of us knew, except for the chief, we presumed. He had some sort of map, but he kept it too himself, as per orders from high up above. In any case, I took the opportunity to relieve the boredom by setting to work whittling some more on my latest creation. It was the last piece of New Haven I still had with me.

The dog wandered over, and nervously sniffed me. Whatever he smelled, he didn't take offense. Just wagged his tail and panted. I reached into my pocket and pulled out the remains of a granola bar. He wolfed it down in one go, then offered to lick my face. I declined.

By this time, the kid was just a few yards away, obviously wondering what to do, whether flight would overcome his curiosity or his reluctance to leave his dog with a foreign devil.

The last thing I wanted to do was to spook the poor little guy, not least because it would only have attracted unnecessary attention, even if it was only from the local villagers as opposed to the jihadis who were really out to get you. We'd already learned that getting into any sort of pissing contest with the locals, merely over the most trivial matters like we'd walked over their pathetic vegetable gardens (or at least what passed for them), was not worth the hassle, notwithstanding the fact that you were usually able to come out on top given the intimidating firepower you packed. I smiled and put my finger to my lips, hoping the gesture made its point in translation. It did. The kid half smiled back, but only for a second.

I shifted my position slightly, so that I could face him better, but it was enough to startle him. He made to run off, but his dog was still fussing around me, begging for another treat, so he didn't seem to know what to do. He whistled a short, high-pitched command between his tongue and his teeth and reached out his hand, but the hound paid no heed. I smiled at him again, but I could tell he was getting closer to panic, and I sure as hell didn't want him crying or screaming, making a holy fuss.

Instinctively, I guess it must have been, I held up what I'd been working on. His eyes latched onto it right away. It was going to be a birthday gift for my nephew, about to be, I realized, close to the same age as the waif before me. He looked at me in the eyes, then back at what I was holding again. It was a model of a miniature donkey on wheels, about four inches or so high and perhaps six long. I tapped the donkey on its head and it nodded up and down.

It was magic. His eyes sparkled; his cheeks ballooned with the onset of a broad gleeful grin. He even giggled, although you could barely hear it. I tapped the donkey's head again, harder this time, making it bobble even more extravagantly, like it was having a fit or something or just being goofy. That did it. I had him.

I slowly got to my feet, then held out the toy to him, shook it slightly like you do when you invite someone to take something. "You like?" I said, although I knew he probably didn't know a lick of English. I stretched out my hand even farther. "It's for you. A gift." I was almost touching him now. It struck me how odd it was that his skin color should almost be the same as mine, like we might have been born in the same place, from the same stock, perhaps.

He twitched slightly, as if he had, after all, recognized the word "gift." For a moment I swear I thought I was back in New Haven again, standing outside the First Presbyterian on a sunny Sunday morning and giving Bobby his dirk, although this wretched soul didn't seem half so cocksure as him. In fact, I almost wanted to hug him, hold him close. Right then, I wanted a son, him specifically. I wanted to take him home, out of this war zone, out of this miserable desert, the dirt, the disease, the woeful lack of all possibility. I wanted to give him what I'd had, what *anyone* should have.

"Brown," I heard the Lieut say. "Time to go."

He was about ten yards away. He was stood with his legs slightly apart, and he had his M16 cradled in his arms, the muzzle pointed in our direction, although tilted slightly down towards the ground. Suddenly, I realized his head looked huge and menacing, like an enormous mutant bug, an alien invader. His helmet made the top of his head seem outrageously bulbous, like it might explode at any second. His darkly tinted goggles seemed as if they might be harboring malicious evil eyes behind them. The outsized antenna on his radio waved in the air like a whip-like proboscis sniffing out prey.

The dog's fur along its spine stood up, like a line of iron filings suddenly subjected to a powerful magnetic field. He barked and set his teeth, curling his lips as threat. He took a half charge towards the lieutenant, but retreated again just as quickly. I looked back at kid; I could sense his fear before I saw it.

I held my hand up to the lieut, afraid that he might pop one off, shoot the dog, maybe even…

"Lieut—"

I felt the nodding donkey being ripped out of my hand, and then the kid was gone, scampering back towards his village as fast as his skinny legs could carry him. His dog made one last defiant lunge before setting off after him. They were halfway back to the village before I could do anything; then they were disappeared and gone, as if they had just vanished into thin air.

I wondered then who he was, what would become of him, whether he would play with the nodding donkey...or throw it away. I wondered if he would remember me, and how. I hoped he would find a place for me in his heart.

I hope so now, especially now. I knew somehow that I may not have much time left.

13
[25 November 2016]

They come to me in rotation, most often pouncing in pairs, even all five of them at once sometimes.

Brave little bastards! Can you believe it? It's then when they jabber to each other on and off in their Urdu cackle, throwing in an English "fuck" or "bitch" or "whore" now and again, along with something about Allah. I feel like my eardrums are about to burst or my head explode. It's a strange thing to say, I know, but being alone down here for hours on end at least spares me having to listen to them and to smell them, although in my dreams, my nightmares, their voices seem louder than ever, their stink ever more nauseating. I wish they would just say nothing when they come, just go about their business and get it over with. But there'd still be the grunts and the groans and the stink from their groins and the…the mess they'd make, wouldn't there?

…

Oh God…oh dear God. For the love of God…please!

…

They all follow the same routine when they're on their own, like it's some sort of ritual. I hear the footsteps first, clomping down the wooden steps, then their slovenly, slippered shuffling across the cement floor towards me. They always wear slippers and they always shuffle like they're either too fat or too goddamn lazy to pick their sodding feet up. But they're not all fat—far from it. A couple of 'em, even the one that seems to be in charge, can't be more than twenty, I reckon. They've still got the bum fuzz and the pimples on their chins to prove it. They may be Muslims, but they sure as hell haven't gotten the beards yet to go along with it!

The last time, I could tell it was him, the Soft One, the leader's chief sidekick it seems from the way he's always right next to him, following him around like a lost puppy, whenever they're down here together or with the rest of their gang. At first, I was surprised that he was alone, but then I realized that he'd come to practice, to gain some cred before he'd have to perform in front of his brothers again. He's much less sure of himself, as if he is almost apologetic, reluctant to be here, to be doing all this. But whatever, he still goes through with it. He's much quieter than the others, like he's treading on eggshells, just the heavy breathing catching here and there as he struggles to stay inside and keep up his awkward, uneven rhythm. After a minute or so he feels more agitated, like he's getting close, and I urge him on as best I can—my arms bound as they always are behind my back to the cold radiator—urging him with my hips to finish, finish, finish—for God's sake, please fucking finish! And then afterwards praying that somehow his rotten seed won't take, or that, miraculously, the last pill I took is still good somehow, although I know it won't be—it's been far too long since...

But if only that's all there was to it, if only...

...

Sometimes, if I try hard enough, if I can somehow suspend all of my senses and allow myself to be totally taken over by my imagination, I am almost capable of making myself believe that it is you—not one of them—who is with me. I'll insist on recalling the feel of you, the signature of your rhythm, the way you shudder and groan and gasp when you come. I'll literally smell you then, inhale the idea of you as a real material presence, at least for a while... But it's not long before the bubble is burst, and the fishy curry stink breaks through once again...and it's not you, not you at all...

...except when, later, you're there in the snippet of a fitful dream that somehow manages to break through my troubled sleep ...and we're on the canal bank again on an early Spring day, my

head in your lap, and you're caressing me…stroking me like I'm your special pet…
…

I knew he'd be back. Once there's a reliable food source, they just can't help themselves. Who wouldn't take a break from the struggle for existence—red in tooth and claw—if they could? Not Johnny Town-Mouse. I was so glad to see him. He got extra rations as a reward, and as a down payment for what I hoped he was going to do for me.

I'd been thinking for some unknown reason about an episode of Black Adder when the insane idea came to me. Remember the series when they're in the trenches in World War One, and Rowan Atkinson has Baldrick cook the carrier pigeon he's shot that happened to be Colonel Melchett's favorite pet? Well, I didn't want to kill and eat Johnny, but it occurred to me that he could come and go as he pleased, could step through his own looking glass just like Alice. So, why couldn't he be my carrier mouse, I thought, and deliver a message to the outside world for me? I knew it was a long shot, but I've learned down here that improbable ideas can become for-sure fixations when the walls keep closing in on you like they do, day after day. Once I'd started my train of thought, there was no stopping it.

So, I tore out a minute scrap of paper from this book I'm writing in and wrote out a plea for rescue in the tiniest handwriting I could manage: "Help. Captive. Paki men house." I knew it was cryptic, that maybe whoever might read it would immediately throw it away, nothing more than the rambling of some crazy person, and I knew that Johnny might not even deliver the note to anyone—perhaps he'd eat it, or it'd come off in his struggle to navigate his way through the hole he used. But I believed in him, I really did. And when I found just what I needed in amongst the rubble on the cellar floor—a partially-used up tube of glue—I just knew that my lucky stars were coming together in perfect providential alignment.

A dab of glue and the missive was stuck to the back of Johnny Town-Mouse's neck, right between his ears. I put him down next to the hole and sent him on his way.

Nothing to do, then, but wait…
Yes, I'd wait this time…not like I'd done outside the Palace. In any case, I'd obviously no other option. And, I realized, it'd been an unexpected option that had tripped me up that night…that horrible night.
I wonder what happened to her? Is she in another room, somewhere, or did she get away? Had she, oh God, had she gone to the police? She must have!
…
Why haven't they come yet?
Why haven't you?

14

[22 March 2016]

It had been a nerve-rattling wait, but the contact had come a couple of days before Jamal was expecting it.

The mobile phone he'd been sent came alive in his trouser pocket at the very moment he was withdrawing his weekly Jobseeker's Allowance from the local post office. The money wasn't much, but it gave him great satisfaction to have the government he was plotting against giving him free money at the taxpayers' expense. He quickly reached into his trouser pocket to silence the vibrations. For some reason, he feared that the postmistress knew about the call he'd been so anxiously awaiting; she'd certainly displayed her innate suspicion of him from the very moment of their first encounter, so who knew what the old biddy might surmise about him? But the middle-aged, blue-rinsed, overweight white woman who counted out Jamal's money for him just gave him her usual disgusted stare while she was doing her well-rehearsed mental calculations. Then she thrust the banknotes at him as if she was trying to stab him with a knife.

Jamal almost flinched in response, but caught himself just in time. He slowly picked up the banknotes and the loose change, note by note, coin by coin, letting the old bag know he was double-checking her math. Stuffing the money into his pocket, he grinned and said, "Thank you very much, *madam.*" He half-turned to leave and then continued over his shoulder: "Oh, by the way, do you know if the *Sword and Scimitar* is open yet? I could use a pint or two." He grinned again, like an alcoholic Chesire cat before a saucer of beer.

    The woman *tut-tutted* under her breath at his insolence and she started to mumble some curse at him. But she broke off in incoherent mid-sentence having no other frustrated choice as an employee of the Postal Service but to turn away, pretending to busy herself with something on her desk. But they both knew she had heard him, and that she had no option but to hand over Jamal's ill-gotten gains as long as some lazy-assed, apathetic civil servant didn't get around to checking Jamal's claim and striking him from the rolls forthwith, which was not very likely as she *knew* only too well. She could have ratted on him, she supposed, but the holy hassle of it, all the red tape and review panels and testifying under oath. And no one would thank her for it—least of all the bureaucrats who'd have to fill out the paperwork and render some unpleasant judgments; administration, as far as they were concerned, was meant to be a nice quiet life, wasn't it?

    "Ah, never mind, ma'am," Jamal shouted in farewell, as he stepped through the post office door into the street, "the pub's open. I can see from here. Thanks again—for *all* your help!"

But Jamal didn't go to the pub. He was drunk enough already with excited anticipation that even a gallon of alcohol could not match, notwithstanding the fact that he'd sworn off the stuff for well over a year now in any case. He quickly stepped into a narrow alleyway off the street and activated his phone. There was just one voicemail.

"Tomorrow. Ten-thirty a.m. Main entrance, British Museum. I will know who you are. Walk to Mornington Crescent tube stop. Train to Leicester Square. Walk, Piccadilly Circus. Train to Embankment, and then Monument. Take subways to Bank. Buy ticket to Mile End. Go through barrier, then exit. Walk to the Museum. *Do not reply.*" Jamal turned the phone off and snapped the clamshell shut. He knelt down and placed the phone on the ground. He looked towards the entrance to the alleyway: no one in sight. He picked up a broken brick, and with one well-aimed blow smashed the phone. He tossed what was left into a half-full skip behind what looked like a builder's yard.

As he watched the broken phone fly through the air on its way to its early grave, he began to think about the detailed instructions he'd been given. He wondered, given their complex circuitousness in getting him to the British Museum, if he was already being followed by the police or the intelligence agencies (the interview at immigration had certainly left him unsure about that), or whether the instructions were merely precautionary, designed not to arouse suspicion just in case anybody *might* be contemplating tailing him.

Either way, the directions filled Jamal with mixed emotions: trepidation that he might be arrested at any minute, but, at the same time, elation that the world was taking him seriously for once. He'd certainly been told many a time at the camp in Pakistan that he was a chosen one, a martyr for jihad, but even so he wasn't sure he could quite believe it as he hadn't exactly graduated from his training there with flying colors. But now he was starting to seriously consider the possibility that maybe he really was somebody after all, someone to be reckoned with, a man of consequence—and soon, God willing, a man of the "Deed," a true martyr just like they'd said he'd be.

Could it really be so? A pity, then, that the thrill of purposeful action that he was just beginning to taste would be, most likely, so short-lived. But then he remembered: jihad by its very nature could only be a momentary thrill, but, in being so, it was also *the* mother of all acts of martyrdom, the one that opened the gates to Paradise!

Jamal strode back into the street, daring "them" to come get him, whoever they were. He surveyed the growing crowd, gathering now to do their shopping, shuffle off to work, or drag their sorry asses to school. No one paid any special attention to him, the white folks in particular who, he figured, sensing his alien presence, tried to pretend he wasn't there, an invisible, smelly vapor that insolently insulted their being as members of an obviously superior race. Jamal farted as loudly as he could. He grinned like a Chesire cat again, relishing in the pleasure of relieving itself of some beer-induced intestinal gas.

"Inshallah," he blurted out, involuntarily, as if he had a mild case of Tourette syndrome. An old man passing by just at that moment turned and looked at him as if to say "What? Are you talking to me?" But Jamal just looked at him, wondering whether the old geezer would turn out to be one of his victims when he finally did his deed for Allah, and whether the arthritic codger would still be so smug when he realized at the very last moment that his life was just about to be extinguished—just like that—by the little Paki fucker he'd dissed in the street just a few days before. Jamal couldn't decide, but he loved the idea that he would soon have the opportunity to render final judgment like this—yes, judgment: Judgment with a capital "J"!

But still, such power…such *power* in his small, untested hands? It made him tremble before God.

It made him momentarily weak at the knees.

15

[Late September-ish 2015 CT]

The fallout from the drone attack at al-Adrum continued to reverberate around the world like a loose and irate ball bearing in a metallic echo chamber. I heard it as loud as anyone, even from way up here.

The "Arab Street" — as they insist on calling it — remonstrated loudly, chanting "Death to America" (original, uh?) and burning papier-mâché replicas of Uncle Sam and knock-off threadbare versions of the Stars and Stripes (made in China, and shaken angrily — in blissful innocence as opposed to subtle messaging — upside down). In solidarity, I suppose you could call it, and taking the opportunity to vent their own particular grievances against so-called American "imperialism," those made in my image (or is it the other way round: I was made in theirs?) in places such as Venezuela, Russia, and Zimbabwe all jumped on the bandwagon of global anti-Americanism, thankful to be demonstrating against *something* for once since their own governments rarely let them do so against them—at least not without serious repercussions. (I'd like to hold the God-fearing dictators back, but what can you do? Original sin among so many has my hands tied, right?) But in the theatrics of the occasion, oh-so-predictably, the paradox seemed to be momentarily lost on all those involved—except yours truly, of course.

Still, as you might have expected, in the self-satisfied smugness of the liberal-democratic West, enraged voices of ignorant dissent were heard just as loudly too, although less so the nearer you got to Lady Liberty herself, from whence the drone had come. Indeed, by the time you got to Middle America it almost became a criminal offense in the popular, patriotic American mind even to mildly consider that what allegedly passed for a legitimate tactic in the war on terror might actually constitute a war crime—a crime, God forbid, against humanity. It was considered thoroughly un-American to be so un-American! (I almost couldn't agree more—if you get my drift.)

What kind of being, they screamed, couldn't see the obvious, inherent righteousness of the Great Exception's cause in the world, that shining city on a hill spreading its beneficence munificently even if it did so with great, forced-by-the-circumstances, reluctance at times from the explosive warhead of a shock-and-awe-inducing missile? (The logic's almost perfectly Aristotelean in its *consistency*, isn't it?) And even amongst the ultra-liberal Yankees on the east coast and the die-hard hippies on the west, the indignation about the drone strike turned out to be just that: a largely professorial armchair critique that presented a great "teaching moment" about the equally inherent evils of empire, whether formal or not, but which quickly lost its resonance in the ether of fear of another probable 9/11 attack soon thereafter. (Hippies, long hair, flowers, peace signs and all, like to save their asses just as much as Wall Street bankers do when it all comes down to it. Bad shit is bad shit, regardless. *Love* the moral equivalency in that, don't you? Or is it hypocritical equivalency? Mmm, is there a difference, I wonder?)

But for the Islamists hell-bent on carrying jihad right to the Great Satan itself, the attack at al-Adrum was a magnificent propaganda coup. Ever since 9/11 they had been trying to goad the United States and their allies into massively over-responding to their largely pinprick attacks, and they had succeeded to a degree, drawing the US and its "coalition of the willing" into what became the quagmires of Iraq and Afghanistan. But, as a part of their propaganda mix, the jihadists badly needed the US to answer terror with terror, to respond to suicide bombers and knife-wielding executioners with the slaughter of guided missiles launched from afar and lighting up the night sky, a Fourth of July fireworks show like you've never seen before. The drone attacks were fitting the bill, especially when they went astray, inflicting "collateral damage" as at al-Adrum.

And then, to top it all, the supposedly smart president opened his stupid goddamn mouth promising to do "whatever it took" (what else could it be?) to destroy the very hornets he'd roused from their nests in places like al-Adrum. And the jihadi trickle soon became a flood (Hey, don't look at me!

Out of my hands at this point) as sleeping Muslims the world over flocked to the Black Flag of IS, flying over more and more of, first, the Middle East, then Africa, and even here and there in the cities of Europe, too, where Charlie Hebdo was struck down in the sanctuary of his own blasphemous home, and then, inevitably, in the Land of the Free and Home of the Brave — on Christmas Day, 2016, no less.

But that's for later.

Spectacle! — you know I like spectacle, the really big stuff, too wondrous to behold? I don't mean *Cirque de Soleil* tricks, although for your sort I'll admit they are pretty impressive. No, I mean really fucking huge stuff — like a universe billions and billions of light years across and still expanding like a bat out of hell, that sort of thing. Now, *that's* what I call a spectacle.

Unfortunately, when I gave you the gift of language I didn't anticipate that it would be so ambiguous at times, many words given over to multiple, even contradictory, meanings. So, there's *Spectacle*, and then there's spectacle — your typical sort. Let me give you a for-instance. How about this for a spectacle?

"My fellow Americans," the president solemnly says one day a week or so after al-Adrum, interrupting the viewing of *The Voice* much to the annoyance of millions of those who both had and had not voted for him. "I want to speak to you tonight about a grave threat to the country's national security…*blah, blah, blah.*"

Get to the point already, the chorus to this tragedy of Greek proportions says, waddling to the fridge for another super-sized drink and a second round of high-calorie, high-sodium content snacks. *Turn it down*, they demand through mouths filled with crushed crackers in a soup of Diet Coke or some sort of "light" piss-water beer. Listening at best only half-heartedly to the droning voice telling them something of supposedly great import, they turn to the article in *People* magazine that they have not finished reading—some salacious scuttlebutt about the president's wife or Brad Pitt's "illegitimate" daughter, a juicy tidbit still to be enjoyed as popular history *as it really happens*.

Blah, blah, blah…and on the president drones, eight minutes seeming like an eternity already. But then comes his coup de grâce, suddenly striking ears that have been tuned out to him just moments before, and by the time he's said his final words the chorus is back on side, committed now to a wholesale war on terror. He'd said "terror," verbal red meat to a nation freaked out by 9/11 and bent on revenge.

"And so, my fellow Americans, in response to these gruesome—medieval—acts of barbarism, I am committing our nation to finding and destroying the perpetrators, no matter where they are, no matter how long it takes… As I speak to you right now, actions are underway to eliminate some of those who have been responsible…*blah, blah, blah*… God bless you, and God bless these United States of America."

Hell yeah! the chorus cheers, turning up the sound again, expectant now that *The Voice* will soon resume shortly—after the look-at-me news anchor's *instant* analysis of what the prez has just said and the hard-to-differentiate commercial break, that is.

And somewhere in the skies over Yemen another drone already hovers. And somewhere in Florida its operator locks it onto its intended target. And somewhere amongst the band of evil-doers below a young girl and her mother are enjoying the last minute of their lives. And then in a great blast of destruction, the medieval meets the modern — perhaps the postmodern, but who can tell the difference anymore? I certainly can't. Terror, it has to be said, is unbounded by time and the arbitrary way by which your historians slice human history up into neat chronological packages, supposedly demarcating the primitive from the civilized in a nice linear progression. Who do they think they are, these so-called Masters of the Human Historical Record? God or something?

But this "truth" is lost in the contentment that the chorus feels, just that little bit safer now — at least for a while. But it is not lost on those who rush to join the struggle against the infidels, the Crusaders, and the apostates, especially those from the West deploying their own brand of terror in their global war on Islam.

It's an eye for an eye and a tooth for a tooth now, as the Donald prophetically yells — 'til death do us part...as it surely will.

Now, *that's* what I call an oh-so-sorry looking spectacle. But there you go? What can you do? What should *I* do? You tell me.

WWJD? He'd probably say something like, *Let he who has not sinned cast the first stone.*

Now, he was a talented kid. But the trouble is who's going to admit they've sinned — at least *first*, that is? And I'm not sure anyone needs to be advocating throwing any more stones, sinner or not—do you?

Too many glass glasshouses out there.

16

[May-June 2015]

On graduation day from the University of Bologna, Ayaan Pellegrino knew that the world lay at her feet and that before long she would yet again conquer every challenge that might be set for her, would seize every opportunity that might come her way.

She had already surpassed expectations by a country mile: among many other things, she was the first female to graduate at the top of her class in chemical engineering, previously an all-male bastion typical of the enduring patriarchy that still persisted in Berlusconi's Italy. She felt seven feet tall, a beacon to the world! She felt as if the blood of some indefatigable desert warrior flowed through her Somali veins, perhaps that of the infamous mythical Somali queen, Arraweelo, who, she had recently found out, had castrated all her male subjects and ruled her realm with an iron hand. Literal castration might be overdoing it a bit, Ayaan readily admitted, but surely a mass castration of sorts wouldn't go entirely amiss in male-dominated Italy, and neither would she mind taking the lead in such a worthy "operation," if she could.

So off she set for the brave new world of the American giant DuPont, her banner unfurled and flapping furiously in the wind. So violently in fact that it seemed to her sometimes that it might well carry her away and subject her to great danger, just like the early spring storm in the Mediterranean had done off the island of Lampedusa so many years ago. It had taken a miracle to save her then; she had been the "Miracle Baby," hadn't she?

Ayaan wondered if she'd need another miracle someday, in order to turn her promise, her huge potential, into concrete reality. Berlusconi *was* still prime minister, after all—*bunga, bunga!* Would he ever finally go away without some form of divine intervention to make him do so? But her science didn't let her believe in miracles any more—*did it?* And yet, so-called scientific certainty, how certain was that when it really came down to it? So certain that in the end you still didn't need some kind of "faith" to be able to forge on ever forward, even if the belief was in something her kind routinely referred to as the so-called iron "laws of nature"? But who had written those, who or what had been their great lawgiver: Nature herself...or perhaps a miracle-working God, after all?

Suddenly Ayaan felt only her true five feet, six inches tall again—give or take. She scratched her neck, the same spot as always, just right behind her right ear, the spot that when she looked at it in the mirror never showed the slightest sign of irritation or abrasion, just the redness from her worrying at it so.

If there was any sort of infection there, it had to be subcutaneous, perhaps so deep as to be beyond any kind of reach. Whatever else it might be doing, it had certainly disrupted her sense of contentment more times than she'd cared to remember.

That damn itch — wouldn't it ever completely go away?

♠

"Ah, Ayaan," her boss at DuPont said. "Now you're here, perhaps we can get started. Would you be so kind as to make coffee for us all? You do it so well. Cappuccinos, everyone? Luigi, Giovanni..." Her boss held his finger up as if he was hailing some sort of flunky waiter.

Ayaan bit her tongue and got up again. She quickly made the drinks; cupboard doors slammed, drawers squeaked loudly on their runners, steam *whooshed* so loud that it seemed she might be trying to blow the kitchen up. When the coffees were ready, she ungraciously plonked them on the conference table in front of her male colleagues, spoons rattling and liquid spilling into the saucers.

"Er...Thank you, dear," her boss said. He looked across at Luigi and Giovanni, sitting opposite him. They were already returning his knowing look. Giovanni raised his eyebrows slightly as if to say "What's up with her?" Ayaan's boss pursed his lips in response, signaling: "Who knows? You know how women can be." All three men thought to themselves "Must be that time of the month. It's not the first time she's been in a huff like this — for no apparent reason."

Ayaan sulked throughout the meeting, and the men had free rein of both the agenda and the conclusions to their discussion, of which she took little part. What was the point? Now and again during the meeting she'd let her mind entertain fleeting thoughts about exacting revenge of some sort, but nothing had come to mind except Arraweelo's impossibly radical action, the sort that might have brought her immense satisfaction, at least theoretically, but which, it went without saying, would have ended all of her dreams, forthwith. It was all so infuriating, so…unjust. Just a few weeks ago she'd burst through the glass ceiling at the university, and had felt so free, so full of promise. But now another ceiling had presented itself to her, looking very much like it was made of much sturdier stuff than mere glass, perhaps made of one of the new synthetic plastics that DuPont's scientists had a real knack for inventing.

After the meeting was over, Luigi asked whether he could help her with the coffee cups. Ayaan declined his offer with a weak smile. "No, thank you, it won't take a minute," she quietly said.

But it took ten in fact.

She had more than washing-up suds to wipe away.

♠

One more look like that and I'll… It was the sixth time at least in the last five minutes that Ayaan had caught Luigi staring at her breasts.

Sensing her gaze, Luigi raised his eyes and saw Ayaan looking at him, tight-lipped and obviously irritated. He feigned that he'd been looking at his notes lying on the laboratory desk next to him, even flipping a page back and forth in the hopes that he'd be more convincing than he knew he was being. He felt himself flush with guilt. He ran a finger inside his shirt collar, as if to suggest that it was hot in the room, but with the kind of heat-sensitive experiments they conducted there everyone knew that the climate was so carefully controlled that at least two layers of clothing under the lab coat were necessary in order to stop oneself from constantly shivering.

Ayaan looked down at her chest. Even under her three layers of protection against the chilled air there was still no mistaking the imprint of her erect nipples beneath them. Ayaan closed her eyes and pinched her brow just above her nose with the fingers of her left hand. Would they never stop? What was wrong with them? She almost began to cry, but refused to do so. She trembled, trying to compose herself against the swelling anger that was roiling inside her. She wrapped her lab coat more tightly around her, as if she were trying to strap her breasts down. But the effort served little purpose. When she looked up again, there he was, still lusting after her, apparently even more titillated by the way she was squeezing and squashing.

"Want to see more?" Ayaan erupted. "Here! Take a good look!"

Ayaan stood up and ripped open her lab coat, sending two buttons flying in Luigi's direction. One popped him on the forehead; the other narrowly missed his left ear. Ayaan thrust her chest out, cursed, and then stomped out of the room.

Seconds later she burst into her boss's office without knocking. The brief encounter was volcanic. Ayaan's astounded boss stared at her in shocked disbelief as she poured forth a torrent of invective he'd never heard come from such a young woman's mouth, especially one so petite as she. Was the job getting too much for her? Was she too young for such responsibility? Was she perhaps…unhinged? She clearly had no right to talk to him in such a disrespectful manner!

In the end, the sexual harassment allegations Ayaan made against Luigi failed to pass muster with her boss, who also had his problems concentrating on the inquiry at hand when he had Ayaan alone in his office, flustered and flushed, and well…heaving like that. What, he surmised, was so bad about appreciating female beauty? Hadn't God given it to man for a purpose? Even the prime minister, Berlusconi, knew this as well as anyone. *Bunga, bunga* — as natural as…well, as just about anything.

He felt like saying to her "Take it as a compliment, Ayaan. I'm sure Luigi meant no harm. Enjoy the attention. Think how ugly girls get treated! Your beauty will open doors for you — open them!" but he didn't. All he said was: "Look, you have a very bright future here. Last thing I'd do if I were you is to spoil it all by pursuing a complaint for which there really is no independent evidence, and which, at the end of the day, is no more than a minor nuisance, really, in the larger scheme of things. Men love beautiful women — their attentions to you just come with the territory, I'm afraid. And it is all harmless — can't you see that? Besides, if Luigi denies everything, you have to know that really all we have is your word against his, and he is superior to you. Focus on your career, my dear, on what will get you ahead; don't let silly episodes like this take you off course. Alright?"

Ayaan stared blankly at her boss and said nothing. Her parting gesture was to slam his office door closed as hard as she could on her way out. The door rattled violently in its frame; then the glass in its window *cracked!* For a second, Ayaan thought someone might have just fired a gun at her. She fingered the back of her neck: nothing—just a strange numbness, a dead spot; no itch at all.

Luigi never suffered for his transgression, no matter how hard Ayaan tried to make him pay. She attempted repeatedly to entrap him into making an approach that could pass muster as sexual assault, but, on guard now, Luigi failed to take her bait—he took nightly pleasure, instead, in the fantasies she had teased him with earlier in the day.

In the end, Ayaan's tricks came back to haunt her; before long she'd earned the reputation as the office tease, well on her way to slutdom. Even her father's vast resources couldn't help her this time; DuPont turned out to be much bigger than he was, and they refused to fire Luigi despite Piero Pellegrino's financial shenanigans against the company. Luigi's stock continued to rise as Ayaan's tragically began to fall.

In the Sermon on the Mount, Ayaan remembered, Jesus had preached: "Blessed are the meek, for they will inherit the earth." But meekness was not much of a part of her repertoire, and so it came to pass that she inherited much less than she had bargained for, that she believed she had a right to. Or, rather, she inherited much more than she had ever wanted, an inheritance that soon began to weigh her down with increasing self-doubt, even self-loathing at times. Initially convinced of the flagrant vindictiveness of the rumors about her harlot-like reputation, in their persistent repetition her confidence soon began to falter, nibbled away at like a lie that, repeated often enough, eventually takes on the aura of objective truth merely in its repeated telling. She stopped wearing makeup, tried to avoid looking in the mirror any more than was absolutely necessary, as if she was afraid of what, or whom, she might see there.

♠

"Well," Ayaan's boss said to her one day several weeks later, "I'll get right to the point."

He looked as if he was going to go right on, but suddenly he stalled. He went to his office window and looked out over the city below. Whatever it was he had to say to Ayaan would have to be echoed back to her off the huge window he was facing. His words would reverberate in her mind on many occasions long afterwards.

"After...after due consideration," he finally continued, "taking *all* factors into consideration, I'm sorry to have to tell you that it's Luigi who will get the promotion to Chief Scientist...and...and not you." He paused, as if trying to sense Ayaan's mood. Behind his back, his fingers twitched nervously in his lightly clasped hands resting just above his rear end. "But I want you to know just how much we value you here in the GM division at DuPont, Ayaan. Your work is exemplary, and we look forward to many more great things from you in the future. Your time will surely come, my dear; just be patient, okay?"

He paused again, but Ayaan still made no sound. He slowly turned around and looked at her. She was staring blankly at him, offering no resistance, no sense that she was about to explode. "You're still so very young, my dear," he went on, more sure of himself now. "I'm sure Luigi will be a great mentor to you, if you can, well…let bygones be bygones. Yes? Do right by him, Ayaan, and the sky's still the limit!" Ayaan looked up at him and appeared to weakly smile; at least the upside down-U of her mouth leveled out a little, he was sure. Encouraged he was going to get away with it, he maneuvered himself alongside Ayaan's chair and put his arm around her shoulders, giving her a gentle squeeze.

But she resisted, freeing herself before he could get any more familiar than he already was. She suddenly realized that for all the male chauvinism that still resided in the University of Bologna's chemical engineering program, of which there'd been plenty, it was *nothing* compared to that which she hadn't realized still stalked the halls of industry.

Glass ceilings? No, it was more than that, much more. Glass could in fact be shattered; what she faced at DuPont was impenetrable—a steel curtain, no less. She'd been living in a cocoon, a loving and nurturing one in good measure thanks to her parents, but it had left her totally unprepared for the stark reality that now faced her. She felt hopelessly alone, as if she was lost at sea with no hope of rescue.

"I cannot continue working here any longer," Ayaan wearily said at last—no drama, no wrath this time. Part of her still very much wanted to let her boss know just how she felt, but she didn't have the energy any more, worn down by the irrepressible forces arraigned against her, resigned now to what she knew *must* happen. "I *know* I deserve to be Chief Scientist, and I *know* that you know that, too—everyone does, if only they'd admit to the truth, but you all won't. I can't work under Luigi under any circumstances. I need to move on, to where I'll be appreciated for what I can do, not for what sex I am, what 'entertainment value' I have for the likes of Luigi, maybe even—"

"If that's the way you feel, then perhaps it's best if you resigned right away!" her boss angrily interjected.

Ayaan stared at her boss, vacantly again, as if the world had just lost all of its promise. She slowly got up to leave. Just as she was about to open the door to his office, her boss said: "You won't find any better company to work for than DuPont, Ayaan." He was visibly shaking, his face flushed with anger. "You know *why*? Uh?" Spittle sprayed from his lips, almost hitting her.

Ayaan didn't turn around, but just stood with her back to him, her hand on the door knob, silently waiting for his pearl of wisdom.

"Because you're a troublemaker, Ayaan, that's why! Sooner or later, you're going to realize that fact. And for your sake, I hope you discover that about yourself sooner *rather* than later. It'd be a great pity to waste such talent as yours." He was breathing heavily now, gasping with the effort to put Ayaan in her place.

Don't worry, Ayaan thought to herself, *talent like mine will never be wasted, even if I have to die proving it*. As she opened the door to leave, Ayaan noticed that the window glass, puzzlingly, had still not been repaired. She looked at the jagged lines where the glass had cracked. Then she saw her own reflection behind them, fracturing her face into a dozen distorted pieces.

Ayaan went back to her office and packed up her few belongings in a cardboard box, just like she'd seen other DuPont employees do over the time she had been working there when they had, for some reason or another, curried disfavor with a superior in the corporate hierarchy. Out in the street, she turned one last time to look at the building that had once housed such great expectations for her. Thankfully, she suddenly realized, it was located far from downtown Bologna where its architectural philistinism would have disgraced the medieval beauty that still bravely hung on there.

But Italy was still Italy. How many non-chauvinistic, greener pastures could there be in a country such as that? Ayaan set off for home, despondent about her future prospects and nervous about what to tell her parents. Rather than struggling with her box on the crowded Metro, she decided to take a cab.

"Where to, Signorina?" the driver asked, when she'd settled herself into the back seat..

"What?" Ayaan replied, as if she had somehow not expected the question.

"Where do you want me to take you?
"Oh...home...I guess."
"Address?"
"I'm not sure." Ayaan stared vacantly, straight ahead of her. She caught sight of a reflection in the driver's rearview mirror. At first she didn't recognize that it was her own face; the eyes lacked sparkle, and dark smudges underlined them on the high cheekbones, suggesting mild disfigurement rather than the intoxicating beauty they had once exhibited. Then she saw the driver's eyes reflected there too, a look of puzzlement waiting for a different answer. Ayaan smiled weakly. "Oh, sorry. Via di Casaglia—"

"Colli?"

"Yes, that right." Ayaan knew what he was thinking, a girl like her living in Colli, the Beverly Hills of Bologna? Bit of a stretch, wasn't it?

Yes, she thought, perhaps it was.

17

[September 2015]

It's not long when you're in a combat zone, that's not so much a raging battlefield as a desertscape of a minefield laced with God knows what waiting to go off, that you start to dream of going home. What brought you to such a godforsaken place – dulce et decorum est pro patria mori *in the long shadow of 9/11 – now seems like a Fool's errand, like you've been had.*

You and your new best buddy Delta from Dumas, Arkansas, feel like the two biggest suckers in the world. "Jo-Buck," he says for the thousandth time, "how the fuck did we let ourselves get mixed up in this shit?"

So, you make calendars showing the days you have left, scoring them out one by one with thick black X's as they oh-so-agonizingly go slowly by. Delta teases you every night when you jointly perform the ritual, about how you have fifteen more days to do than him. He says, "Poor Jo-Buck, his ass'll still be shitting in this desert, when Delta's big black hiney'll be sashaying down Main on his way to Banjo's Bar and Grill!" You tell him to fuck off, but all he *does is to guffaw even louder. Then he hums, like he always does when he's fixing to turn in,* Tie a Yellow Ribbon Round the Ole Oak Tree. *You always turn away from him then, not wanting him to see you tear up, and wondering, fitfully wondering...*

I'm wandering through an airport somewhere stateside.

I'm coming home. Some old blue-rinse from the local community, a DAR most likely, waves a miniature Old Glory at me, a gaudy yellow ribbon tied in an outsized bow and lopsidedly stuck on the top of her head like a drunken angel on a Christmas tree. "Thank you for your service!" she shouts out. As I exit the Jetway, she hobbles forward. Her arms are outstretched; it's clear she's gonna hug me.

But I *have* to take evasive action, there's no way I can let her touch me, and I dodge her like a running back. I hear her groan behind me as she tumbles to the floor; then the collective murmur of the waiting crowd at the gate, shocked to see the old gal go down like that. A shout rings out: "Hey! What do you..." But I pay no heed and run on, headed for the end zone. Nothing but a yellow flag can stop me now.

Thank you for your service, she'd said. The phrase echoes in my brain, each reverberation seeming to get louder and louder — grating, *searing*.

Outside the terminal I pause for breath. *Service?* What can she possibly know about that? What can any of them know, nodding and smiling at me in my uniform, taking a second or two away from their precious cellphones to pay homage for the security they think I provide? But it's the same second or two I take to half believe the sentiments they express, before I remember what I did—back there in that desert.

I hadn't known I was capable of such a thing. But then I remember Bobby and the bee on my last day in New Haven and realize that, of course, I had always been as mean of a-son-of-a-bitch as he was. That reptilian trait had lain mostly somewhere deep below the surface, but, I then knew, had still been capable of breaking through my civilized veneer when the "right time" might have conspired to turn me into someone I didn't recognize. And that moment had indeed come, the very moment I'd realized my ambition—to become a patriotic holy warrior...

...You see, they'd taken Delta one day, cut his head off, just like that. I'd failed him; I hadn't had his back. So...you see, I had no choice. *An eye for an eye,* after all, the Bible says. And no one is the wiser, anyway; you'll never be found out, although you wonder now and again just what God might do...

We were alone when it happened, just me and him, some Belgian punk, a mercenary Muslim kid from Molenbeck, or maybe an Algerian immigrant from one of those *banlieu* ghettoes near Paris. Wherever he was from, it didn't matter in the end. Like a stuck pig, he just made a gurgling noise when his throat opened up like that, like a piece of smooth liver slickly sliced in two...

You realize it's Delta. He's lying flat on his back, snoring like a buzz saw.

You look at his throat, but there not a scratch. He's as clean as a whistle.

You realize you've been dreaming, you're sure you have. But there's a seed of doubt. You're not really sure at all. Not sure that it hadn't really happened, that you hadn't actually done it.

You've been in the desert too long, just long enough to become a tad unreliable as to knowing what is fact and what is fiction, whether you've ever been Jo-Buck Brown from New Haven, Nebraska, all-star quarterback, and whether you've really sought to go off to war. You can't tell a fake mirage from the real thing. You're in a Hall of Mirrors.

You pinch yourself until you're blue in the flesh, but you still don't know. It almost makes you feel dumb.

18

[24 May 2016]

Mo and Saeed walked aimlessly down darkened street after darkened street, eyeing the passing cars mournfully. What they wouldn't have given for access to a set of wheels! But no, they were totally out of reach. Saeed's dad had a motorized conveyance of sorts—a banged-up banger of a rust bucket, if ever there was one—but even if he'd been gracious enough to let them use it now and again (which he most emphatically wasn't), neither of them would have been seen dead in it. At least that's what they supposed right then in that wretched moment of despair.

Inevitably they meandered slowly in the direction of the town center, but with little more conscious intent than homing pigeons. The dilapidated town center held few attractions now, but it still hadn't quite lost its draw—after all, where else was there to go? And at least *something* a little out of the ordinary was more likely to happen there than anywhere else in godforsaken Rotherham. Neither Mo nor Saeed said a word to each other, both consumed by their own thoughts, their feet—on autopilot—doing the walking and whatever navigation was necessary.

Saeed's musings flitted from subject to subject in quick succession, cycling over and over. First, he would entertain fantasies about his application to university to study computer science in America being wildly successful, being awarded not just a place but also a prestigious and generous scholarship to help pay for it. Then he'd see himself "bending it like Beckham" and scoring an impossible last minute goal to bring the World Cup back to England for the first time since 1966, to be followed by a visit to the Palace and bowing his head before the Queen as she presented him with an O.B.E. for his "meritorious service to the nation."

But, more often than not, he'd arouse himself with his ultimate desire: to capture the heart—and the knock-out body—of voluptuous Kathy Green, the gorgeous blond daughter of one of Rotherham's wealthiest businessmen. Ah, the sex—the glorious, no-holds-barred screwing! Hot, naked Kathy: a totally uninhibited sex-slave to all of his most wanton, lascivious desires. And then there'd be the prospect of a filthy rich future father-in-law to boot, showering his largesse on the newly married couple and landing Saeed a cushy job with the family business where *he'd* be ordering white folks around rather than vice versa for a change. For a brief scintillating moment he'd feel his penis stiffen and maybe something seep into his underpants. He'd look down at his crotch and then across at Mo to see if his best friend had cottoned on to what he'd been thinking. But no, Mo would just be plodding along too, oblivious to Saeed's aroused state of mind. And then Saeed's moment of self-gratification would be as quickly over as it had come on, and he'd remember that he'd have chores to do when he got home.

Shit!

Chances are that Mo's thoughts would have paralleled Saeed's on any given night before this one, but, for some reason he couldn't put his finger on quite yet, Mo thought of neither fame, nor fortune, nor fornication. Mysteriously, Kathy Green was nowhere to be found in Mo's addled state of mind, but, incredibly enough, that verse from the Koran that Saeed had pulled up on his computer screen sure was. He couldn't remember all of it, of course, but what he could recall kept eating away at him, nagging at him to take it more seriously, to probe its deeper meaning.

"And what is wrong with you that you fight not in the Cause of Allah" — Mo saw the words shimmering in the puddles left over from the rain earlier in the day as he splashed through them — "…raise for us from You one who will help."

"Mo?" Saeed suddenly said. "Hello, Mo? Earth to Mo!"

"Eh? Oh, sorry. What?"

"You almost walked into that lamppost, you dick."

Mo stopped and looked up. Above him the streetlight was extinguished, probably had been for months now. The full moon revealed that its glass casing had been smashed, most likely by some bored, unemployed youth such as him throwing rocks at every breakable thing that represented distant, uncaring authority or opportunity denied. Maybe it had been him who had targeted the unoffending light; it certainly wouldn't have surprised him to find out that he'd been the culprit, but he wouldn't have cared, been ashamed. Far from it, in fact. Who gave a flying fuck? Light, darkness, what did it matter? A new dawn was just another day of despair for the likes of him—over and over. He kicked the lamppost—*Fuck!*—and moved on, hopping on one leg until the pain eventually subsided.

Saeed almost dared to laugh, but quickly thought the better of it.

Mo felt Saeed tug at his shoulder. "What's up, Mo?"

"Nothing's up. Just fucking bored as usual. God, I hate this stupid town."

As Mo and Saeed turned the corner onto Main Street, a wash of pale yellow light slanted across the pavement ahead of them. A sign of life at last: some kind of emporium that had somehow managed to weather the latest financial storm that had recently lain waste most of the country to the far north of London.

Mo and Saeed stopped in front of the shop's illuminated window and looked in. The store was closed and in darkness, except for the lighted window that still tried to tempt passersby to come back on the morrow and buy the item or items their nocturnal perusing had convinced them they just had to have, even if, most likely, it would mean they'd have to rack up even more debt in order to procure them.

It was a home electronics store. Behind the large plate glass window, tiered shelving arched in a concave curve facing the street displayed a veritable cornucopia of the tech world's latest gadgetry, most items having names beginning with what was by now the most iconic "**i**" the world of commerce had ever known. Mo wondered whether the letter stood for "I" as in "*I* must have it." Despite his well-rehearsed denial of lusting after such electronic baubles, enforced in large measure by his unemployed status and lack of access to easy credit, Mo nonetheless found himself staring longingly at the latest iPhone that stood in center stage, just a thin sheet of plate glass between him and the prize of prizes. He could almost reach out and touch it...

Mo fingered his dated and dinged-up mobile phone in his hoodie pocket, but it was mostly mute these days since he wasn't able to pay for network service any more. The cheap, muffled piece of plastic reminded him of just how embarrassed he had been to use it whenever somebody, especially someone of his own age, might have witnessed him doing so. How could he expect to stand a chance with Kathy Green sporting such a piece of crap? He didn't want much, God knows, but if only...if only he could just have one decent thing in his life, how things would be so much better. But...

"Shit," Saeed said, "look at the price of that new iPhone!" It was an eye-popping £349.99. "How can they charge that? Amazon's got 'em for less than three hundred! Fucking Jew. They wouldn't let that happen in a Muslim country."

"What? Jews?"

"No, stupid—rip-offs like that! It's un-Islamic, contrary to *sharia*—Islamic law to you. Someone gouging folks like this would be hauled up in front of the imam in short order and most likely get a good stoning for his trouble." Saeed laughed maliciously, although what he said was meant more as a joke than as a statement of theological fact, let alone actionable desire.

"A stoning?" Mo repeated.

"Nah, not really. You only get that, I think, for adultery or being a faggot. Still, it might not be a bad idea—the bloodsucker!"

They both returned their gaze to the iPhone and ruminated in alienated silence together, like two orphaned waifs abandoned on the mean streets of Rotherham. They didn't ponder the ways of justice exactly, at least not in so many words; the concept was too philosophical perhaps, or wrapped up in the mysterious ways of bewigged, red-robed, old white guys sounding far too serious and hoity-toity to be understood by the likes of them. But they did think about and know "fairness," at least in the sense of what some folks had and they didn't, in the ways some folks were treated and they weren't. What law, what divine ruling, said they couldn't—shouldn't—have the latest iPhone too?

Mo looked up at the barely illuminated sign above the store window, where the words "Green's Home Electronics" met his gaze. Kathy Green's dad, Mo silently mouthed, and then thought, "Might have fucking known! The old bloodsucker's got Kathy and the iPhone both!" *Nothing...he had nothing...not a goddamn thing...*

Saeed was just about to say something else when he heard the loud crash. In just a couple of swift, silent movements Mo had picked up a half-brick from the gutter and launched it through the shop window. Shards of glass showered them both. Saeed saw an arm reach in and grab the iPhone. He turned to Mo, but he was already bounding off down the street as fast as his legs could carry him, yelling "Run! Let's get the fuck out of here!" For a second or two Saeed was transfixed by the sound of the shop's burglar alarm going off until it finally dawned on him why it was. "Fuck!" he said, and the next thing he knew he was chasing after Mo as if his life depended on it.

They just managed to reach the bridge over the river Don when they heard the unmistakable wail of a police car's siren in the distance, but getting louder by the second. By the time the police car reached the store, Mo and Saeed were safely hidden in the overgrown vegetation beneath the bridge. They collapsed together in one heap, panting furiously. Mo held up the purloined iPhone like he was hoisting a trophy, and smiled broadly at his accomplice.

"Allahu Akbar," he whispered. *Yeah, God is great!*

19

[17 December 2016]

This is what it's like, as much as I can remember...
  ...
  ...the Soft One's still inside me grunting away, but I can easily tell he doesn't know what he's doing or that he doesn't really want to be doing what he's doing at all. It's a matter of pride with him, I suspect, peer pressure from the gang of gang-bangers he's hooked up with. I can feel him weaken just a bit, like he's run out of gas, can't make it over the edge. He thinks about quitting, withdrawing, I know he does, but just then he makes one final lunge like his life depends on it and lets out a weird "Aiee" before collapsing on top of me. He breathes heavily in my ear as if he is totally depleted, but I know he isn't. I know when it happens with a man, and that wasn't it, not even close.
  He's faked it.
  He pulls out and quickly pulls up his underwear and trousers, as if he's afraid I might suddenly open my eyes and see something he's not too proud of. I can hear him struggling with something, so I half-open my eyes, able to see something of what he's up to if I look straight down beneath the bottom edge of the blindfold. He's fumbling with his belt buckle, somehow incapable of threading the tapered end of the belt fully through it, like he can't master the necessary motor skills all of a sudden in order to fasten it

properly. His shirt tail hangs half out at his waistband. He's clearly as mentally disheveled as his physical appearance suggests. He rips the blindfold off and looks at me with pleading, then angered eyes.

"Please," he gasps. "No trouble, no lies. My brothers when they come, you tell them I did it—good, real good, OK? If not, they joke me very bad. Then make bad, very very bad for you. You understand? Zzzzt!" He makes a slashing motion across my throat with his forefinger. Our eyes lock and neither one of us moves while we test each other out in this way. It seems like neither one of us knows exactly what to do next, but out of nowhere my knee comes up and rams him in his crotch, crushing his scrawny, pea-sized nuts. It's exhilarating to spike him like that—I'd never done that before, I didn't know I had it in me. He wails like a stricken banshee. I feel a rush, like I'm an Amazon. I think about taking a huge swipe at him, to finish him off, but I hear noise coming from upstairs. They're on their way.

My victory, such as it is, will be merely momentary, a looming defeat in essence. He's not faking it this time—and neither will his brothers when they get to me.

...

I'll be honest…nothing to lose now, I suppose, but I did fake it with you—a few times. But I think you knew, didn't you? I could tell by your mood, afterwards—you just got up or rolled over, no hugs, no nuzzling, no heavy sighs of total satisfaction, like you could have wrapped me in your arms and legs forever, your face buried in my neck, softly kissing my skin, over and over…

But now you know, anyway. Well, if you ever get to read this, that is. I didn't want to, please believe me, it was nothing to do with you, nothing; but the last couple of times it'd hurt, and I guess I just wanted to help you come as quickly as possible, to get it…over with.

...

"Be careful what you wish for," my Mum always used to say.

...

I'm sorry…
…sorry I didn't wait.

...

But Katie, or whoever, insisted everything would be all right. "See this?" she said. She got a can of mace out of her bag. "One squirt of this fucker and anybody who tries to mess with us will start screaming his fucking head off, wailing like a baby!" It had a small flashlight at the other end. I never did know if she got to use it. But if she did, fat lot of good it did me.

...

Well, I found Johnny Town-Mouse yesterday. He hadn't made it.

It was the long trail of ants that suddenly showed up that told me that something was wrong. I hadn't seen any ants until then. I felt the soft tickle of a scouting outrider's feet before I saw the weaving line of ants passing backwards and forwards across the basement floor. At first I didn't think their presence meant too much of any real importance, but then I realized that the frenzied activity had to signal something novel.

I was bound to the radiator again, so I couldn't move. I followed the trail carefully with my eyes, wondering where it would end. It disappeared on the sill beneath the small window high up on the basement wall. Something I hadn't noticed before was lying there. Even in the gloom, I could see the ants swarming all over it, like an enraged mob. And there, I suddenly realized, lay the rotting carcass of a small animal in the early stages, it looked like, of decomposition. I don't know that it's Johnny Town-Mouse for sure, of course, but it must be. I just feel it in my bones.

And beside him, I think I can see a few tiny shreds of mangled paper.

...

I mourn a mouse? I mourn that which used to terrify me? But he'd been my only silly hope, so, yes, I mourn poor little Johnny Town-Mouse.

I mourn a lot of things these days...

...

I shouldn't have gone to the Palace. I should have stayed home—with you.

We should have talked more…we could have worked it out…

Maybe you showed up, though—if you did, I'm sorry, but you were late, and Katie I think she said her name was—I'd never met her before—persuaded me to walk home with her.

She said it'd be safe, she'd walked home lots of times before.

…how was I to know it wouldn't be—that night?

…

"No point in crying over spilt milk," my Dad always used to say. He was right, of course, but sometimes it's easier said than done…

I never really knew whether he really meant it, anyway…

…he's a milkman—never dropped a bottle in his life, he's always boasted.

…

A bottle of milk, ice-cold milk!—Johnny Town-Mouse would have liked that…

20

[25 March 2016]

The more he thought about his anonymous caller and the instructions he had communicated, the more Jamal became convinced that he was now a wanted man.

Wanted no doubt by the security establishment, but also, and this was the real kicker, wanted — chosen — by God, the one and only god, Allah. Paradise beckoned now, lying just around the corner somewhere, a mere suicide attack away from certain martyrdom. His training in the camp in Pakistan had exposed his questionable ability to engage in feats of significant physical endurance, but he had more than made up for this lack, his instructors had repeatedly said, by his new-found commitment to the Faith, a steely piety that he had never felt before. His former Islam-lite, pre-Pakistan, persona had been transformed into the turbo-charged variety, the sort that could decapitate apostates with a knife, just like Jihadi John. At least that was the theory, the presumption—that's what he thought he could now do, quite possibly...*Inshallah*...

...*If only he had found Sayyid Qutb in his wayward youth, before a wasted two years at university pretending to be a sociology student, but all the while consumed with chasing "various pleasures of the flesh," as his imam would have put it. At university, he had been either drunk or stoned more times than he now cared to remember, being so hungover most mornings that going to class had been the least of his concerns. For several months his professors had let his poor performance slide—they got paid whatever he and many others like him chose to spend their taxpayer-funded grant money on. But when he'd failed to show even for the year's final examinations, well, even lazy academic accounting had finally had to take notice. The chair of his department had reprimanded him (mildly, of course, since student retention had meant maintaining current levels of funding) and the Provost had sent him a so-called "warning letter" that he might be put on probation if he didn't soon mend his errant ways. He'd gone cold turkey, then, but all that had served to do was to subject him to frequent bouts of* delirium tremens, *rendering sleep and concentration well-nigh impossible. Classes had continued to be missed, his troubles had continued to pile up, and the Provost*—finally—*had kicked him out*...

Sleep, if only he could have slept at night back then...

...if only he could sleep, now.

Still sleepless at the crack of dawn, Jamal set out a full three hours before his designated rendezvous time, not just because he did not want to be late, but also because he would need more time to get there, since he had decided to ward off the chances of being followed and arrested by altering the route by which he would reach the main entrance to the British Museum. The method he chose omitted the Tube altogether. He worried about the inevitable delays, especially during the early morning rush hour, and the train drivers' union was threatening yet more "interruptions to service," as the authorities liked to call their strikes in some sort of incredibly transparent denial as to what was really going on.

Instead, he decided to ride his moped, a secondhand Honda Hobbit, and take a long, circuitous route to his destination. It would give him a better sense that he was in control of his destiny, not a bunch of Bolshie train drivers. Moreover, his trusted steed was nimble, able to navigate through even the densest of traffic jams, and, if necessary, dodge down narrow alleyways and back lanes, even descend flights of steps, if he needed to be elusive or make some kind of escape, or even just, as he intended, to make it all that much more difficult for someone to trail him.

He'd also removed the license plate and replaced it with a fake one he'd made up the night before while he was without sleep. On close inspection, he knew anyone would be able to see it was a pretty poor fake, but at a good distance he figured it'd do the trick well enough. So, even if the legions of CCTV cameras around the city picked him up, no matter—the police would most likely end up looking for a number plate that didn't exist.

And even if the cameras got a decent portrait shot of him, no matter either—his beard would be covered up with a scarf, he'd be wearing wrap-around sunglasses, and his hair would be completely hidden by a black stocking hat. And if all else failed—well, he'd be packing a passport to martyrdom, wouldn't he? Yes, let them come and get him! *Allahu Akbar.*

He stroked the knife he had in his pocket, testing the sharpness of the blade with his fingertips. He pressed the blade against his skin, gently at first, then harder, and hard*er—harder!* The pain hurt alright, but the more its sharp intensity grew the more he wanted of it, the more it thrilled him. Soon, he felt the tell-tale sticky wetness of blood. He let out a loud satisfied sigh. He felt his heart pounding furiously, his knees shaking in that weak-kneed way that release brings you. He remembered the time back in camp in Pakistan when he'd finally managed to stick the feral cat in the gut, as he'd been ordered to, over and over until he had somehow managed to muster the courage to follow through. It had felt *good*, almost arousing, almost... It felt good now. It felt so good it would be a majestic way to die, to sink the blade into one's own gut, to bleed out the suffering of this world, and to slowly and serenely drift off to ... *Paradise.*

The knife was sharp, but would it be enough for the big show when the time came? *Had he ever been...*

...enough up for it—especially "it." "It," huh, why was he so consumed with his sexual prowess—or lack thereof, rather? Why did he let it be the mark of his manhood? He really didn't know, but the facts—his obsession—spoke for themselves. He just did, *like he was subject to an inviolable law of nature, trapped by some*

uncontrollable urge, like an addict. How many times had he examined his penis, measured it with a ruler, urged it, when erect, to be harder and thicker and longer still, its tip twitching like a baby bird stretching for a worm in its mother's mouth? And how many times had he been disappointed—a five, rounded-up, inches at best, even on a good day when was hornier than hell?

The booze and dope, though, had always given him the courage to make a play for the girls nonetheless, and they had certainly shown some interest in him when he was brave enough—high enough—to engage them. Intoxication had had the effect of making him incredibly funny, although he hadn't been always entirely sure whether it was incisive humor or just his plain stupidity that had made them laugh so hard. But he hadn't cared back then, especially when in their uncontrollable mirth they had touched his arm or fallen against him, doubled-up with laughter. The physical contact had encouraged him even further, both in falling prey to the temptresses and in imbibing even more intoxicants so that he could keep up the momentum. But when "the moment" had finally arrived, the moment he had been driving so hard for all night, he hadn't had enough—nowhere near enough in fact. His lust diluted with alcohol, his motor control inhibited by hallucination, and his expectant five inches rounding down rather than up, he had always sputtered to a stop, like a dying engine coughing and wheezing on its last drops of petrol...

Jamal prepared to start up his motor scooter, but as he went to insert the ignition key his hand started shaking so much he couldn't complete the simple task. He had to grab his right hand—holding the key—with his left in order to steady it. After a couple more wayward attempts, he finally succeeded in ramming the key home. By now, he was sweating profusely. He could feel his confidence draining away with the loss of his bodily fluids.

Oh... Was he taking too much upon himself to change his instructions so radically, or would he be commended at some point for his forward thinking, his—what he considered to be—crafty initiative? In camp in Pakistan they had mostly been subjected to disciplined training, carrying out orders from above without deviation and without question. But before they had graduated the instructors had also told them that out in the field, especially back in Europe where they might be "lone wolves" without much in the way of serious backup or reliable communication with headquarters thousands of miles away, they might well have to show flexibility, an ability to think on their feet, to act alone. When some had asked how they might do this, the answer had come back that, normally, such skills could only be effectively honed through direct experience, but that, if they were really the true believers they said they were, then Allah would surely show them the way!

Yes, Allah would—wouldn't he? Jamal mumbled to himself as he desperately fiddled with the ignition key, as if he believed that merely turning it harder would somehow magically transform electro-chemical inertness into powerful combustion. But as he let the clutch go, the engine almost stalled. *Inshallah*! Jamal insisted, jiggling the key even more insistently, and suddenly, from what had seemed like the moment of final expiration, the engine sparked back into furious life again—ready to take Jamal to his rendezvous with destiny.

Jamal pulled out into the endless flow of slow-moving traffic that always seemed to be on the verge of a once-and-for-all choking off of the city's transportation system. All of a sudden, he realized that if inconspicuousness had been what he'd been after then he'd badly miscalculated. Having been away for so long, he'd forgotten just how rare mopeds were on the streets of central London these days. Riding one, as with a bicycle, was like laying your life on the line, and few observers could resist gawking in the expectation of seeing the rider come a cropper. Far from disappearing into the maelstrom of traffic, as he'd intended, Jamal attracted the attention of every Londoner whom he happened to pass by that day…

The stares, the glaring—he'd seen those eyes before, felt their distaste. *Why did they always have to look at him so? Especially the ones he'd paid for. They were always the worst. He hadn't gone to them often, but there were times when he'd just had to. The heavy makeup, the micro-skirts hitched high towards the groin, the mountainous cleavage billowing, thrusting, popping… But the payment at the sordid false beginning of it all, and then the final stare before they left. He'd felt like killing them, there and then, just like that… If only he'd had a knife to hand…*

Hitting a pothole he hadn't seen almost made Jamal lose control of his moped. He wobbled for a few precarious seconds, but managed to regain his balance. He reflexively felt for his knife again, as if something had told him that he might have forgotten to bring the thing along, after all. But it was where it was supposed to be, although in his near-accident the blade had come uncomfortably close to his genitals. He steered the tip of the blade to a more comfortable—and comforting—position, flat against his hip. He looked ahead and suddenly realized he was almost there.

He turned right off Great Russell Street and into Coptic Street. He found a place to park his moped about fifty yards down the road, but he didn't chain it to anything as he normally would have done, just in case he might need to make a hurried escape. And if anyone wanted to steal it, well, good luck to them, it might not be quite the bargain they'd hoped for, and, in any case, his material possessions seemed ever less meaningful to him now, and he'd prefer martyrdom to flight if push came to shove, he was sure.

He dodged into a doorway and faced the door. Off came the hat, the glasses, and the scarf, which he stuffed into his pockets. Recognizable again for his contact's benefit, Jamal walked back to the corner of Great Russell Street from where he'd be observable from anywhere in the vicinity of the main entrance to the museum. At the corner Jamal took up his position and waited, every now and again surveying the crowds of tourists queuing up to get in the great repository of imperial theft, hoping against all the odds that he might spy his contact before he spotted Jamal. But as much as he tried to concentrate on his surveillance, the imposing Ionic colonnade and pediment of the museum entrance before him kept capturing his attention…What treasures lay behind those walls? he wondered, such that such multitudes should wait out on the dusty street for so long…

Treasures?

He'd sought a good many in his time, God knows. Bought some, stolen a good many more—what else could you do on a student grant, and, besides, he wasn't the only one, just about everyone he'd known had been up to it back then. It had been almost a rite of passage, a thrill to relieve the tedium of studying coding, or at least pretending to from time to time. And the bravado of it made up for the disappointments, the letdowns with the girls...At least it was something he was "up to," had enough mettle to see through to the end, thank God. And in any case, what he'd learned in camp in Pakistan about the theft—the grand larceny indeed—of the imperialist Crusaders made his stealing seem at worst mere petty filching, and at best just retribution by comparison. Those walls housed the loot of the Mother of all Thieves, the crusading crooks of...

A sonorous *bong!* broke through the urban cacophony.

It was Big Ben sounding out the hour. Ten o'clock already and still no one had approached him. Soon, it was ten-oh-five, six, seven...*what was going on?* Ten-fifteen, and Jamal's perspiration was in full flow yet again. Then he noticed a male figure making his way agitatedly, it seemed, through the crowds, as if he was looking for someone, panicked almost.

As the figure got closer Jamal recognized it as a brother, a fellow Pakistani. Jamal could hardly constrain himself, eager for his wait to be over and desperate not to let his contact miss him. It was already almost ten-twenty and there appeared to be no other likely candidate in sight.

Jamal stepped out into the street, oblivious to the traffic. The honking at his reckless behavior turned several heads in his direction to see what was going on. A couple of folks screwed their eyes up and covered their ears in anticipation of Jamal being mowed down by a large truck barreling towards him. Someone yelled "Watch out, mate!" pointing a finger at the lorry behind Jamal's back. As Jamal leapt back onto the sidewalk to avoid the truck, his presumed contact's eyes met his. The man flicked his head in the direction of Montague Street which ran up the east side of the museum. Jamal followed him, twenty yards in his wake and ignoring the "Fucking Paki!" curse that the lorry driver yelled at him from the open window of his cab.

His wait was over; the moment had finally arrived. Would he have enough, now that he needed it more than ever? Would he be up to making the truck driver and his ilk eat their words? The old man from the other day outside the *Sword and Scimitar* — what he wouldn't give for the old fart to show up now!

Of course he had enough; he almost had a hard on.

Jamal smiled, and made no attempt to conceal his aroused condition. He imagined his penis was showing him the way, pointing towards his jihadi destiny — at last.

21

[15 March 2016]

At first—just like his Joint Chiefs and his National Security team who had briefed him so convincingly on the need for them—the president of the United States hadn't worried too much about the collateral damage that he was told would inevitably result from his authorization of the use of drones in order to go after the big ticket items on his list of the world's most wanted terrorists.

Politically (no semi-covert body bags returning to the airbase at Dover), economically (no astronomical off-budget expenditures for yet another ground war to add to the national debt and to the fiscal burdens of generations to come), and strategically (no boots on the ground to be lost in battle and tallied by the news media like they'd nothing else to play math with), drones seemed to be his only ace in the hole in this global war on terror—at least for the foreseeable future, whatever that was. And, indeed, when the first reports came in assessing their success, these initial drone attacks had answered his prayers beautifully. The jihadi movements were being decapitated of their most senior leadership almost monthly, and it seemed it would be a matter of only a few more months—perhaps a year or so, allowing for the inevitable fog of war—before he'd be able to announce to the American people "Mission Accomplished," and put the scourge of global terrorism to rest, or at least make it a much reduced side-show.

But then there'd been (inevitably? he now wondered with 20/20 hindsight) al-Adrum.

A decrepit Arab village that was so small and remote that it hadn't even appeared on Google maps no matter how much one might have zoomed in, was now, after the attack, one of the best-known places on earth, getting as many "hits" as Kim Kardashian, if not more, at least as long as the rubbernecking worldwide audience couldn't get enough of the YouTube video that went viral soon thereafter. Who could forget the gripping footage of the wailing, bereaved parents carrying their limp, lifeless children above their heads on the way to burial, and then the heartbreaking climax—a final, lingering, slow motion shot of a child's severed, bloodied hand still holding onto the tether of a wheeled wooden nodding donkey? Even he, so distant as he was from the deserts of the Middle East, could not. In the end, being Commander-in-Chief of the most powerful nation on earth did not, after all, make you immune to scruple, to severe moral self-questioning, to the fear that you'd just committed the most egregious sin mankind had ever indulged in. For all the power at his fingertips, the president felt sickeningly weak on this grey, gloomy morning.

The politics of drone attacks had come back to haunt the him, too; catastrophic "blowback," arrogantly omitted from the strategists' initial calculations, was now, he suspected, only a matter of—a very short—time away. *What, in God's name, might it be?*

He feared the Twin Towers might pale by comparison. The chattering classes had started to babble incessantly about a coming "Big One," grilling him about the prospect every chance they got. He tried to bat the idea away, that his administration was doing "everything imaginable" to make sure another, much bigger, 9/11 had no chance of happening on his watch. But his use of the word "imaginable," plus the scaremongering of the talking heads on Fox News, only served to spook the entire nation, too. From sea to shining sea, imaginations fueled with existential angst imagined every devastating possibility, even the entirely implausible, which soon took on the status of predictable fact—any fool could see that!

The "Big One" became the "Big Question," became the new buzzword of the year, getting its own entry in online dictionaries, and consequently creating in that quintessentially American way a whole boat load of entrepreneurial opportunities, from "AA Super-Premium Life Insurance" that covered you against "Acts of Allah" (although you'd better read *all* the fine print), to "Muslim Look-A-Like Conversion Kits" that could make you look Islamic-kosher in less than two minutes, to "Armageddon-Proof" underground compounds in the mountainous backwoods of Idaho and Montana that promised "to offer your kids a chance to rise again after the End of Days." It was all enough to raise GDP by another two percent that year, and inflation by six.

But right now, the president had more immediate problems. His presumed trump card had self-destructed in the loud wail of global, breast-beating public opinion. It was chasing him down, hemming him in. Lilliputians of all races, creeds, and political persuasions were gathering up their ropes, lassoing him with moral contradictions and then tying him down with impossible policy choices doomed to failure, one way or another—he couldn't, as they said, *win for losing*. He felt as if the so-called "most powerful man" in the entire world had just had his hair cut off, delivered up like a castrated Samson before he'd had any chance of being anything like the mightily hirsute one—pre-Delilah, that is.

It was 7 a.m., and the dawn was still struggling to break through the rain-swept skies over Washington D.C. The president was alone in the Oval Office. As usual, a stack of files, memoranda, and official government papers lay on his desk awaiting his urgent attention. But, uncharacteristically, he didn't immediately delve into them as was his custom. He knew his chief of staff, Bob Hammerschmidt, would soon be with him, badgering him for instructions and hectoring him with his own, often just-a-bit-too-strident, advice. But it was no good, he just couldn't concentrate. He looked at his computer monitor yet again, his right hand fiddling with the mouse, his forefinger hovering—*to click or not to click?* He licked his lips and then navigated the cursor on the screen until it settled over the browser icon.

Click. Restore tab? *Click.*

For the fifth time that morning the viral video filled the screen: ...*the bloodied hand*...

Click. Breaking News: House Republicans threaten federal government shutdown over—*Fill in the blank*! he cursed to himself.

He got up and walked to the large windows overlooking the south lawn. He stared out into the pelting rain. He knew the viper's nest of naysayers were just up Pennsylvania Avenue to his left, so close that if they so chose they could have come to see him and worked things out, but the other end of the iconic thoroughfare might as well have been a million miles away right then—preferably in some other solar system. Al-Adrum felt much closer—just there, just beyond the security fence and lying in ruins... As he turned from the window, his eyes lighted upon a framed photograph on a credenza next to the office door: two healthy, smiling daughters hugging their pet dog, living free...*safe.*

"Good morning, Mr. President!" It was Bob Hammerschmidt, barging his way in as was his wont, with such a short tap of a knock on the Oval Office door as for it to be practically inaudible in competition with his booming voice. "I—" He immediately spied the untouched pile of documents. He pursed his lips and gave his boss his customary schoolmarm look of disapproval.

"I know, I know," the president said wearily. "I'll get to them as soon as we're done—noon at the latest." He slumped down into his chair; Bob took up his position hovering over the president's right shoulder, ready to get down to business. "Okay, what have you got?" the president continued, wearily.

Hammerschmidt launched into his usual rapid-fire presentation, but the only thing the president heard was an unrelenting stream of irritating squawking, as if there were a giant, hectoring parrot on his shoulder.

"Sir?" Hammerschmidt queried, some three minutes into his spiel.

"Uh?"

"Are you all right, Mr. President?"

"I'm sorry…"

"I know these accusations are patently absurd, but *politically*…"

"Accusations? What accusations?"

Hammerschmidt looked at the president incredulously. *Was he losing it just a bit?* The old man was over six years into his stint, but maybe the lame duck was more mortally wounded than he'd figured. "That you're a—*huh!*—'war criminal,' sir. As I say, it's patently absurd, and it won't go anywhere legally, but…"

War criminal? Could he have been? If not guilty of outright criminality, then culpable of something close to it like…

"…and of course, that video of the unfortunate child and his toy, it's—not surprisingly I'd have to say—helping IS recruit more foreign fighters by the hundreds, if not thousands…"

But what choice did I have? And…and the Joint Chiefs have already insisted upon more drone strikes! A grey, billowy cloud mushroomed before his vacant eyes, obliterating an unknown desert village… *And the Navy Seals...was it too late to turn them back, abort the mission?*

"...including even US citizens!"

The president turned to look up at this chief of staff, ashen-faced. "Is it too late?"

"Too *late*? Of course not, Mr. President. Are you feeling—"

"It isn't?"

"No...why—"

"Good...that's good." The president patted his chief of staff's arm and tried to smile. "That's good," he sighed again, but without much conviction.

Hammerschmidt had rarely seen his boss look so low—*never* in fact. The president seemed so completely out of character, nothing like the cocky state senator he'd met just a few years ago. "Look, Mr. President, I can *guarantee* you the war criminal issue has no real legs—none at all. Obviously, the Republicans might try to make some hay out of it, and there'll be a good deal of yelling and screaming from your enemies abroad—that's all par for the course. But the American public won't buy it—they're too concerned about destroying terrorism once and for all to worry about such preposterous allegations. We're at war; we *all* know that. Rumsfeld had it right for once: 'Shit happens!' It's unfortunate, but that's the truth, God knows. *Trust* me, sir, I'll take care of it—haven't I always?"

The president nodded his head affirmatively—*yes he had, God knows.* But then he thought, what exactly did God know? God knew a great deal, unsettlingly so. (Right on point, Mr. President, right on the money!)

Hammerschmidt was relieved to finally close the subject, at least for the time being; he almost wished he hadn't raised it now, and he wasn't all that consoled by the president's rather half-hearted nod of consent that he would in fact take care of things—indeed, he knew the "war criminal" charge would be like candy to the president's enemies, both at home and abroad. He wondered if he might need to consider resigning, moving onto more financially lucrative pastures, perhaps, with a top-notch lobbying outfit or corporate law firm—he'd had a dozen such offers in recent months. The last thing he wanted was to go down with a sinking ship, and the captain, it seemed, was uncharacteristically showing clear signs of losing his renowned mettle. And mettle, spades of it, was what was sorely needed these days. He knew he ought to be loyal to a man who had given him just about everything, but...*so* much was at stake.

"Is that everything?" the president said hopefully, almost pleadingly, breaking the momentary silence between them.

Hammerschmidt hesitated. He hated to leave the issue in the air like this, not knowing if he really had the president on board with his claim to competence. The wounded beast needed help, needed lifting, but if he was really too weak to stand at that moment, then it might not be too long before he fell down for good—a lame duck lame in *both* legs. But there was nothing for it; the world moved on, things couldn't wait. If the president wasn't up for it anymore, then he, Bob Hammerschmidt, Chief of Staff, would just have to take over, become the *real* power behind the throne, the Chief of Operations, like he'd never truly been before.

"Not quite, Mr. President," Hammerschmidt finally said. He placed some documents on the president's desk, and then proffered him a pen. "I need you to sign these executive orders right away, if you would, sir?"

The president looked at the one on top, but he couldn't read what was there. It was all a blur. "What are they for?"

"The drone attacks and air strikes General Graves briefed you on yesterday afternoon. They need to be executed *today*, sir. IS, unfortunately, continues to close in on several key towns in both Syria and Iraq. They could well take them *all* by tomorrow if we don't act right away." Hammerschmidt proffered the pen once again. "Sir?"

The president looked at the photograph of his two daughters on the credenza again, then signed the documents—but without his usual final flourish.

"Thank you, Mr. President," Hammerschmidt said, then made his hurried exit, before his boss might change his mind.

The president walked back over to his office window and looked out. The fallen rain had by now formed several large puddles in the White House driveway. Three birds—what species he couldn't tell—were taking a bath in the largest of them, obviously enjoying themselves like young children playing in a paddling pool. Suddenly, something fell from the branch of a tree nearby. The president flinched. Two of the three playmates immediately took to flight; but the third tarried just a moment too long, and the president saw it nabbed in its brief moment of carefree joy. A cat carried it off in its mouth. A bloodied feather floated to the ground.

Nature, red in tooth and claw, the president recalled. *A Law of Nature, a Law of War: laws, both, beyond moral reach? – Beyond God's too? What had he just signed? Death warrants of sorts for sure, but whose exactly? And would he be judged an executioner or a savior? Could you –* must *you – be both, especially when you were the president of the United States in times like these?*

The incident at al-Adrum, the president now realized, was the very thing that might finish him off once and for all *as a man* – as a moral being – if not as a politician, the commander-in-chief of a nation frightened to death and armed to the teeth. An explosive brew, if ever there was one. He looked at the picture of his daughters again, and then started to sing softly, mournfully, a lullaby more tragic than consoling:

Al-Adrum: for the want of a nail a shoe was lost...

Al-Adrum: from little acorns do mighty oak trees grow...

Al-Adrum, al-Adrum, al-Adrum...

But the rhyme remained unfinished. He didn't know what came next. His daughters' image dissolved into a watery blur.

That night the president sat in his private office alone and ruminated for a long, lonely time, trying to fathom where the intersection of moral obligation and political power might come together in some sort of harmony, or at least settle at an equilibrium point that might just be sustainable. He considered "just war theory," trying to figure out whether there was something hopeful there, or if the whole doctrine was one gigantic oxymoron, riddled with contradictions that couldn't be resolved, circles that couldn't be squared. *What, in God's name, was the "proportionate" use of force, or the definition of "self-defense" as opposed to "offensive action" in a fight like the global War on Terror?* He wrote scribbled notes on his pad and drew diagrams with arrows going this way and that, desperately trying to make the whole thing work, come up trumps.

He couldn't do it; the calculations proved to be irresolvable. There was no Benthamite "felicific calculus"—if only there was, if only two and two in the complex moral universe added up to four, every time, reliably! If he underestimated the real threat of IS, he would expose his own citizens to the high probability of ever more terrorist attacks; but if he exaggerated it, not least in order to get the public support necessary for aggressive response, then his heavy-handed reactions, as he had already seen, might well further strengthen the terrorists' cause and their determination to strike back ever more stridently—go for the Big One, sooner rather than later.

But he felt powerless to be able to do much to stem the flow of the IS's apparently intoxicating appeal. It was obvious that the group's allure was unbreakably magnetic for many a troubled soul, but he found their fanaticism for jihadism incomprehensible for anyone fortunate enough to have been born and raised in these United States of America, even if they were—*especially* if they were—the children of Muslim immigrants. And if he couldn't "get" what these wretched beings were after, then how could he win the propaganda war being played out so expertly in the social media by his adversaries? How could he marshal convincing arguments in opposition to a world view he did not begin to understand, let alone appreciate?

And even if he could square all these vicious circles somehow, would his political enemies, even his so-called political friends and allies, let him practice what he might now preach: that America should show restraint in the face of terror and not insist on an eye for an eye, and a tooth for a tooth, and admit, perhaps, to the terror of its own empire-building, the crimes of its own expansionist past and hegemonic present? Would the American people—his "fellow Americans"—thank him for the effort to re-found the republic in this magnanimous way, especially if his new-found wisdom and moral compass somehow created another chink in the country's defensive armor and a second 9/11, the Big One, took place, leaving thousands more Americans dead—*their* blood on *his* hands, too, let alone on all the little nodding donkeys that their slain children might be holding on to in their moment of death?

No, he had to conclude, they undoubtedly would not.

He'd been right—hadn't he?—to sign those authorizations that morning; he'd literally had no choice! And, hadn't it been a *moral* imperative too, constitutional obligations aside, to protect his countrymen and women, something he'd sworn an oath before God to do not once, but twice? And if so, then the Chiefs had been right all along—collateral damage *was* collateral damage, an inevitable consequence of this hard-to-bear moral equation, and he couldn't shed too many tears over it lest it deplete his will to carry out his presidential responsibilities. Innocents would be killed; American boys and girls would die fighting. And he owed those he sent into battle the consolation—the approbation—that they were doing their patriotic duty...as he was doing his. He'd had his patriotism questioned before and he was determined not to pour any more unnecessary fuel onto that particular fire, this time around.

And then, as Bob Hammerschmidt had so often counseled him, there was the truly *evil* nature of the enemy to consider, those Jihadi Johns who severed heads in their thousands as casually as if they were merely slicing bread, who cut out the tongues of those who dared to practice the quintessential American freedom, our hallowed constitutional protection to speak as freely as we wished. How could there be much, if any, moral consideration of acts such those? How could one battle such barbarism short of a no holds barred response of one's own? He didn't usually much take with Old Testament creeds, but, damn it all, maybe it really was "an eye for an eye, a tooth for a tooth" this time, after all.

But then he saw the nodding donkey and a child's severed hand waving at him again. It was then for several minutes that he shed all the tears he would, before an aide came in with yet another executive order for him to sign; and on the morrow, a second al-Adrum would transpire, and a blood-spattered child's sandal would fly through the desert air somewhere in Mesopotamia.

But the president would do his damnedest this time not to think about it—at least not too much. He couldn't afford to. Besides, he couldn't stand feeling that Bob was doubting him now, questioning his mettle, the very thing that had brought them together in the first place. They'd been through hell and back as a team, he Castor to Bob's Pollux.

It was no time to quit now.

22

[25 March 2016]

Jamal Shirani entered Russell Square, still some twenty yards behind his contact.

The man crossed the road and entered the gardens in the center of the plaza. He scared up a gang of pigeons foraging around a wastebasket at the entrance. They were pretty much the only occupants of the grounds that day, the spring weather being rather more winter-like than an enervating forerunner to the inevitable short English summer that may or may not eventually make its fitful appearance sometime thereafter. Just one other tenant as far as Jamal could tell: a bum crashed out on a park bench. He was covered with sheets of cardboard for bedding—and warmth, such as it was. Beneath the bench were a couple of ratty shopping bags, presumably containing the sum total of the sleeper's worldly possessions. The bags were so filthy that even the pigeons made sure to give them a wide berth as they scavenged for food.

Jamal's contact proceeded to another bench some thirty yards farther on from the sleeping—most likely comatose—vagrant. The seat was relatively secluded, partially obscured by overgrown bushes and trees. He took a seat and waited, staring straight ahead, until Jamal got close. He patted the seat beside him, two light, almost imperceptible, taps on the wooden slat next to his right knee.

Jamal looked behind him: still just the tramp, dead to the world; beyond him, the pigeons fighting over a minute crust of stale bread, somehow missed in their free-for-all until now; and, out of view but within earshot, the bustle of pedestrians and traffic circumnavigating Russell Square. It occurred to Jamal that his companion and he were virtually alone in the *middle* of London in the *middle* of the day. The city was a teeming metropolis of some eight million souls—and counting—but, he was willing to wager, not one of them had any inkling as to what was about to go down right under their noses! Incredible, he thought: they haven't got a fucking clue. He took a deep breath and sat down.

"Good to meet you at last...*Jamal*," the man said, still facing forward.

Hearing his own name suddenly spoken by this stranger sent goosebumps rippling across Jamal's skin, although he knew from the phone message that his contact would be able recognize him. But there was something about the way the guy said his name that seemed a little odd, almost alien in a way, but as to how exactly Jamal couldn't say right then—he was too excited at the momentousness of the occasion to let a trifle such as this consume him for more than a second or two. He wanted to say "You too," or something like that, but every alternative phrase that flashed through his mind at that instant seemed wholly inept, untoward, or a violation of whatever unknown protocol he ought to be pursuing with such a person at a time like this. In the end he only managed a half-embarrassed, half-articulated grunt of an indeterminable nature. He squirmed in his seat, afraid of what the fellow might be thinking of him. He had to make a good impression, and he was already off, he feared, to the worst possible start.

"Relax," the contact said.

"I'm...I'm fine," Jamal mumbled.

A prolonged pause. Jamal desperately wanted the conversation to continue, to get down to serious business, but he didn't know what to say, let alone be brave — or foolish — enough to dare to take the initiative. He shifted his position slightly, hoping that the resultant shaking of the bench might spark things into action.

"Good," the man said, "wouldn't do for nervous nellies in our line of business, would it now?"

Nellies? Jamal puzzled. He slowly moved his eyeballs sideways without shifting his head, so that he could steal a furtive glimpse of his companion. But his contact was still looking straight ahead, cool and calm as you like. He obviously knew what he was about, completely sure of himself. That, at least, was somewhat comforting, as was his appearance — as British Pakistani as they came: olive-brown skin, jet black greasy hair, scraggly beard, open-necked white shirt, and a baggy, ill-fitting suit, concertinaed at the trouser cuffs, which were draped in a slovenly way over a pair of rarely-polished shoes. But the accent, the lingo he used, especially at a time like this? A bit odd? Perhaps not, Jamal quickly concluded. Like himself, the guy had most probably been born and raised in England; Pakistanis with some sort of an English accent were two a penny these days, especially in London. Anticipating that they most likely shared similar life histories, Jamal relaxed a little.

"I'm told you're ready. Are you?"

"Yes," Jamal replied. "I'm ready…Inshallah."

"Of course — Inshallar."

Inshallar?

"Um, I'm told that you had, shall we say," the man continued, "some 'difficulties' with some of the training, particularly with demanding physical exertion — scaling walls, climbing ropes, that sort of thing?"

That sort of thing?

"Well, at first perhaps," Jamal lied, "but I…I started to get the hang of it just before the end. I'm sure — I really am — I could do just about anything that's required now. I'm ready…as God is my witness." Jamal cleared his throat. Suddenly, it felt incredibly dry.

"Quite so," the man said, and then almost as if was adding some kind of scripted afterthought he said "Inshallar" — *again.*

A muscle spasm made Jamal jump, as if he'd just been electrocuted, making the bench wobble enough to discomfort his companion.

"Ah," Jamal quickly said, "damn cramp. Always get it when the weather changes like this. Ah! There it goes again." Jamal stood up putting his weight onto his left leg, and flexing his knee slightly. He bit his bottom lip in the fake effort to rid himself of his phony discomfort. "Ah, I think I've got it." He sat down again. "Yes, that's it." He smiled at his companion as convincingly as he could.

The man smiled in response, but the smile looked forced, a cover, as if he was wondering already who in God's name they'd sent to him this time. Nonetheless, he said, "Good," like he'd forced himself to keep playing along, it being too early in the game to give up on Jamal just yet. "I sometimes have the same problem," he continued, but the way he said it sounded pat, and the air in the space between them suddenly chilled and thickened. He quickly changed the subject. "So, let's — "

"Were you at Pashteek...Daqtoum perhaps?" Jamal could hardly believe what he was saying. The words seemed to come out of his mouth of their own volition, like it was some *in-your-face* alter ego who'd taken charge of his vocal cords, all of a sudden.

"What?"

"Which camp did you train at in Pakistan?" Again, the ballsiness of it all; where was it coming from?

The man stared at Jamal, as if he had just grossly insulted him. But he kept his calm. "Um, Daq...Look, we haven't got time for all that. And ...and...that's not information that—"

"Daqtoum? You were at Daqtoum?"

"Look, I said—"

Jamal leapt up from the bench, and before his companion had time to utter another faltering word Jamal had the knife he was carrying up against the man's throat. How he'd managed to be so quick on the draw, he'd no idea. He seemed to be on some sort of highly-energized autopilot, as if his training had miraculously just kicked in and taken control of him just at the right, critical moment.

"You're a fucking cop, aren't you?" he hissed through his clenched teeth. "*InshallAR? Daqtoum?* — there is no such place!"

Jamal pressed the blade of the knife ever harder against his companion's Adam's apple, creasing the flesh and threatening to draw blood. He put his knee into the man's groin, trying to pin him down, lock him in place. But as he did so, Jamal immediately felt himself falling backwards. In a flash, he was flat on his back, a pair of handcuffs dangling before his face. His contact was on top of him, and yelling. Over the man's shoulder, Jamal saw the telltale flashing lights of a police vehicle suddenly appear over the top of the bushes that enclosed the park. The sound of booted footsteps racing up the gravel pathway soon followed.

As Jamal felt the pinch of the first cuff being applied to his left wrist, he saw his dream of practicing jihad melting away before his eyes. He'd been duped; he was done for. All that training in Pakistan, and it now it was all well and truly over before it had barely begun. What humiliation! A Jihadi John in the making — *him?*

Something — the powerful rush of adrenalin in unbounded flood, the irrepressible drive of divine inspiration, the panic of unrestrained fear? — surged through Jamal's body, concentrating his mind on singular purpose and steeling his muscles with unknown strength. He threw off the hands trying to cuff him just before the pounding feet finally arrived. He picked up his knife from where it had fallen, and ran off, determined to escape his pursuers.

But someone blocked his path—it was the hobo, aroused now from his drunken stupor and apparently, so it seemed, ready to make a half-assed attempt at a citizen's arrest. He was mumbling incoherently and waving his arms about as Jamal literally ran over him.

When the knife had gone in, Jamal hadn't really known what was happening, what he had done. He'd felt the unexpected pressure of the blade puncturing flesh, and then the scraping of hard bone as it had slipped through the hobo's rib cage, although in the moment he hadn't realized specifically that that's what had happened. All he'd instantly known was that he'd clattered into somebody and he'd been carrying a knife, and then there'd been these semi-conscious sensations shortly thereafter. His moment of unexpected jihad had come and gone in an instant—just like that.

Pushing the hobo with the knife still stuck in his abdomen to the ground, Jamal took off in full flight, putting an increasingly good distance between himself and his pursuers. He could hear them shouting at him to stop, that they would shoot if he didn't. But as he barged his way through the throng on the pavement outside the gardens, he knew the police wouldn't fire, afraid of risking the lives of innocent bystanders. Nobody attempted to stop him or bring him down—they were all too consumed fiddling with their cell phones or just gawping at the spectacle he was making of himself for that. He realized he was safe, getting away. Suddenly the thrill of what he was engaged in sank in; his disappointment at the apparent mundanity of his jihadi act dissipated. "Allahu Akbar!" Jamal yelled delightedly. *God is Great!*

Jamal turned back onto Great Russell Street again, thinking that maybe he could retrieve his moped and make his escape once and for all. But up ahead, he saw more police racing towards him. He knew he was running straight into a trap, but he didn't care! The thrill of the chase was everything now. He was one against many; impossible odds that would surely guarantee him his longed-for martyrdom. Incredibly, dozens of people were literally dancing to *his* tune as he dodged and weaved through the crowd of terrified onlookers, who were screaming, some crying, and desperately grabbing onto each other—practically shitting themselves at *his* behest. If he went left, they *had* to go right; if he careened right, they *had* to scramble to match his move. He was the choreographer of hundreds, if not thousands! What power! What a fucking rush!

Jamal dashed toward the main doors of the British Museum, the panicked crowd parting before him like the waters of the Red Sea had done for Moses. He crashed through the simple barriers that were meant to guide the queue's formation, as if they were made of nothing more than matchwood; in the process, an extended family of Chinese tourists, who'd been at the head of the line for hours, collapsed like ninepins bowled over by a perfect strike, Granny finding herself staring up at Jamal through the bars of the barricade now on top of her, as he raced by, a veritable bull in a China shop. A growing cacophony of protest assailed Jamal, but he paid no heed; his adrenalin feasted on their jeers, as if they were egging him on rather trying to restrain him. He was having the time of his life!

Just as he arrived at the main doors of the museum, they opened, as if someone inside had been anticipating his arrival. He darted past the startled staff and bounded up the wide marble steps in front of him. At the top, he soon realized that he had run into a dead end. Alarms were going off and doors were slamming shut. Soon, he'd be well and truly cornered—like a rat.

"Freeze!" Done for—except for one last jihadi gesture.

Jamal calmly reached out towards a huge ceramic vase sitting on a display pedestal to his right. He had no idea as to its provenance; all he could see at that moment was that it was truly huge for a vase—the size of young child—and brightly painted. He slapped it with his hand, making it wobble slightly; he hit it a second time, and the vase gyrated a couple of times on the rim of its base before falling to the ground and shattering into a thousand-and-one pieces. Shards of ancient pottery splattered like sparkling shrapnel against his legs. Then he froze, but the shot he'd been anticipating did not come. Instead, an arm clasped him in a stranglehold; a hand roughly forced his right, then his left, hand behind his back. He willingly gave in to the forces that were governing his entire bodily movement now, and he remained silent—strangely at peace, satiated. He let himself be cuffed and brusquely led away.

A job, some sort of deed, had finally been done. Perhaps—who knew?—a Crusader theft had been destroyed; the blasphemous images on the vase denied further worship by secular apostates letting their academic aesthetic appreciation besmirch the integrity of his faith. No doubt the *kuffar*, the unbelievers, would be enraged, as at Bumiyan and Nimrod, but that, as Jamal had been instructed in Pakistan, was an outcome "that in itself is beloved to Allah."

And that...that was more than enough, *Inshallah*.

♠

Well, it wasn't really, it never is—I see to that. You see, I'm not very often *willing* to settle for less when there can be more—even if it's as dumb as can be.

Here's the real scoop, the bigger picture. It'll make you want to gag; it does me, although I've seen enough of such shit to last me a lifetime. I never cease to wonder...

Some six months later, after their oil dumps had been blown to smithereens by American airstrikes, denying them millions upon millions of dollars in much needed revenue, the leaders of IS came to appreciate that preserving their *cultural* inheritance, no matter how offensive it might have been to True Believers' religious sensibilities, was now very much in their own financial interest. Under the guise of a theological gloss of sorts (*Do they really think I believe them?*), but in reality a sleight of hand rather too clumsily concocted that it wasn't long before it failed to pass careful learned scrutiny, they carted off load after load of "blasphemous" antiquities from the Syrian city of Raqqa, which they controlled, and put them up for *sale* in the international art markets!

Had God and Mammon gotten too close, perhaps, you might wonder? No—not at all. Listen to this:

"You see," Abu Bakr al-Baghdadi insisted one day during Friday prayers, sporting a perfectly straight bearded face in defiance of his critics and naysayers, "there's nothing sinful in this at all—far from it in fact. For, from the vast proceeds of such sales, we extract *khums*, a religious sales tax of some 20 percent. And this tax, you see, goes towards *zakat*, alms-giving, for such as the poor bereaved families of al-Adrum…"

(Oh, thank you, that's very nice…)

"Oh…and to buying the weapons of war, holy jihad, as well—after all, there's a caliphate to win, and it's a dangerous, *costly* business."

(I'm sure it is!)

Meanwhile, back in London at the British Museum, a curator assessed that Jamal had cost the museum some £85,000, quite likely much more at auction, enough to equip around one hundred holy warriors with a Kalashnikov each.

Luckily for al-Baghdadi, there were still plenty more vases that had escaped Jamal's wayward, dumb-ass hand.

Unfortunately, Jamal was not acting alone.

…

Had enough now?

"*What more could there possibly be?*" *a fool among you might ask.*

"Plenty," an even bigger fool might reply. *"Hadn't forgotten about the Big One already, had you?"*

23

[September 2015]

"Hush," she says, stroking my brow, slicked with perspiration. I can't see her clearly yet, but the sound of her silky voice—it's in a register lower than I'm used to back home, like a great male radio announcer's—calms me down.

But I can still hear it, and it's right over me. *Look,* can't she see? It's hovering right there! Is she not afraid?

Wake up, Jo-Buck, she softly says. *It's alright.* Like she's an angel.

The fog begins to clear; the world sheds its blurriness and struggles into focus. The cacophony in my ears clatters away, dissipating. It's going away. I'm safe. We're safe.

I see her now. She's beautiful in her white cap, wisps of blonde hair framing her smiling face. Something's spinning behind her head. I realize it's a ceiling fan, located directly above the bed I'm lying in. Something's trying to drown out her voice; but it's only the AC working overtime to keep out the desert air.

I remember now where I am, and the pain returns.

She reaches up and adjusts something, a plastic bag hooked onto a stand, a tube snaking down from it into my arm. "This should help," she says. "Go back to sleep now."

And I do, slowly, without knowing it.

24

[May-June 2015]

It was the height of the tourist season, and Bologna was jammed with foreign visitors gorging on the old city's medieval charm. Necks strained in the direction of the top of the Asinelli Tower, some ninety-seven meters high; cameras of all shapes and sizes clicked furiously at the architectural delights of the Piazza Maggiore and the Basilica of San Petronio; feet splashed in the cooling water while inevitable selfies were being snapped at the Neptune Fountain.

Summer fun was in full flow—for most, if not all.

Ayaan Pellegrino was there, deep in amongst the throng, weaving herself through the annoying crowds on her way home from her new job, but as to summer fun, she was having none of it. It was stiflingly hot and humid, the cobbled streets were dusty and littered and hard on the feet, and the tourists…well, why couldn't they go home already, or at least pay attention to what they were doing?

Yet another overweight American suddenly stepped carelessly into Ayaan's path, desperate to get just the angle he wanted for his thirty-fifth shot of, no doubt, the sculpted Neptune's bared genitalia, dangling there for all the world to see. Great art reduced to twenty-first century mass titillation, Ayaan scoffed to herself, wondering just how long it might take for the American's upload to his Facebook page to go viral, amusing the hordes of philistines she just knew made up his network of family and friends back in the United States. Suddenly, all the heads around her looked like "thumbs-up" emoticons; she had the urge to break the joints of every one of them!

Ayaan deliberately leant her elbow into the wayward American's back in protest at his gross invasion of her space and his seemingly *willful* ignorance as to how to comport oneself in a crowded space. She grimaced with the contact, fearing contamination from the bodily fluids that coated him, and recoiling from the feel of her elbow sinking in the fatty folds of his outsized bulk. But the American was so encumbered by his weight and engrossed in his photography that she made him stumble nevertheless.

"Whoa!" he drawled in some sort of dumb-sounding southern accent, it sounded like. "Beggin' your pardon, ma'am." He apologetically tipped the brim of his baseball cap, but the hat's loud, boastful logo—*Everything's Bigger in Texas!*—did nothing to assuage Ayaan's disgust.

Ayaan grumpily moved on, irritated by his sweaty, heaving presence, but even more incensed at the continuing hurt she felt at being passed over for

Chief Scientist at DuPont in favor of that asshole Luigi. Bubba here was just another painful reminder of just how much big fat America was standing in her way, denying her what was rightfully hers.

"Hey, stop him!" she heard Bubba yell after her. "He's stolen my billfold!"

Ayaan turned around and suddenly found herself grappling with a small boy. He was dirty and ragged, clearly one of the growing number of street urchins who were plaguing Bologna these days with their petty criminal presence, feeding like lice on the blood of the careless tourists. The kid struggled to free himself from Ayaan's grasp, but his desperation to escape merely triggered her almost automatic response to hold onto him ever more firmly. The boy kept yelling at her angrily in some foreign language she didn't understand.

Realizing that he was hopelessly trapped, the boy looked up at Ayaan and spat in her face. At first, she was repulsed by his action, but when she saw the look of defiance in his eyes something told her that fear lay there, too. He was so small, not much more than a toddler, really. A crowd started to gather around them, jostling them like they were mere flotsam on the sea. "It's alright..," Ayaan started to say, but before she could relax her hold to let him know she meant him no harm, someone suddenly tore the boy away from her. It was a policeman.

"*Grazie, signorina,*" he said, nodding and smiling in recognition of her service to law and order. But before Ayaan had time to say anything, he was gone, dragging the kicking and screaming boy with him, and disappearing into the rubbernecking crowd.

Just before he was finally swallowed up by the throng, the boy broke one arm free and waved it furiously in the air, as if he was trying to grab onto something—for her perhaps; his mouth opened wider and wider, gulping furiously like that of a stranded fish, but his screams soon went silent; then his legs fell limp and his feet scraped across the cobblestones, as if they were useless to him now.

"Miracle Baby," a voice said. Ayaan looked around her, wondering who had said those fateful words. How did they know? But everyone was just looking at her—*she* had said them.

"*Miracle Baby?*" an old woman in the crowd echoed. "More like the menacing little brat he truly is!" she proclaimed indignantly, to everyone's acclamation.

"That's right," her companion said. "Somalis! We should send them all back."

So, the boy's a Somali refugee, Ayaan thought, now a petty thief carved out of pure desperation. Or was it because of his blood, his biological inheritance, as some in the crowd indignantly claimed, shaking their heads in disgust and applauding the policeman's swift removal of the offending presence from their midst?

Somalia, Ayaan wondered, what does it make of a child? Orphans both, but I am here and he has been taken…who knows where? *There but for the Grace of God…* But why? What kind of 'Grace' is that?

Where had the poor child come from? What had brought him to Bologna? Somali—what difference did it make; what did it *mean* to be Somali?

What did it mean to be her...to be Ayaan Pellegrino?

♠

"Ayaan?"

Piero Pellegrino was outside his daughter's bedroom door for the fifth time that morning. "Ayaan, wake up! You'll be late for work!" He knocked on the door yet again, hard enough to hurt himself this time, but there was still no clear sign that Ayaan had either heard or heeded his summons. But he knew she must have. They'd been engaging in this morning ritual for several days now, and he could almost see through the thick wood of the door that Ayaan was still, most likely, in her bed, covers hauled up in a great pile over her head and feigning sleep ...or, more likely, she was just flat out refusing to engage him, being in some inexplicable funk—the amount of ruckus he's generated already surely must have woken her up by now. "Ayaan..." Piero tried the handle, rattling it hard with irritated insistence; it turned, but the door would not open. The deadbolt was holding it fast. Time to have it removed, he thought to himself. Enough was enough.

"Piero," his wife, Pia, whispered loudly from the end of the hallway, "leave her be." She waved her hand, indicating that he needed to join her. She herded her husband down the stairs and into the dining room. Breakfast had already been laid out over an hour ago for the three of them by Maria, their long-suffering cook and housekeeper. It already looked unappetizing: the mortadella, salami, and Montasio slices were already drying out and curling up at the edges; the bread looked on the cusp of becoming stale; and the coffee was insipid-looking, barely even at room temperature now.

The whole repast looked as wretched as his mood, Piero thought, as miserable, in fact, as his whole family's state of mind these days. What had happened to their joy? Of course, the whole row with DuPont had been traumatic enough, but Ayaan had another job already, and they still enjoyed good health and great fortune. Why couldn't that be enough? Why couldn't Ayaan snap out of it? He felt like he and Pia were losing their "Miracle Baby." Maybe, he suddenly feared, they'd lost her already. But why? What could he or Pia have possibly done wrong?

"I'll have Maria bring in fresh food," Pia said, as they took their seats at each end of the large breakfast table.

"Oh, don't bother," Piero glumly said. "I'm really not hungry." He looked over at the place setting where Ayaan used to sit every morning; it was undisturbed and crumb-free, had been for going on almost a week already. He looked up and saw that Pia had followed his glance. There were tears in her eyes.

Suddenly, they heard the front door slam. They both knew that it was Ayaan; she'd developed a distinctive signature as to how she slammed it shut these days: indignant, dismissive—frigidly cold, like the rush of morning air that swooshed into the entryway before the door crashed and rattled against its frame. She'd clearly been up for some time and had just ignored her father's summons, all the while waiting for the perfect moment to make her escape. But from what? What had they done to make her so angry, to alienate her so suddenly? It felt as if she was drifting away from them on some inexorable tide, perhaps swimming away, even, as if she was trying to desperately escape from something...from *them*, her parents, Piero and Pia! But why? Why wouldn't she talk to them? She always had before. What was so different now? Why was *she* so different now? Piero feared he didn't know his own daughter anymore. He feared that perhaps she didn't know herself, either. Maybe what had transpired off the coast of Lampedusa some twenty years ago hadn't been all "miracle" after all. Clearly, some unfortunate chicken had apparently come home to roost.

Pia looked at Piero in alarm. "She'll come back, won't she?" she blubbered.

Piero just looked in the direction of the front door in silence. He wasn't at all sure that she would.

♠

"Wake up, Pia!"

Piero shook his wife by the arm. "Wake up, you're having a bad dream!"

Pia writhed in obvious distress. She was mumbling incoherently. Piero shook her arm again, more aggressively this time. Her eyes sprang open; she looked terrified. "Help her, help her!" she cried.

"Who?"

"Can't you see? The baby!"

"It's all right. You're just dreaming. You're here with me in our bed." Piero embraced his wife. "There..."

"Let me go!" Pia struggled to break free. "Oh my God, she's going under...don't let her go!" Pia broke free of Piero's grasp and stretched out her arms.

She rolled off the bed and onto the bedroom floor. She got on her hands and knees and started searching for something on the floor. "Oh...oh...she's gone!"

Piero helped his wife back onto the bed. "Lie down, Pia. Everything's okay. You've just had a bad dream. Look, look at me. You're safe."

"But the poor baby! She's gone. She went under the waves. I *saw* her! Ayaan..."

"Ayaan's in her room. She came home."

She had indeed come back home...to the house...eventually. And someone called Ayaan was there under its roof. A Somali girl was, he knew, in their daughter's room.

But where was their Miracle Baby...where was *she* now? That was an entirely different question.

Ayaan was in the Land of Punt via Wikipedia and Google images, trying to trace the roots of a life—*her* life—that hadn't at all seemed important until just recently. She couldn't stop thinking about the boy on the street, *that* boy...her *brother* of a sort, perhaps. Where was he now? she wondered. Lost somewhere in Italy's juvenile detention system? Lost, like she was?

As to what her parents were up to, she didn't much care anymore.

They weren't really her parents, anyway.

♠

Her skin seemed to be getting darker by the day, Ayaan was convinced of it.

But it wasn't because of exposure to the sun—that was for sure. The headscarves and the shawls and the long cloak-like dresses she'd taken to wearing recently just about covered her from head-to-toe. She knew her change in fashion was making her stand out in the crowds, but that was not her intent. She was, in fact, trying to retreat, hide almost — go back to the beginning, start over, find a closeted space to be...herself, somehow. She was trying on a different Ayaan, trying to find a shell that fit, a home that didn't crimp at the edges, pinching you. It wasn't easy; moving house never was.

But the large dark glasses she'd also started wearing helped, and in that same paradoxical way that her clothing did. When she saw her reflection in shop windows she knew the glasses made her look like some bug-eyed insect, or perhaps like one of those silly-looking secret service guys who couldn't make up their minds whether they wanted to try and conceal their identity or signal it to the world as loudly as they could. Nevertheless, behind the dark lenses she felt safe somehow, even though she could see the way all the white folks were looking at her, like she had a horribly infectious disease or something. But the compensating beauty of it was, no one could see *her* eyes, see where *she* was looking. She could give her detractors all sorts of evil eyes, but not one of them was any the wiser to that fact. Best of all, perhaps, in the gloom she could at least pretend she didn't have to put up with the lustful stares of the legions of Italian males who seemed to find gawking at her so totally irresistible, no matter that the shape of her figure had disappeared now beneath the multiple layers of her clothing, and that her sapphire-blue eyes had turned to pools of impenetrable blackness behind their black plastic shields.

Different.

Ayaan was not only feeling different, she was actively seeking difference out. Difference still felt alienating at times, but the more she cultivated it the more liberated, the more authentic, she felt. She didn't know quite why it made her feel this way, at least not yet, but it did. And she was getting hooked. She'd never felt this sort of addiction before, and she had little idea as to where it might lead her.

And now, she didn't care.

♠

"It's almost as if she doesn't *care* anymore," Adriana said.

Adriana and her friend, Carmela, were talking over coffee in the lounge at their workplace. Ayaan Pellegrino, their co-worker, was sitting by herself across the room, apparently engrossed in whatever she was looking at on her iPhone. She didn't look up once during the whole time Adriana and Carmela were there, which was a good thirty minutes, some ten more than they were supposed to be away from their work stations on mid-afternoon break.

"I don't think she does," Carmela confirmed. "Just look at her. What is all that get-up she's wearing? If I didn't know any better, I could easily belief she's become a Muslim or something!"

"Well, look!" Adriana said, stroking her fingers on her Adam's apple, and flicking her eyes in Ayaan's direction. "Haven't you noticed?"

"What?" Carmela queried, frowning.

"Around her neck," Adriana whispered.

Carmela furtively looked across the room where Ayaan was still engrossed with her iPhone.

"Oh yes!" she suddenly said, fingering her own neckline now, like her friend had just done. "It's gone. Don't know how I missed it. Maybe it's hidden underneath the scarf."

"No, she's not wearing it anymore," Adriana replied. "I'm sure of it. When we were in our Pilates class yesterday, she wasn't wearing her crucifix then, and she's always done so in the past. It was so big, you couldn't miss it, could you?"

Carmela thought for a moment. "You don't think she has...do you?"

Adriana shrugged. "Who knows? Who knows anything about anyone these days?"

"Including me?"

"Yeah, including you!"

The girls laughed. Ayaan either did not hear them or chose not to.

"She does look different, though," Carmela continued, "and I don't just mean the clothes. Can't quite say what exactly..."

"Yeah, I was thinking that too. Her complexion, hmm—I don't know, is it different somehow?"

"Maybe. She looks like she's filled out a bit, too—she always looked so skinny before."

"Expect the clothes don't help."

The girls looked at each other. They knew they were suddenly thinking the same thing. Adriana put her hand to her mouth, looking shocked.

"You *think*?" she said.

"Didn't even know she had a boyfriend!"

"Fat chance she doesn't, I bet," Adriana said, sneeringly. "You know there isn't a man in this building who can't wait to get in her pants. It's disgusting."

Carmela nodded in agreement. "Now I come to think of it, though, I haven't seen them sniffing around her quite so much lately."

The girls looked across at Ayaan again. She certainly didn't look like the Italian sex-goddess she used to, but, then again, despite all the get-up, they knew that she still had a special something about her. It was infuriating.

"Well, whatever," Adriana said, as she got up from the table. "Banged up or not, she's more than likely not going to be here too much longer."

"What do you mean?"

"Signor Carlucci, I overheard him the other day talking about her. He's finally had enough, apparently. She's just not pulling her weight anymore. 'Chief Scientist?' he said. 'How on earth did we ever seriously consider it? God knows what's happened to her? But I can't wait or afford to find out any longer. Now I know why DuPont *really* let her go!'" Adriana grinned.

"Good riddance to bad rubbish!" Carmela said with a flourish. The girls laughed out loud again, but even then Ayaan still paid them no heed.

The girls took their empty coffee cups to the adjoining kitchen, and then went back to work. Ayaan stayed where she was. Even though she hadn't heard very much at all of their conversation, she was confident that she *knew* exactly whom they had been discussing and in what manner, too. But the girls' gossip didn't concern her anymore; it was all water off a duck's back to her.

Ayaan put down her iPhone and pondered. Should she just leave without warning one day soon, or should she have a parting moment of triumph with Carlucci and tell him to stick his job to his face? Chief Scientist? What could she possibly want with that now? Great change was coming to her life — she could sense it, *see* it already starting to happen. It was at once startling and confusing, yet irresistible. It amazed her that what once had seemed outrageous exotic novelty — *impossibility* in fact — had so quickly become almost "normal," as if things had always been that way.

A storm was approaching, the first waves of it already beginning to toss her to and fro. Right now she was surfing with them, feeling the exhilaration of the ride, their ceaseless power. She prayed that when the eye of the storm finally hit her that she would still be able to swim to the new shore that would hopefully beckon.

But as she felt for her crucifix she realized it wasn't there anymore, around her neck where it had always been. She panicked.

Would her prayers be answered without it?

Of course…of course they would.

♠

Ayaan, satiated by a teeming dish of *Cambuulo* — a Somali dinner favorite of *azuki* beans and *qamadi* wheat mixed with butter and sugar, opened her browser again to begin surfing the web, a new consuming passion that had gripped her ever since the encounter with the street urchin.

Click.

A nation's tragic history: ethnic strife, colonial oppression, a failed state, *Al-Shabaab*, US marines wading ashore with CNN waiting, black hawk down. A people thrust into a black hole of history. Refugees, like her, dispersed to the four corners of the earth. A diaspora with nowhere to return to.

Click.

Disease, poverty, drought. Warlordism, rapine, and murder. Illiteracy, repression, genital mutilation. Old at thirty-five, left to die at fifty. The arc of life stunted by famine and deprivation. Humans without rights, not even the right to live out the meager lives they'd been dealt by uncaring history.

Click.

A young Somali bride—barely twelve years old it looked like—staring into the camera, more in sorrow than joy in the expectation of her wedding day. Piercing blue-green eyes and high cheek bones—just like her own! What is she thinking? What does the future hold for her? There, but for the grace of God…there it goes again, that grace that God is so famous for. A mouse click in the stream of life: I am here, she is there. But for the Miracle, I'd be there too, no doubt.

Click, click, click…

…drawn into the algorithmic labyrinth of Google's making. Impulse ensnared by the traps of hyperlinking in a moment of weakness.

Suddenly, a chat room; a call to arms. *Come build the Caliphate! Your Muslim brothers and sisters need you!* What on earth is this?

Click.

A video clip showing soldiers of the Assad regime in Syria beheading her Muslim brothers, so the caption read. *Let us end such suffering! Will you join us?* Shall I? Am I really one of them? I've forsaken religion; God doesn't exist. I'm a scientist, an atheist!

Are you truly? Then why are you here? What brought you here?

I don't know…

Don't you? Can't you feel it, daughter? Can't you feel the pain you see before you? Look! Look again, admit what your eyes tell you! Ask yourself, sister, why does Allah bring you to such witness?

I…

If you feel the hurt, then you have heeded Allah's will. Allah has brought you here. Submit, Ayaan, submit!

It was true. Something *had* drawn her here.

She hadn't realized it at first—she had been just surfing, like everyone did—but then something had drawn her in, tunneled her deeper and deeper from one link to the next, as if she was on a roller-coaster, dragged along for the ride. Why hadn't she gotten off if she hadn't liked it? But the truth was she did like it; it was thrilling in a weird sort of way. It made her feel giddy.

An unexpected clarity, Ayaan realized, had broken through; some force beyond physics, beyond chemistry, yet still beyond serendipity, had lifted the existential fog that had enveloped her entire being, body and soul, over the past several weeks. But she was still a scientist. She knew the universe was ordered and not random, at least fundamentally, even if the ultimate nature of that ordering was still mysterious in its finest detail, and despite what many quantum physicists had to say about the quirky nature of quarks. Even Einstein had continued to insist 'til his very end that God did not play dice, hadn't he? There *had* to be a deep order to life, no matter how chaotic it might seem on the surface, living it from moment to moment, and tossed and turned in the process. Hadn't the storm-tossed sea brought her rescue rather drowning? A miracle, or a conspiring, ordered Nature with specific purpose in mind? And if there was order, then how did it come about? Via the bootstrapping Laws of Nature or through God's mysterious omnipotent will, his Creation? She wasn't at all sure, neither one way nor the other. But did it really matter? Life had a purpose, *must* have a purpose, and you couldn't live life, you couldn't be your true self, until you found it…or it found you.

She once was lost but now was found—a poor wretch like her!

♠

Piero and Pia Pellegrino were astonished at the dramatic turnaround in their daughter's mood. She smiled constantly, and bustled to and fro from their home with great urgency, as if she had so much to do. What exactly that was, they had no idea—and they almost didn't care.

They knew that she wasn't going to work anymore, and she still wasn't talking to them all that much, except to say good morning and good night, and other such pleasantries, and to request that Maria purchase special foods and spices for the feasts she now prepared for herself, totally forsaking mealtimes with them. They desperately wanted to know more about what she was up to, to get her back as the daughter she once was as soon as possible—if indeed it was possible. But for the moment they were prepared to let her have her space, as wide and yawning and mysterious as it, disturbingly, still was. Ayaan *seemed* happy, something that they'd thought she might never be again just a few short days ago; it was better, Pia convinced Piero, to let sleeping dogs lie. Except, they soon realized, she wasn't exactly sleeping all that much. The *endless* hours in her room on her computer, days at a time almost, plus her bizarre new wardrobe, her extreme reclusiveness…

When should they say something?

Dare they, oh God?

♠

Cambuulo again.

It was the third time that week that she'd prepared it for herself. But it was *so* good. She wondered how she could ever have eaten so much pasta and pizza in her former life. Just thinking about it made her feel sick and bloated now. And the wine? Gone forever. She was convinced that the blood in her veins had new life and energy, like a pure mountain stream, an unpolluted gift from the heavens.

Ayaan looked at the floor between her feet. She imagined her parents seated in their usual places in the dining room below and picking at the food Maria had prepared for them, occasionally looking across at the empty chair where once she would have been sitting. How much longer could she keep shunning them so? She would have to leave soon; there was no other option.

Her parents. But they weren't. She could just about still remember that she'd truly believed they had been once, but it was an increasingly faltering and displeasing recollection. She knew that they still thought they loved her in their own misguided way, but she'd come to realize that their love had been built on lies, and perhaps even a sense of unwarranted privilege to reorder—arbitrarily reshape—another's existence and identity. Yes, they'd given her material comforts fit for a princess, and opportunities almost beyond measure. And if they hadn't adopted her, who knows where she might have ended up?

But...

They'd played God with her. All the privileges and luxuries had turned out to be false idols. DuPont had rejected her, insulted her womanhood; everything that money could buy had failed to save her soul—had cheated it, in fact. They had tried to make her Italian when she just hadn't really fit the mold. She was their colonial prize, a purloined treasure from Italian Somaliland smashed on the shores of Lampedusa, and then refurbished as a faux East African antiquity in modern Italian garb, and ensconced in pride of place in their palatial museum. *Miracle Baby?* Miracle "cure" more like, for their...impotency. Worst of all, they'd poisoned her with apostasy—of a Roman Catholic kind. All this was a fake "love" that just couldn't be requited. It *had* to be forsaken, rather.

For the first time in many years, Ayaan began to cry—for herself...and perhaps for them, too.

♠

Submit?

It wasn't in her lexicon, so why did she keep going back to what he'd last said, implored her to do? But the more she tried to resist the injunction, the more it seemed to entice her, draw her to its flame. Was this mysterious Kifat from the chat room she'd stumbled into teasing her, or was he serious? Islam? She didn't know anything about it. She was an avowed atheist! Her rationalism told her that there was no God — no *provable* one at least. But lately, well, she had been feeling a bit strange, to say the least. Strange not in an entirely bad way, like she was ill or something, but odd in the sense that she'd been feeling that her sensibilities — especially when she was intensely pensive or dreaming — had been taking her to a part of the universe she'd never been to before, somewhere where it seemed like she was communing with something — call it a god, if you like — fundamentally powerful and all-encompassing, a mysterious ether indecipherable to scientific explanation but nonetheless palpably real and intoxicating for all that.

This Kifat, what was he doing to her? Whatever it was, she didn't particularly want it to stop. Why was he so sure of himself, so certain about everything? He seemed to have the zealotry of an absolutist — a scientist perhaps! Ayaan smiled. What was so bad about that?

She wondered what he looked like, this man she'd never met but who drew her closer to him every day? A beard no doubt; perhaps long flowing white robes, sandaled feet, and a long curved scimitar sheathed at his waist. An Omar Sharif astride a magnificent camel and dominating the desert horizon—but with Peter O'Toole's sapphire blue eyes, please! She dismissed the phantasy with a giggle, she was being too silly for words, but she knew full well that it would be back before long.

Ayaan looked across to her bedside table. Her alarm clock was winking 3:15 a.m. Its green glow in her dimly lit bedroom intermittently illuminated the framed copy of Caravaggio's *The Taking of Christ* her mother had given when she'd been confirmed, long before she'd become the scientist she was now. The pulsing green made Christ look as if he was feeling sick, as if Judas's kiss were poisoning him somehow.

She thought of Kifat again. She imagined his lips circled by his facial hair. Thick lips, a perfect Cupid's bow... Her computer beeped, signaling that someone was messaging her.

— *Ayaan! Ciao, come va?*

It was Kifat again; the third time that night. She hesitated; perhaps he was coming on a bit too strong. Besides he lived hundreds of miles away, at least a thousand. The index finger of her right hand gently stroked her computer mouse: to click or not to click? She involuntarily twitched, as if the mouse had somehow just given her a mild electric shock.

Click. *E bene.* It's good. You know Italian?

— Ah, no, I looked it up! Only English, apart from my native Arabic, that is.

Ayaan smiled to herself. It pleased her to know he'd made the effort, minimal though others might have argued it undoubtedly was. She saw cute now, to go along with the handsome hirsuteness she'd assumed he must have.

— *Certo.* Okay. Perhaps I can teach you.
—Would you? I would like that.
He would like that. She would like that.
— *Perfetto!* That's perfect.

Ayaan's cursor blinked at her, as if it was counting the seconds waiting for Kifat's next reply. He began to type, then abruptly deleted what he'd being composing. More seconds, more metronomic monitoring, went impatiently by. What was he having second thoughts about? Ayaan readied her fingers over her keyboard. Should she say something?

His words, when they popped up, startled her a little. She wasn't entirely surprised by what he said; just that he'd so quickly gotten back into his rather didactic chat room persona. She'd rather hoped they'd just get to know each other a bit better first, take things slower. But Kifat seemed in a hurry, anxious to get beyond the to and fro of the innocuous flirting that she was expecting, indeed perhaps hoping for.

—Tell me about your name—*Ayaan.* Unusual for an Italian, no?

Ayaan stared at the word "Italian." Suddenly, it seemed odd to her, almost alien, as if she'd just seen it for the first time. She hesitated to reply, wondering whether Kifat might be disappointed that she wasn't from Italy after all. What picture of her did he have in his mind? The hourglass figure of a leggy model hip-rolling down a runway, long brunette tresses cascading down her back, full lips pouting at the world as if to say "Look all you want, but don't even dream of touching"? Would Roma, even Roma *chic*, do—even for someone, she presumed, who might be well

177

used to such looks? But she couldn't hide it for long, and there was no point in lying. Enough falsehoods were stalking her world already.

—I'm Somali. I was adopted by an Italian couple when I was a baby. I lost my parents in an accident at sea.

—I'm so sorry, Ayaan. I had no idea.

—Oh, I was lucky. The "Miracle Baby" they called me. My adoptive parents are quite well off. I've had everything money can buy.

—Everything?

—Well…

—It's ironic, isn't it?

—What?

—That you've had Italian parents when you consider what Italy did to Somalia. You do know about all that, don't you, Ayaan?

—Yes, yes I do. At least I do now.

—How do you feel about that?

Ayaan didn't reply. Tears were beginning to form in her eyes.

—The Catholic fascist Crusaders seized your ancestral home, Ayaan, slaughtered tens of thousands of your own kind in the interests of empire. "Italian Somaliland"—what apostasy!

—Stop. Please stop.

—I'm sorry, Ayaan. But the Truth has to be told. I'll pray for you.

Ayaan closed the window to the chat room, and Kifat was gone. But his words lingered on like burned-in pixels resistant to deletion. "Erase History" was fake, as she already knew, no matter how many times you switched "Search History" off, no matter, she feared, if you actually smashed your computer into a thousand pieces—there's all that stuff in the cloud now, and who knew who really had control of that?

History was here to stay, warts and all.

♠

There was a new message in her in-box. She knew it must be Kifat. Ayaan had avoided the chat room for the last twenty-four hours, so she suspected he'd be keen to reach her.

—Where have you been? I need to congratulate you. K.

Ayaan read the message over and over, looking for clues as to Kifat's intent, and pondering what on earth he wanted to commend her for. He intrigued her, that much she had to admit, but as to why exactly she couldn't say, at least not with any certainty. All she knew was she couldn't erase the image she had of him from her mind, even when for the few hours she managed fitful sleep—sometimes even especially then.

But what he'd said about Somalia, about her ancestors, had upset her. Despite the fact that she'd done her own research about her home country, for some reason Kifat's confirmation as to what she'd already discovered seemed to rub excessive salt into her newly-found psychological wounds. Why? Because, she now realized, the Truth, as he put it, hurt; and its consequences demanded a response. The Truth had to be confronted; history had to be avenged. Her own life, her search for her sense of self, seemed to depend on such a grandiose sort of scheme now. The thought seemed incredulous, but it also felt exhilarating, and all she could think of was how she was going to find an effective way forward in such a startling scenario.

And in that moment, Kifat was there.

Click.

— Congratulate me — what for?

— I see you graduated first in your class at Bologna. Well done! ☺

Ayaan smiled. She'd never seen Kifat do that before, add the Smiley Face.

— How do you know that?

— Never heard of Google? :-7 WTF

She laughed out loud this time.

— Why are you checking me out?

— Because you are so interesting, so talented. Chemical engineering, right? :-D MVP!

— Yes.

— How is it going at DuPont?

— I've left DuPont.

— Left? What happened?

Ayaan hesitated. She really didn't want to talk about it, but after she'd offered her first few vague words about the context of her resigning, the torrent of the truth came gushing forth. She couldn't help herself. She hammered at her keyboard furiously, composing three pages of invective at warp speed.

Click.

It was several minutes before Kifat replied.

— You did the right thing, Ayaan.

At a measured pace, Kifat explained himself. Ayaan read along, letting his every word speak to her, as if she was hearing a truly revealing sermon for the very first time in her life. He was fully on her side, without reservation. He surprised her with his enlightened views on gender equality and the perniciousness of patriarchy. His analytical comparison of Italian imperialism to DuPont's decades of economic exploitation of a whole slew of Third World countries, along with their environmental despoliation and massive destruction via the company's manufacture of chemical weapons like Agent Orange in Vietnam (neo-imperialism, he called it), not only confirmed her own worst suspicions of her former employer, but also convinced her she'd under-estimated her new acquaintance far beyond measure. Kifat was truly someone worth listening to—and he was her *brother* if truth be told, part of his, *their*, family, not the fake one she'd been brainwashed into loving all these years.

Kifat's long message finally came to an end. He waited for her response, but none came. If she was angry, he surmised, she would have vented already. Her silence, therefore, could only be that of someone in confusion, or agreement—at least perhaps ripe for the picking.

—It's time for change, isn't it? To destroy the DuPonts, the imperialists, and the Crusaders in this world, to bring God's grace to the True Believers, the exploited, and the downtrodden!

Before she knew what she was really saying, Ayaan had typed:

—Yes…but how?

—You're a chemical engineer. You can help us here where the struggle has already begun. Will you come and join us?

—How? Where? When? Tell me.

—Come to me here, Ayaan. You can help us make the desert bloom, can't you, bloom big, very big? It is Allah's will that you do so. Do you hear him calling you?

Of course, Ayaan suddenly realized, she *really* could help them. With her scientific expertise in GM, she could, like the Israelis had done, make the desert bloom, at least with a lot of help and a dose of good fortune. She could feed the hungry, millions of them—how much bigger could it get than that? As big and as miraculous as five loaves and two fishes— at least! Oh, at last...

—Yes, I hear him! I will come.

—Perfect! I am waiting for you. Abu Bakr al-Baghdadi commands you. He has commanded thousands like you and they have come. Ghazalan, Parsa, Dinar, Sajjad—follow them, ask them what it's like to submit to Allah. H2CUS :-)=

The beard. He had a beard!

Perhaps she was ready to submit, after all— now that Kifat had shown her a way.

♠

And so, it comes to pass, that Ayaan chats with Ghazalan and the others, and they fill her full of hope and purpose. And like them, she frequents *Inspire*'s website and is...*inspired*.

But a bit unnerved too, to be honest. All the stuff about holy jihad, the occasional reference to the End of Days, and the constant appeals to justice at the point of a sword, so to speak, frighten Ayaan, the hint of nihilism seeming rather at odds with making the desert fecund with a mountain of food for the starving multitudes. But, in the end, she assumes that she will not be consorting with any of the violent sort of thing, at least not directly; she'll have a special kind of jihad of her own—the *struggle* to get her alchemy to transmute arid sand into nutrient rich soil, to sprout new crops where only lifelessness has persisted before. Ayaan knows that there'll have to be some taking of an eye for an eye for her people, her Somali kin, to finally get their just desserts; but she'll leave that agenda for the Kifats of the world, and assume that Allah will render final judgment on all of that when the time comes. Now that she has found real purpose, she is loath to let it go. Like the proverbial ostrich, she will bury her doubts in the imagined sands of Syria—at least for as long as she can, that is.

Physically, Ayaan still remains in Bologna, in the home of Piero and Pia Pellegrino. But existentially, spiritually, she is already a million cyberspace miles away, cocooned in an electronic brave new world that eggs her one and reshapes her mind. She is a Miracle Baby again, reborn this time for jihad, although she doesn't fully realize quite how yet.

And then one day: **Click. Click. Click.** Just like that—impulsively, and a one-way flight to Istanbul is booked. A farewell gift charged to her parents' credit card, she rationalizes. It's the very least they can do—let their Miracle Baby freely fly.

That night, her parents are in troubled sleep, Ayaan unknowingly gone.

The next day they discover her empty room: just her backpack and a handful of clothes missing. No note, no explanation; just her crucifix lying on her pillow. Are they to pray for her, request another miracle, or is she really lost to them, to Christ?

They pray, not knowing what else to do after the police finally tell them where they believe she's gone, and what it appears she is set on doing when she gets there.

But will their prayers be enough?

We'll see. But there's a darn good reason why you lot often say "on a wing *and* a prayer," isn't there?

25

[Late June 2015 BCT (Beyond Christian Time-Date Unknown)]

Ayaan knew she must have seen such a landscape before, many years ago when she was a very small child—not much than a few weeks-old baby, really—somewhere in Somalia; but although she felt some sort of primal recognition of what now lay before her, she was in truth totally unprepared to find herself in such a vast, relentless desert. It hurt her eyes to search the sun-blazed horizon. What was lying there, and then beyond it? *Anything*?

     But despite the barrenness all around her, there was no mistaking the urgency and the directness by which she was being propelled forward—the driver knew *exactly* where he was going, it seemed, and what he expected to find when they arrived there. He was driving at warp speed, and as straight as the crow flies homing in on its roosting place, as if it was being drawn directly there on a long piece of string being rapidly wound in. So, she kept on looking, shielding her eyes and looking, looking—waiting for that moment when some sort of oasis, she hoped, would mirage itself into view on the far horizon, like a magical genie emerging from a lamp. But as to whether the genie would be a kindly one or not, she was very much uncertain now. In fact, she was very much beginning to fear the worst. Every-thing was moving much too fast, and those seemingly innocent clicks on her computer mouse now appeared to have sucked her into a maelstrom of unanticipated activity in which she didn't know up from down, or dangled promise from real potential danger. What had she *done*?

Of course, her research back in Bologna had informed her that where she was headed would be such a desolate place; she'd seen scores of images of it during her Google searches, and, yes, here it was, as vast and unforgiving as you could imagine. But it hadn't been that easy to deeply—existentially—transport herself in the mind or online to a place that was just about the total antithesis to her home town back in Italy. No towers or basilicas in this place; no winding medieval streets packed in tight by imposing architectural gems, one after the other, and linked by expansive piazzas decorated with fountains, and drawing vast crowds to them by day and by night in equal measure. Just a world of sand and rock here, undulating to the horizon and scorched by an unrelenting sun, and bereft of trees and almost of any sign of human habitation.

From Istanbul, Ayaan had traversed Turkey by train and bus, as Kifat had instructed her. She'd been met at the point where her last bus went no farther by one of Kifat's aides, who'd had then smuggled her across a remote part of the border into northern Syria, or what Kifat had referred to as Mesopotamia, the center of the new caliphate he and his comrades were in the process of building there. It was a vastly critical project with which she was, she thought, committed to assist him, although the longer her journey from Italy had gone on the less sure she'd begun to feel about it all. But that was understandable, Ayaan had told herself—*wasn't it?* She was on a great mission, one she could never have had any earthly idea she'd be on one day. Who wouldn't get a little nervous, scared even?

And scared she undoubtedly was now. When she'd finally met him in person, just a few steps inside Syria, Kifat had looked exactly as she had imagined him—fantasized perhaps, she'd then suddenly recognized. But, inauspiciously, he'd immediately seemed not at all to be the attentive, caring friend she'd thought she'd found online. There'd been no Smiley Face at all, not even any kind of welcoming embrace, just a wave of the hand and a "Come!" as he'd about-faced and started to head off for their vehicle, leaving her to struggle as best she could to keep up with him, tired and burdened by her baggage, such as it was. But, then again, they'd been entering a "war zone," he'd unceremoniously advised her. They were on really *serious* business—genuinely life-threatening, it had then finally hit her. Oh God, *what* had she done?

Ayaan redux, Ayaan reborn: she was to be Islamic State's Chief Scientist, but just exactly what they expected her contribution to be she still wasn't altogether quite sure. Growing genetically-modified food, she'd still assumed. At least that what Kifat had discussed with her online, she remembered—"making the desert bloom," all that sort of thing, *just like the Israelis had done*.

The Israelis? For all their obvious apostasy—and their litany of crimes against humanity, especially against the Palestinian Muslims, it suddenly struck Ayaan that Kifat was in actual fact envious of them, wanted to emulate them in great measure. A Jewish home?—a Caliphate for the *umma*, as well; a blooming Negev?—likewise the Shamiyah, too; a Haganah for the Jewish state, then a DAESH for the Islamic one in parallel—ferocious holy warriors, both. Was she about to embark on the very *same* sort of crusade the Israelis had begun well over half a century ago?

Ayaan shook her head; she hated how her thoughts kept leading her into such expansive and disturbing realms of supposition. *Food*, she insisted to herself, genetically-modified food, to feed the women and children—that's what I'm here for! But when she looked out at the desert again, relentlessly passing by like the endlessly looping-around background of a cartoon strip, she couldn't avoid the obvious conclusion: making all *this* bloom? There was no way—at least not in her active lifetime, while she was actually here.

Ayaan knew now that she wouldn't be of much use to Kifat *at all*. The challenge he'd set for her would be Herculean, impossible, given what she knew about such things. And, even assuming that perhaps she might be able to make it happen *sometime* in *some* very limited measure, at the very least would have meant that she'd need a great deal of technical assistance, masses of equipment, an army of workers, all costing in the millions and millions of dollars. Could Kifat really provide all of that—*here*? What would happen when he found out she might not be able to do it after all? Would he find something else for her to do, or would he just send her home? Or, she barely dared to think of it, would he just…like Jihadi John? She *had* to succeed somehow or she *had* to escape—she just had to. If only the click of a mouse worked in reverse, and you could undo everything. But there was no erasing of your history…in the end. Digital footprints were fundamentally material, when all was said and done, and the cocoon of your online world had consequences—real concrete consequences—whether you realized it at the time of your impulsive web surfing, or not.

    The pick-up truck they were riding in hit yet another rock or pothole—she just couldn't tell the difference anymore. The trip had been so hideously bumpy she'd been feeling rather nauseous for at least the last hour, but she hadn't dared to ask Kifat to get the driver to stop. She slumped against Kifat's shoulder one more time. It felt like he had a rock in there, so large and firm were his deltoids. A globule of bile sourly invaded her dry throat, and then, thankfully, melted away in her saliva. "Ah!" Ayaan grunted, but Kifat made no sound. He just sat there next to her, impassively, staring straight ahead. He'd barely said more than a half dozen words to her since he'd met her just inside the border. She wanted to look at him again, but forced herself to resist the temptation.

But his physique, at least two meters of superb athletic masculinity; his presence, immediately commanding and authoritative, so wildly magnetic that you succumbed to his will almost spontaneously, as if there was absolutely nothing you could do to stop yourself, even if the charismatic attraction was as much born of fear as it was of adulation. And he was incredibly handsome. She assumed he was probably a Syrian or an Iraqi, perhaps a so-called "foreign fighter" already hardened by the jihadi campaigns in Bosnia, Afghanistan and Yemen. But to Ayaan, he *looked* decidedly Somali, almost a male version of herself: clear, olive-brown skin, high cheekbones, and searing, sapphire-blue eyes. So, it dismayed her to find that his only physical feature that was at all off-putting was his thick black moustache and beard. They'd once been the center of her fascination with him, but now in real life they reminded her of Bluebeard from the Grimm's fairy tale her adoptive mother had read to her as a child. Assuming he might have been married already, how many of Kifat's wives were still alive? she suddenly wondered. Was he like Bluebeard in this murderous manner, as well as in looks? By the look of him, she was now beginning to suspect that he might.

The truck hit another bump, the biggest so far, disrupting her increasingly disturbing reverie. Ayaan bounced from Kifat's shoulder to the driver's, and then back again. She felt claustrophobic; the bile, more voluminous this time, returned and managed to wet her lips. She was suffocating.

"Stop! Please stop!" she begged. "I'm going to be sick."

Kifat said something in Arabic, and the driver brought the truck to a screeching halt. It slid to a slaloming halt, kicking up a huge cloud of desert dust in its wake. Kifat opened his door and got out, roughly dragging Ayaan with him. She fell to her knees and threw up. The flying sand only added fuel to her already violent fit of coughing. "Ohhh! Ohhh! Oh, God." Ayaan's vomiting ceased, but she remained on all fours, gasping for air. Kifat ignored her plight; he leant against the vehicle's hood and lit up a cigarette for what must have been the fiftieth time that day. He took a couple of long drags on his cigarette, and then casually removed a speck of loosened tobacco from the tip of his tongue with his fingers.

"Finish? We must hurry. No more time here," he said. He stubbed his barely consumed cigarette out on the wheel hub behind his legs, and then flicked the crumpled tube of extinguished tobacco out into the desert, discarded casually as if it was suddenly surplus to his addictive requirements.

Ayaan shook her head, still gagging and coughing. Kifat grabbed her under her armpit and hauled her to her feet. But rather than helping her back into the cab, he took her to the rear of the truck, opened the tailgate, and then pushed her unceremoniously into the cargo bed.

"You stay here," he said. "Until you're better." He slammed the tailgate shut, and then fished around for a length of rope. He began to tie her wrists to a safety bar at the front of the cargo bed. "Better to be safe than sorry—we wouldn't want to lose you, would we?" He hacked up a wad of smoker's phlegm, and then spat it into the dust. It barely missed Ayaan's crouching frame. "Not much farther," he continued. "The women are anxious to meet you, *very* anxious."

      Ayaan thought she heard Kifat laugh, the kind of laugh she imagined Bluebeard might have had, right after disposing of one of his many wives. Kifat got back into the truck's cab, and they were off once again, bouncing into what now seemed a very uncertain future, as the sun, thankfully, began its descent into night. In the cargo bed, Ayaan flopped around even more violently than she had before, up front. Back there, there was no muscular Kifat to cushion her, and the rope around her wrists began to burn into her skin. She yelled for Kifat to get the driver to stop again, but the truck just continued to pick up speed. The engine roared so loud, Ayaan could barely hear the sound of her own desperate voice.

      But within a half hour, the road suddenly smoothed out and the truck slowed down. Much to her surprise and relief, Ayaan surmised they were approaching the outskirts of some kind of settlement, presumably their destination. Buildings began to line the road, sporadically at first but then continuously. The structures became more densely packed and multi-storied. They were obviously entering an urban center of some significant size, one big enough, given the vast number of what looked like bombed-out buildings Ayaan saw, to be a major strategic target for some military force or other.

At last, Ayaan was able to get reasonably comfortable. The friction from the rope ceased to burn her wrists. She managed to sit up; she could now see over the truck's sides. She desperately searched for any living soul who might be on the street, someone whom she might be able to signal to for help. But deep in the middle of a dark, lightless night the streets were deserted—no more life than the desert itself.

She looked up at the night sky; not a star or constellation to be seen. God knows what direction they were traveling in, or what direction they'd come from. They'd come from somewhere on the Turkish border, that much she knew, but how on earth had she managed to get herself there in the first place? Why had she bought the airline ticket to Istanbul? Why had she left home? Why had she abandoned her parents? All those horrible things she'd thought about them, the way she'd pushed them away, she was sorry for all that now. Why had she gone to that chat room, met Kifat, be lured by him to come here? Here, of all places!

She marveled at the seeming surreality of it all. Looking back, it now felt as if she'd been in a time machine over the last few weeks. Surfing the internet was just like taking an airplane to a far-off land. When you by the ticket and set out on the long journey, you don't really have a good sense of the magnitude of just what's going to happen to you; that you're going to travel thousands of miles in just a few hours, and then fetch up in a strange and foreign land. But suddenly, you're there and there's someone there to meet you. He's a complete stranger, but he has your name on a hand-held sign, and he's local and knows what to do, how to navigate through the alien throng swarming the streets outside the terminal. Then you're in a car and being whisked away, and in your uncertainty, in your nervousness, you clutch onto the nearest branch that seems to offer safety, guidance—and Kifat appears, taking charge and you follow. He commands and you obey; there's no other choice. You're on autopilot now. What's done has been done in a weird sort of vacuum where the decisions and choices you've made have not been fully grounded in your immediate, physical, lived experience. You've made them in a cyber-bubble—and then it bursts on you, just like that!

She could retrace all the steps, make all the causal connections between one action and another in reverse, in retrospect, but the end result, as logical as it might seem when you thought about like this, like methodically reconstructing the historical record, still didn't make any sense—*none* whatsoever. Surely it was all a terrible dream, but the ropes around her wrists punctured that forlorn hope as soon as she'd beseeched it.

She had been first in her class in chemical engineering at the University of Bologna, and had an IQ of 145; she also had enough scientific and technological expertise to be able to genetically modify crops. She was *that* smart that she now found herself bound by the wrists in the back of a pickup truck somewhere in a mythical land called Mesopotamia, the future home of some equally utopian Islamic caliphate? *That* smart that she now was Bluebeard's prisoner, for all intents and purposes? But it had been *she* who had made the choices that had brought her to such a predicament. It had been *she* who had been foolish enough to let herself be cocooned in an online toxic echo chamber and be brainwashed by the constant drum beat of its poisonous jihadi groupthink. All this was how, Ayaan realized, the emotionally vulnerable, the mentally ill, and the angry alienated plunged over the edge of normalcy, of civilization, to become paranoid conspiracy theorists and murderous maniacs, even in so-called "mature" democracies, let alone alienating autocracies.

Choices? Free will? Intelligence? What price them all, now? Did they really exist, and if they did, just how fallible were they in moments of self-doubt, of emotional crisis? In the end, for all her smarts, she had been as impressionable, as *imprintable*, as a baby gosling instinctively latching onto the supposedly first emotional safe harbor that presented itself to it. And *somehow* that "safe harbor," she'd once incredulously believed until her arrival in Syria, had been Kifat—and here she now was—sucked into a black hole.

Oh God…

Suddenly she heard the clop of a horse's hooves just ahead of them, and it was getting nearer. Ayaan leaned over as far as she could, so that she could see over the side of the truck closest to the center of the road. The truck began to turn slightly; it was about to overtake the horse. Ayaan strained to make herself as visible as possible from the road.

A rickety cart piled high with the city's stinking refuse came into view, then an old man seated up front holding the reins, and finally the horse itself, an emaciated, flea-bitten beast, looking as wretched as she now felt. The driver was slumped over, apparently half asleep, letting his trusty charge find their way on autopilot.

As the truck pulled just ahead of the horse and cart, Ayaan began to jiggle her body as best she could in order to attract the cart driver's attention, but to no avail. He just sat there, head hanging down, and swaying slightly to the rhythm of the horse's arthritic clomping. Ten yards quickly opened up between the truck and cart. Ayaan kicked the side of the truck, then again, even louder this time. It did the trick. The old man looked up and stared right at her. His face expressed shock, but whether it was because he'd been rudely awakened or because he hadn't expected to see such as Ayaan tied up in the back of a truck in the middle of the night, she couldn't tell.

Ayaan mouthed "Help!" over and over. She tugged against her bonds hoping that he would understand the nature of her plight. The old man stood up and stared at her. Yes, he could see now, surely! But then his head shifted slightly — he'd caught sight of something else.

The black flag of Islamic State was flapping on its pole attached to the rear bumper of the truck. The old man sat down again, gave the horse a couple of sharp flicks with his whip, and then commanded it to turn down an alleyway to his right.

"Keep it quiet back there," she heard Kifat shout out. He'd opened his cab window and was leaning out of it. "Or I'll take care of it for you."

Ayaan slumped back into the bed of the truck and began to quietly cry.

Mama, Papa, she moaned over and over.

♠

Ayaan awoke the next day with the sun, already high in the sky, streaming through the window of the room she was in.

But the bright light and the sun's warmth did little to lift her spirits. Her cheeks felt clammy with dried tears; her head complained of a low-grade headache. Someone must have undressed her and put her to bed, as she couldn't remember a thing after they'd arrived at Kifat's quarters, and she'd been handed over to the custody of an overweight, middle-aged woman who'd fed her. The food had been delicious, but now she wondered if the woman had slipped something in it—a drug of some kind to make her sleep. She hadn't slept so deeply in weeks; and she'd not dreamt at all. But now everything came flooding back: the long ride in the truck across the desert; Kifat's rough treatment of her; the brief, impossible, moment of rescue...

"Ah, you finally awake!" It was the fat woman. She had a bowl of water in her hands. She came and stood by Ayaan's bed, put the bowl on the small table next to it, and then placed the palm of her hand against Ayaan's brow. "How you feel?"

Ayaan was surprised to hear her converse in English, but then she realized that the woman had an accent that didn't belong in that part of the world. She sounded almost French; perhaps she was Algerian or, more likely, of Lebanese descent. "Where am I? Who are you?"

But the woman didn't answer her; she just retrieved a small washcloth from the bowl and began to clean Ayaan's face. She was gentle enough at first, but then she began to almost scrub Ayaan's skin, stretching and pulling it roughly, as if she already had some kind of grievance against her new charge. Ayaan winced; for a second, she heard her mother saying: "Keep still, Ayaan. Look at how dirty your face is!" And then it suddenly came to her. *Ransom!* She'd been kidnapped; Kifat and his gang wanted her parents' money. What a naïve fool she'd been!

Satisfied that she'd done a good enough job of washing Ayaan's face, the woman looked her once over with palpable distaste, handed her a headscarf, and commanded: "Get up — quick! Dress. For head, cover hair." She ripped the blanket covering Ayaan off her in one fell swoop, with all the exuberance of a matador teasing a bull. "He here get you soon! Be ready, no make him angry." She wagged he finger at Ayaan. "No — no make him angry!"

♠

Just as she'd finished dressing, the driver of the truck from the night before showed up.

He was as surly and mostly uncommunicative as he'd been then. He said almost nothing; his face displayed little emotion of any kind, just a look of "I'm not enjoying any of this anymore than you are"; his actions were strictly utilitarian, like a gruff master roughly ordering his dog about by yanking its leash — whatever, in other words, was minimally necessary to get his orders through, and that would keep Kifat off his back. He spoke in Arabic what few words he uttered. The only one that Ayaan could make out was "Fatima," her fat caretaker, she supposed. His hand gestures did most of his talking, like he was a signer for the deaf and dumb.

The driver took Ayaan by the arm and hustled her out of the room where she'd spent the night. They crossed a courtyard where a gaggle of children were playing, while four or five young women went about their daily chores. They all stopped and stared at Ayaan as she was briefly paraded before them. They looked at her as if she might just have landed from another planet. It suddenly occurred to Ayaan that it'd been a long time since anyone, including her once doting parents, had looked at her as if she was a "normal" person, someone that you could easily relate to, someone who was not alien, unsettling in some disturbingly exotic way.

On the other side of the compound, the driver opened an imposing looking door, one completely out of character with all the others that Ayaan had seen thus far. He thrust her through the opening, as if he was a prison guard in the movies returning a prisoner to her cell. He closed the door behind her, before going off to take care of his next assignment.

"What do you think?" a voice said from behind her. "Will this suit your needs, our cause?" Ayaan turned around. It was Kifat. He nodded his head and gestured with his arm, inviting her to examine the room. He was obviously proud of it.

It took a few seconds for Ayaan's eyes to accommodate to the subdued lighting; the room, though quite large, had no windows, and at that moment whatever artificial light was available had been turned off for some reason. Soon, however, recognizable objects began to come into focus, like ghosts emerging from a thick graveyard fog. A large workbench came first, followed by a row of high stools. Ayaan slowly stepped towards the bench. A deep sink appeared, stained by a foul-looking green and an almost toxic-looking orange. Then, in quick succession, she made out racks of test tubes, then a computer, and finally a smorgasbord of electronic detection and measuring devices, some that she recognized, several that she didn't. She realized she was in a laboratory of sorts, primitive with respect to the construction quality of the room it was located in, but so unexpectedly full of modern-looking scientific equipment that, in fact, it all suggested something quite sophisticated was nonetheless expected to take place there.

"My needs?" Ayaan hesitantly replied.

"For your work," Kifat said. He stepped towards her. Ayaan looked puzzled, as if she had absolutely no idea what he was talking about. Kifat's expression turned sour, and he stared right at her. "Don't play games with me. You know why you're here!" He pointed towards a large metal door in the rear wall of the lab. It looked out of place, too imposing for the obviously much older and much less forbidding wall that accommodated it. "I think you'll find the key ingredient you'll need to do your work in there."

Ayaan looked at the door. A black skull and crossbones on a yellow background glared back at her. She jumped. Then she saw the telltale symbol for the presence of radioactive material—a sort of black-and-yellow, circular, three-winged angel of death hovering above the pirate symbols. Ayaan turned to look at Kifat, stunned.

"In...there?" she mumbled.

"Yes, of course. Where else?"

"But...what is in there that I need?"

Kifat frowned. "The uranium compounds we procured from the university in Mosul when we captured it. You knew about that — we talked about it before you came."

"Uranium?"

Kifat sighed heavily. "Yes — for the bomb."

Ayaan almost fainted, slumping back against the bench. "Bomb? When—"

Kifat furrowed his brow even deeper, the creases bending wavelike with annoyance. "The 'Dirty Bomb,' the one you *promised* to make for us."

"I did? When? I don't know anything about such—" Suddenly, the penny dropped. "'Make the desert *bloom*,' you said. Oh my—"

"Don't play the fool with me, Ayaan! You knew perfectly well what I was talking about when I said that."

"But I thought...Oh, what a fool I am. What a perfect idiot!" Ayaan collapsed to her knees as if someone had just sliced her legs off right below them.

Kifat grabbed her by the stray strand of hair that had escaped her headscarf. "I'm warning you, Ayaan." He yanked her head back so that she had to look right at him. His eyes flamed with rage. "What do you take me for? You worked for DuPont, and we know they are at the heart of the American nuclear weapons program—"

"What?" she croaked.

"Manhattan Project, Savannah River, Hanford. We know all—"

"But that was fifty years ago! And, in any case, I'm in GM like I told you, genetic modification, not… I don't know anything about *bombs*!"

Kifat glared at Ayaan as if he was looking right through her. She had told him she was in GM—he'd known that—but he'd thought she'd just been playing along with him in order to fool the Crusader spies who would have, undoubtedly, been trying to intercept their communications. He may not have tricked them, but now it appeared he had certainly inadvertently tricked Ayaan—and *himself* as well. What an incompetent fool he'd been! Kifat let go of Ayaan's hair; then he slapped her across her face as hard as he could. "You *will* submit to Allah's will," he threatened. "You *will* make the bomb. I command it as your husband!"

Ayaan, clutching her face, looked up at him in horror. Kifat looked down at her, and then pronounced, as if he was an imam leading Friday prayers: "The *Holy Koran* commands that you are now my wife. The Prophet says that 'those that your right hands possess,' you may take as your wife. I have captured you in battle, in holy jihad, Ayaan. You are mine, and you will do as I say."

Kifat turned to leave. At the door, he said: "Tomorrow. We start tomorrow." But just exactly what he thought they'd start, he was not at all sure now. Jihad wasn't supposed to be like this.

26

[24-25 May 2016]

The Rotherham police searched in and around the area of Green's Home Electronics for a good long while after its latest break-in, but they did not find Mo and Saeed cowering in the out-of-control vegetation beneath the bridge over the river Don, just a hundred yards or so down the street. Nor did they hear the boys trying to muffle their nervous giggling, a mixture of glee and trepidation at their unexpected triumph in nicking the iconic iPhone.

The police were also unable to detect any clear prints at the scene of the crime; Mo had jettisoned the brick he'd used to smash the shop window into the river. And whatever footprints might have been left behind by the thief or thieves had quickly dissipated in the rain that had just begun to fall at the moment of the impulsive burglary. When Mo and Saeed finally came out of their hiding place, the police were nowhere to be seen, having long given up on cracking much of the case that cold, damp, drizzly night. Discovering their amazing good fortune, the two comrades in arms high-fived each other; they were home scot-free, it seemed. *Shit!*

When he got to his house, Mo went straight to his room in order to hide the iPhone under the floorboards where he kept his most private possessions. There almost wasn't any room for it. For someone whose life had been so wretched and deprived, he'd amassed a good deal of private stuff over the years. He took everything out of his secret hiding place, thinking he needed to put the phone as far out of view and reach as possible in case any no-good snooper, especially his old man, might take it upon themselves to violate his privacy one of these days.

Mo checked off the inventory of his prized possessions in his head as he took them out of the underfloor cavity, one by one. There was the cash he'd stolen from his dad's wallet, the crumpled banknotes secured by a rubber band into a tight, cylindrical wad; his stash of porn, his favorite pages dog-eared from frequent, perhaps excessive, *addictive*, viewing; the lascivious "love letters" to Kathy Green (just about porn itself, in its own amateurish way) that he'd never dared to send to her, she never having shown even the slightest interest in him; the school report detailing all his failing grades that he'd made sure his dad had never seen—he'd tried changing some the "F's" to "B's" but had achieved little more than making it perfectly clear what he'd been trying to do; his dead mother's cheap wedding ring his dad thought he'd lost; a miniature Koran still in its cellophane wrapper, sent by a distant great aunt in Pakistan—perhaps he'd take a look at it now, someday soon when he had the time; a ticket stub to see Sahal Salaam, a comedic rapper from Egypt—a bit blue and blasphemous, he knew, but, God, he was *so* fucking funny; a moth-eaten skull cap he couldn't quite remember why he still had it; and—the greatest prize of all—a pair of Kathy Green's panties he'd stolen from her washing line just a few days before he'd stepped up to nicking expensive consumer electronics to add to his petty criminal repertoire. Gratifyingly, everything was there as it should have been. It looked like his old man still didn't know about his hidey-hole, thank God.

Mo picked up the iPhone and looked at it again. In the moonlight shining through his bedroom window, its black shiny sleekness contrasted so sharply with the shabbiness of not only his surroundings, his dad's shambolic house, but also of his equally disheveled self. Billions worldwide hankered for such a treasure as this, and now he had one. He fingered the smooth edges, caressed the glassy screen, wondering what opportunities it might bring him—if there was ever a chance that he'd be able to keep it, to use it. Such a tiny thing, but you only had to touch it here and there, and before you knew it you could go anywhere the World Wide Web might take you, even if your bodily self was forever stuck in godforsaken Rotherham! It was cool, so fucking cool; so cool, in fact, that it'd give him amazing street cred for once, to attract wads of admiring attention, perhaps even to finally be able to seduce the likes of Kathy… What magic! *If only…*

Suddenly, the moon went behind a cloud. The phone disappeared into darkness, as if someone had just turned it off. He pushed the power button, once; then harder and longer a second time. Nothing. Of course, it needed charging up first! Something else for his old man to complain about: *D'ya think my money grows on trees? Find your own 50p's for charging that thing. Where'd you get it, anyhow?* He'd just have to know, wouldn't he, stick his scabby nose into where it wasn't welcome… Mo carefully wrapped the iPhone up in Kathy's underwear; symbolically he figured, he'd just put what he'd stolen from old man Green right back under his nose. Better yet, right next to where his precious daughter's pussy once was!

Mo heard his dad's slippered footsteps slowly shuffling up the staircase, then begin to slouch across the landing towards his bedroom door. *Shit!* He quickly stuffed the panty-wrapped iPhone as far back in his hidey-hole as it would go, then he crammed everything else back in front of it. He was just replacing the loosened floorboards when his father's shuffling paused right outside of his door. Mo stopped what he was doing. Silence. He sucked in and held his breath.

"Mo?" his father's voice softly said.

Mo concentrated on keeping his lips tightly sealed. He began to feel the strain of not breathing, not even through his nose.

"Mo? Are you awake?" the voice said a little louder this time.

More silence, the kind that seems to be dead set on betraying itself and everything around it, like it can't help but sooner or later giving away those who are trying to hide under its cover. Mo was about to burst, but, thankfully, the shuffling started up again, and began its retreat in the same arthritic manner as it had approached.

Mo finished carefully replacing the floorboards and got into bed, still fully clothed. He lay there for a good long while, unable to sleep. He could hear his father pottering about in the kitchen below him. He thought he heard a chair scrape across the floor, then creak as if someone was stepping up onto it, trying to reach for something. What was the old sod up to now? Could he somehow see his hidey-hole from down there? What if he'd dislodged some ceiling plaster in the kitchen when he'd been jamming the phone into the hole? Had he inadvertently done something to the electrical wiring, making the kitchen light flicker? He could almost feel his dad glaring up at the very spot where the incriminating evidence lay. Then he heard his dad crawl up the stairs again, but this time he went straight to his room. Thank Christ! Mo said to himself, and then quickly fell to sleep, although one harried on and off by the haunting secret beneath his bed.

Throughout the night, Mo kept dreaming that he was squashed inside his hidey-hole like a breached, near-term fetus in a shrunken womb. He could barely breathe; the underfloor wiring would keep wrapping itself around his neck as if it were a live snake bent on constricting him. It'd be terrifyingly claustrophobic; he'd frequently feel close to complete suffocation, but every time he'd try to turn around and climb out of the hole his limbs would remain jammed up against the floor joists, and the bounds around his throat would just get tauter and tauter as if they were self-tightening nooses. A thousand grasping hands would reach out to him from all directions, clawing at him, tearing at his clothes. Raspy voices would keep calling out, louder and louder "Give it to us. It's ours, *our* precious! You stole it, you filthy thief!" He'd desperately look around him, searching for Kathy Green's panties, but wouldn't be able to find them. Then he'd see Saeed up ahead, sitting on top of a bridge over a river. He'd be grinning and dangling his feet over the stone parapet. He'd be holding something in his hand, out over the rushing waters below. It'd be the iPhone! Saeed would toss it two or three times into the air and then catch it, teasing Mo. Then Mo would burst free of his bonds and struggle forward, but, on seeing this, Saeed would toss the iPhone into the air one more time and let it fall into the river below, unleashing a surge of gurgling water towards Mo. He'd be drowning, going down,…*going down…drowning…a loud ringing*

in his ears, getting louder and more insistent. It was the doorbell downstairs, he suddenly realized. It had been ringing for the last five minutes, non-stop.

Mo looked over at his alarm clock: 5:45 a.m. "Oh, shit!" he hissed. He feared it was the police come to get him. But when he peered out from behind his bedroom curtains and looked down at the front porch below, all he saw was an agitated Saeed, pressing the doorbell with his thumb so fiercely that it looked as if he was trying to gouge someone's eye out.

Mo jumped out of his bed, and scrambled downstairs as fast as he had fled the scene of the burglary the night before, anxious to head off his nosy-parker father before he got to the front door before him. Mo almost knocked his father over as the old man emerged from the kitchen, a huge mug of inevitable milky tea in his hand. Mo flinched as a few drops of the hot liquid splashed onto his bare arm. But soon he was at the front door snapping back the multiple bolts and frantically turning the double locks to open it.

"Hey!" Mo's father complained. "Watch what you're doing! Almost knocked me over, you little…" He held the mug out in front of him, trying to make sure no more of his tea spilled. "What's the big rush, anyhow?"

Mo opened the door, and immediately put his finger up against his lips. He grabbed Saeed by the arm and herded him back up the staircase, pushing and shoving his friend as if he was a boxer practicing on a punch bag. It was all Saeed could do to stay upright, tumbling forward unsteadily on his way to Mo's room.

"What the hell's he doing here at this time of the morning?" Mo's father demanded to know.

"Mind your own fucking business!" Mo shouted in reply.

Inside his room, Mo slammed the door shut behind him, jamming a chair under the doorknob to prevent his father from opening it from the landing. He hushed Saeed again. Saeed obeyed, but his lips twitched and he clenched his teeth as if he was bursting to say something of the utmost importance. Mo raised his hand and grimaced a frowning "Don't you dare!" He put his ear to the door and listened intently for any sign of that his father might be pursuing them. None came. Mo nodded his head, indicating to Saeed that it was safe to speak. "Keep it down," he cautioned.

"What the fuck are we gonna *do*?" Saeed burst out in a loud whisper, pacing the room like a cat on a hot tin roof. "I can't get caught. You've gotta get rid of that thing—right away!"

"Calm down, calm down," Mo said, as calmly as he could. He put his hand on Saeed's shoulder, encouraging him to sit down. The floorboards were squeaking with his friend's every agitated step. "We're *not* going to get caught. If we were, we'd have been so by now." Mo scratched the side of his nose.

Saeed recognized the gesture, the tic, what it probably signaled. "Are you sure?" he queried. But that scratch—there it went again.

"…Of course I am," Mo finally insisted. His fingernails prepared for a third scratch, but just at the point of contact Mo suddenly dropped his hand to his side, his fingers still fidgeting slightly, as if they were still itching for something to do, to assuage some sort of disquieting impulse.

"Well, maybe you're right," Saeed reluctantly conceded, "but I still say we've gotta get rid of that fucking phone." He looked at Mo, tears starting to well up in his eyes. "My chance at university's at stake, goddamn it. I know it's a long shot, but without that I'm done for—life's over, as good as." His eyes glistened now, truly moistened. "Mo, *please*—we've got to get rid of it!"

Mo considered his friend's request in silence, weighing his increasingly limited options the more he thought about them. But the iPhone—he'd never be able to afford something like that. He went over to his bed and crawled underneath. With his fingernails he jimmied up the section of loose floorboard. For a second or two he hesitated to reach into the hidey-hole, afraid that the phone had indeed somehow been removed from it during the night. He half-expected to feel liquid, but, after pushing through the logjam of his other treasured possessions, he soon felt the comforting presence of Kathy Green's underwear, then the shape of the phone inside them.

He took a deep sigh of relief as he removed the iPhone from its makeshift camouflage. He crawled back out from under the bed and stood up, holding the phone in his hands like it was some sort of Holy Grail. He held it out to Saeed, but his friend recoiled, as if he now feared the thing. Mo smiled. *The iPhone* — a gift — an Ark of the Covenant almost, as he saw it — sent down from Kathy Green, the price her father deserved to pay for the sin of his Jew-boy miserliness. Mo considered it poetic justice that it had been old man Green's daughter's underwear that had provided his new iPhone with protective warmth during the chilly winter's night.

"Mo," Saeed cried, "stop it! Just let's go now, and get rid of it. Throw it in the Don. For God's sake!"

Mo held the device up to his ear. What deals could he do with a device such as this? Maybe...just maybe it might get him into the crack game. No more fucking about with second-rate weed on windy, rain-swept street corners. With this baby, he could really be in the know; what the market conditions were, where the best suppliers hung out, maybe go international if he wanted to! He could be the big dealer he'd always dreamt of being. And then he'd have the cash, oh yes sir, would he fucking ever! Enough one day for a car, a red-hot sporting one, flash enough to pull Kathy Gr—

"Mo, stop it! What are you doing?"

Mo had taken the phone down from his ear, and was fiddling with it. He'd already taken the SIM card from his own phone and was about to insert it into the iPhone.

Saeed sprang to his feet and knocked the phone from Mo's grasp. It flew across the room, landing on the pillow on Mo's bed.

"*No!*" Mo screamed. "You stupid..." He rushed to retrieve the iPhone. He picked it up gingerly, and then turned it over slowly between his fingertips, as if he was looking for wounds. "Oh...you better not have fucking broken it! I'll kill you if you have!" He took out his handkerchief and began to clean the screen with the gentleness of a mother wiping her child's hurt tears away.

"For fuck's sake, Mo! You activate that thing and they'll know where it is, right away. Don't you know it has GPS on it?"

Mo blinked, as if he was waking up from a trance. He looked stupidly at Saeed. "What?"

"I said, if you use it you'll tell the police exactly where it is." Saeed took the phone from Mo's hand. The screen was blank. "Thank God for that," he breathed, "it's still off. Your card probably won't work in it, anyway. Your account's been cancelled, hasn't it?" Mo nodded. "And the battery's not even charged up." Saeed flopped onto Mo's bed, the i-

Phone in his hands held high above his face. "But we've still got to get rid of this thing, Mo—and *soon*."

Mo looked at the iPhone, still desiring it, wishing he could keep it. Even without electric life, its power to bring the world to him, to potentially transform his life, still mesmerized him. But he suddenly realized that Saeed was right, that it was in the end of little use to him, apart from teasing him with hopeless—even dangerous—fantasies. He'd have to give it up. Unless...

"Okay, you're right," Mo said wearily, but then his eyes opened wide as if he'd just received a revelation. He took the phone from Saeed and held it up, balanced on his fingertips. "But we're going to get something for our trouble before we get rid of it, you mark my words if we don't. Throw it in the Don? What would be the point of that? No sir-ee, no point at all. No, we're going to pawn this fucker. Old man Green's not going to get off so lightly. Love to see his face if it ever gets back to him one day, especially if he has to *pay* for it. Fuck him! And his little fucking whore of a daughter. Come on, let's go. We've got no time to waste."

"Wait—" Saeed said, but it was too late. Mo had thrown the chair barring his bedroom door aside, and was already gone, thundering down the stairs three or four at a time. Saeed followed, still wailing his feeble efforts to get Mo to stop. At the foot of stairs, Mo abruptly halted. Saeed barely managed to avoid crashing into him. When he regained his balance, Saeed realized that Mo was transfixed by something on the loudly blaring television in the front room that led off from the downstairs' hallway. It was the early morning news on BBC One reporting on an American drone strike in some place in the Middle East neither Mo nor Saeed had ever heard of.

Mo slowly walked through the open door to the front room, listening intently. Saeed followed. As they entered, the scene of devastation that filled the TV screen switched to footage of a speech the American president was making. He was going on about destroying the terrorists wherever they might be, and by whatever means necessary. Saeed knew that he'd heard all this stuff before, although he couldn't tell you where or specifically when—he didn't care much for the news, all too depressing, and, quite frankly, excruciatingly boring. Saeed was fascinated less by the report than by Mo's totally unexpected fixation on it.

"What is it?" Saeed said.

"What?" Mo replied. He blinked, as if his consciousness had just been abruptly switched back on again. "Oh…nothing. Just the fucking Americans again—blowing things up as usual." He put his hand in his hoodie pocket and fingered the iPhone, as if he was trying to recall what mission they'd been on before the TV had sidetracked him. "Come on, let's go!"

Mo rushed out to the hallway, Saeed in his wake, but one final thought about what he'd seen on the television still momentarily preoccupied him: *He's black. Why would he do such a thing to black folks? And he's a Muslim too, isn't he?*

But, as quickly as it had come to him, the puzzle ticker-taped out of his mind, already reabsorbed with the potentially gratifying task still left undone.

Old man Green, they were going to stick it old man Green—*again!*

27

[19 December 2016]

God, did he howl!
 He put his hands over his wounded crotch and drew back his hips, as if he was trying to take evasive action. But it was already far too late for that—I'd nailed the little Paki fucker, a bull's-eye right on his bollocks, rendering him, I hoped, the last of his degenerate, malignant line. He stumbled away from me, bent at the waist and gasping, like he was suffering the most gut-wrenching pain imaginable, the sort that lays low even the biggest of blokes, Samsons with their hair—their balls—suddenly cut off. He wailed like a frightened little kid, but in that moment, strangely, I despised him for not fighting back like a man. Behind my gag, I almost cried with delight, although I knew my moment of triumph would be short-lived, and that they'd inevitably make me pay an even higher price for my attack on his pathetic so-called manhood. But I didn't care anymore. What more could they fucking well do to me than they hadn't already done? We'd all—them and me—crossed a Rubicon many days ago. I certainly know I had.
 What about you, Robbie…what about you?
 Then, as predicted, came the cackling Urdu again, followed by the thunder of feet galloping down the cellar steps. The voices sounded panicked, asking each other something over and over and over, then getting angrier and angrier, feeding off each other. The

Soft One kept on whining and blubbering. I tried to take some measure of delight in the precious moment of his humiliation, but it was only a half-measure at most—the compensation of getting my own back seems less uplifting by the very act of it now, like it's losing its luster from overuse It seems as if there's no possibility of taking pleasure in anything, anymore...never again. Rescue, escape...what will they bring me now?; what kind of life can I expect to have after this nightmare is over? God...

The chief's voice suddenly emerged loud and clear from the babbling din they were all making, and the others settled immediately into obedient silence, except for the sniffling Soft One trying to regain his composure, now that his mates were here. The chief began to think out loud it sounded like, as if he was posing questions, weighing up options, as opposed to giving directions. Then I heard the shift of gears in his voice, and his orders came fast and furious. Shuffling feet scampered off in all directions. The leader's garlicky, curried breath suddenly washed over my face—he was close. He made a sound with his thick lips, as if he was blowing a kiss at me, the curry-slurping fuck. I heard him giggle. "Fucking bitch," he cursed. "Inshallah," I think he said, as if he really meant it. "God willing?" Could he be serious? Of course, by now I knew he was.

Surely he'll burn in Hell one day, right?

Slap! *My head whiplashed violently to one side, almost, it felt like, as if it was about to come off. My cheek burned, like it was literally on fire. I knew what was coming next—he was staying faithful to his script. "For the love of God...it's Jihad for Dummies," you'd told me, Robbie, before they took me and brought me to this place, and you were right of course. But the dummies right at that moment had the upper hand, no matter how stupid they were. They could do whatever they wanted, and there was nothing anybody, not even God, could do about it. And their god, Allah, was one their side, sanctifying whatever they found it fit to do to me. How in the fuck did it ever come to all this?*

The others returned. "Inshallah," the chief said again, as if by repeating the word made what they were about to do all right in Allah's eyes–a call to jihad, if you can believe that? Well, of course you can, you know about these things. Then the chief's voice changed; he started kind of half-chanting, half-singing. He sounded like one of those "call to prayer" guys they have—a "mooah"-something or other, I think they're called. But he wasn't very good at it; he kept coughing when he tried to make that high, wailing noise those "mooah" guys do. Then he stops, and all the others start chanting in unison, like they're answering his call or something like that, and then off he goes again. It's then when I realized that they were really praying...really praying! For what exactly right at that moment, I didn't know. It'd only be later that I'd realize they were most likely praying to Allah in order to sanctify what they were about to do to me. Sanctify...God would do such a thing? Anyone's god would?

Someone jerked my head back, ungagged my mouth, and then forced it open. Another squeezed my cheeks together, shaping my lips into a puckering funnel. The smell of their curried fog disappeared and I smelled the burning sweetness of whiskey, instead. I gagged and gurgled, almost drowning, as the liquor flooded my mouth, then my throat. I was being waterboarded—with alcohol! Payback for Abu Ghraib? Fucking Blair, fucking Bush!

Damn them all.

I lost consciousness then, I suppose.

I think you can guess the rest...

...

You probably never would have guessed this though; nobody would have—not in Rotherham!

Kathy seemed to know what she was doing, that she could take care of herself. She told me about this Paki guy who she thought was really into her. She'd noticed him several times in recent weeks; he kept popping up wherever she was, even at her Pilates class once. He just seemed to be hanging around, but she kept catching him staring at her. She said that the next time she saw him she would let him have it. She patted her purse again, and laughed. She opened it up to show me. She switched on her little flashlight, since it was pretty dark walking through the park, and said, "Take a look at this little baby!" She had a can of mace in there; it was lying right on top of all her junk—ready for use. Fat lot of good it did me, though. Seems like she never got the chance to use it in all the mayhem.

And that was the last time I heard her voice. Her laughing again, right at the moment I felt something come down over my head. I immediately started to suffocate, and then I must have lost consciousness, for the next thing I know I'm down here—kidnapped!

I wonder what happened to her, whether she's nearby, perhaps in this building somewhere. Whether she's still laughing now...

And that can of mace...what I'd give to have one now.

...

It's been a while since we've had much to laugh about, hasn't it? Was it just the sex that came between us? Or did we start to drift apart earlier than that?

...I can't remember the last time we laughed.

And I'm trying not to remember the stupid hurt we did to each other.

That's why I was at the Palace on my own in the first place...

28
[15 April 2016]

"Ice cream?"

The boy had just stared at him, then given him the merest nod of his head. He'd slid the bowl across the table between them, a large plastic spoon, something that would have easily snapped if it had been used as a weapon, speared into the over-sized portion of ice cream. It had been the kid's favorite kind: banana split drenched in chocolate sauce and sprinkled generously with hundreds-and-thousands. It had already started to melt around the edges. Their stand-off had lasted a good ten minutes already, and he'd still been debating whether to give in—yet again, or not. But he'd had to try to get the kid to talk, curry his favor somehow. But he'd have to wait another minute or two more, though—his antagonist's mouth had already been full of ice cream within seconds of his having been given it, and the beginnings of his usual chocolate moustache had begun taking shape, along with its customary comedic effect. It'd always made the kid look really dumb.

As the kid had kept lifting the spoon to his mouth, his Guns N' Roses tattoo had kept flickering in and out of view. Maybe he'd better do some research on the band, *he'd thought. Perhaps there might have been a point of entry there. Perhaps his son, Ahmed, might have been able to school him on the group; it might also have had the additional benefit of bringing them back closer together a bit, heal their increasing father-son estrangement—well, it had been a thought anyhow, no matter how hopeless it had turned out to be. In any case, how convincing a Heavy Metal fan might he have been able to act out, anyway? He just didn't look the part, to say the least. As Ahmed had kept telling him ad nauseam, he was "such a stiff."*

Imam Khalifa stared at the ring stain on the table where a bowl had sat just a couple of hours before, pondering the "Ice Cream Kid," as he liked to call his latest case. The dirty-cream color of the solidifying ring of melted dessert had started to yellow, like it had developed an infection of some sort. But the shape of the ring stain intrigued him; it was nearly a perfect unbroken circle, just one minor break in the otherwise pleasing Pythagorean perfection: directly opposite to where Jamal Shirani had sat. Imam Khalifa wet his finger with the tip of his tongue, then made his repair, dragging a bead of liquid from one side of the break to the other and making it whole again. But his surgery enjoyed only momentary success; the surface tension of his repair failed to hold for more than a second or two. The gap in the ring's circumference re-appeared—if anything, it was even bigger this time. He took a tissue from his pocket, and made to erase the stain once and for all, but suddenly thought the better of it. Perhaps it was too soon to give up so easily.

Jamal Shirani was proving to be a tough nut to crack. Not the hardest he'd ever had, but then again the program was still relatively new, and he'd only had a handful of referrals so far. No doubt some severely hard-boiled assignments would come his way soon enough, the way the intelligence services were going after the jihadis these days. He suspected he'd been seeing only some pretty low-hanging fruit so far: the novices prone to carelessness and enough nervousness to give them away at any moment, so that they had been arrested before they could do too much damage.

The kid had burped and wiped his mouth with the back of his hand, smearing what had been left of his chocolate moustache across his left cheek. He'd touched his own cheek, and had said, "You've smeared—"but the kid had just grinned and shrugged his shoulders.
"Would you like to tell me about what happened in Russell Square and at the museum?"
The kid had shaken his head, no. "Only Allah needs to know about that," he'd said. Then he'd wiped his index finger around the inside of the bowl, and licked it clean. "Good," he'd said. "Just the ticket," he'd then added, in an obviously fake, British upper-class accent.
He'd bitten his tongue, while fleeting thoughts of "punching someone's ticket" had almost snapped his cool. He'd immediately gotten up, and had walked across to the window. Through the late afternoon mist, he'd been able to just about see the dome of St. Paul's cathedral. He'd noticed suddenly how lonely and diminutive it had looked, surrounded and hemmed in by Gherkins and God knew what other architectural abominations. Iconic? For how much longer? he'd wondered.
Above the cathedral dome a large bird had appeared, and he'd watched it circling there as if it had been

lost… turning and turning in the widening gyre…as if it couldn't hear the falconer's call.

He'd turned back to look at Jamal; he'd been leaning back in his chair with his eyes closed, most likely feigning sleep. He'd started to mouth some words, silently at first: Things fall apart; the centre cannot hold… *Then he'd gone on to softly mumble:* Mere anarchy is loosed upon the world… *but it'd been loud enough to have roused the kid from his slumber. Jamal had looked at him as if he had recognized the lines.* The best lack all conviction… *he'd soldiered on…*

…while the worst, Jamal had interjected,
Are *full* of passionate intensity!

They'd stared at each other in silence then for a few seconds, both wondering what exactly it was they had just shared.

"Don't come much worse than me, do they, imam?" *the kid had finally said, before closing his eyes again.*

Worse than him? Who had the kid thought he was? He'd known all about him; his dossier had been an inch thick, and there'd not been a whole lot to suggest that he'd been much of a real bad ass at all. The kid had spent over a year in Pakistan, but to what effect?

He'd closed Jamal's file, recognizing that there'd been little more to be gained in trying to get the kid to re-engage again that day. Jamal had started to softly snore, but whether he'd been faking it or not, he hadn't cared to know.

He'd looked through the window again, as he got up to leave; the mist had to turned into a thickening fog, and night had made a good start on finally erasing all signs of life out there in London. He'd not even been sure if the dome of St. Paul's still existed anymore.

That Jamal was clearly a jihadi neophyte, Imam Khalifa already knew from the police reports, although the stabbing of the vagrant was troubling, nonetheless. Turned loose too early and without some rehabilitation, he worried that Jamal might one day really do some serious harm, even as a rather bumbling lone wolf. The kid appeared committed, brainwashed—passionate even; and a fanatical Curious George with a bomb and a Kalashnikov to hand could inflict an awful lot of carnage, even if he wasn't terribly efficient at using them to full effect.

The world was full of angry young men—and women—these days, but the difference was clearly this in the modern era: their anger was just a few clicks and a few moments of emotional incontinence away from being vented with the aid of literal weapons of mass destruction. Not the biggest of such, like the real nuclear bombs dropped on Hiroshima and Nagasaki—although you could never be entirely sure about that, at least not in the long run—but clearly big enough to take dozens, if not hundreds, if not thousands of lives in one impulsive fell swoop. Dozens dead in a movie theatre at the hands of a lone wolf with a semi-automatic and a couple of high-capacity magazines was still mass destruction, however you looked at it. Serious homicidal threats had thus become almost a dime a dozen. It was truly frightening; how could *all* the angry ones be stopped? There was, he feared, no way to do so; but if he could prevent one or two or three, it'd be worth something, wouldn't it?

Besides, Jamal was getting his goat far too often, making him look inept in front of the guards. Just like his son Ahmed made him appear in front of his wife and daughter. It was all just too much!

Peace, he needed some peace, to be left alone. Was it too much to ask? In his own house?

Apparently, it was. From just above him, in his son's bedroom, *Guns N' Roses* were answering him loud and clear, although the only thing that was clear to him was their earth-shattering, ear-splitting volume—he couldn't make out a single word they were singing, if that's what their caterwauling was.

But he didn't really have to; he knew the signal his son Ahmed was sending him. He knew it ad nauseam.

"Tell me, Jamal, what does it mean to be a Muslim? What does the word literally mean?" Like he, the imam and counselor and the PhD in Comparative Religion, had really known anymore. All that learning and learned erudition, yet he'd felt clueless in the Age of Radical Jihadism, the time of the so-called "Global War on Terror."

The kid had turned his head away and had just stared at the bare white walls of the room they'd been in. No pictures, no decoration, nothing to have suggested anything other than that the small box of a room had been designed with only the brutal utilitarian function of interrogation in mind. The room right then had reminded him of the tunnel he took under the Thames every day, to and from work: the pallid artificial lighting; the sense of claustrophobia, drowning almost; the longing to re-surface again—the proverbial light at the end of the tunnel.

Jamal had snorted, as if he'd been clearing snot from his blocked nostrils. "You tell me," he'd finally said. "You're the imam."

"All right, it means 'submission,' submission to the will of Allah, as I'm sure you already know—"

"So, why are you asking me, then?"

225

He'd bitten his tongue, before continuing. "I want to help you, Jamal. You are facing some very serious charges. The stabbing alone—"

"Help me? What help do I need from an unbeliever?"

The kid's face had turned angry, and he'd fingered for the alarm button under the table between them, just in case.

"I know what you are!" the kid had thundered. "You're a copper's nark. Imam? What do you know of Islam, you traitor?"

That he was an apostate and a traitor were charges against him that Imam Khalifa was well used to by then—it seemed like it came with his job, was part of the deal you just had to accept in trying to rehabilitate jihadis—and sometimes, lately, he'd come to half believe them himself. They'd grown and grown, just like an itch that just wouldn't go away, but had only gotten worse, become more irritating, increasingly debilitating. In his line of work, he'd learned that he needed to develop a thick skin, and he'd tried to, but whenever these epithets were slung at him they always hit a sore spot, made him wonder about his faith. Why?

He'd been a pious Muslim for as long as he could remember, and he'd worked so hard to become an imam. It was his vocation, a gift from Allah, something that you could never abrogate, except on the pain of eternal damnation. He'd come to accept that in doing what he was doing at the center, he was consorting with the so-called enemy, taking up with non-believers, apostates, and Crusaders, as the jihadis liked to call them. But his consorting—this temporary "marriage of convenience"—such as it was, was unavoidable, wasn't it, if he was to continue to be able to submit to Allah's will? For Islam, he truly believed, was in deep, deep crisis. In his mission to help save it from the radical jihadists, he *needed* the police and the courts and their prisons in order to first corral those whom he wished to save. His sort of sermonizing no longer seemed to do the trick in returning the wayward Believers to the cautious, quietist, and nonviolent fold he'd so fervently subscribed to all his life. He needed, too—didn't he?—the state's financial resources and the imprimatur of its secular sovereignty if he was to be allowed to gain access to his fallen brothers and sisters, to stand any chance of combatting the evil—the apostasy—the extremists were brainwashing them with.

But then, caught in the midstream of such musing, he'd stop thinking like this, suddenly realizing he was like a dog chasing its own rationalizing, self-justifying, bull-shitting tail. Or was he?

He just wasn't quite sure anymore.

Traitor? The barb had hurt, but he'd kept his composure. Losing his cool would have had only added fuel to the flames of an already contentious relationship. He'd counted to ten, and had then tried another tack.

"Life is hard, a struggle—for all Believers. We all know this, right?"

The kid had raised his eyebrows at him, not in surprise so much as in "Duh! Thanks for that, genius. How would I have ever figured that one out?" He'd immediately realized that he'd sounded too sanctimonious by half, like the preachy dad his son so often had railed against.

"I mean," he'd bumbled on, like he had always done, not having known, really, anything other than his usual stick-in-the-mud modus operandi, "we have dreams but often we are disappointed, frustrated. For instance, I dream of building a new Islamic Cultural Center where I live in East Ham. The current one is small and in bad repair, but we are too poor in our community. I fear it will never happen." Oh damn, he'd thought, wincing at the sound of his own boring voice, what would Ping-Pong, cold pizza curling at the edges, and a couple of verses from the Koran have meant to such a kid as him?

But, unexpectedly, the kid had looked up; no raised eyebrows this time, but a face that had almost expressed mild inquisitiveness. It had looked, for the moment perhaps, as if he'd struck a chord with him at last, against all the odds. Jamal had pushed his empty ice cream bowl to his right, as if he'd needed more room to ponder. He'd looked at the vacated spot on the table, expecting to have seen the usual ring stain left behind. But there hadn't been a trace of anything—except, he'd thought somewhat hopefully, a change of dynamic, some wholly unanticipated irregularity in the laws of nature.

Poverty—maybe that had been something they might have shared, something on which they might have begun to construct a better relationship. At the time, it had seemed to be worth a try...

But maybe not.

Imam Khalifa knew enough already to know that real radical jihadists didn't always naturally grow in materially-deprived soil—far from it, in fact. Several of his cases so far had been poor enough, and had suffered sufficient discrimination and alienation to fuel a million revolutionaries, whether secular or religious. But even in their relative poverty, they'd had enough financial wherewithal, even if it had come to them only in the form of welfare benefits, to assimilate quite thoroughly to many of the physical comforts of modern British life, and they'd been content enough in the end to "amuse themselves to death" in front of the TV or hooked up to their digital devices, again. They'd caved in before long to his entreaties, ready, after their brief thrill-ride with what had been little more than a rather armchair jihadism, to settle back into the soft, material life of a Muslim in name only, especially if not "going along with the imam" had meant staying under virtual confinement in some sort of half-way house, having to do chores and having access to their "digital playthings" severely rationed. Was Jamal one of these jihadi wan-nabes in name only, or was he of the type, whether poor or not, who'd become captivated by the dangers, the risks, and the promise of doing some-thing *really* big for once?

In any case, what did he know of poverty anymore, enough to be able to relate in any mean-ingful way about it with the likes of a Jamal? He'd known some measure of *relative* poverty once, during the first dimly-remembered years of his family's immigration to England, when his father, poorly educated and barely semi-skilled, had struggled for a while to get a good-paying factory job. But England had begun to boom shortly after their arrival, and all his family had known since had been constant, if challenging and often still limited, upward mobility, for Khalifa himself most of all. He wasn't fabulously rich by any means, but poverty, the kind that might move someone to jihadi anger, was nowhere in sight for him anymore—if, indeed, it had ever been.

There'd also been a time, even so—not so long ago in fact—when he'd thought he'd had a pretty good handle as to what it was like to be poor in England, albeit indirectly. A good many of his congregation in East Ham knew severe deprivation, and he'd led efforts to help them try and alleviate it, as he ought to have done as a pious Muslim and a spiritual leader of their community. But, he now realized, that "indirectness" had been a barrier to empathetic imagination as to what living in poverty was really like, not necessarily an enabler of it.

He'd ladled soup in his Center's squeaky-clean and well-equipped kitchen, all right, and he'd handed out food parcels to his senior citizens every week, among several other such *zakat*-mandated charitable endeavors; but he'd never visited the homes of the poor, or ventured out much into the backstreets and projects of East Ham. After his day at the Center had come to its usual close at around three or four p.m., he'd routinely gotten in his car and driven *directly* home—to a leafy, well-situated, suburb to the north of the Thames, a fact that he hadn't advertised much at all to those he ministered to every day! Within ten minutes of locking his front door behind him, East Ham had always seemed a thousand miles away. And just yesterday, as he'd hung his coat on the hall stand, he'd wondered again whether there might be *some* significance in the fact that the road he took between home and work tunneled *under* the river, rather than bridged *over* it…

No, poverty wasn't what he and Jamal might have in common, at all; it was "caving in" that they shared. It was a hybrid religion they both subscribed to, a syncretic mixing of both intoxicating mundanity and the spiritually elusive: first, getting high on the secular consumer comforts and titillations of modern Western high tech society, and then not knowing what to do when the episodic highs inevitably wore off, and sent them plunging back into the miserable existential reality of their lives—not knowing who they really were, not knowing what they really wanted, and feeling abandoned by something they'd at one time so eagerly, addictively, sought.

If there was a poverty he and Jamal shared, it was truly a poverty of *spirit*. Yes, spirit—something they'd both incorrectly believed they'd had a wealth of, in one way or another! Or perhaps, what they both lacked was how to cultivate the *right level* of that precious substance. Jamal and his ilk clearly had far too much, at least of a bastardized, debauched kind; and he...well, he wasn't sure if he had *any* at all, anymore—of any meaningful description.

"True Believers can only be poor in spirit*!" the kid had spat out. "Allah will provide everything that we need."*

"Indeed, he will," he'd lamely said. "But only if we focus on our piety, look deeply within ourselves, test our faith."

"Struggle, you mean?"

"Yes...struggle!"

The kid had smiled. "Jihad!" he'd said. "I know all about that. Would you like me to tell you?"

No, he hadn't wished for that—not then at any rate. He'd already known what was going to come next. It'd become Jamal's signature gesture when he'd believed he'd had the upper argumentative hand over him. With great meticulousness, the kid had wiped his finger around the inside of the bowl on the table between them, making an annoying squeaking noise in the process, in an effort to retrieve the last dregs of melted ice cream left there. Then he'd stuck his finger in his mouth and sucked it off, smacking his lips exaggeratedly.

"If you'd really like to know what's going on with me, imam, you know where to look. It'd save you a whole lot of grief trying to deal with me. Save you on the ice cream, too." The kid had burped, and then had slid the bowl back towards him. It had left a ring stain on the table.

A perfect circle of liquid again—but this time, unbroken.

But what had the Platonic form portended, he'd pondered later on, as he'd approached Tower Bridge in his car on his way to his Islamic Cultural Center in East Ham? An undivided truth; that there was no God but God, neither Christian nor Muslim nor anything—no denominational brand whatsoever, just God, a one size fits all?

Or might the perfect "O" signify just what it did arithmetically—not oneness, but nothing? A big fat zero? The End of Days, an Alpha canceling an Omega out in one great, final act of nihilism?

But he hadn't had time to answer his own question. His train of thought had been disrupted by the traffic suddenly having come to a complete stop in front of him. Tower Bridge had been in the process of raising the great spans of its elevated roadway in order to let shipping through on the river below. The span on his side of the river had already almost reached its most perpendicular point, blocking his view of the north bank of the Thames. He'd looked at his gold watch; he'd already been running late because of Jamul's uncooperative behavior. There'd

been several vessels on the river making headway for the bridge.
Would he ever get to the other side? he'd wondered.
He'd pointlessly honked his horn in frustration. It'd sounded just as tuneful as Guns N' Roses, *and it had gotten him no nearer his destination.*

Imam Khalifa switched on his computer. As he logged into his Internet account, the opened tab he hadn't closed the last time he'd been online popped immediately into view. It was the home page of *Inspire*, the online magazine of Al-Qa'eda in the Arabian Peninsula. "Inspire," it announced with slick Madison Avenue graphics, "...and Inspire the Believers."

Inspire? That was clearly the key. That's what Jamal had kept saying: "Go on, imam, inspire me!" and then staring at him defiantly, the same look, Khalifa recollected, that his son Ahmed routinely gave him when he'd take him to task about staying out late, or not helping out his mother more around the house—all those adolescent irritations that needled him just as much as his frequent hemorrhoids did. "*God*, you're such a bore, Dad…you're such a bore, Dad…such a…
...*bore!*
Imam Khalifa wondered when was the last time he'd truly inspired anybody, as opposed to just having bored them with his predictable sermons, replete with admonitions about being pious and, in the end, being like those supine Christians who took Jesus too much to heart by not doing too much more than rendering unto Caesar what was Caesar's, and settling into that all-too-comforting, lazy-assed

religious comfort zone: a Christian in name only—especially when you needed the pretense in order to feel okay about getting married in church, about having your kids baptized (just in case), and about making sure you went to heaven when you died by having a priest at your graveside mumbling a prayer over you (just in case, a second time). He suddenly realized that he might well have been as much a part of the problem as of the solution when it came to defanging radical jihadism. "Listen to yourself," Jamal had said. "Do you know what you sound like? Like a salesman for Western depravity and a herald for capitulation—not to Allah's will, but to sin!"

Indeed, Imam Khalifa thought, his own contribution to the so-called propaganda war with the jihadis must have seemed, especially from someone with Jamal's point of view, no more convincing than the toffish prime minister's call to persuade young Muslim minds to imbibe the elixir of so-called "English values," a soppy, ill-defined mix of moderate, tolerant liberalism supposedly sexed up with the promise of a life for all in an English country garden, where everything was in its proper place and nothing unduly disturbed the carefully tended herbaceous borders—not a weed in sight, just the comforting sound of the buzzing bumblebee as it carefully went about its business of kindly pollination.

He liked the idea of a paradisiacal Garden on Earth—it was *so* quintessentially Islamic—although he had something more like the *Alhambra* in mind, not so much a red rose- and ivy-adorned, thatched roofed, stone cottage somewhere in Cameron's Cotswolds. And when he thought about East Ham, there was barely sign of any plant life beyond weeds or a wretched tree trying to make it in an island of concrete and a fog of traffic fumes. He knew that must be Jamal's experience too, being a fellow Londoner. "Stuff the garden," Jamal had said, when he'd asked if he wanted to take a walk there while they talked one day. "Nothing out there for me. I have all I need in *here*." Then he'd tapped his forehead with his finger, and grinned. In any case, it was usually raining or freezing cold whenever they'd had one of their "rehabilitation sessions."

But what the prime minister's nice, decent, pasty liberalism didn't fully understand, Imam Khalifa increasingly recognized, was that it would always fail as a social glue if it did not somehow — no doubt contrary to its presumed founding principles for pluralism and open-ended tolerance — validate the far more universal need to *belong* to something much bigger than oneself, even the forging of a tight in-group of true believers committed to an uncompromising call to arms, a fervent chauvinism sanctioned by an at least half-imagined deity. Indeed, the English themselves were susceptible to such radicalism, as the UKIPers' jingoism over the EU and immigration seemed to prove. But it was that inspirationally — if not exactly spiritually — uplifting state of affairs that *Inspire* promulgated, that neither Cameron nor he got, that was *precisely* what the jihadis were promising the likes of Jamal, and delivering on, at least on the battlefields of Mesopotamia, in the offices of *Charlie Hebdo* in Paris, and at the airport in Brussels.

The much vaunted "Arab Spring" had brought down dictators all right, Imam Khalifa had even applauded such apparent victories at the time, but the only carrot to fill the resulting vacuum that the West and Islamic moderates like himself had dangled before the Jamals of this world had been an insipid liberal-democracy, a decidedly chaotic, non-comittal, messy, and underwhelming prospect as opposed to the Manichean absolutism of the imminent re-establishment of the triumphant Caliphate—*the* harbinger of the End of Days and the return of the Mahdi—that IS was vowing to usher in. Now, all *that*, Jamal had repeatedly lectured him (although not exactly in so many highfaluting words), was a cause really worth fighting for, coming alive for. It was, indeed, worthy of martyrdom!

Of course, Imam Khalifa knew that IS most likely would never be able to fully deliver on its promises—surely they couldn't carve out a so-called caliphate and hold on to it, could they?—and that sooner or later disappointed and battle-fatigued Jamals would eventually give up on the ghost of militant jihadism. But even so, he reluctantly conceded, even that likelihood was probably months if not years away, more than enough time for the global war on terror to have wrought such destruction on all sides that any sort of decent rapprochement between different peoples and their supposedly antagonistic faiths might no longer be possible then.

What was it the German Jew Karl Marx had said? *Religion is the opiate of the masses*? Well, Imam Khalifa knew his Islamic brand might well be such a soporific substance too, just like Cameron's secular religion of "English values." But even if the jihadis gave out opiates of their own kind, they were nonetheless truly of a very different order. They were hallucinatory all right, but, he just had to admit, they were inspirational too, to a degree he'd never thought might be possible. And it was truly frightening—and not just for Christians and Jews and atheists.

For where did *he* stand in the jihadists' world, before jihadi judgment? It was a question Jamal had often put to him when he was especially talkative or animated: "Are you ready, preacher? For Judgment Day? It's coming—and *soon*." Intellectually, he knew Jamal's threat wasn't literally true, but even if Allah was not quite ready to pass judgment on him yet he still very much feared what Jamal's might be if he ever got out of prison before being rehabilitated. And losing his livelihood and his nice three-bedroomed house might very well not be the worst of it—not by a long chalk...

Imam Khalifa caressed his neck and then lightly fingered his Adam's apple, as if he was searching for something with his fingertips. An image of Jihadi John—or was it Jihadi Jamal?—flashed before his eyes. He was wearing a black ski mask and staring straight at him. His eyes, tightly framed by the opening in the mask, seemed to be twice their normal size. They looked like two deep, dark, cold wells, devoid of all emotion, all feeling. They accused with terrifying finality.

In his left hand, the figure held a crimson-dripping knife; blood was smeared three-quarters of the way up the sleeve of his black tunic. But it was what he held up in its right hand that made Imam Khalifa recoil with horror. That gruesome severed head, drained ghostly pale with the rapid loss of blood; those eyelids closed like a blind man's, as if they had brought down the final curtain on the wretched victim's life in brutal anonymity; that hair matted and unkempt where it had been grasped by the exe-cutioner's hand; those clumsily butchered remains protruding from the neck where it had been cut off from the body: straggly pieces of arteries, muscle, and flesh looking as if they'd already been feasted on by ravenous scavengers. Imam Khalifa retched; sour bile invaded his throat, enough to finally make him vomit. He'd seen it all before, but it always had this effect on him, even more so this time as for a moment he'd thought the ski-masked villain might have been Jamal.

Then he remembered Jamal was safely locked up in prison. *Oh God!* he gasped, wiping his mouth with his handkerchief. But he still felt the need to nervously look over his shoulder, to make sure that no knife-wielding maniac was really behind him. But he was alone. "Oh…" He turned around to face his computer again, then poured himself a glass of water from the decanter on his desk. He drank it all in one go. He felt his pulse; it was still racing, but palpably slowing down now. He sensed perspiration starting to dry on his neck; it felt almost pleasantly cool, soothing.

He grasped his computer's mouse and scrolled to the next page on *Inspire*'s website: it was a letter from the Editor.

> In the Name of Allah, the Most Gracious,
> the Most Merciful.

All praise is due to Allah the Lord of the Universe, and may His peace and blessings be upon his Messenger Muhammad and those who follow his footsteps. To proceed: Whenever Al-Qaeda is mentioned, the American citizens' mind thinks of vest and car bombs. Bearing in mind that none of these weapons has struck them since 9/11. So why would they relate Al-Qaeda to these bombs? Simply because they fear these weapons and have seen enough of their destructive power in Afghanistan and Iraq.

Many Feisal Shahzads are residing inside America and all they need is the knowledge of how to make car bombs. They are all yearning to fulfill their duty of Jihad.

The American government was unable to protect its citizens from pressure cooker bombs in backpacks. I wonder if they are ready to stop car bombs!

Therefore, as our responsibility to the Muslim Ummah in general and Muslims living in America in particular, Inspire Magazine humbly presents to you a simple improvised home recipe of Shahzad's car bomb.

And the good news is ... you can prepare it in the kitchen of your mom too.

The opening invocation, of course, Imam Khalifa had fully expected. It was, a secular English friend had once told him, the "standard Islamic boilerplate," something he'd used himself just as formulaically in his prayers and sermons. But, he could tell somehow that there was an unusual fervency behind the words he had just read. These guys really *meant* it—that everything they were doing they truly believed they were literally doing it in Allah's name. He'd like to think he was doing the same thing too, but now he was not so sure. He didn't know whether his piety could withstand such terrifying passion. So, what chance for impressionable and alienated kids like Jamal? "They speak the simple, plain Truth," Jamal had lectured him. "It's as clear as a pure mountain stream—no dark shadows by the banks where lies might hide; no clogging silt to obscure revelation; no twists and turns—no disorienting deviations." He knew Jamal was parroting this stuff, but, still, parrots could bite, and bite hard—if they were hungry enough, angry enough, had something to prove.

But the jihadis' real hook over the likes of Jamal Shirani was more than all this, he realized. In the end, to serve God, to submit to his will, was intrinsic to all believers, an inherent part of their faith as Muslims. It was boilerplate at times, if you like, but, critically, it was boilerplate at the heart of one's religious DNA and, therefore, supremely important, notwithstanding his friend's secular cynicism. But, although all this was a core component in establishing one's piety, was it any more than that—was it truly *inspirational*?

No, it was not. It was what came next after the routine invocation that mattered most, when it came to rousing the pious, actionable fervor of kids like Jamal. The editor had expertly played on the almost inherent hatred of America among Muslims of many stripes, including even himself: on the one hand, a sometime beneficiary of the fruits of American civilization—computers and Disneyland, he had to admit, not being the least of them—but at the same time appalled by the country's idolatrous love of money and its commercialization of just about everything, including the worship of God, of *faith*.

The real inspirational jihadi kicker was surely this, *Inspire*'s editor was simply yet convincingly saying: the United States, for all its imperialistic power, its vast arsenal, and its control of the inter-national financial system, was weaker than most folks realized. It had an Achilles heel that even someone like Jamal in his mum's kitchen could get at: Americans' abject fear of the lowly car bomb. And what was true of America was true of its sidekick, Britain, too. No matter how downtrodden you were, no matter how much a pawn in the Great Satan's games, you could nonetheless be a David to America's Goliath, and hit him where it really hurts most—right in the nuts, at home, where he's most vulnerable and most fears it.

Terror was *not* the monopoly of the United States or the mighty British government any longer; it had now become "democratized," the weapon of choice for all the so-called "angry little men" the world over. Just how *inspirational* was that? How were the likes of Imam Khalifa supposed to combat such an irrepressible force, if all they had to offer were the dull counsel of moderation, to supinely accommodate one's faith to the injustices of the secular status quo? Words were just words no doubt, but his must have seemed pathetically vacuous compared to those accompanied by real action, the swashbuckling derring-do of outfits like IS.

Imam Khalifa scrolled to the next page, unsettled by what he might read next. If he could feel some of the allure of what he was reading, then what might others less savvy than himself feel about what they were being told and encouraged to do? *Inspire* was offering a way out, a road to respect and empowerment, some kind of justice and revenge in a world so many of Jamal's ilk had struggled to root themselves in. And even if they didn't enjoy any of this for long, getting killed in the process perhaps, no matter; for a martyr's death—if you *really* believed it—was not really death at all, just the mortal sort, a pale shadow indeed compared to what was to come in Paradise.

He continued to scroll through the next few webpages, finding ever more nuggets of plausible truth in what he saw written there. He felt like he was walking through a minefield of startling, disturbing revelations. First this:

> The western media endeavors to portray the American empire as old favorite, the defender of peace, the number one human rights protector and that it has values and principles that they call to. Is this the feelings of billions of people? Do people really buy this? Or is the reality different?

Imam Khalifa blinked—he thought the United States did a pretty good job on human rights, at least mostly so, despite his disgust at some of the Americans' sins, like gambling and pornography, and Abu Ghraib and Guantanamo Bay. But now he wasn't as sure as he'd supposed he'd been.

> Do you think the Japanese have forgotten what happened in Hiroshima and Nagasaki? Do you think America's atrocities in Vietnam and Panama could be forgotten?

Panama? What... Oh yeah, Noriega. But he was a drug runner, wasn't he? But Japan, Vietnam—atrocities? Yes, of course, of course. Sixty thousand instant deaths at least at Hiroshima, plus over 130,000 more in the aftermath. And My Lai in Vietnam—he recalled the pudgy lieutenant Calley standing trial, and then President Nixon's pardon. Number One human rights' protector? Hardly, when you really thought about it like that.

Another page: a Q & A with Sheikh Anwar Al-'Awlaki, an American citizen assassinated by an American drone armed with an appropriately named Hellfire missile for spreading false propaganda and advocating holy war against the Great Satan.

> It wasn't the Muslims who dragged in civilians into this war. It was the Americans, and on a scale that is astronomically different than ours. They killed millions of Muslim civilians in cold blood during the embargo of Iraq which was before 9/11.

Imam Khalifa slumped back in his desk chair, staring at Al-'Awlaki's words. He wanted to challenge some of his assumptions—hadn't the US been forced to embargo the brutal dictator who'd gassed his own Kurdish citizens at Halabja, and had then invaded Kuwait?—but soon realized that "who did what, first" didn't really cut much mustard, or get you very far when it came to international politics or the apocalyptic call to radical action. For every crime against humanity, there was more often than not another such crime that had pre-dated it, perpetrated quite possibly by the very so-called innocent targets of the latest round of atrocity. Assigning innocence and culpability in the larger scheme of things only rendered you a confused dog futilely chasing its own tail.

Where had it all begun? Where would it all end? With God, he supposed, but the thought brought him little solace. And in any case, even if Al-'Awlaki was biased, did only look at one side of history's ledger, he still had a critical case to make, a case moreover that could easily inspire the likes of Jamal Shirani to take up arms for Holy War. Maybe these kids like Jamal really did believe in the rewards of jihadi martyrdom, a place in Paradise with seventy-five virgins, no less. He just didn't know. *Anything* seemed possible these days. He still believed that fundamentally the jihadis were wrong, engaging in mortal sin. But...but ... but what could he hope to do about it?

It seemed like Jamal was already lost to him, just like Ahmed was. He was feeling rather lost himself, almost hopeless. But still, this War on Terror had to be stopped somehow, and he was too deep into the process of playing his (limited) role to step out now. The jihadis most likely had him on their target list already, and quitting the rehab program would only raise the hackles of the intelligence services and the police, make him a prime suspect for them, too. And then there was his family and the mosque and the house and...

Why couldn't they just shut sites like *Inspire* down, or at least block them, if they were such a threat, such an effective jihadi recruiting tool? The Chinese seemed to know how to censor the Internet with their Great Firewall of China, didn't they? How hard could it be for GCHQ or some such to do something similar? Technically, it ought to be a no-brainer.

For a few seconds, he was intrigued, then inspired by this—what should have been obvious—revelation. But it didn't stand much scrutiny for long, the more he thought about it. There was the not-so-little complication of free speech, free expression. How much would you want to mess with those? It was true that he'd sometimes felt a sympathy for so-called "blasphemy laws," but he'd always recognized in the end that they were both open to serious abuse and, thusly, to be a cure worse than the disease. And how could you really *force* someone to believe? It was oxymoronic.

Moreover, jihadi websites were not just recruiting tools; they were also repositories of critical intelligence. Shutting them down would only result in cutting your nose to spite your face. *Curses!* He was back to trying to out-progagandize the jihadis again, a contest he knew from first-hand experience he and the government were losing, and might indeed never win.

His desktop icon for *YouTube* suddenly filled his field of vision. He must have been staring at it for some time without realizing it.

Click.
Sign in: IKonic66. **********! *Click.*
Search: Jihadi John. *Click.*
About 109,000 results.

Not all complimentary, of course, but still. *YouTube* was like a sieve, filters be damned. Famous or infamous, it didn't seem to matter. And *YouTube* was just the tip of the iceberg. He looked at his hands: so many holes in the dike, so few fingers.

Imam Khalifa turned off his computer and began to fiddle with his worry beads.

One more shot, he sighed. I'll give him one more shot.

What could he lose? At least he had an unlimited supply of ice cream and bananas. And the notion that *Guns N' Roses* might have given him entrée as something of a fellow traveler in Jamal's world had proven to be a total dead end. He just didn't "get" the music, and the idea that he liked the lyrics of their songs was too preposterous for words.

Besides, Jamal now claimed that he no longer liked them, too. The kid was as emotionally slippery as an eel.

Would he ever catch him?

29
[October 2015]

There's an eerie quiet before the battle begins, a surrealistic calm before the terrifying storm that's to come. You're like a subatomic particle in superposition, neither here nor there, teetering on the edge of two parallel universes, waiting nervously for God to measure you, flip you like a piece of flimsy flotsam on a storm-tossed sea. And when he does, it's like nothing you've ever fucking imagined it would be. Not even close.

When hell breaks out, your first thought, if you have one, is that you'll shit yourself or cry like a frightened kid, call out for your mommy like they do in the movies. But then there's an almighty fucking rush, and you're firing like a maniac, getting off on the power you feel coming out of the end of the barrel of your gun, blowing your biggest load ever. There's a lightshow that's as big and beautiful as anything you've ever seen. You're painting a Pollock canvas on a mega-scale, swirling trails of color like you're waving giant fireworks in the air all around you, having a real riot of a fucking good time.

And then the party's over, just like that, and it starts to register what you've just done, been a part of. A hangover's coming; you can suddenly feel it. You were probably hit several minutes ago, but it's only now that you start to realize it.

It's only later, much later, when you've regained consciousness and you're in the hospital wondering if you'll ever walk again that they tell you what happened to Delta, your buddy from southeast Arkansas. You recall his big black shiny face, always happy, like he's high on life all the time, no matter where in the hell you are. You remember asking him about it, was he using, but he'd always said no, that it would be against his faith. And besides, he didn't need anything like that, not even booze; he had God, or Allah as he called him.

He was a Muslim, you remind yourself, and suddenly it seems like it matters in a way that it hadn't ever mattered before. It's then when you really get religion, and you're a wannabe Pat Tillman no more.

30

24 December 2016]

I coughed and gagged, spitting out half of the alcohol they were funneling down my throat. But within seconds—thankfully, I guess, in a weird sort of way—I passed out. The last thing I remember hearing were their prayers starting up again, more animated now, now that they were almost ready…

I don't know for sure, of course, what happened next, not all the gory details at any rate. I just have the sickening feeling a drunk has the morning after, that something bad had happened the night before, but he can't quite remember what exactly, although, given the signs and the fleeting, half-visualized flashbacks—he fears and kind of knows instinctively that it's the worst…the absolute fucking worst.

I hurt like hell; I've barely been able to move for days. The swelling and the rawness down there … and I have the crabs now, too. I'm trying to clean myself up and tend to the damage, but they've only given me some paper towel and a jar of some sort of cream—I've no idea what it is; the label's in a foreign language. But it stinks alright, like everything of theirs does. I tested the cream on the back of my hand first, and it didn't seem to do any damage. So, I've just put a little on down there for now; we'll see soon enough whether it works or not, I suppose. At least the stuff alleviates the soreness a bit. But I sense, oh fucking God forbid, a sort of indescribable knowing in my belly already, perhaps... perhaps an unwanted gift from one of them. I know that it's far too early to know such a thing....but I just have this feeling...I just know, somehow.

Tell me, Robbie. Tell me that I'm wrong! A sign... anything!

It can't be anymore, for us now, can it?
...

"Inshallah," I hear the dumbfucks say when they come to check on me—over and over, as if they actually wanted what I most fear, as if God wanted it, too. If I pinch myself anymore, just to confirm what's going on down here is really fucking happening, I'll swear I'll have a whole slew of bruises on my arms and legs to last me a lifetime. I look like a black-and-blue leopard!

Huh, a lifetime? Is that what all this is? Feels more like purgatory, if not literal hell. Looks like Father O'Malley might have been right, after all, although I doubt even he would have wished all this shit on me. When...if...all this comes to an end one day, one thing's for sure, though, I'll not be skipping confession as much as I have been recently—well, at least not as much. It might be good for both of us...to confess, brings things out into the open, deal with them, instead of...well, you know...

Life, not sure I want it anymore, anyway...not a "new" life in any case, if you know what I mean? That, I want to end before it begins...if God can forgive me.

What have they done to me, Robbie?

Where are you? For God's sake, where are you?!

Where were you...?

The end may be near now. Will you ever know what happened to me? Will you ever get to read this? God willing, you will...but what is he willing?

All this?
...

Where are the fucking police? They must have her, too. Katie, Kathy, are you here somewhere? Send me a sign if you are. I hope they're not...but they must be...I suppose.

What else would they do with you, the fucks?

...

Just a short cut across Jubilee Park, that's all it was. Another quarter of a mile and we'd have made it. Why us? Why then? I can't stop thinking if only I'd waited at the Palace, not trusted that Katie, or whatever her name was, especially at that time of night, not blithely cut across the park like that—it's got no lights, for fuck's sake! Just one little decision to do something else, just one moment of delay, and maybe they'd have never even seen us. And all this shit would never have...

I also can't stop wondering why they kidnapped me, are still keeping me down here after all this time. I thought at first it was the sex they were after, and it obviously is... But it seems like there must be more, but what? Why didn't they just do their sordid business right there in the park and have done with it, run off before I could even see who they were? And then there's all the chanting before and after—what's that all about?

What the fuck do they want? Why won't they let me go now? I'm used up...so used up. What's the point anymore? God, what's the fucking point?

...

In the end, I guess I started to let you go, too—didn't I? And now, after all this, there's likely no going back, getting back to where we were.

I missed my chance. We both did.

...

I wasn't expecting this particular turn of events at all, not by a long chalk. Still, don't know if it'll lead to anything. He is the Soft One, after all. Doubt he's got the spunk to really help me—get me fucking out of here!

Yesterday, he found it—yes, this, my scribblings.

He'd brought me to the toilet, as has become the routine by now for whoever's turn it is to put me down for the night, make sure I'm not going anywhere. Since it was him, I knew I'd get away with sneaking my journal out with me, so I could write in it some more overnight while they were all asleep or had gone home or whatever.

Anyway, inside the bog, I'm making sounds like I'm having trouble trying to shit, while, at the same time, I quietly get up onto the toilet seat in order to fish out the plastic zipper bag the notebook's in from the cistern. But I must have been overdoing my grunts and moans, because suddenly the bog door flies open, and there he is. "What's wrong?" he says. "Are you okay?"

We both freeze, him, in the open doorway, looking like he's seen a ghost, and me, I'm standing there perched on the toilet seat, my hand still in the cistern.

Then he whispers—like he's more afraid the others might catch him falling down on the job than he's ready to announce that he's caught me red-handed trying to pull some sort of trick—"What are you doing? Get down."

I turn my head to face him, thinking I'll tell him I was just trying to adjust the ballcock, 'cause the toilet wasn't flushing right, but it's too late. I'm so disoriented I forget to let the zipper bag go, and the next thing I see are his eyes moving to zero-in on my hand. I turn and look, too, and there it is, as large as life and dripping water all over my shoes.

"What is that?" he says, but before I can answer he's already looking back over his shoulder as if he's as guilty of some malfeasance as I am. He's clearly starting to panic.

I decide I may as well fess up, I figure he's going to know soon enough, anyway. "It's a—"

"Put it back!" he commands. He's still whispering, but louder now. I can sense the fear in the slight elevation of his voice. I let the bag drop back gently into what remains of the water before it was turned off, and get down off the toilet seat. My knees tremble slightly; I'm still not sure what he's going to do. It's clear that he seems caught in two minds, and that whichever way he jumps—turn me in or turn a blind eye—he's sure to catch hell for it. He's breathing heavily and he's running his hand through his hair, over and over. He's hesitating, he doesn't know what to do. I have what feels like a flash of inspiration, and I realize that there's the slightest of an opening right in front of me. So, I seize it. There's not much time; the others, I just knew, would be there soon, wondering what was taking him so much time to shut me up for the night.

"Listen," I whisper. He turns to face me, already looking like a child that needs comfort. "Say nothing to the others about this"—I nod towards the cistern—"and I'll keep your secret, too." He blinks like he doesn't get it, so I glance at is groin and raise my eyebrows. "You know," I say, like a prosecutor sure of his case. "Think what they'll do if they know you can't—"

"Okay! Okay!" he replies, gasping almost, as if his life depends on his agreement to my proposal.

I hold my hand out, wanting to do something reassuringly ritualistic in that moment of great consequence. I know now that it was perhaps silly of me to expect that such as him would be bound by such a gesture, but at the time I felt that it was all I had to try to affect him, get him at least enough on my side as to make a difference. I was literally grasping at straws, as well as hands.

He looked at me for a couple of seconds, then took my hand in his. One shake, and that was it. But his hand felt warm, its skin soft, almost like a girl's. I can't be certain, but I'm almost sure he had the slightest crack of a smile on his face, not a supercilious thing or an unconscious reflex, but a real one, the genuine article.

I smiled, too. For a fleeting moment, I almost felt sorry for him. And I've started to wonder how a kid like him can end up where is now. I mean, I know he's a Paki and all, but still, he seems like a frightened kid, most of the time he's with me. He's just a boy, really: stupid, can't control his dick, impressionable, easily led—a dummy, in all but name. But maybe he's more than "just a boy," if you know what I mean. Maybe he could get it right, if only he had the chance, some guidance. I realize now that I know nothing about him, what has brought him to such a place. Surely, he couldn't have done all of this of his own free will, could he?

In any case, I've gotten to keep my precious notebook! It's been the only thing, I reckon, that's kept me from completely losing it all this time. And I keep wondering now if perhaps one day he'll finally take the next step, eventually find some moral momentum from the brief act of human recognition we felt for each other in that oh-so-brief moment. But I'm not betting on it.

31
*[July 2015-June 2016(?)FBCT
— Far Beyond Christian Time]*

In the makeshift lab in Raqqa, nervous hope had turned into morbid fear, an alchemy as radical in its transformational effect as the one she was supposed to engineer in turning the crude ingredients that had been procured for her into an even cruder Dirty Bomb. Ayaan felt as if she had fallen off the face of the earth, had been sucked into a black hole from which there could be no escape, only obliteration of one sort or another. That night, all alone, she waited…waited for the inevitable.

It was well past midnight when he finally came.

She'd been staring at the heavy curtain all night long, ever since Kifat's men had brought her there. When it finally ruffled, then flapped, Ayaan gasped and inched back on the mound of pillows she was lying on.

Kifat slowly emerged from behind the curtain. He had a look of grim determination on his face. He glared at her, a falcon locking onto its prey. Ayaan inched back even more; she was right up against the wall now, no further retreat possible.

"No! Please…" she begged.

Kifat stepped towards her, lifting his *dishdasha* up a few inches by grasping it in both hands at knee height. When he was right in front of her, he knelt, and then sat back on his haunches. He adjusted his robe at his crotch with his right hand. The clothing bulged, as if something was secreted there. Ayaan stared at the fold; she knew what it had to be.

"Please!" she begged. "I will do as you say. I will make it."

Kifat continued to glare at her. He smoothed his moustache with the tips of his thumb and forefinger, and then pursed his lips.

"I promise! I promise!" A muffled sob caught in Ayaan's throat. She coughed.

Kifat lunged forward, his arms stretched out in front of him. Ayaan threw herself to her right, trying to escape him. She landed face down, burying her face in the cushions. She froze, waiting to feel the powerful grasp of his hands gripping her hips tightly, but she felt nothing. She heard Kifat's voice, but she had little idea what he was saying. It sounded as if he were almost singing, chanting. Still no hands clutched her. She turned her head slowly, until one eye could see him. Kifat was almost prostrate now, his face to the floor, and his arms stretched out in front of him as far as they could possibly reach.

He was praying. *Oh, my God! Thank God!* Ayaan turned her face back into the cushions again, and remained still. Kifat seemed to be deep into prayer; she could sense the passion in his singsong voice, modulating, it seemed to her, with some genuine choral skill. She was almost soothed by it; that such beauty could come from such a man... *Maybe, just maybe...*

The chanting stopped. It ended with a crescendo, a sustained, lilting cry to Allah. Ayaan heard Kifat moving, the rustle of his *dishdasha* as he got to his feet, the slight grunt of the effort to unbend his knees and stand up. There was a pause; she could only hear his breathing. It sounded like he was out of breath; maybe from his praying, she thought. The breathing became heavier, getting closer; she could smell his breath — the foul stench of tobacco.

A hand grabbed the back of her neck and forced her head deeper into the cushions; another lifted her *abaya* and then tugged at her underwear, dragging them down to her ankles. Ayaan felt Kifat thrust himself into her buttocks, forcing her thighs apart. And then he was inside her, grunting fiercely with every lunge of his pelvis. The pain was unbearable, so much so that even though her mouth was wide open little sound emerged from it; it was as if the stab of his penis had ruptured her lungs, depriving her larynx of the air it needed to perform its function. She felt as if he was tearing her apart.

Just at the point when she felt she could take no more, when she thought she was going to lose consciousness, Kifat shuddered, groaned loudly, and shook again. He moaned once more, the satisfied grunt of being well spent. Ayaan felt Kifat's weight lift from her, but she couldn't move. She quietly wept, letting the cushions absorb her tears and mute her sobs.

Kifat got off her. Ayaan heard the rustle of his *dishdasha* again, then the movement of his limbs. She heard him begin to pray again, although his invocation this time seemed subdued and much less melodic than before, as if he barely had the energy to get through it. When he finished, she waited for what might come next, but she was strangely unafraid, too depleted to feel much of anything except a deep numbness.

Kifat looked at Ayaan lying on the cushions. She looked truly pitiful, he thought, and for a moment he was tempted to touch her lightly on her shoulder, in consolation perhaps, but he stayed his hand. In the time of the End of Days, he quickly remonstrated with himself, she was, as the Holy Koran commanded, a trophy of war — nothing more, and certainly nothing of sentimental consequence. She was a mere broodmare; a convenient womb, God willing, for the breeding of future holy warriors. Beyond that glorious task, her life had no meaning. He dug his knuckles into his thigh; he *had* to keep himself focused on that!

But as he turned to leave, like an iron filing drawn irrepressibly to a magnet, he couldn't help but look back over his shoulder at Ayaan one more time. He could see her shoulders shake in response to her muffled sobbing. He went back to her, bent down, and drew a blanket over her up to the back of her neck; even a broodmare needed warmth, he rationalized, some minimal level of protection at least, if it was to be of any use.

But as he did so, he suddenly realized that Ayaan had not been cut, like all his other conquests had. His entry had been too smooth, and the path to orgasm too easy. He wondered what it might mean for his hoped-for offspring, that they would emerge from and have the blood of an impure mother. Still, there was no doubt he would have her again; no, no doubt at all about that. And if Allah had a problem with Ayaan's purity, he would surely take matters into his own hands, sooner or later.

♠

For the next several days, Ayaan didn't see Kifat.

Presumably, she thought, he was giving her time and some space to recover from her ordeal. God knows, she needed both. Maybe Kifat did too; given the injury he'd done to her, it seemed quite possible that he'd damaged himself in the process as well—at least she wished as much. She spent most of her days and nights confined to her bed, sleeping mostly, perhaps with the "help" of some local potion. Who knew what Fatima, Kifat's third wife who tended to her, was putting in her food and drink, but surely it wasn't an accident that she almost immediately fell into a deep sleep after every meal.

Still, recover, to a degree, she did. The pain in her groin slowly subsided as the swellings went down and the abrasions healed. She'd resisted at first when Fatima had tried to apply some strange-looking salve to her genitalia, but when she'd finally given way—she couldn't match Fatima's almost manly strength—the coolness of the ointment had instantly soothed her. Thereafter, she allowed her nurse to do whatever she pleased, and was thankful she did. Ayaan didn't suppose that Fatima had had any formal medical training, but whatever Fatima did seemed to do the trick.

In return, Ayaan tried to be the best patient she could. Apart from getting well, she so very much wanted Fatima to warm towards her, befriend her if at all possible, enough such that she might one day soon help her, help her to...*escape*, get back home. Home, she *must* get back home—back to Mama and Papa and Bologna!

To think that just a few days ago she'd been so determined to leave her home behind, and now just the very *idea* of it was so delicious, a yearning desire almost beyond measure! But could she possibly get back there now? The very thought of what dangers such an escapade might entail horrified her, immediately punctured the fragile bubble of her hope for escape. Could she, would she be able go through with it, if the occasion presented itself? Could she, should she have much, if any, faith in Fatima, even if she was the only person she was having any interaction with?

Most likely not, it seemed. Fatima's nursing skills were not at all complemented by her unnecessarily brusque bedside manner. She was a strictly utilitarian nurse, who asked no questions and expected automatic compliance with her commands, signaled mostly by her unforgiving physical movements—a poke here, a prod there, a twisting of a limb somewhere in between them—rather than by the calm, reassuring vocal requests of someone well-attuned to the Hippocratic oath. Her remedies were effective, but administered roughly, as punishments almost. Ayaan tried to get Fatima to engage her in conversation, to look at her in the eyes, but had no success whatsoever. Fatima had obviously taken an instant dislike to her, and was ministering to her only because Kifat, doubtless, had ordered her to. There were moments, indeed, when Ayaan thought Fatima's aversion to her might have been bordering on the pathological. The way she held her scissors as if they were a dagger; the waterboarding-like manner in which she gave Ayaan her medicine; the technique she employed to examine Ayaan's abdomen, kneading it aggressively, almost puncturing her skin...

Escape? What chance of that? She was friendless, virtually alone in the world. She'd been friendless and alone before, in the surging seas off Lampedusa, she supposed, but only for a moment. She'd been quickly saved then. But there were no God-fearing Italian sailors out patrolling where she was now. She'd needed a miracle then, and she desperately another one now — but from whence would it come, if at all?

But life seemed *full* of miracles, didn't it? Life itself was a miracle.

The only problem was that far too many of them had been rather bad miracles as opposed to being fortuitous ones, in her case. She was lying in a bed in the middle of the Syrian desert after having been raped by a Muslim fanatic — how miraculous was that? Well, about as much of a marvel as an orphaned Somali baby floating in the Mediterranean Sea being rescued, and then adopted by an Italian billionaire and his wife. Her miracles seemed to come in strange pairs, beneficial *yins* and malicious *yangs* dialectically feeding off one another in some kind of tragicomic cosmic dance that couldn't quite make its choreographic mind up. In her case, the miracle of being pitched parentless into the sea had been matched by that of being plucked out of it again, equally wondrously, by an unsuspecting mariner, who'd then found safe harbor for her in the arms of a new barren family suddenly made whole by her arrival. Would, could, the dialectic work beneficial wonders like that again for her? Why not? Who could predict such serendipitous things?

Predict? Was life predictable?

She thought of all the millions of Italians whose lives were thoroughly foreseeable, at least in their broad outlines: lives spent almost entirely in the places of their births, attending the same schools their parents had, pursuing similar careers too or at least having jobs close to home; then marriage to a local, perhaps even a distant half-cousin, and the raising of families to start the whole generational cycle over again. But her life had not followed that pattern at all! Why? Why should her life trajectory have been so wildly different, so incredulous? God's will? Chance—pure serendipity?

Her life had not only been thoroughly capricious, it could also easily have been *so* very different, so much so that she wouldn't have found herself lying there in the Syrian desert *at all*. What if she'd been adopted by a different family who hadn't lived in Bologna, and had been poor? What if she hadn't been adopted at all, but had spent her early life in an orphanage? What then? What if she'd never worked at DuPont? What if she hadn't bumped into that street urchin and then hadn't wondered about her Somali heritage?

What if she hadn't gone on line, hadn't clicked so impulsively on those links to the chatrooms? What if...

*Oh God...*was there no way out of the labyrinth she'd entrapped herself in? No possible avenue of escape at all...short of blowing the whole thing to smithereens, herself along with it?

♠

Some weeks later, Ayaan was in her lab.

After she'd recovered from Kifat's assault, he'd ordered her to immediately get to work on the Dirty Bomb. The caliphate was in urgent need of it, he'd proclaimed. Ayaan's initial inclination had been to repeat her assertion that she knew nothing about how to go about building such a weapon, but she'd soon thought the better of it. If she had any chance of coming up with an escape plan, she'd figured, at least appearing to be useful to Kifat might just give her enough latitude and opportunity to do so.

But exactly what sort of an opening she might have been hoping to come across in this way, she had had absolutely no idea. But if she'd have admitted to her uselessness to him right away, then Kifat would have no doubt imprisoned her forthwith, perhaps even summarily executing her shortly thereafter. And the idea that she might end up in an orange jumpsuit, blindfolded and on her knees, with a sack over her head... Well, meeting her demise even in a totally futile attempt at flight seemed immeasurably preferable to that. The Don Quixote in her just had to keep on going, tilting at windmills until...

A pile of manuscripts stood on her desk next to a computer, and surrounding them both, covering most of the rest of the large table top, were a scattered set of blueprints of various kinds. The computer screen flickered occasionally, the result of a combination of erratic electricity supply and a less than optimal internet connection. Somebody or other was bombing Raqqa almost every day, no doubt exacerbating her connectivity problems. She presumed it was the Americans, but who knew for sure? No one would tell her anything, and she still understood little Arabic. English was the lingua franca in her world now, but it was only used sparingly, restricted mostly to giving her instruction as to what she should do and how quickly she should do it. At first, Kifat had been her main interlocutor in these matters, but recently he'd handed over the task of supervising her to a subordinate, so she rarely saw him anymore. She wondered what greater tasks he now had to take care of: presumably one of them was finding a delivery mechanism and a suitable target for her bomb—which was still far from completion.

Ayaan made an elaborate show of supposedly engaging in her appointed task. She suspected that the guard, who was always in the lab with her, was there not only to stop her running away, but also to monitor her behavior and report back on it to Kifat. She was determined to put on a good show for him, and that she *could* do.

She maneuvered her mouse and clicked it furiously; web pages came and went, albeit slowly, illuminating her feigned fierce concentration from time to time in the glow of their initial projection onto the computer screen. She constantly got on and off her stool in order to circumnavigate her desk and consult yet another blueprint. She looked terribly busy—making as little progress as possible without, hopefully, raising suspicion that she was in fact doing such, although she knew this game could only last for so long before Kifat would cotton on to what she was about. But by then, maybe…

She doubled down on her performance, slapping her pencil down onto the drawing she was scrutinizing and muttering angrily to herself. Out of the corner of her eye, she saw the guard flinch. He gripped his weapon as if he was preparing to ready it for use. Then he settled back into his customary slouch by the door. Ayaan smiled to herself—apparently her performance was doing the job.

She pulled another one of the designs toward her and spent some time altering and annotating it. She coughed and looked up, her usual procedure when she wanted to alert her guard that she needed his attention. He was still lounging against the doorframe, consumed with the task of picking his nose. His Kalashnikov was resting now against the front of his legs at an angle, and the muzzle, Ayaan noticed, was pointing teasingly toward his groin. *If only*, she thought. She dropped a heavy book to the floor. The loud *thwack!* made the guard spear his nostril with his finger, but, unfortunately, the gun remained in place, and silent.

"Sorry!" Ayaan exclaimed. The guard was reaching for his gun again. "Book," she said, pointing to the floor. He followed her gaze, and then nodded, contemptuously. He waved his rifle muzzle in the direction of the offending volume.

Ayaan bent over and picked up the book. Then she reached for the drawing she'd been working on and began rolling it up.

"Engineer," she said. She secured the scroll with an elastic band, and held it out towards the guard. He gave her an indignant look, wiped his nose with the back of his hand, then sauntered over towards her. He held out his hand, but just at the moment Ayaan was about to hand the scroll to him, he snatched it away. The document fell to the floor. He smirked at her. Ayaan tried to hold eye contact with him, but soon gave way. She retrieved the drawing and held it out towards him again, eyes down. She felt hot, flushed. The guard made no move, then snorted loudly, as if he was gathering up phlegm in his throat. Ayaan squeezed her eyes closed in distaste. Still he did not take the document. She gingerly inched it toward him. Finally, he ripped it out of her hand, spat into the sink next to her desk, and left. Seconds later, she heard the telltale sound of a key turning in the lock from the other side of the lab door.

Ayaan waited as long as she could before looking up. She knew she wouldn't have long before the guard would return, most likely with the engineer in tow, perhaps even Kifat, too. It wouldn't take the engineer more than a couple of minutes to realize that the drawing she'd sent him was bullshit. She quickly tiptoed over to the door through which the guard had exited, and put her ear to it. No voices, just the sound of booted feet pacing the corridor outside. She went back to her desk, and manipulated the mouse of her computer.

In the address bar she typed "Google," then hit return. Nothing yet again, just "الوصول تم رفض" — "Access denied," she knew by now it just had to have meant. It was clear that the only access she had was to the files that she had instructed her computer tech, Amin, to download for her several weeks ago—she hadn't been allowed to do so herself, unsupervised. So why was the browser still there, if she couldn't get to any website that Kifat clearly did not want her to? It didn't make sense. She quickly closed the page, and then deleted the search inquiry from her history.

Ayaan wiped a tear from her eye and took a deep breath. She was determined not to break down, but to keep considering and reconsidering her options for finding a way to escape Kifat's iron grasp. She began to go over yet again several possible stratagems she'd entertained over the weeks since her arrival in Syria: flight under the cover of a dark, moonless night; contacting the Italian embassy in Damascus, somehow; perhaps even killing Kifat in some manner in a surprise attack—but each avenue quickly became a cul-de-sac of hopeless impossibility.

Flight? She would need accomplices, but who? The embassy? How would she make contact, get there? Was it even still open? Murder? How might an opportunity present itself, would she be able to go through with it when the time came? How could she make sure she'd be prepared? Where would she get a weapon? Wouldn't Kifat be just too strong for her, anyway?

"Oh..." Ayaan's head slumped to her desk, her face buried in her folded arms. The fleeting thought about exacting vengeance in lieu of impossible flight returned to her thoughts, gathering brightening flame now. She *could* escape in a tragic, morbid way, and in the process, yes, given the skill set that she already had, she could—

"Not asleep, are you?" It was Kifat.

She had not heard him enter. She straightened up immediately, slowly turning around to face him. He was alone—had the engineer not told him yet, perhaps? "Oh...no, I...I was just, um, thinking about something, that's all...The trigger. What sort of triggering mechanism to use."

"Ah, I see. Good...good."

Good? Did he know, or didn't he? That second "good"—what did it mean?

Kifat stepped up right in front of her. He put his hand underneath her chin and raised her head, so that she had no alternative but to meet his gaze. He locked his eyes on hers; in another time and place he might have been her lover with such a gesture, but his cold stare projected suspicion as opposed to endearment. A draft of chilled air coming from the air conditioning vent above their heads brushed Ayaan's neck, making her shiver.

"It's good to know that you're not thinking about other things—distractions of one sort or another—keeping you from your work."

Kifat let go of her chin, but not before giving the underside of her lower jaw a firm tap with his knuckles. Ayaan involuntarily bit her tongue in reaction to his touch. She grimaced and then licked her lips. The chilled air wafted against her neck again, but her shivering had already given way to perspiration. She thought she was going to be sick—she'd been having these sensations with increasing frequency lately.

"Tell me, Ayaan," Kifat continued, stepping around behind her so that he could get a good look at her computer screen, "do you miss Italy? Do you think about your family? Do you want to see them?" He reached for the mouse. The cursor on the computer screen meandered towards the menu for her search history. *Click. You don't have any history.* "Mmm," he murmured.

"I...I've been working on these blueprints today," Ayaan blurted out, indicating the drawings on her desk. "They're for a trigger design. We'll need to build a prototype, first."

"A what?"

"Have a go at making one, to see if it'll work." Ayaan could feel the chilled air wafting her neck stronger than ever now, but the more it blew the more she perspired. She just couldn't help it; she felt as if her nervous system had just been overloaded by a surge of electricity. Kifat, by comparison, looked as cool as a cucumber, like he always did, in command, on top of things, in the know...

"Oh, yes, I *know*," he said. He pulled one of the designs towards him, and made a pretense of studying it. "All very complicated stuff. Yes, very complex, indeed." He stepped around Ayaan again, all the while looking at her. He perched himself on her desk, facing her. He was so close to Ayaan that his left knee, positioned between hers, was almost touching her

268

groin. He leaned right into Ayaan's face. "Are *you* complex, too, Ayaan?"

But before she could answer, the room shook; there was a muffled boom from somewhere outside, but quite close by. Glass lab equipment rattled; a piece fell to the floor and smashed.

"Hear that, Ayaan? Feel that? They're back. They're getting closer. We're going to need you to deliver very soon, or it might be too late."

"Soon, I promise. It's just that—"

Kifat grabbed her wrist. "Never mind, it doesn't matter anymore, Ayaan. We already have what we need—and it's not your so-called trigger. The engineer's already told me about that. Silly girl, Ayaan, *very* silly." He felt her surprise transmit itself from her wrist into his hand. "Shocked? Don't be. Did you really believe that we ever needed you to build our Dirty Bomb?"

Kifat got up and went to her computer again. He logged onto a website: *Inspire*, it said, *and Inspire the Believers*. Kifat scrolled down several pages. The face of a bearded man appeared. It belonged to a Samir Diyala, a French citizen of Algerian descent, the caption said. He was a nuclear scientist, formerly part of the A. Q. Khan network that had once engaged in the illicit proliferation of nuclear bomb know-how, the accompanying comment elaborated. "He's our man, Ayaan," Kifat declared, "Not you."

"But...but why did you recruit me?"

Kifat scrolled some more. This time her own face appeared. Kifat stepped back so she could read what had been written about her.

The apostates and crusaders have cowered before car bombs, backpack bombs. Let's see how they will react next? Ayaan is a great scientist, unwittingly trained by DuPont Company, the forger of many weapons of mass destruction. But now Ayaan has come home. She is building for us a Dirty Bomb. It is time to avenge Hiroshima and Nagasaki.

Are they ready? Are the apostates and crusaders ready? Ayaan is asking this question. Are you ready to answer her call, follow her example?

Ayaan looked up at Kifat in puzzlement.
"You still don't get it, do you?" Kifat said. "Aren't you *inspired*?"
"Propaganda?"
"Of course. Only partly at first. We did think that maybe you would be of some technical use, but we were wrong. Naturally, we had to test you, make sure you were fully trustworthy, a true jihadi. But you failed that test, Ayaan. You tried to hide from us the fact that you were trying to make contact with the Crusaders—"
"The browser. Is that why—"
"Surely you should have known that merely deleting your browsing history would not fully cover your tracks. We may be poor, ignorant Muslim fanatics in your privileged eyes, Ayaan, but I'm afraid we're a lot smarter than you think. Amin has been able to tell us every search you've made."

Ayaan started to tremble. She tried to control herself, but still couldn't. The walls of the lab seemed to close in on her; Kifat's presence loomed over her like a billowing, malevolent genie emerging from a lamp. She thought she was going to suffocate.

"What will you do with me?" she bleated.

Kifat pursed his lips, as if he was actually considering various options. But Ayaan only sensed a deliberate teasing, that he'd already made up his mind. And that could only mean one thing...

"Do you know what we do with traitors, Ayaan? It's obvious, isn't it? What do you think traitors deserve?" Kifat turned back to the computer, and manipulated the mouse again. A video clip sprang into life. It was Jihadi John, knife in hand, standing next to a kneeling figure in an orange jumpsuit, waiting...

Tears filled Ayaan's eyes. She mouthed some words, but no sound came. Kifat just looked at her dispassionately, as if he was no more than mildly scientifically interested in her overly-sentimental reaction to what, after all, was an appropriate sentence for her having transgressed Allah's will — at least with respect to the Dirty Bomb.

"Stand up!" Kifat commanded. Ayaan got shakily to her feet. Kifat reached out towards her. Ayaan flinched, although it was clear he had no knife in his hand. Kifat hesitated, then he rested the palm of his hand against Ayaan's belly. She sucked in her breath and flinched again, but the gentleness of his touch surprised her. She drew in a second breath, but it was much shallower than the first. Kifat slowly moved his palm around her mild swelling, pressing down here and there.

Suddenly she knew what he knew—that she was pregnant. In a few weeks, she realized, Kifat would be the father of her child.

"Ah, just as I suspected. You've been keeping another secret from me, haven't you?" Kifat stroked her belly, trying to discern the shape and size of what might lie within. There wasn't much to detect, but it was clear enough. "Your sisters have told me about your sickness. They know what it means. Quite the deceiver, aren't you Ayaan? Where did your parents go wrong? But this time, *Inshallah*, your deception has saved you."

Ayaan collapsed to her knees and flung her arms around Kifat's legs. She pressed her face against his thighs and began to sob.

Kifat allowed her a few moments to indulge herself in this way. Himself too; he took more than some pleasure in seeing her submit to him so abjectly. Then he pushed her to the floor, and left.

♠

Ayaan was subsequently relegated down the ranks of Kifat's ever-expanding harem, and she was pretend-Chief Jihadi Scientist no longer. She was demoted to being a lowly wife number six—the very bottom—of the spousal pecking order, though she was not so much the genuine sacramental article as a thoroughly *expendable* concubine-cum-prostitute—when the time might come. She was a mere temporary incubator for Kifat's future progeny, an inconvenience that he *had* no choice but to tolerate—at least until she came to term.

Kifat largely ignored her now, except to check on her pregnancy every once in a while; and in the harem she was offered no quarter from his other wives, who all ranked above her. They ostracized her, unless there were orders to be given to her; they beat her whenever they judged she'd made some egregious error—which was often, almost every day it seemed, even if her usually innocuous offense was nothing more than the accidental spilling of a cup of milk, or her forgetting to arrange her *abaya* strictly according to their pernickety specifications: a sloppy tuck here, an incorrect fold there, a cowlick of hair inappropriately uncovered.

The only measure of tolerance they afforded her was to protect her pregnancy. Slaps to her head there certainly were plenty, but any sort of assault on her abdomen or groin was avoided with the utmost care. She was also given ample, nourishing food, albeit grudgingly, but only in meals that she consumed alone. Kifat's other wives knew perfectly well on which side of the bread their butter was spread. They, like he, had no concern for Ayaan in the slightest measure, except for the new life she was hopefully carrying. After its birth, all bets placed so far, Ayaan knew, would be off—except for the one that placed its entire stake on her eventual demise, that is.

One night, a couple of weeks after her demotion, Ayaan was alone, as usual, in her sleeping quarters. She was wide awake. It was sometime in the middle of the dark, cold night. All the other women were soundly asleep; through the heavy curtains that enclosed her space, she could hear Fatima snoring like a freight train, and occasionally a mumbled word or two from some of the others, no doubt in troubled dreams of some sort. Even those wives at the top of the hierarchy had plenty to worry about, even if their lives were not in quite the kind of precarious balance hers was.

She felt the movement in her stomach again, but more animated than anything she'd felt before. Then there was another stab of pain, and yet another. She shifted her position, hoping that it might quieten things down a bit, but to no avail. The movements had become truly discomforting lately, disturbingly painful at times. Were there complications with her pregnancy that they didn't know about? From what she could tell from their conversations (she'd acquired a decent amount of rudimentary Arabic by then), no one, including the doctor, had said anything other, she was sure, than that everything looked fine. But the pain from this latest attack was making her double up so much that it was all she could do to not cry out. Then the episode was over; as suddenly as the attack had come on, it just as abruptly dissipated. Ayaan straightened out her body and relaxed back into her bedding, breathing heavily.

Ayaan felt her stomach, began to caress it, moving her hands in wide arcs over the mound that housed her baby. What kind of life would it have? Would it follow in Kifat's footsteps? What kind of life would *she* have after the birth? Would she have one at all? Her belly complained again; she was sure it was a kick. Was her unborn child trying to tell her something? Another kick, like an enraged assailant's—How much more of this could she take? It had to stop. Please God, make it stop!

Ayaan managed to sit up, so that she could look around her. There was little to see in her sparsely furnished space, and she had very few personal possessions. Nonetheless, she scoured the room over and over, as if she knew that whatever it was she was looking for *must* be there, somewhere. She slowly got off her bed, and, bent at her waist again, she hobbled over to her makeshift dresser. For a few moments, she just stared at a long-handled hair brush that lay on top of it. She fingered the handle, taking the measure of its shape and heft. She picked the brush up and took it back to her bed.

She lay back on the cushions again and spread her thighs as far apart as she could. She bent her knees upwards, allowing her to bring her feet up towards her abdomen; her pelvis pivoted slightly in response, making it easier for her to reach down and touch her genitals. The tip of the brush handle was cold, and it made her wince as she pushed it gently in. She held it in place for a few moments, readjusting her grasp slightly so that it was firm. She shifted her feet an inch or so to find any extra purchase that was still available to her. The stabbing recommenced, drowning her in a tidal wave of excruciating pain.

Now, she gasped. *Do it. Now!*

Fatima woke with a start. First, she heard something that sounded like glass breaking; then soft moans blubbering up into an aching, desperate sobbing. It was coming from Ayaan's quarters. She got up. The other women were waking up now, too. Fatima led the way into Ayaan's sleeping space. A shattered mirror lay in several pieces on the floor; a long-handled hair brush lay amidst the shards of broken glass.

"I couldn't...," Ayaan softly blubbered. "I just *couldn't.*"

♠

Against considerable odds, Ayaan eventually bore Kifat three sons.

He had triplets! Holy warriors, one day, for the next generation of jihadis to come, and testimony, Kifat believed, to his divinely-inspired virility. He was convinced that he literally had jihadism in his genes, the only bastardized bit of Darwinism he unwittingly subscribed to, along with, of course, the conviction that Islam's battle with the West was certainly "red in tooth and claw," and that its final outcome would surely be determined by the "survival of the fittest," which, God willing, meant Muslims like himself building a Sunni caliphate in Mesopotamia, and, eventually, far beyond.

For the moment, though, Kifat settled into the role of a distant fatherhood, physically and emotionally, patiently biding his time until they'd been weaned off their mother's milk, and were ready for his schooling. Under Fatima's close supervision, he was content to let Ayaan play out her final jihadi function. And, Ayaan, against all her expectations, gladly picked up her motherly mantle. It was as if she'd been preparing for such a role all her life.

Indeed, by the time her baby boys had reached three months old, Ayaan had completely succumbed to devoted motherhood, the only thing she had now that gave her any reason for living. Even a degree of hope, too, if she could raise them according to her own designs, as opposed to Kifat's—*if only*. But as for escape, what hope lay there? Any? Precious little, even the most rudimentary of analyses quickly concluded for her, and he'd kill her, she didn't doubt, for just making the futile effort. But there was still a jihadi role of sorts that she could and *must* fulfill—submitting to God's will in the struggle for motherhood, the nurturing of new lives, of propagating desperate new hope in an ocean of pitiless tragedy. Could the Miracle Baby perform miracles in turn—for her sons?

As to what happened with the Dirty Bomb, Ayaan never heard any more of it. She was no longer on the "need to know" list. She was ordered to clean up her lab, and prepare it for her successor.

On her last day in her old lab, Ayaan took one last lingering look at her laptop computer. She cleaned the greasy, smeared screen with a cloth, rubbing so exaggeratedly that it seemed as if she was trying to rub right through it, to exorcize the evil spirits, the nightmares, of her long torturous captivity.

Oh, she suddenly sighed, a near sob catching in her throat. *Oh...*

She stared at the blinking cursor through her moistened eyes; its incessant beat, like digital Chinese water torture. She grasped the mouse and maneuvered it: one last time—just to be sure.

Click. Access Denied.

Click. You have no search history.

And no history of anyone searching for me, either, she thought. Her parents, had they even tried? *Surely...*

A flash of bright blue: the screen had gone blank. *No internet connection.* They'd cut her off altogether now—completely severed, once and for all.

Oh...

She gently fingered the magical device in front of her, as if she couldn't quite believe that such a powerful creation was really dead. A metaphorical pull of the plug, that's all it had taken, and the startling power of its bits and bytes, its hyper-connectivity, and its deep-learning algorithms, those very attributes that had enabled Kifat, incredibly, to seduce and to recruit her to jihad, now lay entirely prostrate, offering *no* hope of escape at all! Impossible, but it was true.

Ayaan slammed the laptop lid down. *Useless! Or was it?*

An eye for an eye, a tooth for a tooth...

Jihadism—two could play at that game ... *Inshallah.*

She opened the laptop up again, thinking earnestly now, futility giving way to eternal hope in the guise of the human spirit...

Maybe, just maybe...

...and human ingenuity.

She hadn't been top of her class in chemical engineeering for nothing.

32

[22 April 2016]

Imam Khalifa entered their usual interview room.

He felt like a man on death row — condemned. Not literally to death, but in the sense of being about to engage in something as close to utter futility as you could possibly imagine — even more so than it had been in his most recent interactions with his ever more wayward son. Despite the fact that he, Imam Khalifa, was free and Jamal, a convicted felon and his most troubling referral, was not, he nonetheless felt that in the game they were about to play the deck was stacked very much against him. When Jamal looked up at him as he entered, the kid grinned as if he'd been dealt four aces already.

Imam Khalifa took his usual seat across the table between them, with Jamal's back to the room's only window. But there wasn't much to see, as Khalifa could have told him — just the low grey clouds banking up over the Thames in the distance, shrouding the tall buildings and threatening yet more rain. His chair, as per regulations, was "cushioned" with precisely one and one-eighth centimeters of foam padding, while Jamal's was made of just an unforgiving thin sheet of hard plastic, the intent being, Khalifa knew, to instigate just enough physical discomfort to loosen the Jamal's tongue in his desperation to get the interview over with as quickly as possible. And that meant, he'd warned Jamal on more than one occasion (although not exactly in so many satirical words), that the canary would have to soon start singing, get down off his mighty perch and be a nice, cooperative little birdy, or these cozy "ice cream socials" would soon cease altogether. But whether Jamal viewed his warning more as a sign that he was winning the battle between them or as the threat it was intended to be, he really had no idea. That said, as the sessions with Jamal had gone by, he'd increasingly feared the worst.

Today, though, it was his rear end that was incommodiously situated, not Jamal's. Despite his chair's so-called padding, his latest bout of hemorrhoidal irritation was not only making him squirm in his seat, it was also threatening to shorten his fuse. He cinched his buttocks together with a self-induced contraction of the muscles, as if he was trying to take command of his wayward bodily malfunction. But the attempt brought him only temporary relief; before he had time to draw another breath, the irritation flared up again.

He really must stop by the chemist's on the way home, he thought. It was annoying, to say the least, this problem of his; annoying like everything else seemed to be these days: the exorbitant mortgage payments at the end of every month; the hassle of commuting on crowded tube trains (now that his car had recently broken down) that only seem to run when the unions took time out to be reasonable for once; his kids, those strangers who grew stranger every day, cocky Brits now, almost totally lost to him; his wife, "she who must be obeyed," the incessant nagger-in-chief about matters oh-so-domestically trivial (he'd even dreamt of throttling her at times); and, lately, his thankless job trying to so-call "rehabilitate" the likes of Jamal Shirani. *God, how had it all gotten to this?*

He carefully rearranged himself on his chair one more time, and, finding what he thought to be a comfortable position, he took the plunge and opened up the conversation.

"This is *it*, Jamal," Imam Khalifa began, trying desperately to concentrate on what he wanted to say. "This is our last session together, unless I can show that you—we've—started to make some progress."

Jamal scratched his throat before, contemptuously, making a "sad" face. "No ice cream, today?" he said, mimicking a little-boy voice.

Khalifa looked at the table. The ring stain from before was still there, although much faded. It was smeared; presumably a cleaner had at least made some half-assed attempt to remove it.

"I'm afraid not." He looked up at Jamal, trying to appear authoritative, but he knew he didn't look the part—never had. An imam was not a pope after all; he was at best a mere fallible guide, an uncertain teacher, a self-doubting mentor, or, at least, his sort was. "We're, as they say, down to brass tacks now,

Jamal. Quite possibly at the end of the road for you and me. There are only two ways forward: either you work *with* me, or you go back to court where, I can assure you, a judge will be more than ready to give you the longest sentence he can. Twenty years at least, I should think—and, no, definitely no more ice cream."

Jamal pursed his lips, and then smirked. "Well, maybe that's just as well." He grabbed a small roll of fat just above his waist and jiggled it. "It's playing havoc with my figure, anyway."

"I'm serious, Jamal. Are you ready to...talk to me, or not?"

Jamal thought for a moment. Unexpectedly, he said, "Okay, you've been patient. As patient as an imam! And since you say this is my last chance, I'll do the decent thing and give you yours, too. What can I help you with? What would you *really* like to know?"

Khalifa felt himself tense at Jamal's cockiness, and he almost lost his cool. But he held on, determined not to be goaded into lashing out. He knew he couldn't win in the long run with Jamal, but he hated the idea that his last meeting with him would end in such an unprofessional, demeaning way. He shifted his buttocks again; Jamal looked at him as if he was intrigued by all his squirming commotion, that maybe he thought he'd gotten him on edge, at a distinctly nervous disadvantage. The kid's smirk, if anything, grew wider, enough to irritate Khalifa into trudging on, as opposed to succumbing to capitulation.

"If I ask you where you were really from, Jamal, what would you answer: England, or Pakistan?"

"Hah! That's easy," Jamal quickly declared. "Neither! I am from the *umma*, as you are too—or at least you would be *if* you were a True Believer."

"But what does your passport say?"

"My passport is of no consequence, except to ease my way into and out of this infidel land."

"Well," Khalifa said, "it'll not be easing your way anywhere at all, soon—except to a long stretch in prison. The *umma* may well have to get along without you for a good while."

Jamal looked momentarily stumped, but his customary smirk soon returned to his face. He said, "The *umma* is always the home of True Believers, no matter where they may be—even in prison!"

Khalifa knew what Jamal was saying were true—at least in a broadly spiritual way. But, he also recognized that the theological claim was largely fatuous with respect to most Muslims' everyday material existence where most of them lived most of the time, especially in places like London. He'd done his bit to build a meaningful Muslim community—a mini-*umma*, if you like—in East Ham, but, to the limited sense that it existed at all, it hadn't fared too well against the powerful countervailing allegiances of drug gangs and football supporters' clubs, along with the daily grind of just trying to make it as a Muslim in modern, thoroughly secular, Britain.

Even where one might have expected Muslim solidarity to be the most resonant of all, in the many countries of the Middle East and beyond, the Sunni-Shia split, among many other rather petty divisions, had, he had long believed, made a mockery of the Islamic pretense to "a worldwide community of believers," even when there hadn't been a Christian, a Jew, or a profane Western secularist in sight to have maliciously stirred the pot of sectarian hatred for their own narrow advantage.

"*Think*, Jamal," Imam Khalifa continued. "Consider what you're giving up, what you're throwing away. I know it's not easy as a young Muslim in this country, but it's given you much more than you believe."

Jamal began to lightly drum his fingers on the table. He squirmed in his seat, now, his smirk abruptly giving way to silence.

In the momentary hush, Khalifa realized his voice seemed jaded, his words amounting to little more than routinely parroted aphorisms he no longer really put much stock in. He hated the fact that he felt and sounded so pathetic when so much was at stake.

"England's brought you much more than ice cream," Khalifa nonetheless trotted out, as if either he couldn't help himself or he didn't know what else to do at that point. But his attempt at mild humor fell flat. Jamal's face showed no sign of even the slightest crack. Khalifa changed tack, tapping into what he desperately thought might be a more promising line of attack: "What do your parents do?"

Jamal was puzzled by the question. What did they have to do with anything? He remained silent, wondering where the imam's questioning was headed.

Khalifa took out a folder from his briefcase, and shuffled through the papers it contained. He pulled one out, and read it. "Your father's a foreman in a car factory, right? And your mother, it says here, is a primary school teacher—a good one, it seems."

Jamal shrugged his shoulders. *So what?*

"What did they do in Pakistan, before they immigrated to England?"

The question jilted Jamal's cool, triggering him to involuntarily recall memories of his family's history of upward social mobility ever since they'd left the Swat valley behind back in the early 1950s. His parents had been poor peasants then, bound to virtual enslavement by the quasi-medieval social structure that had managed to survive Pakistan's emergence as a supposed modern nation-state, albeit one also self-described as an Islamic Republic. And his Nanny Laila, his father's mother, was still there, mired in the poverty that her son and daughter-in-law had escaped, despite the remittances they'd occasionally managed to send her over the past few years. *He really ought to have visited her...*

Khalifa thought he could sense that Jamal knew what he was driving at, even though he remained stoically mute. The restless squeaking of Jamal's plastic seat told him all he needed to know. It was time to press whatever advantage he felt he had, home. Maybe this time, his logic might win the day—for once.

"They've done well, haven't they?" Khalifa continued, feeling he had an unusual amount of traction now. "Made a nice home for you, gave you everything you needed, wanted?" Jamal's finger-drumming became louder, staccato almost. "They've worked hard, haven't they? They sacrificed at first, and now they're reaping their just rewards. And they've stayed true to their faith through it all, making *zakat* even in their leanest years. Your father managed to save enough money to do the *hajj* three years ago, didn't he?" Khalifa paused. He was feeling almost triumphant now. "Quite amazing, really, since neither of them had the good fortune to go to university."

Jamal snorted. "Ha!" he exclaimed. He grinned and shook his head. "University? Ha!" He very much wanted to follow up with a diatribe about the evils of Western education, just like his brothers in Boko Haram in northern Nigeria did, but the pain of the memory of his own failure at university abruptly paralyzed his vocal cords.

"You went to university, Jamal, didn't you? Engineering—right?"

Jamal turned his head ninety degrees to his left. His eyes had begun to water.

Khalifa saw a dewdrop of a tear below Jamal's eye, in silhouette against the darkening sky he could see through the window, slowly spill onto the kid's cheek. He knew all about Jamal's failure at university, and for a moment his compassion almost got the better of him. He'd known failure in his own life; humiliation, too. They were gut-wrenching in the worst possible way. *She'd been the one, the only one. Oh Maimoona, why did you...?*

"I'm... I'm very sorry things didn't work out for you, Jamal. But it's not too late. I could help you get another chance. And it wouldn't cost you anything. There'd even be a living allowance for you, a flat—somewhere to call your own; some training—software engineering, whatever you like; and help finding a good job afterwards." *A second chance. Had it been too much to ask?...*

Khalifa was standing up now, leaning across the table, desperately trying to get Jamal to turn his head, to look at him. "What do you say to that, Jamal? The English, in their own way, believe in *zakat*, too. Believe me, they do. But for *all* their citizens, Jamal — regardless of their faith." *Regardless...regardless of everything you meant to me?*

But Jamal kept his eyes averted from Khalifa as much as he could, his chin slowly sinking down onto his upper chest. Every now and again, he grimaced as if he was suffering from indigestion. He started to rock slightly in his seat, making it squeak again — louder and louder.

"We live in a generous, peaceful country, Jamal," Khalifa persisted. "Can't you see that? Your parents and you have been given opportunity here to lead a good life, free of the indignities of poverty and political repression. No, England is no utopia — it's not a Muslim country, for a start. But it is not an apostate country either, not at its core. Do it and its people really deserve the terrible violence you want to inflict upon them? 7/7, what was the point of that?" *What had been the point of it, Maimoona? Rejecting me for him?*

Jamal's rocking continued to pick up momentum. He put his hands over his ears.

"*Salaam*, Jamal, that's how Muslims greet each other every day. It's the first thing we say on meeting, whether it be a friend or a stranger. Peace, peace — isn't that what our faith stands for at its core? Isn't that what Allah wants for us *all?" Why don't you leave me in peace, you'd said... But what had I done?*

Jamal leapt up from his seat and began to pace angrily around the room. He shook off his despondency like a bull tossing a careless matador in its flailing horns. His ashen face flushed crimson, and the onset of a searing rage boiled away his tears in an instant.

Imam Khalifa sat back down in his chair, his hand searching desperately for the panic button under the table.

"*Peace*? You call all this peace?" Jamal spluttered, spittle spraying his face. "This peace you talk about—it's *violence*! For Muslims, it's a violence embedded in discrimination, police brutality...the *humiliations* heaped on us every day." Jamal saw giggling white girls dance before his eyes, pointing at him, at his... He was shaking violently. He reached across the table and grabbed Khalifa by his throat. "*Allahu Akhbar!*" he yelled.

Khalifa fell backwards out of his chair, but not before he'd managed to press the panic button. "Warden!" he screamed. "Help!"

Jamal lunged over the table, but Khalifa managed to scramble away into the far corner of the room. The door burst open and two guards hurried in. They quickly subdued Jamal, although he didn't give up without a brief furious struggle. The guards cuffed him, and held him down on the floor until he calmed down. As Jamal lay there, Khalifa suddenly realized that his tattoo was no longer on his forearm.

"The tattoo," he said, "where is it?"

The guards allowed Jamal to sit up and face Khalifa. As much as his cuffed wrists would allow him, he slowly clawed at the wounded skin with the fingernails of his left hand where the logo *Guns N' Roses* had once adorned the top-hatted skull. Only abrasions, a few drops of dried blood, and the fuzzy remains of the tattoo lay there now.

"With your bare nails?" Khalifa asked, incredulously. "But the pain?"

Jamal grinned, his eyes sparkling with the pleasure of making his proud pronouncement. "Pain? No, it felt *good*!"

Khalifa felt empty, a lost child again in a world he just didn't understand. He nodded at the guards, indicating for them to take Jamal away. It was Pontius Pilate time, he conceded—what else more could he do?

But that did not prevent Jamal from offering up his parting shot. The more the guards grappled with him to drag him off, the more he resisted and raised his voice. It was all the guards could do to restrain him.

"*Peace?*" he screamed, his spittle flying everywhere. "Not at *any* price!"

"Button it, Shirani!" the burlier guard commanded, pushing Jamal's right arm way up his back, as if he was trying to break it. But Jamal paid no heed, and kept on struggling to get free.

"And you know what, imam?" he yelled, the veins purpling in his neck and pulsing like hosepipes threatening to burst. "I *am* somebody! I'm a holy warrior, a jihadi. *Allahu Akhbar! Allahu —* "

Imam Khalifa heard a sickening thud, and Jamal disappeared from view. The two guards and Jamal were in a heap on the floor now, their fight finally ended. Jamal, it appeared, had said his last.

Khalifa was slouched against the wall of the interview room on the other side of the table from mound of entangled bodies, his chair toppled over beside him. He was stunned, unsure of what had just happened, or where he was. He blinked stupidly, as if he'd just regained consciousness after recovering from a trauma. He looked at the toppled chair. He noticed its padded seat was ripped; pieces of foam stuffing lay like newly-fallen snow on the tiled floor.

But at least the burning in his rear end had finally let up.

♠

Imam Khalifa remained slumped in the corner of the interview room for several minutes after Jamal had been dragged off. He'd truly feared for his life when Jamal had lunged at him. Such rage, such ferocity! The kid had seemed manic, out of his mind.

Mental illness of some sort, perhaps—now he thought of it? It must have been in part; Jamal's crazed condition had to be more than just common-or-garden anger or frustration, surely? But, then again, not every mentally ill person behaved like Jamal had—or like Jihadi John had for that matter. And if Jamal was mentally ill, then what could he have done with him, anyway? No chance of rehabilitation under those circumstances, just continued incarceration; per-haps, in a best case scenario, in a high-security hospital rather than a maximum security prison. But, even so, to what effect even *that* outcome—in the end? Nothing more than just a single jihadi warrior temporarily out of commission, but with tens of thousands more of them to go. Sisyphus had an easier time of it.

He sighed deeply, as if it might be his last. He felt like the Dutch boy with his finger in the dike. He looked at the second finger on his right hand; it seemed awfully thin, and water, he well knew, would find a way through if there were only just the slightest chance of doing so.

Radical ideology, then? Was that the primary causal factor? (The idea that it might be *the*ology, he just couldn't subscribe to.) No doubt about it. The jihadis were quite clear about that; all you had to do was read *Inspire*. And he knew that personal and collective grievances fueled, fertilized, and ventilated by any absolutist philosophy of a Manichean, good-versus-evil, kind, and orated by a charismatic leader, had always been a perfect brew for any sort of call for genocidal Holy War, from the Nazis' Final Solution to the Americans' Manifest Destiny to the Greater East Asian Co-Prosperity Sphere of the Japanese Empire.

But he was sure Jamal and thousands like him didn't really fully understand the dogma they spewed—not even many of the originators of such lies did, as he well knew from his research for his doctorate. But if they believed *fanatically*, how could you possibly argue with them, rationally persuade them to think otherwise? Rehabilitation? Candy bars and consolation; computer coding and a job on the software engineering assembly line? More like *dis*-habilitation, a sense of deshabille of the worst alienating kind for the likes of Jamal, he feared.

Or was Jamal's derangement fundamentally biological, perhaps, less mental *illness* that might be subject to treatment than an *innate* condition, an unfixable permanency? Something reptilian, hardwired, buried deep in the brain, always there but needing a perfect storm of some kind to bring it out into the open, a knee-jerk instinctual response on automatic tripwire and beyond conscious moral restraint? Something like the sex drive—much less prone to easy, constant arousal no doubt, but much more explosive when it happened? Or a Nietzschean "will to power," if you like, that drives lost souls to engage in holocaust fantasy, *übermensch* wannabees with access to weapons of mass destruction?

It all seemed so incredible, so unbelievable: such phenomena in the twenty-first century, after millennia of human progress and cognitive evolution? But was such thinking too deterministic, too fatalistic? *That* simple?

So, if it wasn't so much nature, then might it be *nurture* instead? He knew the nature-nurture debate was a sterile one, that nature and nurture enjoyed a dialectical relationship, that they were not root and branch binary opposites. Environmental factors triggered human behaviors in *conjunction* with the genetic instructions that one's genome encoded. They obviously had a significant role to play.

He remembered that one of his psychology professors in graduate school had been keen on a theory that argued that those prone to engage in atrocities, like decapitation and other forms of torture leading to death, were acting out childhood traumas that they had been subjected to, most often by their parents. So, on that score, had Jamal, perhaps, suffered from gross parental abuse early in his life, and was now reacting to it extravagantly, all these years later? He'd certainly refused to either name or talk about his parents; it had been quite obvious that he had no love or respect for them, either. But again, it was clearly *not* the case that every sufferer of child abuse automatically became a potential genocidal maniac later in life. The theory was too simple and reductionist; there had to be more to it.

He thought of Jihadi John again: decapitation, an act so simple and so final, yet so hard to explain. What was Allah playing at?

It was probably a bit of everything, Khalifa finally concluded, but when you mixed all these factors together, created a perfect storm, well, the mixture was explosive, titanic, beyond rational argument, sober reasoning, and human compassion.

He thought about Sayyid Qutb, the founding father of the Muslim Brotherhood, to which he had often felt a strong allegiance. The Brotherhood had taken care of the *umma* in its many times of desperate need. Indeed, he'd tried to replicate, albeit fitfully, many of the Brotherhood's social programs in East Ham. Qutb had been an intelligent being as well as a compassionate one, and he had earned advanced degrees, and had written books as erudite and inspiring as you could possibly have imagined. He'd truly been a man of great peace. But in the end, when Nasser had turned secular push into repressive shove, Qutb had nonetheless advocated jihadi violence, too. Like Jamal, he'd not striven for peace *at any price*. A university education, in and of itself, did not necessarily commit folks to non-violence or prevent them from falling foul of becoming psychotic, pathological killers. Far from it.

What *was* Allah's will? Would he ever truly know?

For most of his life, he'd questioned man's ability to know the mind of God; he presumed that it was sacrilegious to even try to. He believed that the Koran was indeed Allah's literal word, but words were often ambiguous, even more so when combined in phrases and sentences, and not least in inscrutable *surahs* and *ahadith*, so the best that one could do was only to *try* and merely *interpret* them, fallible and contestable in some measure, though, those interpretations would always inevitably be. That's why he'd subscribed to *ijtihad*; that's why there were at least three main competing schools of Islamic jurisprudence with numerous offshoots, belonging to so many sects and branches of the Faith. Islam was for all its much-vaunted monotheism, a veritable Tower of Babel.

Ambiguity and uncertainty were at the heart of Islam, weren't they? Of course they were; but they had routinely led to great discord, the search for a pure and simple *compelling* Truth. And in that struggle, absolute truth, a Manichean black-and-whiteness concerning matters theological, had become literally a life and death contest of great tragedy — and it had resulted in the orgiastic slaughter of innocents that he saw all around him today.

Ijtihad, he now realized, would never be enough for the alienated Jamals of this world — maybe not even for himself anymore. For, if imams were fundamentally uncertain as to the will of God, then how could they light the way for the unwashed pious—how could they reliably *lead*? Why would the faithful follow a blind man, or at least a man with questionable vision? On the other hand, what if the imam who claims to know the mind of God gets it wrong, or renders His Word much too simplistically, wouldn't it be just as dangerous, perhaps catastrophically so, to follow him as well? Perhaps—perhaps, most likely so, but that was *precisely* the kind of clarity that appealed to the likes of Jamal.

Was there no way out of this jam?

Maybe, he thought despondently, it was time to quit. After all, he'd quit on just about everything else that he'd thought had once been important to him: his ambitions, his wife, his kids, his heritage, maybe even his own faith now ...and he was going to quit his job, what he'd once proudly called, his career, his *calling*. Nothing was calling him anymore, except despair.

Except...but it was so long ago. *Maimoona*. She'd really ever been the only one, if truth be told.

But she'd *quit* on him.

He'd thought he'd forgotten about her—until today.

He got up, and looked out the window. Heavy rain clouds were scuttling across the sky towards him. He couldn't see the Thames at all now; in fact, he couldn't see much more than his own fuzzy reflection, cast in shadow and warped by the impurities of the cheap glass.

33
[25 May 2016]

One of the few types of commercial establishment to have been doing a roaring trade in recent months in Rotherham had been the pawn shops.

Perversely though, for Ajmal Patel, owner of "Patel's Pawn Shop," this sector's rapid commercial expansion meant that his inventory was growing at a bit of a worrying pace, given the near-term unlikelihood that anyone who might peruse his mounting stock would be able to afford to buy anything of significant value from it. True, he was getting a fair bit of new stuff at bargain basement prices these days, given the sellers' extra degree of desperation for ready money, but his cash flow was pretty much flowing all in one direction as a result—*out*.

To make matters even worse, he had a growing list of baying creditors to deal with, and, like Ajmal himself, they wouldn't be too shy about demanding what they were due soon enough, even threatening a lawsuit—or perhaps something even physically worse. Gianni "Johnny" Del'Vecchio, in particular, had been known to crack a knuckle or two when folks hadn't toed the line, as Ajmal knew well from previous direct experience with his go-to creditor of last resort. The small scar on his left forearm was a daily reminder that he needed to pay close attention to his "hobleegay-*shuns*," as Johnny liked to forcefully put it in his best Italian-accented English. Mercy in Ajmal's dog-eat-dog business world pretty much only resided with Allah, and Allah, unfortunately, tended to stay above the fray in these kinds of mundane monetary matters. And even when Allah, via the sayings of the Prophet Muhammad, had deigned to dip his toe into matters commercial, he more often than not had left Ajmal totally bewildered.

    Quite how Muhammad had squared the circle of staying in business and making a profit, while also not charging interest and not listing items for sale above something mysteriously called a "just price," and then, to top it all, to give a good ten percent of whatever was left to charity, Ajmal had no earthly idea. He'd tried in his early years as a businessman, when he'd still had some idealism left in him, to follow scripture in these matters, but it hadn't lasted long. He'd soon discovered that if he wanted to stay in business, his piety, or what was left of it, would have to take a back seat from time to time—well, perhaps just about *all* of the time, if truth be told. Economic necessity decreed that he'd have to honor Islam rather more in the breach when it came to earning a living.

In the end, he'd consoled himself with the thought that even Allah must have *surely* known there were only "certain" ways—sinful though they theoretically might be—to make a decent go of it in post-Thatcherite Britain, and that in this sense his own "sin" *really* had lain with others, non-believers of a so-called Christian and Jewish sort, who ruled the system in which he had no choice but to struggle *as best he could*—Inshallah. And *they* certainly hadn't let religious sanction bother them too much when it had come to running a business, so why should—or, rather, how *could*—he be expected to? Thereby, Ajmal had claimed exculpation from the unforgiving demands that living in *dar al-Garb*, the House of the West, had necessarily imposed upon him, and he had hoped that Allah might buy his argument about it all when Judgment Day finally came. And in the meanwhile, there were mouths to feed and bills to pay and the need to build a nest egg for his retirement—if he ever lived long enough to see it, that is.

Ajmal looked at the pile of invoices on his desk, demanding payment forthwith on pain of prosecution. *Inshallah*, he said to himself counting yesterday's takings one more time.

"…ninety-ni—"

The shop's doorbell clanged complainingly, disturbed by the impatient entrance of two male Pakistani youths in hoodies. He quickly stuffed the banknotes he'd been counting in the till, and locked it. He tensed, ready to push the alarm button under the shop's counter if need be. The two young men ambled slowly around the shop. They picked up an item or two and briefly inspected them. Ajmal could easily tell they were not interested in buying anything.

Ajmal wondered if his wife were back from the supermarket yet, whether she'd hear him if he had to call to her for help. The youth by the door coughed. It was forced, falsely modulated—a signal to his friend? He was just about to ask what they wanted, when the other, more confident-looking one, stepped towards him, retrieved something from his pocket, and put it on the counter in front of him. It was an iPhone; brand new, it looked like. Ajmal knew right away: it had been nicked—it was "hot."

"How much you give me for it?" Mo asked, nonchalantly, as if he engaged in transactions like this as a matter of course, as if there should be no question that he was the lawful owner of the device.

Saeed turned from his lookout post at the door, anxious that the deal should go down quickly, without any hitches. He turned back to look out onto the street again, bladder-irritated with nervousness, and just as he did so a passerby looked at him full in the face for a second or two, as if he thought he knew Saeed. Saeed looked away and pulled his hoodie tighter around his face. He heard Ajmal stammer his reply.

"Um, well, let's..." Ajmal dropped the phone just as soon as he had picked it up. He searched for the alarm button under the counter, wondering whether he ought to stop this show before it got any further, but for some reason he couldn't locate the damned thing.

"Whoa!" Mo admonished. "Be bloody careful. Know how much this cost me?"

"Sorry. Um, a fair bit, I suppose...but this looks brand new, and I'm not familiar with the model. Do you... I mean, perhaps you have a receipt or some-thing?" He searched for the button again. *Where the hell was it?*

"Look, I haven't got all fucking day. Want this or not?" Mo demanded.

"Okay, okay," Ajmal said. "I'll, er... I'll just go back into the house to see if my wife can come and watch the shop while I look up a list price—"

"I said we're in a hurry. You got cloth ears or something?" Mo suddenly realized that he was sweating like a pig, and smelling just about as bad.

Over at the door Saeed was fidgeting more than ever, not knowing whether to follow along with the exchange between Mo and Ajmal, or whether to concentrate all his powers on keeping lookout and controlling his bladder. He *desperately* needed to go pee.

"Okay, okay, alright—no problem," Ajmal said. He needed to calm this kid down. He did a quick calculation in his head. "Two hundred...No, let's see... like to think I'm a fair man. Two-twenty-five do it? You won't do better than that, trust me."

Mo knew the old bastard was screwing him, but Saeed's fidgeting told him that it was already way past time to go. He gritted his teeth, for a split second thought about cussing the old man out, before thinking better of it and settling for a final, if nonetheless exasperated, "Done!"

Ajmal open his cash drawer and grabbed a wad of banknotes. He quickly counted out the money, too fast for Mo to keep up.

"Mo!" Saeed suddenly said. "Come on, let's go!"

As Mo grabbed the banknotes and turned to go, a couple of them fell out of the pile and wafted gently to the floor behind the counter where Ajmal was standing. Ajmal had seen them drop, but Mo had not. As the bills hit the floor, Ajmal quietly placed his foot over them.

Mo dashed out of the shop in pursuit of Saeed. Thankfully, the street was deserted: folks at work, in school, or back home already after their morning's errands. A couple of hundred yards down the street, Saeed, leading the way, dashed into a narrow alleyway, crashing through the row of rubbish bins lined up there and waiting for collection. Mo had no choice but to follow. Just ten yards down the alley, Saeed abruptly came to a halt and stood facing a wall, his legs apart. He was groaning and panting at the same time.

"Aaah…ohhh…"

Mo heard the tell-tale sound of a jet of urine splashing against the brickwork. A rivulet of steaming yellow piss appeared between Saeed's feet, snaking its way over the cobblestones.

Mo went back to the alleyway's entrance and peeked around the corner, looking in the direction of Patel's Pawn Shop. Nothing: no people, no sirens, no cops.

"Shit," Saeed said, "glad that's over. Think the old fuck cottoned on?"

Mo glared at him. "Are you fucking kidding me? The way we ran out of there?" Saeed looked crestfallen. "Ah, don't look so worried," Mo continued, "he ain't going to say nuthin'. How much stuff do you think he's got in there that's nicked? Tons of it. Nah, he'll keep his fucking mouth shut. The profit he's gonna' make on that iPhone means too much to him. Besides, more than likely he's paying off the cops anyway to turn a blind eye to what he's up to. Why do you think I took the phone to *him* in the first place?"

Saeed grinned stupidly. "Oh, yeah. 'Course."

"Come on," Mo said, "let's get the fuck out of here." As they turned to go, Mo whacked Saeed on the back of his head.

"Ouch! What the fuck was that for?"

"For using my name, you dufus."

"Sorry, I just didn't—"

"*Think*. Yeah, I know."

Back in his shop, Ajmal Patel waited a good minute after Mo and Saeed had fled his premises before moving. Assuming they'd definitely gone, he retrieved the banknotes that he'd hidden under his foot. *Forty pounds.* He put them in his pocket, a little extra off the books—not that it mattered all that much anyway, since he cooked them as a matter of course. He walked over to the shop door and silenced the still ringing bell with his hand. He gingerly looked out into the street. Deserted. He went back inside the shop, closing and locking the door behind him. He pulled the window blinds down and flipped the Open/Closed sign to "Closed."

He needed time to think.

34

[The Void, **Christian Holiday Season***, Alpha-Omega 6]*

Is there anybody down there? Are you listening?
  It's Christmas; let's sing! (You know the words, I'm sure!)

It Came Upon A Midnight Clear

*"Peace on Earth, goodwill to men,
From Heaven's all-gracious King."*

♠

It had been almost fifteen years since the Big One—9/11.
  Well, the Big One for Americans in any case. They like to believe they know all about what "big" is, especially the Texans. But Big Ones—*really* big motherfuckers—of various descriptions and causes are all just a normal part of the cosmic terrain for me.

Big's my middle name. Just wait until I decide to have the final Big Doozy of them all!

Still, politically, what had happened was of enormous significance for the young, American president, elected a few years later with just about no experience in foreign or national security affairs at all. Yet, despite all the carping of Darth Vader, the former vice-president, about the neophyte president's lack of national security *cojones*, he'd been the one to finally authorize the successful mission to take out Osama bin Laden, the spiritual leader of the nineteen assassins who had taken down the Twin Towers, seriously damaged the Pentagon, and had come close to slamming a fourth plane into the Capitol or the White House on that fateful day. And, despite all the odds, Dick baby, he had somehow kept the nation safe from another such devastating attack, or worse—at least, thus far.

True, the threat of a second 9/11-type disaster hadn't entirely gone away—far from it, as his top intelligence advisors had kept warning him. There had been the Boston marathon bombing, plus the rise of Islamic State, and any number of publicly-known and unknown lone wolves within the lower forty-eight who had (fortunately, I guess) been apprehended before their terroristic plotting could have done any serious damage.

But most Americans had felt safe enough in a weird limbo-like sort of way, despite all this turmoil. It was the kind of "security" they'd come to know during the Cold War, when a nuclear holocaust had surely been a distinct possibility. (There had been so many close calls then, I'd almost felt obliged, sometimes, to step in before the whole planet had gone up in smoke. But I always managed to stay my hand in the end.) Americans had actually lived their lives in those troubled times as if the prospect of nuclear Armageddon had been little more than one residing only in Dr. Strangelove's paranoia-induced fertile imagination, something possible in a satirical movie, perhaps, but surely not in real life? Well, all I can say is that I wouldn't have bet on it. Not sure I can always see the difference between a Strangelove and Joe Sixpack most of the time—can you?

In any case, when "12/25," as it came to be known, happened in 2016, so-called Christian Time, few in America were really ready for it.

In the fall of that year the number of lone wolf terrorists had kept increasing. It was interesting to see, I'll admit, this, somewhat perhaps, unexpected development. Evolution never ceases to amaze me—I mean, I like surprises as much as any deity, and I'm a bit of a Trickster myself, if I may say so, but some of the stuff that natural selection throws up, like your brains...well, I just have to scratch my head in disbelief. It seems as if just at the point a particular species comes to dominate an ecosystem (nation-states with standing armies in the millions and lots of WMD, for instance), a new minnow of a species—like the lone wolf, in this case, with just an assault rifle or a homemade bomb and a helluvan attitude—pops onto the scene like a pernicious deus ex machina and disrupts everything, turning the world completely upside down.

And then, evolution being what it is (shit—you can't make this stuff up!), suddenly groups of these new guys started to coalesce into marauding gangs, seemingly randomly and unpredictably at first, bootstrapping themselves into existence like some emergent property from the myriad chatrooms on the Internet, and they'd soon become far too numerous and scattered for the intelligence services to be able to effectively keep tabs on them all. These so-called "packs" of lone wolves didn't slip under the radar so much as overwhelm it, stretching the resources of the intelligence agencies, law enforcement and Homeland Security so thin that murderous rampages somewhere in the United States began taking place almost on a monthly basis.

In late August, the Golden Gate was shut down for months after a sizeable hole had been blown in a center section of the bridge; by mid-September, it had been no longer safe to ride Amtrak between Washington D. C. and New York City, derailments due to various forms of sabotage occurring just about every week; and, in October and November, the NFL season had been temporarily suspended after stadia in St. Louis and Kansas City had thousands of seats blown up shortly before hordes of excited fans were about to arrive.

But it was Christmas Day that delivered the coup de grâce, the mother of all Christmas gifts from those bent on bringing imperial America and its imperious federal government to their collective knees. The "enemy of my enemy being my friend" guiding the formation of the unholiest of unholy alliances (you've gotta believe me, though, I disown them *all*—I've given up having favorites, "chosen ones," any more), a group of home-grown jihadis

306

(American-born Caucasian converts as well as Muslim-born immigrants) joined forces with a confederacy of long-established so-called "Patriot" militias of a libertarian, anti-federal government bent.

Together, they were determined to trigger Armageddon, the slaying of the Beast that oppressed them all, expropriated their fundamental freedoms whether religious or civil, or just plain gun-toting American. They called themselves the "Holy Alliance of Faithful Patriots" and they gave you all a Christmas like I'll never forget. American intelligence sources claimed that the mastermind behind this novel, hybrid alliance was a certain Samir Diyala, a sometime jihadi bomb-builder, and IS in Raqqa quickly tweeted that that was indeed the case (al-though, I can assure you, Samir was more talk than real action for the most part, and, as you'll soon see, his fame didn't last a whole lot more than a Warhol-ian fifteen minutes, in the end).

What this ragtag, gaggle of jihadis served up was another 9/11-style attack from the skies, but this time not with hijacked civilian airliners. Rather, in keeping with the times, it was launched with a squadron of ten drones purchased in the mother of all globalized marketplaces, as laissez-faire as a libertarian's fantasy could aspire to: the dark, satanic, global arms market where just about any weapon of choice could be had for the right price—and, of course, there always *is* one: the equilibrium point, as the economists still insist on saying, where unlimited, cornucopian supply meets voracious, determined demand. Or, to put it in my terms: where faith in me is really nothing more than faith in yourselves; where my word is supposedly yours. *Made in my image?* I don't think so; I'm just a Trojan Horse with your own narcissistic portrait poorly hidden inside me. Anyway—whatever: back to the Christmas story.

The drones were small enough to escape radar detection, but big enough to carry missiles (newly-invented miniaturized kinetic devices), and they swooped down while you all were celebrating the birth of your Lord and Savior. At the moment when you might have been pondering momentarily on the sins you'd committed for which He, my supposed son, had died, the drones released their ordnance to devastating effect. The Capitol dome, newly refurbished at great taxpayer expense, was punctured by ten massive explosions. It collapsed like some giant punctured balloon. Into the rotunda below, shattered into a million pieces, Brumidi's deified Washington (by the way, he looked *nothing* like me, thank God), flanked by Liberty and Victory, lay prostrate and destroyed. Your self-proclaimed American exceptionalism had been hoisted by its own—less-than-exceptional-now—petard. Six guards joined the first president and his nubile female friends: they were killed instantly. Few in number perhaps, but each lost life shouldered a symbolism that broke the hearts of over three hundred million bereaved souls, from sea to shining sea. (For the record, it brought no pleasure to me, either.)

The response to the attack was, as I fully expected, apoplectic beyond measure. The prideful beast had been badly wounded and it bayed for all-out revenge, claiming, without divine sanction I might add, that it was doing so on my behalf, too. A fervid yellow fever took over the land: ribbons—canary, golden, lemon, cyber—were festooned on every tree and lamppost, flapping in the wind, symbolically shaking with rage. The president—willingly now, regardless of the complexities and ethical nuances of the global war on terror he'd fretted about just a few months before—took up the cudgel that his compatriots demanded he do so forthwith.

It was total war, and the nation was mobilized like it hadn't been since 1941 when that first "day of infamy" had visited it. The lame duck president in a time of great national emergency quickly became a lame duck no more, but morphed miraculously into a ravenous bald eagle. Predictably, the intellectually incestuous "inside-the-beltwayers" and the faltering "liberal establishment" wailed against executive overreach and the president's serial abuse of their constitutional rights and privileges, but the coalition soon fell apart, fearing for the safety of their own asses and shouted down by The Donald and his Stormtroopers, of which there were now many tens of millions. Saw it all coming, of course, a trillion miles away; anyone from my vantage point could have.

Here are some of the worst details.

The Patriot Act was resuscitated, renewed, and strengthened. Government surveillance was raised to levels never seen before, enough to make even Edward Snowden's revelations look like little more than schoolyard tittle-tattle. At first hundreds, then thousands were rounded up on the slightest of suspicions concerning their supposed "un-American activities" and were held over indefinitely, habeas corpus be damned, à la Abraham Lincoln. Guantanamo Bay became a small city, very much open for business again. Rand Paul, this time, said nothing (thank God), and libertarians of all stripes ditched principle like it was a deathly contagion, eagerly joining the great trans-ideological chorus screaming for the government to *do something* to save their sorry asses. Freedom, they finally realized (how come it took so long?), needed the very Leviathan they had for so long so virulently hated. And if freedom for them— *you'll love this*—meant none for others, then so be it. Come to think of it, they soon concluded, if just saving their asses meant none or very little liberty for *everyone*, then bring that on too! On 12/25, Ayn Rand was proved to be the false prophetess she'd always really been, a simpleton like all the other dummies practicing whatever form of jihad they happened to subscribe to. Makes you wanna weep, but I'm rarely the crying kind...well, until now perhaps.

In the end, al-Adrum had merely been a beginning point, a first stumbling half-measure, of what now transpired, and many wondered just what winning this new *total* war on terror might ultimately entail, not least the jihadis who felt America's wrath like they'd never felt it before. One hour after the multi-pronged—both domestic and international— counterattack had been launched, the president spoke live from the Oval Office telling you all that the *last* showdown with terrorists of all stripes was now underway. It was going to be a long destructive fight, he somberly warned, "but we will prevail, God willing." (If he'd been listening, he'd have known I wasn't.) He neglected to mention Armageddon or the

End of Days directly, but the subtext was clear—everyone soon got the picture.

The next morning the president went to the National Cathedral for a special "War against Terror" service. The bishop sanctified the president's actions on my behalf, for he *knew* that I was surely on *their* side. Indeed, CNN that morning had already salivated incessantly over the "great news" that the 12/25 Mastermind, Samir Diyala, had been killed at almost the same time as the drone attack on the Capitol the day before. It astonished Wolf Blitzer that Diyala had apparently blown himself up in his lab in Raqqa—a booby trap, his panel of experts speculated to no end (correctly this time, in fact—it really wasn't fake news, *contra* The Donald). Was this a sign, Wolf gushed, that at the moment of its latest triumph IS was indeed coming apart at the seams? Were there rival factions within the Caliphate, struggling for power? Would the world ever know who had planted the device that had killed the notorious bomb-builder? Who could the brave, heroic savior possibly be? (He never conceived that the he might well turn out to be a she.)

Encouraged and gratified by this welcome news, the congregation at the National Cathedral somberly, if nonetheless lustily, sang "Onward Christian Soldiers," perfectly comfortable in the assumption that theirs was a Holy War—*the* only one—fully deserving of a rousing, spiritualized call to arms. The president closed his eyes and mumbled along with the bishop at the final benediction. He needed the holy man's imprimatur (he erroneously assumed) and he was mightily grateful for it, but his sanction had never really been in doubt. Separation of church and state there may well have been somewhere in the Constitution, but when the state asked, especially at a time of great national need, the church dutifully followed along—it always had; faith and patriotism had always gone together like a horse and carriage (it doesn't take a whole lot of omniscience to see that, does it?). Church and state are, at times like that, one and the same, *e pluribus unum* for real—for once.

But as the president rode back to the White House in his armored car he said another prayer, beseeching me to show him the way, and then remembered what his old preacher back in Chicago had once yelled to his African-American congregants: "Not God bless America, but God *damn* America!" (Indeed, the old black preacher boy was right; I'll admit, I've often felt that way, myself.) And on every continent, the reverend's blasphemy was taken up as a rallying cry for war—the last war, at the end of which God, or Allah (or whatever my real name was supposed to be), would choose his chosen people at last and whisk them off to Paradise, safe and sound and having the time of their post-material lives (sorry, no virgins for you—just a handful of raisins, like the original text said, before succumbing to egregious mistranslation). Anyway, at least *everyone* could agree on all that. Perhaps Holy War, jihad, was not just for dummies after all—or perhaps it was for *all* of you, without discrimination, bookoos of book learning or not, notwithstanding. Yeah, that sounds more like it.

But, you might wonder, could the dummies be stopped before it was all too late?

♠

Come on, let's try! One more time!

> *"O hush the noise, ye men of strife,*
> *And hear the angels sing."*

35
[November 2015]

Nurse Sally Carter had been warned it might happen, but that if she knew what was good for her she'd do well to check her emotions at the hospital door—*every* time, without fail. *Just do the job, Sally,* she'd been admonished. *That way, no one gets hurt any more than they need to. There's more than enough hurt to go around already.*

And for six months, she toed the line. She surprised herself with the mettle of her newly-discovered stoicism in the presence of the horror she came face to face with every day. But mettle was more like metal than she had supposed...

...it corroded and weakened with time, too...
...

He'd been stretchered in just like all the others, a groaning mass of bloody pulp, his odds of pulling through—even wanting to—looking pretty goddamn awful.

The thing was, though, he was one of theirs—a jihadi. Fucking IS.

They'd had no choice but to place him amongst all the others, their guys, including the "coalition of the so-called willing." Neither place, nor time for any thought of segregation or quarantine right then. But it irked her, stuck in her craw. He was right there, along with her boys, crying for comfort, *their* medicine, *her* attention. He'd obviously been in the firefight with them, a wretched casualty now, too. Had it been him who'd gotten the mangled marine next to him? This— she checked the American's dog tags—this *Brown, John B.*? This beautiful American boy, this Christian (*Presbyterian, AB Negative*) warrior?

The jihadi had coughed, choking on his own blood.

She'd looked at the scalpel where the surgeon had left it before he'd had to rush off to attend to another in acute cardiac arrest. The blade was so sharp it took no pressure to slice through tissue like a hot knife through butter. A skilled surgeon made it look so easy, so clinically precise.

A crude jihadi made it look easy, too, she'd thought, like those ski-masked Jihadi Johns butchering apostates in the desert. A calm proclamation; the straightforwardness of obeying God's will; the logical, one-and-only, conclusion. Quickly, the deed is done, like it's routine, "standard operating procedure," paragraph 19(c) of the sharia version of the laws of war.

Perhaps she could have, too. It would have only taken a moment, and she'd been alone right then.

But the jihadi had coughed again; he'd clearly been going down fast.

"Doctor!" she'd yelled. "He's…"

She'd never forget the look on his face, the look of a dying young man, a universal soldier of sorts in that way.

Her job had been, first, to do no harm…

…

He knew was dying. He could feel it in his bones. The hushed and huddled conversations just out of earshot; the worried frowns struggling to transition even into fake half smiles anymore; Nurse Sally's just sitting there by his bed, long after he knew her shift must have ended, fidgeting and twitching as if she was expecting something to shock her at any second. The fact that she'd stopped talking about when he'd go home, back to New Haven.

When the end came, it felt like he was sinking into a warm bath. They must have shot him up real good; he almost felt happy. Except for one thing: the kid and the nodding donkey. He just couldn't get them out of his mind, the way he'd snatched it like that, and run off; the way he'd disappeared so suddenly—all of it just unsettled him, although he couldn't quite figure out why. Perhaps, he now realized in the clarity that they say sometimes accompanies one's death, it was not so much the kid per se but what he symbolized: the tragic choice he'd made to join the War on Terror, and, in its hubris, the price one had to pay for one's sins, among other things the unblinking buy-in to American Exceptionalism, *his* supposed exceptionalism: New Haven's star quarterback and his status as an all-around, all-American boy. A regular Billy Bud, warts and all.

Apropos of nothing, he'd suddenly thought, why had he made the toy donkey so goddamn goofy-looking? What had been the point of that?

Then his head had just slumped onto his chest, like a flower's half snapped off in the wind, and now just hanging there, lifeless.

His last physical movement roused Sally Carter from her semi-slumber. She'd gasped, but the emotion of the moment had caught in her throat, making her cough. Her eyes had watered, but she'd refused to cry.

Her American boy was dead, but the jihadi had survived. And she, in one way or another, had had a hand in both of those outcomes. She wondered about the justice in all that. She wondered what the folks in New Haven, Nebraska, would say when they heard the news...

36

[Christmas Day, 2016]

My reckoning says it's Christmas Day, but of course I can't be absolutely sure. Nothing around here, not a goddamn thing, that would indicate such. Same old cereal (quite stale now) for breakfast, and I haven't been fed since. In fact, no one's been down here today since this morning. I wonder where they all are? Surely, they're not celebrating Christmas, are they?

In a way, I hate it sometimes when they don't come down. If I'm not careful, being alone with my thoughts is almost just too much to bear. So today, I decided to read some more of what was already written in this old exercise book that I've been writing in. Don't know why I haven't read much of it before—looked like it was just some kid's schoolwork, I suppose. Turns out, though, that I couldn't have been more wrong. Well, it is schoolwork, boring history I thought at first, but then I soon realized after reading a page or two, that if this was history, it was far from being boring. I've never given much thought about "history repeating itself," as old Crusty Crutchfield used to say at school ad nauseam, "the first time as tragedy," I think it went next, then "the second time as..." What was the second time? I've forgotten. What on earth could be worse than tragedy, anyway? Whatever, though, I realize now that I'm living proof that history, in fact, does repeat itself—sometimes right under your nose! And more's the fucking pity for it, is all I can say.

Apparently, this notebook belongs to a kid called Charlie Buttershaw, a pupil at Rotherham Academy. Before today, I hadn't found too much at all to interest me. Just a few scribbled pages of notes about a bunch of so-called Puritans, who were, as best as I can tell—the story's a bit hard to follow at times—religious weirdos who decided to sail off to America to find new lands where they might be free to practice their cult. They set off in a ship called the "Mayflower"—I've heard of that, I think—in 16-something. The last two numbers of the year are smudged. All so very fucking uninteresting, I thought, until I came across these precious snippets. They look like they might be passages transcribed from a history book or something. They're clearly not the kid's own writing. I've written them out again so that they're a bit clearer. Charlie has crap handwriting—probably as a result of too much texting! The dots are where Charlie's writing is either smudged or indecipherable, or where the page is torn. Here's the first excerpt that started to grab my attention.

> In May 163[?]...the Puritan forces...deep into the Pequot territory to surprise a palisaded villa[ge]...Mystic River...four hundred...women, children, and ol[d] ... ... surrounded the sleeping village and set it ablaze. The Pequo[t] died either in the flames or in flight from the inferno as they...into...gunfir[e]... ... and swords... Captain Mason exult[??] "God was above them, who laughed his Enemies and the

> Enemi[es] of his People to scorn, making them as a fiery Oven..."

Then there's a there's a big missing piece of the page, before this:

> "Sometimes the Scripture declareth...women and children must perish...We had sufficien[t] light from the Word of God for our proceedings."

> ...[W?]illiam Bradford recalled: "It was a fearful...them thus frying in the fire and the...blood quenching the same... ... ... but the victory seemed a sweet sacrifice and... ...praise thereof to God, who had wrought so wonderfully for them..."

Finally, to top it all, there was this:

> ...as a warning, the Puritans stuck the severed head of a sachem, a paramount chief, on a pike on top of the fort at Plymouth Plantation.
>
> THEY GOT WHAT THEY DESERVED! THEY WERE HEATHENS!

This last bit in capital letters, I reckon, must be Charlie's two cents' worth.

Well, I obviously don't know the whole story about these Puritans and the Pequot, but it makes me think. Sounds like Holy War, doesn't it? A Christian version—I'm pretty sure the Puritans were Christian: they say "God" and "Scripture" a lot, and I haven't quite forgotten everything I learned in school, despite Crusty putting to sleep more often than not.

A seventeenth-century Christian Jihad! Not the first, and most likely not the last of that sort. "What goes around, comes around," just like old Crusty had said. History repeating itself—like a goddamned steamroller. And as I thought about it all, I suddenly remembered what Hitler had said: "By fighting against the Jews I am doing the Lord's work." Well, maybe he was no real Christian, but then I recalled that pudgy-faced American televangelist, Jerry Falwell, going on about how the American president, as a Minister of God, was a "revenger"—I think that's right—executing war upon those who do Evil, and that, therefore, he had a right to use the full force of the military to bring wrath upon them. And who could be more evil than the terrorists, especially non-Christian ones? Jeez, "He that is without sin, let him cast the first stone!"

Is that what this is all about, with me down here—payback for the Pequot, and all the other Christian massacres that litter the pages of history? A kidnapping in Rotherham of someone like me is part and parcel of the world's religious wars going back hundreds of years? Bit of stretch, do you think? Too farcical? Well, maybe not. And all because you didn't show up, or I left too early—being in the wrong fucking place at the wrong fucking time?

What did *I* do to deserve it?

Who is this god that they all say wants all of this? No god that I would want to know.

...

Farcical? Of course, the second time's as "farce"! I guess it makes sense when you think about it like that. What else could all this shit be?

37

[25 May 2016]

"Whooo!" Mo yelled as he Fosbury-flopped onto his bed. He and Saeed had just gotten back from their visit to Patel's Pawn Shop.

"Hey, Mo, what a blast, uh?" Saeed joined in. "We did it! We got away with it, just like you said we would. Got one over on old man Green and have over two hundred smackers to show for it, too! Two fucking hundred quid! What are you gonna do with it, Mo?"

Mo considered Saeed's delicious question for a few moments. He'd never had anything like £225 before, and he felt a little overwhelmed by trying to imagine all the tempting possibilities.

"Calm down, Saeed," Mo counseled, like he was some sort of wise owl fully in control of his emotions all of a sudden. "We've got to be careful about all this—take our time. Anyone seeing us getting flush all of a sudden, we'll get nicked for sure." Mo retrieved Patel's payoff from his pocket and threw it on top of his bed. "Let's see, what can we get away with spending at any given time without attracting attention?" He picked up the cash and began counting it. Saeed joined in the count, softly echoing Mo's *twenty, forty, sixty...* But at *one hundred and eighty-five*, they both stopped. Mo laid the last bill he had on top of the pile on his bed, then he stared blankly at his empty hand.

"What's up?" Saeed asked, looking around the room as if he expected to find more money there somewhere. Mo half-followed Saeed's searching, all the while frantically rifling through his pockets. A worried and then an angered look took over his face.

"The bastard," Mo spat out. "The fucking cheating bastard!"

"What?" Saeed asked. "What?"

"That old fucker has ripped us off, that's what! We're forty fucking quid short!"

"Are you sure?" Saeed said, still scouring the room. He got down on his hands and knees and looked under the bed. "Shit!" he continued, realizing that Mo was telling the truth. The boys looked at each other, stupefied.

"One eighty-five?" Saeed said disappointedly. Then his eyes brightened: "But that's still a pretty decent haul. We can still do a lot with that, can't we? Can't we, Mo?"

"Well..." Mo began to concede, sorely tempted by the promise £185 could bring to his materially-deprived existence. But lure of the ill-gotten gain was struggling to overcome the surge of roiling resentment he was also feeling from having been so easily duped by Patel—an old fucking Shylock of an Indian, no less!

"Yeah, we could get—" Saeed interjected.

"No!" Mo exploded. "No, we're not spending any of this money until we get our full fucking due!" Mo grabbed the stack of banknotes from his bed and hurriedly stuffed them into his pocket. "Come on!" he hissed. "Let's go."

"Where?" Saeed asked, perplexed.

"To get *our* pound of flesh—for once!"

♠

Within twenty minutes they were back at Patel's Pawn Shop.

Mo burst through the shop's door, making the bell clang furiously again. There was a white middle-aged male customer in the shop; he was conversing with Ajmal, who was in his usual place behind the counter. Startled, they both looked up. On seeing Mo, the Caucasian quickly assessed that caution was the better part of valor and left the premises post-haste, grabbing whatever it was that he had come to pawn, and without bothering to say goodbye to the pawn-broker.

"What...what do you want?" Ajmal said. He took a step back from the counter and inadvertently backed into the shelves behind him, dislodging some ceramic pieces. One of them—a cheap Chinese knock-off of the Virgin and Child—crashed to the floor, shattering into a half-dozen pieces.

Mo slowly approached the counter, staring straight at Ajmal. He retrieved the money from his pocket, raised his hand high above him, and then slammed it onto the counter. *Thwack!* Mo reached across and grabbed Ajmal by his shirt front, popping the top two buttons. "Where's the rest of my fucking money?"

"I don't know what you're talking about!" Ajmal tried to free himself from Mo's viselike grip, but the more he struggled the tighter Mo held on, pinching the skin and the wiry hairs on Ajmal's exposed upper chest. "Ouch! You're hurting me!"

"I'll *really* fucking hurt you, you old bastard, if you don't cough up the rest of what you owe me, plus another thirty...no, fifty, for all the *inconvenience* you've caused." Mo pulled his free right hand back and made a fist. He let it fly forward as if he was going to punch Ajmal smack in the face.

"Don't hit me! Please, don't hit me!" Ajmal screamed, cowering. Mo's fist came to a halt just an inch from Ajmal's nose. "All right, all right!"

Mo smirked at the shopkeeper. "That's more like it," he said. Then he popped Ajmal one on his forehead for good measure.

"How...how much do you want?" Ajmal asked, palpably afraid now, his left eye twitching furiously, as if Mo had really socked him one right there.

"It's not what *I* want, it's what *you* fucking owe me," Mo replied. "All things considered, and because I like nice round numbers, let's make it one hundred even, shall we?" Mo released Ajmal from his grip, giving the storekeeper a final shove in the chest as he did so. Ajmal fell back into the shelves again, dispatching a second "fine" piece of Oriental statuary—this time a Joseph and a Mary, ass-mounted and very pregnant, on their way to Bethlehem—to join its companion piece in shattered demise on the shop floor.

Ajmal stepped towards the till to get the money. As he opened his cash drawer, he surreptitiously reached with his free hand under the counter and pressed the alarm button. He found it right away this time—no trouble at all. But he'd been practicing in anticipation that Mo and Saeed might well return.

Ajmal took some banknotes out of the till. He peeled off the top bill and held it out; Mo opened his right hand on cue, palm side up. Ajmal began to count: "Twenty, forty, sixty, seventy, eighty, eighty-fi...no, sorry, my mistake." He took the notes back in order to start again, playing for precious time. "Okay," he began again. "Eighty-five, ninety-five, one hund—"

"Mo!" Saeed yelled. "It's the fucking cops!"

Mo grabbed the money and spun around. "Go!" he yelled. He opened the shop door and pushed Saeed through it in one continuous motion. He heard the siren first, and then far down the street he caught the first merest glimpse of the tell-tale blue flashing lights of a fast approaching police car. Mo and Saeed began to run, faster than they ever had.

"Down here!" Mo commanded, after they'd covered some fifty yards or so. He pointed to an alleyway leading off the street.

Saeed did as he was told. Mo stopped at the entrance to the alley, but kept stomping his feet as loud as he could in order to convince Saeed that he was still running right behind him. Saeed soon disappeared around a corner, ignorant of what Mo was up to. By now the police car was almost upon Mo. He looked at the vehicle as if he didn't think much of all its flashing and wailing, as if he was deliberately trying to bait it like a matador teasing a bull.

Behind the car, he could see Ajmal standing outside his shop and pointing in his direction. By the time the police car came to a screeching halt just in front of him, Mo could clearly see the two officers seated in the front. They were staring at him fiercely, clearly incensed by his arrogant bravado. The one in the passenger seat was speaking into something in his hand, and then Mo heard it, a blaring command for him to lie down on the pavement and not move.

Just as the officers made to get out of their vehicle, Mo started to assume the pose he'd been ordered to. For just a split second, the policemen relaxed, believing the chase was over, but it had only just begun. What had started out as a crouch on the way to prostration suddenly turned into the starting stance of an Olympic sprinter. Before the officers knew it, Mo had taken off like a rocket down Main Street again. He rapidly made twenty yards on them — then thirty, forty. The policemen blustered and yelled, waved their arms and blew whistles, but all to no avail. Then they started out after him, and the great chase was back on.

At that moment, Saeed stealthily approached the entrance to the alleyway again, nervously looking for Mo, whom he'd finally realized had not been behind him anymore. He peeked out onto Main Street just long enough to appraise what was going on, and then quickly turned around and went back the way he'd just come, putting as much distance between him and Mo and the police as he could. He wondered how Mo was doing, then panicked at what might transpire if the cops managed to catch his friend. Would Mo squeal? Should he turn himself in? *Oh, shit!* Saeed knew what he ought to do, but he didn't. He went home, laid low, and prayed like he'd never prayed before, hoping to God that there wouldn't soon come an ominous knock on the door from you know who.

Mo led the cops on a merry chase, and he loved every minute of it. He realized that he wasn't fleeing because he was afraid, but because the mix of danger and defiance suddenly thrilled him so! The powers that be were desperately trying to rein him in, but he was defying them, making them dance to his tune for once. No doubt they'd probably get him before long, but not before he'd jerked their chain for a good ten minutes or more, showed them just who Mohammed Khalid Hussain *really* was.

Despite his exhilaration, however, Mo soon began to slow. He wasn't used to such athletic exertion, and his poorly developed leg muscles and lungs started to give out on him. His pursuers, older but in far better shape, were quickly catching up. Just then, the local mosque, a converted Methodist chapel long since abandoned by its aging and dying Christian congregation, came into view. He bounded up the steps to the main entrance and burst into the sanctuary, slamming the door behind him. A startled imam caught a collapsing Mo in his arms.

"Here, Imam Sahib," Mo gasped. "Take this— *zakat.*" Mo pushed a wad of banknotes into the cleric's hands, collapsed to the floor, and passed out.

Although surprised by this unexpected manna from heaven, the imam gratefully accepted Mo's contribution to the needy, and when the police asked him later on if Mo had given him anything, he smiled shyly and gave just one gentle shake of his head—no, the boy hadn't. The police took his holy word for it. But Mo was not so lucky. After the paramedics had managed to bring him back to consciousness again, the police promptly arrested him and he was hauled off to jail at the local station.

When he was alone in his sanctuary once more, the imam retrieved Mo's money and counted it. *Ninety pounds.* An odd amount, he thought, but then again he'd grown used to not asking where donations came from recently, assuming that in one way or another it was Allah's will that they should be offered up in whatever amount the alms-giver could afford. And who was he, a mere imam, to question Allah's will, even if the source of the money might be somewhat, shall one say, "questionable" at times?

Allah worked in mysterious ways from time to time, his wonders to perform. Yes, he surely did— these days more so than ever. And, anyway, money was scarce in economically-stricken Rotherham...and he had a growing family to take care of, bills to pay... *Inshallah.*

38
[Somewhere in Mesopotamia, Fall-Winter 2016 CT]

Kifat, Ayaan Pellegrino's captor-*cum*-consort, rose quickly through the senior ranks of Islamic State. He was a fearless, battle-hardened warrior, a leathery Afghan veteran and, latterly, commander of several of the group's great conquests in both Iraq and Syria. He'd also headed up the mission to build a Dirty Bomb, a General Groves of sorts to the caliphate's own mini-Manhattan project.

But his success, his superiors well knew, would soon mark him out as a prime target for an American drone—if he wasn't, indeed, one already. Thus, there was no other choice. A few weeks after Ayaan had given birth to their sons, he and his entire entourage (his large family, his adjutants, and his bodyguards) were taken out of Raqqa and spirited away to a remote location in the mountains to the north, a network of bunkered caves linked by tunnels and trenches, from where, it was assumed, Kifat would be able to direct his operations in relative secrecy and safety.

He didn't like this turn of events one bit—indeed, his mood darkened by the day after he left Raqqa—but he, too, knew it was *absolutely* necessary. Building the caliphate was just too important to be sabotaged by personal predilections. He reassured himself as best he could by accepting his commanding officer's insistence that his relocation was all according to God's will. But still…it felt like he was hiding, not taking the fight directly to the Crusaders as he'd always done; and there was no mistaking the fact some of his men seemed to carry out his orders with a little less ardor now, as if they were questioning his authority, his jihadi credentials, his manhood. He felt nettled, rattled—unusually uncertain.

For Ayaan, on the other hand, life stayed stuck in the tragic rut it had recently fetched up in. She remained entrenched in her lowly position in Kifat's harem. She was number six now out of five wives and one concubine—herself, his latest trophy of war. Her rock-bottom status meant that she saw little of Kifat and, thankfully, received even less of his attentions. Except that her isolation, her entrapment, just seemed that much more hopeless that way.

Didn't she need him in some fashion if she wanted to be released, be allowed to go back home to Italy? But how could she stand any chance of getting him to let her go if he largely ignored her? On the other hand, maybe his apparent indifference might allow her to slip beneath his radar, so much so that she might eventually find an avenue of escape! But what about her sons? Could she leave without them? Could she even flee *with* them? They were only a few weeks old, and they were *three*!

And, to top it all, there was what she'd left behind in her lab in Raqqa. Would it work? And when? Would she ever find out if it did? Would Kifat, someone, put two and two together and…

She half-wished she'd hadn't left her "calling card" now, after all. At the time, she hadn't considered how her beloved boys might be seriously compromised by her overwhelming desire for revenge. She'd foolishly considered them to be outside the parameters of her plotting and planning; they were *Kifat's* sons, too, as well as her own. But now, oh God, what price might they pay if her surprise went according to plan? Who would have the last gruesome, sickening, laugh, extract the last drop of vengeance from the whole sorry state of affairs that had come about between herself and her husband… between, it incredibly seemed, God and Allah; one and the same presumably, but somehow separated by a chasm as wide as the whole of creation?

♠

Ayaan looked at her three sleeping sons.

They were lying in three basket-like cradles, side by side. They slept in her room, as she was still nursing them, but she knew they would be immediately taken to the communal sleeping quarters when they'd been weaned. For a few months, maybe six or more, though, she'd have them almost exclusively to herself. Those months were going to be a precious time, she already knew that; cherished for the brief moments of joy her babies would bring her as their mother, and treasured because those months would afford her the only sustained opportunity to try and shape their future development, to mold their characters.

Her joy, she fully anticipated, was going to be a fleeting and, most likely, a troubled one. But seeing them in their sleep, she tried to let their tranquility, their cherubic faces, and their tiny balled fists stuck between their gently sucking lips, banish all such concerns from her mind. She was a *mother* now, their *ummi*, as they would come to call and know her. She could barely believe it: Aarib, Bashar, and Kareef were *her* sons! If there was hope, promise of any kind, it lay in them.

Motherhood. Yet another miracle—how many more might there be? Or was it the *last* one? And had this miracle already turned into its opposite, too, taking a more tragic turn this time, as opposed to her rescue off Lampedusa? Her motherhood had effectively trapped her, bound her to her sons—and therefore bound her to Kifat and all that he stood for, whether she was still a willing participant in his schemes now, or not. Her hope for the miracle of flight from Kifat's grasp had to be given up now. Not only was a viable escape plan impossible to conceive, but God knew what might happen to her babies if she left them be-hind with Kifat... or if someone did, in fact, find her "calling card."

But it was still a moment for jihad, a struggle, if only now of a motherly sort—if there was enough time, that is. Occasionally, she carefully asked Kifat if there was any news from Raqqa, but he just scoffed and told her Raqqa didn't concern her any more. She looked for a sign of unease in Kifat's face, for the merest tremor in his voice, but detected neither. It very much looked like her experiment had failed. She imagined it collecting dust on a shelf, untouched, mute, a dud.

♠

For seven-and-a-half months, Ayaan kept her sons as close to her as she possibly could.

Thankfully, Kifat didn't show much interest in his boys during this time, beyond checking in occasionally to make sure they were being well looked after. He was, Ayaan assumed, probably too consumed by the pressing business of the caliphate he was helping to build to be able to concern himself much with what, after all, were considered to be almost exclusively women's domestic duties. Moreover, Fatima and the other wives had their own growing broods of children to look after to be overly concerned with what was happening to hers. So, Ayaan used the time and space she'd been fortuitously given to try to save her sons.

Ayaan well understood the shaping power of early childhood on later adult life, when nurture had the chance at least to lock in some fundamental behavioral traits that might persist over a lifetime, and when genetic endowment, even if part of it came from a father like Kifat, was at its most malleable — primed for fine-tuning from an attentive parent providing fulsome love, ample nutrition, and constant stimulation. True, her own early childhood nurturing hadn't saved her from the allure of jihadism, but it had only failed her in a moment of emotional weakness, and not at all permanently so. Besides, she had no choice but to grasp at whatever slim reeds of opportunity came her way, now.

So, for thirty weeks Ayaan took care of her children's every need. She played games with them. She told them stories and sang them songs. She kissed and hugged and coddled them in a great constant shower of affection. Fatima and the other wives thought she was perhaps just a little crazy, given her zeal; Kifat, if anything, was pleased—his boys were growing up fast, looking more like future holy warrior material by the day!

But, even though Ayaan let nothing slow her down, or any negative thought dampen her ardor for what she was trying to do, there were many times when, lying awake in the middle of the night, she was forced to admit to herself that she was engaged, most likely, in a futile cause. If she was nurturing her boys in a way that might steer them clear of becoming like their father, how could she possibly know? She was an untested mother, still very much feeling her way.

And the human brain was the most complex known thing in the entire universe, it was said, containing at least eighty-five *billion* neurons all firing away and constantly building and rebuilding vast, complex neural networks that even the neuroscientists still knew very little about. What chance, then, she? Even more, she only had a very short while to try and engineer anything that might have a lasting effect on her sons. They would leave her almost exclusive control soon, and be exposed to a much larger battery of influences for years and years to come, not merely a few months. And in the end, any theories that tried to predicate adult behavior upon early childhood influences and modes of nurturance were just that—too reductionist, too pseudo-Freudian to be of any predictive use in any specific case.

In the end, Ayaan was forced to settle on doing the best she knew how. But whether it would be enough to make any positive difference or not, she knew only time would tell, and long after, she feared, when she might not still be around to find out what, exactly. Who knew what Aarib, Bashar, and Kareef would become? But, if there was room for both hope and fear in that wedge of uncertainty, Ayaan couldn't help in her heart of hearts but let the bulky weight of the latter crowd out the slim reed that was the former.

Even so, she still got up every day and went back to her mission, as if banishing her fears was as easy as throwing back her bedding.

♠

Shortly after she'd successfully weaned Aarib, Bashar, and Kareef, they were taken away from her during the daytime, as expected, and placed in the crèche that Kifat's senior wives ran, and from which, given her humble status and the lingering suspicions as to her dedication to jihad, Ayaan was barred from playing any role whatsoever. She feared for the worst—and it wasn't too long before it began to raise its ugly head.

One day, her sons were returned to her in the late afternoon unexpectedly wearing camouflaged combat fatigues. They were too big for them, but when Ayaan queried the decision to dress them in such a manner, Fatima curtly informed her that Kifat had ordered that they should be so attired. The disturbing liveries became the boys' staple clothing—uniforms in the real sense.

On another day, a few weeks later, her sons spent the last half-hour before bedtime crawling after each other and pointing, going *bah! bah!* and burbling, it sounded like to Ayaan, something very much like *Allahu Akbar, Allahu Akbar!* Surely it was just a game, she'd tried to tell herself; surely they weren't really trying to say… were they?

It was all a game…yet it wasn't; they couldn't possibly have been saying it…yet they might have been. When would the truth of it all, she wondered, finally be revealed?

It wasn't long. They played the game frequently, her admonitions for them to stop doing so being too gentle and unauthoritative to dissuade them for long. Then, when they were capable of unsteady locomotion, they surrounded her one day and *pow-powed* her instead, and when she told them to cease, they didn't until Fatima, hearing the ruckus and Ayaan's distressed voice, finally came and took control.

Their eyes… Ayaan would never forget the look they had—icy-cold, manic, terrifying, possessed. It was a look she'd last seen only a few days before.

♠

On that day, Ayaan had been returning from the well when she heard Kifat's voice.

It sounded as if he was drilling his fighters. But as Ayaan turned the corner into the opening where Kifat was shouting out his commands, she got the shock of her life. He was, indeed, drilling fighters…of a sort: young kids, probably aged between three and fourteen or so, she guessed. They were all boys, seven of them, lined up in front of Kifat, the tallest closest to him and the smallest farthest away at the end of the file. Kifat had a rifle in his hands and he was showing the boys how to aim and fire it. A couple of them paid close attention, engrossed in what Kifat was doing, but even so they had blank expressions, as if they didn't quite know whether they should be inspired or troubled by what learning such skills might portend. The rest, especially the toddler, found it hard to focus on Kifat; they fidgeted and looked around, neither inspired nor troubled, just bored and needing to go pee but afraid to break ranks.

Kifat said something to the tallest boy and held out the weapon to him. The kid flinched at the command, hesitated, and then nervously shambled forward. He stopped right where Kifat's outstretched arm ended, but he did not take the gun. He just kept looking at the ground and then at the rifle, back and forth, again and again. Kifat shook the firearm in the boy's face, forcing him to finally take it. The kid's arms buckled with the weight, before he finally steeled himself to try to take charge of the weapon. Kifat kept issuing instructions and his charge awkwardly followed them. Finally, the hapless recruit raised the rifle to the middle of his chest and squinted at the sights rather than through them, at what must have been close to a forty-five degree downward angle. Even Ayaan knew he couldn't possibly be actually aiming at something with any precision at all in such a posture. Kifat grabbed the boy by his shoulders and pulled them back. The barrel of the gun swung wildly up into the air.

"What are you doing?" Kifat yelled, slapping the boy on his head. He grabbed the kid by the shoulders again, forcing him to straighten his back. The boy stumbled, making the barrel swing even more wildly. "Stand firm!" Kifat screamed, roughly maneuvering the boy's hands until he had them where he wanted them on the rifle. "Here, hold it like this, you fool! Now, tuck the butt under your shoulder and—" The kid lost his grip and the gun slipped, pointing towards the ground. Kifat grabbed the rifle's barrel and forcibly pointed it in the direction he wanted the kid to aim. "Here! Like this!" he shrieked. He was red-faced now, clearly getting close to completely losing it.

The boy wobbled and jiggled like a marionette. One or two of the other boys stifled giggles, mildly entertained by the spectacle being played out before them. But when they finally realized that it was all no game, they either looked on in increasing concern or looked away altogether. The little one started to tear up, and then piss dribbled down his chubby legs and pooled between his bare feet. Kifat signaled to Fatima, observing the goings on from the door of her quarters, and she quickly came and carried the by now blubbering toddler away.

After another minute of struggle and exasperation, Kifat finally gave up his efforts to get the boy to execute the drill. He clocked him on the side of his head again, and sent him back to his place in the line. Then he walked behind his charges and gave each one a smack on the head for good measure, too. It must have been therapeutic for him, as by the time he'd whacked the last boy, Ayaan noticed, the redness in his face had all but disappeared.

Kifat resumed his position in front of the boys again. He retrieved a smart phone from his pocket and held it up so that they could all see the screen. He beckoned them in closer, and the boys shuttled forward into a hunched semi-circle around him and the phone, like American footballers in a huddle before setting up for the next snap. Kifat had his back to Ayaan, with the boys, therefore, looking in her direction. Even from her somewhat distant vantage point, there was no mistaking the rapture on their faces as they looked intently at the phone's screen. At one point, their eyes glared as if they had just seen the most incredible thing ever, and then they went vacant and icy as if their emotions had suddenly dried up, zombie-like, like her sons' were to do when they would mock-execute her a few days later. Ayaan wondered — she feared — what those young innocent eyes had just witnessed.

The boys made no sound, and Kifat offered no commentary on what was being viewed. Two or three minutes passed, and then Kifat took down the phone and placed it on the table behind him. "Dismiss!" he ordered, and his neophyte troops scuttled off, jabbering in excitement. Kifat remained a few minutes longer, chin in hand and pacing back and forth. Then, too, he left the scene, as if suddenly seized by a new idea.

Ayaan waited where she was, mulling over the possible implications of what she had just witnessed. As she bent down to pick up her water pitcher, she noticed Kifat's smart phone still on the table where he'd left it. She looked around the clearing; she was alone. She crept stealthily towards the table.

She picked up Kifat's phone. It was still switched on. She swiped the screen, and it popped back into life. The black flag of IS appeared, flapping, like the global icon it now was, in the desert wind. Ayaan immediately knew what was coming next; she'd seen it so many times before, once when it had held a kind of warped fascination for her, the strange, otherworldly titillation of war porn, and then, as now, where it grossly offended her, made her wonder how humanity could stoop to such a level of barbarity and how she could have, even if only for a short while and indirectly, consorted with it. Even now in its offensiveness she could barely resist its magnetic allure; those kids, those wild-eyed boys gone suddenly catatonic, she knew where they'd been in that moment... Was that where Aarib, Bashar, and Kareef were headed, too? But it wasn't, really, all that much of a serious question; she already knew the answer.

She heard footsteps. Ayaan quickly put the phone back where she'd found it, retrieved her water pitcher, and hurried off before she was discovered.

That night, long after she had put her sons to bed, Ayaan studied their sleeping faces. They were still in their cherubic stage, infantile innocence captured in all their fresh-faced glory. But soon she noticed that their eyeballs were rippling their closed eyelids every now and again; and their lips trembled with soft, inarticulate murmurings. What were they dreaming, such small boys?

What indeed?

♠

[26 Rabi Al-Awwal, 1438 AH (Anno Hegirae)]
[25 December 2016 CT]

Christmas Day night was bitterly cold in the Syrian desert, but the pollution-free, cloudless skies hosted as compensation a million twinkling jewels stretching from horizon to horizon.

Up there in those gorgeous heavens, Ayaan tried to divine her boys' future. They were growing up so fast, and because she saw them much less often now that they had been taken from her charge, they seemed to be almost completely different infants every time that she had the good fortune to be with them. Their physical development astonished her; they were truly chips off Kifat's block, already muscular and thick-set. And the evolution of their personalities, too, amazed her just as much; three-of-a-kind triplets were rapidly becoming three unique characters right before her eyes. But she could palpably feel the emotional distance between them and her widening by the week; they were slower now to come to her to be hugged and kissed, and those eyes that beheld her…those Kifat eyes…

Ayaan shivered, as a blast of desert wind buffeted the rocky outcrop she was sitting on. She suddenly realized that she'd rarely shivered or felt the cold in Bologna; but now, even out here in the desert, it seemed like nothing could keep her warm anymore. She wrapped her *abaya* around her as snugly as she could, but the wind had no trouble in continuing to penetrate the flimsy material it was made of.

She looked up at the night sky again, and began to pick out the constellations she knew, joining the twinkling dots in her imagination. She'd looked for her sons' star sign over the past many weeks, to see whether it had been either rising or descending, and if she could discern from such movement what their prospects might be. Of course, as a former scientist—she could just about remember being one once—she didn't rationally have any truck with astrology. But what was left to pin one's hopes on now? Religion? Reason? God's will? Only a fool would rely on any of them. But fools, she sighed, the world had plenty of—including herself.

For whatever it was worth, though, Aries didn't seem all that reliable, anyway. It was hard to spot; and how in God's name anyone thought that it looked anything like a ram, she had no earthly idea. Consequently, she hadn't been able to really divine what the hell the beast had been doing all along. It perhaps hadn't moved at all!

And perhaps, she thought, that was just as well.

In his lab in Raqqa, Samir Diyala, IS's Chief Scientist and Bomb Builder, was in a euphoric mood. After months of hard work, he believed he was close to realizing his ultimate jihadi test: a second and much more powerful Dirty Bomb for Allah. The chilly air in the air-conditioned room fazed him not one bit; he felt sublimely untroubled, warm, almost aglow, luminous like he hoped his latest creation would be on detonation someday very soon.

His first attempt at constructing such a device had been deployed in Kurdistan, but more as a test than a full-throttled operational strike. It had popped and fizzled rather, but that had been intentional, or, so it should be said, nothing more than could have been accomplished at the time given that their stock of radioactive material had been so meager. Still, his baby had had quite a propaganda and terrorizing effect. The thought of just a relative smidgen of radioactivity mushroom-clouding above them had scared the Kurds shitless. The video he'd seen of them scurrying like a swarm of panicked lemmings towards a clifftop had thrilled him, and he had fantasized almost daily thereafter about the torrent of fleeing humanity he'd no doubt foment when his latest creation — codenamed "Obese Baby" in honor of Hiroshima and Nagasaki — dropped its load somewhere, it was hoped, in Dar al-Garb. Over the last year, they'd been able to acquire, via black market agents in Moldova, a goodly (or "Godly," as Samir liked to joke) stash of nuclear juice, enough, he'd calculated, to fry several thousand fleeing Americans' jelly-wobbling asses. The End of Days was drawing near; he could feel it in the very core of his being.

"*Allahu Akbar,*" *he whispered.*
God is truly great.

Ayaan climbed down from her rocky perch high above the cave she had been forced to call home, such as it was. She never knew when Kifat might show up, but he usually did so late at night. It had been several weeks since he'd last visited her, and Ayaan had a hunch that that night it would be her turn to be forced to dance to his vindictive tune, whether it be a beating, a forced copulation, or both. Her own birth sign, Capricorn (her best guess), had dipped lower and lower in the western sky recently.

The sound was so faint at first that Ayaan thought it must be an acoustic illusion — the echoing mountains played tricks on her ears all the time, especially when, like this evening, she'd opened her senses up to whatever signs and signals the cosmos might choose to direct at her. But then the *thud, thud, thud...clatter, clatter, clatter* became unmistakable—a man-made machine moving swiftly through the sky and coming directly towards her. Ayaan was intrigued at first, and then puzzled; it was a sound she suddenly realized that she'd never heard out there in her desert home before. Then it was directly above her, hovering thunderously like a monstrous dragon, and sweeping up great swirls of dust and debris in its whirling wake. Ropes dropped down from its belly and black slug-like figures began to slide down them.

Samir looked at his watch.

He counted backwards in his head. Another fifteen minutes and it would be Christmas Day, as the Crusaders called it, in Washington DC. No doubt, he thought, the apostates would be preparing to celebrate the birthday of their so-called Lord and Savior (a rather minor prophet, though, for True Believers like himself) in their typically debauched manner. Samir could visualize them now, a nation of drunken sots believing somehow that inebriation was some sort of spiritual transcendence, a fitting way to honor Him. Well, they'd find out soon enough—less than three hours from then—that they'd gotten it all so abysmally wrong. Oh yes, indeed!

If only, that is, his proxies, the hastily assembled "Holy Alliance of Faithful Patriots," would be able to successfully pilot their drones with sufficient skill. And he had his doubts about that. But there was nothing more he could do about that now; he needed to stay "silent" at this stage of the game. In any case, the 12/25 operation had always been a rather at arms' length one, as far as he was concerned. Nothing for it then, but to try to get some sleep in the expectation that there'd be some great news first thing the next morning.

Samir reached up to turn the lab lights out, but as he did he caught sight of a laptop computer on the top shelf of a bookcase. For some reason, he'd never noticed it before, and he had no idea why he suddenly did so then. It took it down and put it on the bench in front of him. It had a thick layer of dust on top it; it obviously hadn't been used for quite some while. Whose could it be? He considered various possible options.

"Ayaan's?" he hesitatingly conjectured at last.

The first burst of ear-shattering gunfire, unexpectedly, came from behind her. Even though Ayaan hadn't been hit, the mere sound of the cacophonous uproar, and her own instinctive reaction to it, felled her to the ground, like a tree trunk toppled in one fell swoop in a tempestuous storm.

She heard Kifat's bodyguards starting to frantically yell warnings and instructions to each other: "Americans! Americans! From the chopper! There!" Bullets started to fly all around her, pinging the rocks and kicking up the dirt; the smoke and gases from exploding grenades and smoke bombs began to sting her eyes and blur her vision. But maternal reflex immediately made her get up and run back towards her cave, weaving and bobbing in order to avoid being hit: "Aarib, Bashar, Kareef!" she screamed, over and over. "My sons — my boys!"

Americans? Oh my God, the Americans are here!

Ayaan knew right away that they must have come to get Kifat, but now she quickly realized that her hope for a miracle rescue, for so long seemingly such an impossible fantasy, might well have just presented itself after all. If she could just find her boys and get them to the Americans—they would take them away with them...to safety! After all that had happened, she was going to escape, to go back home! It was the Miracle Baby of Lampedusa all over again—times four.

But where were they?

Ayaan saw a looming, shadowy figure ahead of her, shrouded in a vast cloud of smoke. It stumbled towards her, and then, as the smoke began to dissipate, it emerged into clear view. It was Kifat. He had beaten her to it; he had Aarib, Bashar, and Kareef corralled in his arms. He was holding them tightly, crushing them. They were crying, wailing, terror-struck.

"*Ummi!*" they called out to her.

"My babies!" she cried back to them. She looked at Kifat; he had his trademark wild-eyed stare, precursor she knew to something violent about to happen.

"Kifat!" she yelled. "Let them go! Let me get them to safety. Please!" But Kifat ignored her; he was transfixed on something over her shoulder. "Please, Kifat, before it's too—"

She heard a gruff American voice behind her yell something, but she couldn't make out what. Kifat shook his head emphatically from side to side. Everything went silent, and all movement turned into slow motion. Ayaan cried out for her children once more but she couldn't hear her words; she reached out to embrace them, but her arms never made it. The American repeated his command, whatever it was, but again Kifat shook his head, *no-o-o*. Then Ayaan saw it: the pistol pressed up against Aarib's temple, the barrel threatening to penetrate his skull. Kifat's—yes, *Kifat's*—finger on the trigger, twitching, itching, stroking the cold metal in nervous preparation.

Ayaan, silently screaming, no breath in her body, lunging forward, but...

Four dead, among them infants, unfortunately; a blood-stained stuffed toy bearing witness at their feet.

Samir blew the dust off the laptop in one gusty go, then opened it up.

He switched it on, but the screen took its time to light up. And when it did, Samir got his wish — though not quite in the way he'd wished for it.

There was a split-second burst of luminosity, all right, and a sizeable bang to immediately follow. But there was not enough of either, though, to fry a thousand apostate asses, or to knock down anything like a city block or two.

Just one dead, and one makeshift laboratory partially destroyed.

Luckily for the remaining denizens of Raqqa, the large steel door with a sort of black-and-yellow, circular, three-winged angel of death hovering above a pirate skull and crossbones painted on it, held firm.

The raw material for another "Obese Baby" lived to perhaps fight another day.

♠

[26 December 2016]

"Collateral damage" the official news release from the Pentagon read.

Of course, we've all heard this *yadda yadda yadda* before, haven't we? But, to be precise, here's the official gobbledygook, straight out of the DOD's very own *Dictionary of Military and Associated Terms* (I wouldn't want to be accused of engaging in any semantic tricks, now — would I?):

> "Collateral Damage: unintentional or incidental injury or damage to persons or objects that would not be lawful military targets in the circumstances ruling at the time. Such damage is not unlawful so long as it is not excessive in light of the overall military advantage anticipated from the attack."

So, what do you think? Ready for some parsing, are you?

These deaths: which were they, injury or damage?

These deaths: were they intentional or incidental?

Lawful? According to whose law? Mine, or some other Supreme Being's?

These deaths — *excessive*? In light of what presumed "advantage," military or otherwise — or none at all?

Hard to say, isn't it, when you think about it?

But if you think all that's bad enough, take a shufty at this, the routine military report from GFC (Gun Fire Control) that accompanied the news release (if you bothered to follow the links, that is): Initial Assessment: *3 x WC*.

Uh? Simple really: Three women and children killed. Appreciate the arithmetical precision; but not so sure about the conscience-sapping nature of the bureaucratic rendering, are you? *3 x WC* — what the fuck is that? Three toilets?

...

Beauty, I suppose — or ugliness for that matter — is no doubt in the eye of the beholder, whether he be aesthetically challenged or not.

But blood on a stuffed toy, well...what do we make of that?

...

As for Samir, what do we make of his demise? Kind of collateral damage, too, I guess you could say, if you wanted to be kind — or mean. But if that's what it took to avenge poor Ayaan, then who'd begrudge her such a *post mortem* reward?

I wouldn't.

But, no doubt, a dummy might.

39

[Spring 2016]

Socking Imam Khalifa on his jaw, and then kneeing a guard in his groin as he tried to subdue him, was the last straw. As far as rehabilitation was concerned, Jamal Shirani was, for at least the time being, *toast*.

Consequently, he was bounced out of the London-based program forthwith — presumably, a total lost cause, in addition to facing new criminal charges for assault and battery. With new cases coming into the program by the day and filling up limited bed space, Jamal was transported up north to make room for them. Up there, the assumption was, he'd be well out of circulation, unable to do too much damage, if any at all. How many terrorist wannabes lounging around in a northern jail waiting to be converted to the cause by the likes of a Jamal Shirani could there possibly be? One or two minor dupes perhaps, but Rotherham was certainly no London, the mother of all jihadi recruiting grounds and tempting terrorist targets—no sir, not by a million miles, everyone in the know confidently asserted.

Before he was shipped out of the capital city, a judge in a ridiculous-looking powdered wig told Jamal that he wouldn't see freedom again for a good long while. Twenty years *minimum*. Even though the hobo he'd stabbed in Russell Square had survived, Jamal's known terrorist links and his assault on an officer of the law were more than enough for a severe sentence—although perhaps a bit less with good behavior, the dispenser of Her Majesty's justice reluctantly conceded.

At that very moment, though, Jamal's last inclination was to be a good boy, to suck up to the wardens and to keep his nose clean. But after a couple of weeks in prison, careful observation eventually convinced him that goodness, even just feigning it, brought certain privileges that he could use: access to books, and more time to study in order to further develop his piety, his knowledge of Islam—*among other things*.

And so, Jamal started to play a new jihadi game: model prisoner to all outward appearances, but in reality a jihadi wolf in compliant sheep's clothing. And by the time Mohammed Khalid Hussain came his way a few weeks later, Jamal had already begun to build the basis of a new jihadi movement right inside the walls of Her Majesty's Prison Service in Rotherham, south Yorkshire.

♠

[16 June 2016]

Jamal first saw Mo as he made his way to his cell after having been convicted of theft and trying to sell stolen goods. The judge had said Mo might have gotten off without any time, but his priors for minor drug possession had unfortunately tipped the scales of justice against him: three months inside in order to "learn his lesson," plus a year's probation when he got out. But the judge had no idea just what kind of student Mo might turn out to be, or what lessons he might eventually ascertain.

Mo, as was the routine — the ritual almost, was shuffling along in front of the prison warden accompanying him, carrying his meagre, prison-issue bedding on his outstretched arms, and looking bemused, like a kid on his first terrifying day at a new school. It wasn't unusual for inmates to scrutinize new arrivals as they were ushered into the cell block, but whereas most were looking for potential targets to exploit or possible new kingpins to worry about, Jamal was looking for fresh recruits: short-timers whom he could quickly bend to his will, become his faithful disciples on the outside, while he remained locked up — a persecuted martyr — on the inside. Jamal was planning jihad from jail — what safer headquarters than that could there be, *Inshallah*? The irony of it all — it was so, so sweet.

"In here, Hussain," Jamal heard the warden say. "Room one-oh-one, reserved just for you. Enjoy your stay. Get your bunk made up pronto, and then get out there in the rec space with the others."

Jamal listened to the warden's heavy boots clunking down the passageway as he made his way back out of the cell block, each reverberating footfall emphatically reminding everyone within earshot of the omnipresent nature of his petty-tyrant authority. When the door slammed shut at the end of the corridor and a key rattled in its lock with metallic finality, Jamal made his way slowly to Mo's cell.

"*Salaam.*"

Mo jumped. He was busy making up his bunk, and hadn't heard Jamal approach in his soft-slippered saunter. He spun around. "What?"

"Peace. *Salaam,*" Jamal said, again. He smiled. "May I?" He gestured that he would like to enter Mo's cell, his eyebrows arched in supplication, but before Mo could fashion an articulate response, Jamal was already beside him, proffering his outstretched hand. Mo gingerly took it in his.

"Jamal Shirani," Jamal said.

"Mo Hussain," Mo replied.

"Brothers, eh, you and me?" Jamal continued, gesturing back and forth between them with the forefinger of his left hand.

"Yeah...I guess so," Mo replied, assuming Jamal was referring to their similar skin color.

"I think we're going to get along, you and me. I can just sense it." Jamal smiled again, then covered their handshake with his left hand, as if he was already sealing the bond between them that he'd already—rather presumptuously, Mo thought—proclaimed.

Mo could feel the warm blood flowing through Jamal's fingers. "Mmm...yes, I...I hope so." Mo made to remove his hand from the handshake, but Jamal held on, not aggressively, Mo sensed, but with a sort of calming firmness—an almost caressing touch, a gesture of...what exactly? He wasn't at all used to such a strange sensation...coming from the touch of another man. It made him momentarily feel weird, but, nevertheless, okay. Yes, it was okay. Well, more than okay. It was, he had to admit, *good*.

The door at the end of the passageway squealed loudly on its lubricant-starved hinges, again. The warden was coming back.

"Listen, Mo," Jamal counseled, "anything you need, any concerns, just come to me whenever you can. *I can help you.*" He squeezed Mo's hand in confirmation that his word was as good as his bond.

Mo nodded his head in acknowledgment. "Thank you—I will."

The warden's footsteps started to clatter up the corridor.

"How long you in for?" Jamal hurriedly added.

"Three months," Mo replied.

"Perfect," Jamal said, and then ghosted out of Mo's cell on his slippered feet before the warden caught him.

Perfect? What?

Mo looked at the hand that had held Jamal's, then brought it to his nose and lips.

"Oi!" the warden bellowed. He was standing right outside Mo's cell, arms akimbo, looking like he was in the mood for doing some "funny stuff" with his latest plaything. "What are you bloody well up to? Don't just stand there picking your nose—get that bunk made up, like I told you to do 'arf an hour ago!" He spied something untoward, and stepped into Mo's cell. He poked Mo's mattress with his truncheon. "What do you call this mess?" he said, tapping the sloppily tucked-in sheet at the foot of Mo's bunk. "It's 'ospital corners in 'ere, Hussain." He ripped Mo's bedding from off his bunk, and threw it onto the cell floor. "Now, get to it, and get it fucking right, this time!" He waved his truncheon in the air, the implicit threat more than crystal clear to Mo. Then he about-turned, and marched away down the corridor towards the rec room.

Mo looked at the pile of bedding on his cell floor, then kicked it. The odds were looking pretty certain that he'd be seeking Jamal's comradeship before too long. He'd need his savvy if he was going to be able to deal with the fat-assed warden, who, it was clear, was out to make life *very* unpleasant for him.

Suddenly, Mo realized, there was more than a fat ass that the warden shared with the police officer who'd almost broken his arm that night on the rain-sodden streets of Rotherham. It seemed like just about the whole of the town's law enforcement personnel had nothing better to do than make going after him some sort of collective vendetta.

Fuckers! he cursed to himself. He'd show them.

With Jamal's help, he knew he would.

40

New Year's Day, 2017

Robbie,
    It's been six months now, I know. And I'm sorry for taking off like that after I'd been rescued. I'd just about given up all hope. There must be hundreds of derelict houses like that one in town. It was a miracle they decided to search that particular one. Maybe God's on my side after all, but I don't know, I don't know any more. The police said that someone had tipped them off, one of the members of the gang that nabbed me, apparently. I don't know who it was, of course, but I can't get it out of my mind that it must have been the Soft One. I'm probably crazy for thinking that, but there were times when he seemed, almost, well, that he *cared*.
    It was just little things he sometimes did, but at the time they made all the difference in the world. You know, things like bringing me actual toilet paper, so I wouldn't always have to use the ripped up newspapers the others gave me. And one time, he actually started to tear up when he caught me silently weeping at my plight. He tried to pretend

otherwise, that he'd had something in his eye, but I knew different. It wasn't just the tear he had; his whole face looked pained. Believe it or not, given what he did to me, I actually think he was at times almost genuinely empathetic—which is saying a lot for his sort.

Anyway, I guess it doesn't matter all that much now. We've other things to worry about, to work through. God, do we ever.

After the quacks got through with me they insisted that I go away for a while to recuperate, get myself back together again—like I was, as we were before, before all that's happened. I was glad to see the fuckers get done for what they did to me and so many other girls, even some of their own kind—can you believe that? Well, yeah, I can when I think about it. That's the kind of vermin they are. We should never have let them in in the first place—they're aliens with an alien religion, if a religion's what you can call it. Still, I don't know if I'll...things will ever be the same again. Sometimes I can't see how they can be. I know you want to help me, to take care of me, but, well, we'll just have to see. Give me some space, more time. Please. All right?

I've had some medical issues, obviously—what you'd just about expect after being kept locked up like that and, well, having been messed around with like they did with me. It's amazing I'm almost back to normal again. Well, normal may be stretching it a bit, I suppose. I've kind of lost sense of what normal's supposed to be any more. You can understand that, can't you? You have to know that I don't blame you for anything, how could I? Please, don't feel responsible, guilty in any way. You couldn't be there to protect me all of the time. You had your job, your life to lead. I know that—really I do. It's just that I feel so...so cheated. What did I do to deserve all this? Why did we let them in in the first place? They don't belong here.

It's been very difficult for me, unbelievably hard. It feels as if my emotions, my nerves, have almost been completely shredded. I'm coming back, bit by bit, but it's a very slow go of it. You know I want to see you, but I can't just now. It's still too soon. The nurse told me today that I've actually put on a couple of pounds and that my wounds have just about healed, so, she says, something must also be mending in my mind—these physical signs of improvement, her theory goes, are most likely not possible without a spirit that's not on the mend, too. I don't know whether she's right about all that—she is a bit religious, always saying 'God bless you, my dear" to me whenever she goes off duty—but let's hope so. One thing I know for sure, I'd still be totally freaking out if they hadn't gotten rid of those fucking crabs! The filthy vermin of filthy vermin—one and the same.

There's one big medical thing, though, that I haven't told you about yet. They had to operate—you know, a woman's problem. I couldn't take care of myself properly when the Pakis had me: little soap, no hot water, no Tampax, and you know what my periods can be like, all that...well, I'll spare you the gory details. So, it was inevitable, wasn't it? All of it, what they did to me? Yes, well...so they had to operate, bring it all to an end, *all* of it. There was no choice. You know what I mean, don't you?

Hard to believe it now, but the obstetrician—the surgeon I mean—was a Paki, too. Yeah, I know, one of them! And after we'd gone private too, paying for it out of Mum and Dad's own pocket. Oh, I know, the money, but we just had to, I just had to. I'll tell you one day, sometime when ...things are all better.

He could have been one of them. He had the same curry breath, the same shuffling feet, the same greasy brown skin. You can imagine what I was feeling having one of his sort wielding a knife over me. And when I heard him say

"Inshallah" just before I went unconscious counting backwards as they make you do, I just about flipped out right there and then on the operating table, but I guess I zonked out before I could make any move. It was the last thing I remembered before I came round a few hours later: *in-fucking-shallah*. Still gives me the creeps.

I have to admit, though, he did a pretty good job. He...he took care of it...everything.

There's still a scar, of course. The nurse insists it's healing nicely, but you know how such things can be. They never completely disappear, do they? Some scars can last a lifetime, more than that really, reminding you, shaming you, pricking at you with itchy irritation, never letting you completely go, never letting you really get over it...over and over. Oh...

Tell me it's over, Robbie?

It has to be. I'm tired of all this fucking shit. Aren't we all by now? Maybe what happened in DC on Christmas Day is the last desperate gasp of this stinking bloody War on Terror. Maybe the Americans will really take care of the jihadi fuckers once and for all this time! What have they been waiting for? But it's strange, weird, isn't it? It all seems so far away now, like it's not real, but in a horror movie or something. Even all the shit those bastards did to me is beginning to seem like a bad dream, somehow.

I'm just trying to get one life back—*my* life—to get well, and it's about all I can manage right now. I'm sorry I keep putting you off, but please be patient. We have to get it right. But if you can't wait anymore, I understand. To be honest, I'm not sure I know it'll ever be really right again. Not like we need it to be. And what's been done can't be undone, can it? It'll always be there like a dark, knowing shadow, looming over us like an evil spirit, poisoning our relationship. There *is* an arrow of time, despite what some scientists claim, and there's no reversing it—*ever*.

As for all the rest of it, the global war on fucking terror, it can go to hell.

Take care of yourself. I'll write again soon, I promise.

Jill xxx

41
[16 June-16 September 2016]

Jamal set about the business of cultivating Mo earlier than he'd expected.

To his surprise, it had been Mo who'd made the next move. As soon as he'd entered the rec room on his first day in Rotherham prison, Mo had come right over to Jamal and had sat down next to him before Jamal had even had the time to invite him to do so. It had been almost as if Mo had been behaving like a newly-born gosling imprinting on the first thing to have shown him some sign of concern in what must have been an alien environment for him.

Just what Mo's *specific* motivation had been, Jamal hadn't been at all sure, but he hadn't supposed it was jihad, at least not strictly speaking. But there'd been no mistaking the kid's irritation about something or other. Fortuitously, though, whatever it was that had been already getting Mo's goat would prove to be vexing enough such that he turned out to be a piece of cake—or, rather, a piece of candy—for Jamal's purposes.

Jamal hadn't really anticipated that he'd so quickly become such an effective organizer and recruiter, let alone a leader, but he had. Even though he'd done rather poorly in his physical training in Pakistan, and had totally flunked his first real jihadi field-test in London, somehow his ideological training and whatever latent mentoring abilities he'd actually possessed had finally meshed together to bootstrap into existence the new and improved Jamal Shirani: al-Qaeda's point man in Rotherham, south Yorkshire—AQIR, for short (or so Jamal quietly claimed, unbeknownst to his far away superiors somewhere in south Asia).

By the time Mo had shown up in Rotherham prison, Jamal had already built up a small corps of cadres among the handful of nominally Muslim inmates. There'd been four of them so far, Mo about to become the fifth. Jamal had felt like he was on a *real* mission now, something way beyond the half-assed fracas he'd stumbled into in Russell Square.

What a jackass he'd been! But not anymore. No, sir: he'd really found his jihadi niche now. If London hadn't been "calling," as *The Clash* would have put it, Rotherham certainly was!

♠

"So, tell me, Brother," Jamal said to Mo late one afternoon in the rec space of Rotherham prison, "what are you in for?" He slowly slid a candy bar across the table towards Mo, as if he was playing a well-thought-out opening gambit in a chess game, exposing his queen right from the start in order to draw his unsuspecting opponent into a delicious trap.

It was Mo's favorite: a *Yorkie*, its famous slogan *"It's Not For Girls!"* emblazoned on the packaging for all the world to see. Mo smiled: *How did Jamal know?* After the prison fare he been given over the last few days, he could barely wait to sink his teeth into it.

"Thanks," Mo said. "My favorite!" He tore off the wrapper in one go, and took a large bite. An almost orgiastic combination of dark chocolate, raisin, and biscuit swirled around his mouth and over his tongue. He quickly broke off a second huge chunk, stuffing it into his mouth on top of the, still un-masticated, first one, almost choking himself in the process.

"There's plenty more where that came from," Jamal said. "We may be inside, but that doesn't mean we have to be deprived." He put his hand in his pocket and retrieved something. Mo watched him intently. "Like one of these?"

It was a *Fieldmaster* Swiss Army Knife. "Where'd you get that?" Mo said, his eyes almost popping out of head. "They're not allowed, are they?"

"Technically, no. But regulations, shall we say, are not always enforced in here. In fact, I can get you just about anything you might want that's supposedly off-limits." Jamal put the knife quickly back in his pocket.

"You can? How?"

Jamal gently touched Mo on his shoulder. "The wardens are not well paid, so they appreciate a little backsheesh or a personal favor from time to time. For the right price, they can be very forthcoming. Let me know when you might want something, and I'll see what I can do." He patted Mo's shoulder again, then he gave it a soothing squeeze.

"Thanks. I will," Mo said. "I will." Suddenly, his fear that being in prison was going to be pretty rough started to melt away. *Maybe life was going to better in the nick than out of it!* He smiled at Jamal. Mo could sense already that Jamal knew what was what in the prison, how to get by. All he had to do was to stay close to Jamal, and he'd be alright. And it seemed that Jamal had definitely taken a shine to him: the counsel, the candy, the consolation. It surprised Mo that he didn't even mind Jamal's physicality all that much, something he would have been mightily offended by before he'd walked into Rotherham prison. He took another bite of his *Yorkie*, a more measured piece this time that he chewed rather than gulped down whole.

"So, what are you in for?" Jamal asked again.

"Oh," Mo said, his mouth still full of candy, "um…I'm…um…in for theft. Stole" — swallow, *cough* — "an iPhone." He coughed again and licked his lips, making sure he got each last little crumb that might be stuck there. "Then I got caught trying to pawn it off." *Burp!* He looked at Jamal and smiled again. "You?"

Jamal ignored Mo's question. Instead, he rested his elbows on the table between them and then tented his hands together in front of his face, his thumbs resting against either side of his chin, his forefingers against each side his nose, and the rest of his fingers — tips to tips — splayed out in front of him like the opened blades of two oriental fans, side by side and gently touching each other along their tops. He closed his eyes.

Mo wondered if Jamal was praying or something. The only other person he'd ever seen act like this had been the imam at his local mosque. But that had been years ago, at least seven or eight. Still, Jamal's pose somehow soothed him. He had to pinch himself that he was *actually* behind bars.

After what must have been a full minute, Jamal took his hands down from his face, opened his eyes, and then pursed his lips. Mo was entranced by Jamal's behavior. He waited in silence for what Jamal might say next. Surely, it would have to be something very prophetic, the way he looked like that.

"We're True Believers, you and I," Jamal began with great solemnity, "in the House of War, *Dar al-Harb*, the House of the West, *Dar al-Garb*. In Allah's eyes, we can commit no crime in such a place, we can only sin — that is, fail to submit to His Will."

Mo was thunderstruck; he'd never heard such words before, and said with such authority. He just sat and gaped open-mouthed at Jamal.

"In such a debauched pit of apostasy," Jamal continued, "in the House of War, in the House of the West, our only duty is to commit to jihad, by whatever means necessary, in order to submit them, the apostates, to the House of Islam, *Dar al-Islam*, the House of Peace, *Dar al-Salaam*."

Mo barely understood anything of what Jamal was saying, but the way Jamal so authoritatively articulated the words forced him to listen, to try to comprehend them as best he could.

"Do you understand?" Jamal finally asked.

"Yes...well, um, no...not exactly," Mo spluttered, embarrassed to be such an ignoramus in the company of one so apparently wise and learned.

But Jamal's whole demeanor, his high-flown rhetoric, just bowled Mo over. For the first time in his life he was feeling respect for someone older than himself, and eager—yes, *eager*—to *learn* from him. Mo pinched himself; he was in the presence of a teacher, yet he didn't feel alienated, angry, resentful, or oppressed. But there was more, Mo suddenly realized: he didn't feel as if he was being lied to, bullshitted with the white man's tales of spreading civilization and enlightenment to subhuman savages like himself, the kind of crap his father had succumbed to hook, line, and sinker. No, he could sense that he was being told the truth, perhaps the divine truth if there were such a thing, and it made him feel good—*different* in a weird kind of way that he just couldn't quite explain.

Jamal smiled and nodded his head slightly, as if to say Mo's lack of erudition was not the sin his schoolteachers had always said it was, but, rather, was something to be thoroughly expected of a child living so far from his true home, and being fed the lies of the apostates in the House of the West.

"Tell me," Jamal said, "why did you take the iPhone?"

"Well...I suppose I—"

Mo suddenly realized Jamal had only said "take" and not "steal," and in that moment he was confused by the choice of word, making him wonder if he had in fact stolen the device, after all.

"Did you do so because you coveted it, had greed in your heart?" Jamal gently pressured.

"Um..."

"Come on, you have to face the truth. Did you steal it? You're in prison, aren't you?"

Something clicked in Mo's brain at the bald accusation: the illuminating straw that broke the camel's back of a lifetime of oppression and alienation. "No! I did not steal it!" he boldly declared, as if there could be absolutely no doubt about it.

"That's right," Jamal encouraged, "you did *not* steal it. But why did you take it, then, if it wasn't yours?"

Mo faltered.

"Was it because everything in this *takfir* country has been stolen by the *kafirs* from people like us? Tell me, Mohammed, do you have money, do you have opportunity, do you have hope?"

"No," Mo dejectedly said. His eyes glistened, wetted by the pain that had accompanied him from the time of his premature arrival in a Rotherham maternity ward some nineteen years ago.

"Do you have freedom and respect?"

"No...no I don't," Mo continued, a little louder this time.

"Is this your country, Mo, your home? Are you welcome here, or do they spit on you, call you names?

"Yes, they do! They do!" Mo hissed. He squeezed what was left of the Yorkie bar so hard that it crumbled into a half-dozen pieces and dropped to the floor. "Yes, *she* does!" he cried.

"Who does? Who does such a vile thing?"

"Kathy Green!"

"Who's she?'

"She's the daughter of the shopkeeper I stole the phone from."

"But you didn't steal it, you already know that. What did she do to you, Mohammed?"

"She...she turned me away, called me a 'stinking Paki.'"

"She as good as spat on you, Mohammed, didn't she? She doesn't want you here. Her father doesn't want you here. Nor do all the apostates, the white people. *They've* stolen from you, haven't they? You're the victim, not them. They stole your freedom, your opportunity, your dignity, didn't they? You see that now, don't you?"

"Yes...yes!" *Mohammed.* Jamal had just called him by his real name: Mohammed! He couldn't believe he'd been so ignorant and insensitive about that for so long, that he'd allowed the world to get away with calling him Mo, a stupid, insulting, English-style nickname, like he was one of them when they'd never, ever meant it. Muslim? What a thoroughly wretched one he'd been!

"Well, what are you going to do about it?" Jamal continued, his voice getting louder, more insistent.

Mo thought for a moment, then said, hoarsely: "Do? What can I do? Nothing—least of all from in here."

Jamal leaned across the table between them, grasped Mo by both shoulders, and shook him: "Nothing? *Nothing*? Are you a True Believer, or not?"

Mo hesitated, betraying perhaps a grain of uncertainty. But Jamal's eyes held him fast, commanded him. "Yes," he finally conceded, "yes… of course I am."

"Well then," Jamal said, "what did we say it was every True Believer's duty to do in the House of War, in the House of the West?"

Mo pondered for a moment. Jamal willed Mo's slow-geared brain to crank out the applicable answer to his question. Eventually it came.

"To practice…jihad?" Mo ventured, although he still wasn't altogether clear as to what the phrase might mean, especially—specifically—for the likes of him.

"Yes!" Jamal confirmed. "Jihad!"

"But, how?" Mo beseeched. "I don't know how."

"Don't worry," Jamal counseled, "we'll find a way. *Inshallah*."

Jamal made it all sound so straightforward, so black-and-white. Mo had never distinguished much between right and wrong before, but now they stood clear, shorn of the ambiguities and messy compromises of his down-at-heal existence. He'd always done what he'd done on the spur of the moment, as if he had been nothing more than a ball bearing bouncing around inside a pinball machine. But now…he'd be the Pinball Wizard on the outside flipping the ball bearing instead! At least when he got out, that is.

"All right, you two, keep the noise down," a warden suddenly interjected. "Playtime's over. Back to your cells, and be quick about it." He looked at the floor by Mo's chair. The remnants of the *Yorkie* bar were scattered over the clean tile. "And take that mess with you. Got it?"

Mo bent over to pick up what remained of the candy, but in the process he surreptitiously ground some of the chocolate coating into the tile.

Yeah, jihad, Mo thought. *One step at a time.*

♠

Mo's baby steps towards jihadism took time and endless patience on Jamal's behalf. His student was a slow learner, and he seemed to lack more than a little spine necessary for a potential holy warrior. Jamal wondered for a good while if he had perhaps chosen the wrong kid, but his options in Rotherham jail were rather limited, so he persisted with him. Allah would surely show the way.

A good half of Mo continued to be confused and uncertain about what Jamal was trying to teach him. The idea of jihad, somewhat foggy though it still was for him in all its archaic-sounding theological garb, unnerved Mo, scared him more than a little. He wasn't sure he was up to the test it might ultimately present. But the other half of him remained titillated by the new way of thinking that Jamal's understanding of Islam afforded him: a possible way out of his sorry life in segregated England. He felt a thrill from time to time, the first intoxicating sparks of empowerment, of perhaps someday being a real man with true, meaningful agency—and carrying out Allah's will, no less. It was a glorious nettle he just had to find a way to grasp. And Jamal, thankfully, luckily, was there to help him.

Still, Mo's initial sessions with Jamal did not exactly seem all that auspicious. Jamal had not expected them to. It was going to take a lot of sustained effort in order to finally drive the nail into the coffin that was Mo's untutored, un-steeled mind. But in just three months? Well, why not? Three months was just about ninety days, give or take, and that was at least ninety more sessions Jamal would have in order to work Mo's mind over.

So, for ninety times, Jamal drilled Mo on the teachings of the Koran, as intensely as if they were in a Pakistani *madrassa*. The pedagogy was well suited to Mo: scant emphasis on philosophical reasoning, textual analysis, or exegesis, just a huge diet of memorization and recitation, and a commitment to seeing things in strictly black-and-white, absolutist terms instead — from an exclusively Salafist perspective, that is. Mo ate it all up, as easily and gluttonously as if he were just gorging on one *Yorkie* bar after another. What a blissful diet!

The wardens, as instructed by their boss, the governor, viewed Jamal's intense get-togethers with Mo and the four other Muslim inmates in his coterie of hangers-on as welcome, or at least untroublesome diversions on the whole. Whatever shit was going on in their huddled conflabs, the wardens quickly and conveniently concluded, seemed to keep Jamal's group relatively quietly occupied, a welcome relief for them from having to deal with all the indiscipline and often raucous behavior of the other inmates, who just had to keep on blowing off steam from time to time.

The governor checked out Jamal's so-called instructional materials, but wondered what harm could there really be in the Koran and something called the "200 Golden Haddiths"? He knew, of course, that Jamal had been convicted of terroristic plotting and first-degree assault, but there were no pamphlets on how to make a bomb, or some such activity, amongst his "teaching aids," nothing like that whatsoever. As long as the Koran and the "200 Golden Haddiths" were all they had to work with—and, of course, they had *absolutely* no access to the Internet on the inside—the only damage they were likely to do was to their own feeble minds, trying to figure out what in the hell Islam was all about. He'd sampled a few verses and hadiths, just to be on the safe side, but what in God's name had any of it meant? The stuff was indecipherable! Most likely, he concluded, Jamal was just trying to be Mo and the others' priest, their imam or whatever it was they called it, for some strange reason. Maybe it made Jamal feel good, a bit of a big shot in his otherwise very little world; but, if so, fine. No, more than fine, great! All things considered, then, better to let sleeping dogs lie, he finally resolved.

Like they said: *If it ain't broke, don't fix it.*
And so it wasn't—fixed, that is.

♠

[16 September 2016]

When Mo's day of freedom, and that of his comrades, finally arrived, he was ready—at least he thought he was. Jamal had given him both a plan of action and the inspirational wherewithal to be able to carry it out, he believed. As he made his exit from the cell block, he turned briefly and saluted Jamal, who was observing his protégé's launch into jihadism from the other end of the passageway.

"Go home!" Jamal called out to Mo. "Go to the House of the West and bring it to peace, the House of Salaam."

The wardens, and the other non-Muslim prisoners who were in earshot, wondered what the fuck he was shouting about. Didn't he know what kind of home Mo was going back to? And Mo, a bringer of peace? Since when? The guy must be off his rocker.

"*Inshallah!*" Mo called back. "*Inshallah!*"

"*Shall-ya*, really?" a warden mocked in his ignorance.

"Yes, I shall," Mo mumbled underneath his breath. "Just you fucking wait and see."

42

13 May, 2017

Robbie:

    I'm so sorry, I really am, but I still don't know when I'll be back. I even wonder now if I ever will.

    I know I'm not being entirely fair to you, not telling you where I am, not letting you have some means of communicating with me. But everything's just so difficult, so fucked up. I'm almost afraid to see you again. The thought of resuming our relationship scares me. Emotionally, I just don't think I could handle it now. I guess I'm so nervous that it might not work out as well as we'd like, that I just daren't tempt Fate like that. I don't think I could stomach us falling apart again. And we might, we just very well might now, after everything. I'm scarred, so deeply scarred. I can barely stand to have anyone near me—anyone at all.

    I'm so unbelievably angry, too. Mad as hell all the time. Pissed off at myself for not waiting for you that night, outside the Palace. Annoyed at you for not coming on time.

Furious at those Paki bastards—I just can't get my head around the idea that they thought they could just kidnap me off the street like that, that they had the right to do what they did to me, over and over, that their fucking God had told them to do it! I'm madder now than I was when I was down there in that cellar, as incredulous as that might seem to you. Is this what the rest of my life will be like? Gnawed at incessantly by an anger that can't be assuaged? What kind of life is that...for either of us?

Oh God, I feel like I'm on the other side of some huge, impenetrable curtain, separated from all that went before, and now I'm not able to get back. Am I really still alive? Still Jillian? Your Jillie? Jill? Perhaps you'd be better off without me...especially like this.

Oh Robbie! Where were you? Where the fuck were you?

I'm not the woman you knew and loved before all this shit happened. And I don't think I can become again the woman you would want me to be as your wife. I know you want kids, but who knows whether that can happen now, whether I can go through with it. How can I now? Can I be a mother, a wife, after all that's happened?

Perhaps, ~~Insh~~ Inshaller, God willing, or whatever the fuck it is that they always fucking say. But I wouldn't bet on it.

For your own sake, as well as for mine, Robbie, try to forget about me and move on. You can't afford to be late a second time.

Goodbye, Robbie. I'll always love you, one way or another, but not in the way you might want...or deserve.

Jill.

43

*[8 Dhu al-Hijjah 1437 AH – First Day of the Hajj
(Early September 2016)]*

In the end, and after much agonizing deliberation, it was Mo's fixation with Kathy Green that eventually gave Jamal the plan that he was looking for. He had initially hoped that Mo and his Band of Brothers might carry out a bombing in a public forum somewhere in Rotherham—a sort of pipe bomb mini-version of 7/7, he'd fantasized—but two considerations had ultimately nipped this hopeless dream in the bud.

The first concern was that in economically-depressed Rotherham sizable gatherings in public spaces were few and far between these days, and even if there were still such things taking place, what propaganda value would such a target in a town such as Rotherham accrue? A decent amount, no doubt, if there happened to be *some* human carnage as a result—a shattered limb or two, a blinded eye, but there could be no guarantee of that outcome, none at all. It would be Mo's first, quite possibly faltering, time as a would-be jihadi bomber *in the field*, after all. And look what had happened on his own first time in Russell Square!

No: Rotherham was no London—no Ground Zero, as the Americans liked to call it. The scrubby, economically-depressed town was almost entirely glitz-free—how many would notice whatever relatively minor devastation Mo might eventually foment there, and for how long? Sadly, Rotherham was less, much less, than a prime target; and, even worse, Mo was no "Sid," the infamous Mohammad Sidique Khan, leader of the 7/7 bombers who had taken seven lives in his successful attack on the westbound Circle Line train on that fateful morning in the mid-summer of 2005.

Mo had certainly come a fair way under his guidance, Jamal had to admit. He'd had no doubt when Mo had been set free that he would carry out whatever plot he, Jamal, might have told him to execute. But, although instructions on how to procure the ingredients for and on how to make a pipe bomb were readily available on line, he worried that Mo wouldn't have the organizational gumption necessary to implement even such a minimal plot in the field, out there in the real world.

And if missionary zeal was not balanced by logistical soberness, then did such a jihadi become more a danger to himself and those whom he served, than the enemy? Quite likely, if not a certainly so. No,

Mo as a bomber was just far too big of a risk to take. Jamal thought again about his own botched jihadi action in London. It hadn't entirely been his fault he knew, but, nonetheless, he'd failed and had gotten incarcerated for his incompetence as a consequence. In a way, Mo reminded Jamal of himself back then: eager but green, dangerously green. Mo was nowhere near ready to carry out a bombing—and neither was any of his even less proficient comrades—even if a suitable target in Rotherham could have been found, and sending him out even farther afield had been even more out of the question.

So, with Mo and his gang, Jamal had had to come up with another way, a mission of somewhat more modest means, but still big enough to make a jihadi difference. One that would catch the notice and approval, he'd fantasized, of his superiors in faraway Pakistan, perhaps even resulting in a gushing article about it in *Inspire*, complete with a photo of yours truly, the mastermind behind the plot.

Yes, the Kathy Green idea had fit the bill perfectly: a more than passable act of jihad, yet amenable to the talents—such as they were—and driving passions of his acolyte, Mohammed Khalid Hussain. In all their discussions about the injustices and insults heaped upon Muslims living in England, a session had rarely gone by without Mo venting his rage at Kathy Green and her family.

At first, Jamal had been puzzled by Mo's obsession with her—she was a white apostate girl, after all, and judging by Mo's accounts little more than a whore—but he'd once been enough of a man of the world, whether secular or religious (and sometimes it was difficult to always tell the difference), to know that male lust oftentimes worked in odd, if nonetheless all-consuming, ways. In his younger days, even he, Jamal, had gratified himself over images of naked women of all colors and creeds without discrimination, and he was still haunted by the frustrated, all-consuming lust that had so devastated his tragic time at university.

True, he was doing better now on both of those scores, but he still respected the power that such a formidable drive had over the male sex. If it was a test from Allah of some kind, whereby self-restraint and self-control in the face of such passion was meant to prove one's submission to Him rather than to the sins of the flesh, then, Jamal often wondered, why had Allah set the bar so, *so* high? Was he teasing men unmercifully? Why? He knew the spiritual answer of course, in purely theological terms; but in his loins he still felt he knew a deeper truth sometimes, a Darwinian one red in tooth and claw, and relentless in its control over the reptilian minds of men.

But what Jamal did know for sure was this. There were several dimensions to Mo's alienation from the world, most of which Jamal had instructed Mo in and convinced him of, but chief among them, at least in the boy's own mind, was his grievance against the Green family. That's why, Jamal supposed, Mo stole the iPhone from Kathy's father's shop—it was his way of getting back at her for her disinterest in him. So, Mo would have both the drive and the ability, Jamal further concluded, to take his revenge on the Greens to the next level: sexual assault, the systematic rape of *kafir* women in a time of war. Submission to Allah's will demanded such action. It was there, in the Holy Koran as plain as could be. He knew; he'd seen that very call to action himself—with his own wide eyes. And wide eyes, those of Mo, were what had greeted Jamal when he'd finally broached the issue of violating Kathy Green shortly before Mo's release from prison.

"Kathy Green?" Mo had said incredulously, as if he'd just been given the opportunity of a lifetime.

"Yes, Kathy Green." Jamal had let the silence hang there between them, trying in the midst of the pregnant pause to gauge Mo's emotional reaction to his pronouncement, and hoping that the simplicity of his command, and the two short words of Kathy Green's name, would find the cognitive purchase he was looking for, the emotional hook that would secure Mo's commitment to the cause. For a moment, Jamal had feared that his presumed infallible call to arms had failed; Mo's wide eyes had suddenly morphed from twinkling titillation to what had looked like almost catatonic stupefaction.

"Kathy Green, Mo. It must be done, Allah wills it."

"But..."

"*Allahu Akbar.*" Jamal had raised his right arm, and whatever Mo might have protested in that moment had remained locked deep in his thoughts.

"*Allahu Akbar,*" Mo had meekly repeated, as if there hadn't been anything else he could possibly have said. He had thought he'd been emancipating himself all those weeks under Jamal's tutelage, but his voice, his voice...it had suddenly seemed to come from outside of him somehow, as if really hadn't been his but someone else's.

That four-letter R-word: Jamal hadn't uttered it, but that had been what he'd meant—there could have been no doubt about it. *Could he, though?* God knows, he'd done such a thing many times in his dreams; Kathy had really wanted him, then, voraciously, like a bitch in heat, and he'd taken her, screaming and bucking, into wild orgasm. But then, the thought of *actually* doing what he had so often so lustily desired... He'd felt incredibly hot; his heart had started to thump like a galloping stallion, pulsing blood into an already stiffening penis. *Perhaps he could do it...* Then a depressing thought had pricked his potency: something in the nether regions of his brain had cruelly reminded him that he was still a virgin. He'd begun to tremble; he'd moved his lips like a dying fish out of water, mouthing inarticulateness as opposed to actually uttering it.

"The iPhone," Jamal had suddenly said. "Remember the phone, Mo? Why you took it? Remember what we said when we first discussed the incident?"

Mo had nodded in agreement.

"Good. Kathy Green is another iPhone, Mo. Of much greater consequence, I know, but Allah has made the pathway clear. We jihadis must deprive the apostates of what they hold dear, turn what they treasure most against them, destroy them from without—in battle—and *within*, destroy them from inside, from within their own hearts, like a cancer."

Mo's wide eyes had flared again with the memory of his having hurled the brick through the plate glass window of Green's Home Electronics...the grab...the chase...the shake down at Patel's Pawn Shop...the deliverance of *zakat* to the wide-eyed imam...the whole thrilling shebang...

The theft of the iPhone had given him an almighty rush all round, a thrill he'd rarely experienced before, and now he'd been offered the mother of all rushes: the abduction of a *kafir* woman and his taking of her against her will, as a trophy of holy war!

His lust had become sheathed in hate, but he could get off in a much bigger way than just coming inside her, having enjoyed the orgasm of his life. His seed would join the many millions from brother jihadis in having despoiled the House of the West—and in his case, the House of Green's Home Electronics—from *within*. And what had started out as petty criminality—the taking of the iPhone on an impulse—would be transformed into legitimate, glorious jihad. And if he died or got killed in the process, then so much the better, for then Kathy Green would be of no more consequence to him, replaced in Paradise by seventy-two compliant virgins, a reward fit for a true martyr to Islam if ever there was one.

Just how great could God be?

By God, he was really going to do it, he really was!

44

[November 2015]

Jo-Buck Brown's mom and pop as a rule didn't get many visitors—they really didn't care for many, if truth be told. So, when an unknown car pulled into their driveway they immediately looked at each other across their kitchen table with looks that said this can't be good. Another salesman? What could they possibly need at their time of life?

But when the car door finally opened and the guy got out, they knew that he wasn't selling anything—except patriotism, a chance at glory perhaps, if you were prepared to take the risk. And Jo-Buck had. And now they immediately knew. The one thing they still very much needed wasn't coming back.

Except in a few days' time to a place called Dover, somewhere out there on the east coast, up by Washington, D.C. The nice young marine said it could be arranged for them to be there when he arrived, if they'd like.

Yes, they said, they would.

But when they got there, they didn't see Jo-Buck. Just the box he was being carried in. It came out of the rear end of a huge plane, the likes of which they'd never seen before. It reminded them of Jonah and the Whale. But Jo-Buck had surely never "ran away from the Lord," had he?

But Pop Brown knew about the fog of war, what it could do to the best of men. And what Mom didn't know, he didn't think it was in his place to tell her. Pop took some solace that in the end the Lord offered Noah salvation, after all.

...

Salvation of a sort Minister McKinley presumed he would be able to bring John Buchanan Brown, if he needed it. But he doubted he did.

The flag-draped coffin, the marine escort, the gun salute cracking in the icy air of New Haven's graveyard said it all. A conquering hero had been returned to his home to rest in peace. Minister McKinley loved this stuff, the ritual, the ceremony, whether military or religious. He relished the starched, crisp uniforms, his elaborate robes, the pomp and circumstance; he wallowed in all the solemnity of the occasion, his primary role in orchestrating it. The citizens of New Haven depended upon him at times like this, just like they depended on the likes of John Buchanan Brown for their security.

Despite all the loss and all the tragedy, fighting the War on Terror was still part of God's plan.

And Christians, they were still marching as to war...

...whether that be as holy warriors...or as safe-at-home, gung-ho cheerleaders.

...

And amongst that latter group, of course, no one sang louder, none cheered with any more gusto, and nobody screamed bloody murder about destroying IS more vociferously than Doc Haldane.

But that was his job—to make the good folks of New Haven feel better. It was Hippocratic Oath 101.

And besides, the War on Terror was as black and white of an issue as you could possibly get, startlingly clear in its Manichean clarity as to who was good and as to who was evil. And it was surely no divine accident, was it, that those who were white—literally, as per skin color—were also, without fail, good, really good, chosen. No sir, Doc repeatedly harangued anyone who would listen to him, there was no doubt about that, at all.

Except perhaps, he sometimes worried in his rare, quieter moments when some serious reflection might take a hold of him, in the exceptional case of Jo-Buck Brown, that all-American local boy of Scots-Irish descent. It was so naggingly irritating, like something stuck between your teeth that you just can't help poking at with your tongue although you just can't quite dislodge it. In other circumstances, the ones the Doc would have preferred and tried to pretend was actually the case, the name Brown would have been just fine, perfect in fact. Nothing all that much more Scottish than Brown, was there?

But brown, albeit a lightish shade often unnoticeable in the summer, was also Jo-Buck's skin tone (he just couldn't bring himself to use the word "color"). No one else in New Haven, including the rest of the Brown family, looked like Jo-Buck in that respect.

And as for Jo-Buck's blood type, AB negative, how often had he come across that in his forty years of medical practice? It had been so rare that you might want to conclude that it was un-American.

But Jo-Buck was dead now. Did it all *really* matter anymore?

Better bury the sleeping dog along with the fallen hero, and hope that God wouldn't notice.

...

Miss Brodie, of course, was very upset to hear about Jo-Buck. He'd always treated her with such respect and caring attention. Childless herself, she'd come to see him as a surrogate son long before he'd left for war.

But when Minister McKinley first broke the news to her of Jo-Buck's death, she barely shed a tear. She didn't even inquire too much about what had happened, how he'd been killed, how long he might have been in hospital before the end. Indeed, if Minister McKinley had even told her where he'd been fighting and for what purpose, it wouldn't have made much difference to her. Some place called Mosul — where on earth was that? The War on Terror — oh yes, war was always a terrible thing, Donny had written her all about it in '44.

The only thing that seemed to occupy her mind concerning Jo-Buck's death was whether he'd still been wearing the good luck charm she'd given him on his last day in New Haven. Indeed, she was very anxious about it, as if the answer to her question, asked time and again like she desperately wanted a better response the next time, was the key to the whole puzzle as to why Jo-Buck had not come home, except in a coffin.

"Did he have King George with him, around his neck?" she'd kept demanding, pulling on the chain of her own crucifix like she was pulling on the emergency cord of a speeding train, trying to get it to stop before something very bad might happen.

"King George?" had come the usual puzzled reply, whomever it might have been from.

"Donny's half crown!" she'd berated them, frustrated at their ignorance.

But no one had known; the only thing they could attest to was that such an item had not come back with his body.

"The fool!" Miss Brodie had yelled, louder than she'd done for a good thirty years. "The silly young fool!"

But she'd known that for a long time, deep down in her heart of hearts, that the world was full of fools, but it had always been too much to sustain in her living consciousness for long, to try to deal with such a fundamental truth.

Like the Truth that commanded you couldn't tempt Fate too much, that you shouldn't play fast and loose with Lady Luck. Fortuna Belli didn't always play nice with Fortuna Redux, let alone Fortuna Faitrix.

It made her want to weep: but for the head of King George, a young life had been lost.

...

Bobby hadn't been at Jo-Buck's funeral. He'd been considered still a bit too young to attend. And everyone agreed that, on top of that, his adulation for his marine hero might well have ratcheted up his grief so much that the young guy might well have never recovered. What the eye hadn't seen, they'd hoped, the heart wouldn't grieve. Another sleeping dog to shovel dirt over.

But, of course, Bobby did catch wind of New Haven's great calamity; how, before long, could he have not? He might have feigned disinterest in what the adults around him might have been whispering about recently, but he'd heard enough to put two and two together, at least in the barest outline, enough to suspect that Jo-Buck wouldn't be coming home for some tragic reason. Moreover, on the day of the funeral, he'd seen them all donning their finest funereal gear and had sensed their dismal mood. In the end, one of the adults had finally let it slip, quite obliquely but still, just as they'd been about to set off for the First Presbyterian church. Everyone had paused, a great silence pregnant with nervous anticipation.

But Bobby hadn't so much as flinched: no wailing, no weeping, no tantrum with his arms and legs flailing in denying protest. Just a vacant stare, and then a turning away, ready to be escorted off to his temporary guardian's custody for a few hours, as planned. No one said anything, but they all knew what each of them was feeling. Thank God, looks like he might be alright, they said to themselves, fingers crossed.

Jo-Buck's burial had been held in glorious sunshine, but when Bobby made his own way to the gravesite two days later it was just starting to rain. But the first heavy raindrops were of no concern to him. He was on a mission.

When he first saw the freshly-constructed burial mound and the headstone at one end of it fronted with several bunches of flowers, Bobby couldn't quite believe Jo-Buck was really lying there beneath the pile of dirt. Even though he was in the open air, in the midst of the Great Plains no less, it felt almost claustrophobic. He thought he could even feel gritty dirt in his mouth. But there was no mistaking that this was the spot. He rubbed his fingertips over the engraving: *John Buchanan "Jo-Buck" Brown*. Even though he wasn't a great reader, that was a name he'd known how to spell for quite some time. If he'd gotten a dollar for every time he'd seen Jo-Buck Brown (or just Jo-Buck indeed!) in the local paper, well, he'd have had quite a stash by then.

So, it was true then, at least half true. Jo-Buck was back, but not home; still here, down there, but gone. He'd be able to visit him every day, but never see him in the flesh; talk to him, but never get a response. What kind of cruel joke was this?

Bobby reached into his waistband and pulled out the wooden dirk Jo-Buck had whittled for him. Its blade was blunted now, stained with bodily juices of God knew how many species of insect and animal life. It was even chipped in one or two places. It was in truth a sorry replica of Jo-Buck's original creation.

He felt bad about that, but it was too late now. Only one thing for it, it seemed, although why exactly he thought that was the case, he couldn't really say. Maybe, what he did was more an act of instinct, a gut reaction, than an appropriate ritualistic response of some kind, something like one of Minister McKinley's elaborate sacraments, all that chanting back and forth, the laying on of hands, the swinging of the censer chalice on its golden chain.

Whatever it was, Bobby did it quick, and then was on his way, like he'd seen a ghost.

Minister McKinley recognized it right away when he was shown it by his cemetery caretaker. "Good Lord," he'd exclaimed. "Just get rid of it, please. It's probably nothing," he'd unconvincingly added.

But he hadn't been able to not notice just how close to Jo-Buck's neck its blade would have been if he'd really been lying just a few inches, instead of six feet, below the ground.

45

[16 September 2016]

Saeed kept an extremely low profile after Mo had been arrested.

He made minimal appearances on the streets of Rotherham, and kept himself as much as practically possible within the confines of his room. He certainly did not venture out to visit Mo in prison; he couldn't face being in Mo's company, even if they might be separated by iron bars and a prison warden might be comfortingly nearby. Nor did he want to tempt Fate and put himself inside a place that might just be waiting for him anyway, before long, if his betrayed friend had already spilled the beans on his former accomplice.

So, Saeed felt increasing trepidation as the day of Mo's release got ever nearer. He wondered what Mo might do to him when he got out; for, short of fleeing Rotherham altogether for some undisclosed location, he knew Mo would sooner or later track him down. It was inevitable. The portentousness of this critical moment kept Saeed awake at night and permanently on edge during the day. He didn't know how much longer he could take it.

But when the fateful day arrived, it wasn't so much Fate as fête, although a rather more sedate kind of party than they might have had in their former times together—if they could have afforded it back then, that is. There was no confrontation at all; neither physical nor verbal assault from Mo as Saeed had fully expected. But Saeed could immediately tell that Mo had changed during his short stay in prison, nonetheless.

Mo seemed more assured, confident, even-tempered, although this new, improved Mo was not altogether a totally reassuring one, in some as yet precisely definable way. But what could he, Saeed, do about it, anyway? At least, Mo hadn't done him grievous bodily harm. Mo was still his best friend (pretty much his *only* friend), come what may; and, Mo had forgiven him, just like that it seemed, for his cowardly betrayal.

So, maybe Mo was a tad spooky now, post-prison; but perhaps, Saeed hoped, it would prove to be in a *good* way.

♠

[19 September 2016]

One day shortly after Mo's release, he and Saeed were ambling through the streets of Rotherham, as had long been their comradely, and sometimes therapeutic, habit.

It was an utterly pointless activity in strictly utilitarian terms, as it had always been, but Saeed was glad to get back into the old routine again, such as it was. The almost ritualistic nature of the activity comforted Saeed, such that his friendship with Mo was still, presumably, largely intact. Their silence, too, soothed like an unspoken bond; and the less said about the past, the better, in any case. But Mo, Saeed noticed, was not walking along in his usual signature slouch; he was striding, head held high, as if he knew where he was going, what he was going to do, their apparently circuitous wandering notwithstanding.

But, despite Mo's outward show of being confident and carefree, Saeed knew Mo was deep in thought—that he was itching to say something. Mo's telltale fake throat-clearing still gave the game away as much as it ever had; in that sense, his old friend hadn't changed at all. Saeed waited patiently for Mo's revelation, but on the bogus coughing and wheezing went. It wasn't long before Saeed couldn't stand the suspense any longer.

"All right, Mo, what—"

"I *need* you, Saeed," Mo interrupted, still looking straight ahead. Then he added in a voice that seemed to Saeed to echo back and forth between the house walls on either side of the alleyway: "You know you owe me one, don't you? *Big time.*"

Big time, big time, big time, big time...Big time!

At the very moment he'd almost felt finally rid of it, Saeed's guilt over his betrayal of Mo seemed to reverberate back off the pavement just in front of him and hit him square between the eyes. He stopped dead in his tracks. Mo took a couple of extra steps, and then stopped, too...waiting, insisting, *commanding*.

"Yes," Saeed said solemnly, "I do." He audibly gulped. "I do," he repeated—he vowed.

As to what his consent might be getting him into at that very moment, Saeed had absolutely no idea. And Mo was disinclined to reveal it to him. The disclosure, Mo knew, would have to wait until as near to the last practical moment as possible, when it would be too late for his friend to go weak on him— *again*.

Mo knew steeling Saeed for his jihadi task would be something of a Herculean task given Saeed's weakness over the whole iPhone episode, but Jamal had schooled him well, he believed, in the tricks of the trade concerning turning pimply, alienated youths into burgeoning holy warriors. Mo was sure he could find the hidden jihadi seed within Saeed's frail body and timid mind—he just *had* to now. Just as Jamal had helped him to cultivate his own new-found steadfastness, so now he, Mo, would help to propagate such steeliness in others.

A jihadi chain reaction had been set loose! And there could be no stopping it, *Inshallah*, for Mo had a special tool that Jamal hadn't had to help and guide him on his way. A really special one: the kind, it would be fair to say, that had already repeatedly hoisted the tech-savvy apostates of the West by their own mouse-clicking, Googling, petards.

♠

[20 September 2016]

"Get...off!" Saeed exclaimed, shoving Mo on his shoulder.

"Oh, fuck!" Mo said, playfully giving into the force of Saeed's push.

The knife see-sawed through the skin, then sliced into flesh, a clumsy butcher at work. Liquid crimson smeared its blade; soon the entire hand that grasped it, too.

"Shit!" Saeed stood up and grasped his forehead in disbelief.

"Oh my God!" Mo moaned.

Something inside the hood made it shake, like a live ferret does in a sack. Then it went still. The knife had almost done its job. The crimson was everywhere now, a jugular having been severed.

"Aah!"

The hood came free; a head, bug-eyed and already ashen, was unveiled, held by its straggly hair in lofted triumph. Both Saeed and Mo turned their heads away, but not so much that they couldn't still see what was going on. They were voyeurs of war porn with weak self-denial, and weak—as yet, untutored—stomachs. Saeed felt a glob of bile sour his throat, making him gag, on the verge of throwing up.

"Yikes!"

Saeed reddened and perspired from the combined effects of both embryonic nausea and the wild, synapse-searing excitement that was now engulfing him. He was totally transfixed by what was playing on the screen in front of him.

"Jihadi John!" Mo cried, as if the Savior had just returned.

"Jihadi John!" Saeed enthusiastically joined in.

Mo looked at Saeed. Saeed was hugging himself and rocking backwards and forwards, as if he was at prayer and praying as energetically as he ever had. Or, perhaps, Mo momentarily thought, his disciple-in-training had severe stomach cramps or, even worse, was about to wet himself.

"Amazing; fucking incredible!" Saeed gushed through his discomfort.

"Again?"

"Yeah...again!" Saeed burped loudly; foam oozed from between his lips. "Oh."

Mo clicked on the replay icon, and, on the screen before him, the image of a large black flag flapped and rippled furiously in the desert wind. The heavy fabric smacked loudly at the wind's angry behest, portending both threatening menace and vengeful wrath. Two pairs of spellbound eyes anticipated the black-draped, hulking figure to soon step into view again, and take up its position beside the hooded and orange jumpsuited kneeling form immediately to its right. The ominous presence, only its eyes, mouth, and hands exposed to view, spoke in a commanding, confident voice and waved a knife in its hand, punctuating its pronouncements as to the divine justice of its cause with dramatic jabs, thrusts, and parries.

"A Londoner... a Cockney fucking brother!" Saeed exclaimed. "Can you *Adam and Eve it*?" Saeed grinned at his joke. The bile had receded back down his esophagus, at least for now.

"Yes, I can *believe* it," Mo came back, and then his expression morphed into deadly earnestness. "Can't you?"

Yes, he supposed he could, Saeed thought. He looked at his right hand and wondered what it might be like…to be like Jihadi John. "Mujahid Mo and Salafi Saeed!" he proclaimed. "Butch Cassidy and the Sundance Kid! How about that, Mo?"

Mo rolled his eyes. "It'll do for a start," he grouchily conceded. He turned back to the computer. On the screen the bloodied severed head was dangling by its held hair again.

Saeed made a slow, sawing movement with his right hand. Yes, yes, he just might be able to…one day, maybe sooner than he'd have thought just a few weeks ago. And each time he saw the video, the nearer that day seemed to be approaching—at least that's how it felt. Maybe tomorrow or perhaps a day or two after that, when they'd inevitably have watched the video several times more, he'd be just a little surer. But what did it matter? Surely he'd never have to do such a thing? Whatever it was that Mo was planning, surely it couldn't be that? Saeed looked at his right hand, closed his fingers and thumb into a fist, and slid it silently into his pocket.

"Damn!" Mo said, still staring at the computer screen. "What would you give to be like J-J, eh?" He punched Saeed gently on his arm.

Saeed smiled weakly, but said nothing.

♠

[21 September 2016]

@fatmanK: see sister ayaan on inspire! ☺
@mujahidmo: sister?
@fatmanK: you better believe it. :<>

She was truly stunning; like Kathy Green, but even better. The high cheek bones, the blemish-free olive skin, the piercing sapphire-blue eyes. Even her hair—a bronzed auburn burnished to brilliance in the desert sun—trumped the blonde tresses that had formerly driven them both wild with desire. To Mo and Saeed, Kathy Green's Caucasian allure suddenly seemed sickly by comparison, a dazzling whiteness gone pasty, a casualty no doubt, they surmised, of northern English winters, sunless and relentlessly rain-swept, year in and year out. They gawked at the unknown woman's image on the screen, and then turned to look at each other, mirroring each other's exact movements and thinking their identical thoughts.

"Wow," they said in unison, "...*Wow!*"

"Who *is* she?" Saeed said, turning his attention back to the screen.

The heading on *Inspire's* web page said "**Ayaan**," in big bold letters; just Ayaan, nothing else. And no wonder: what else was there to say when you looked at her stunning portrait right below it?

"Ayaan..." Mo said huskily, as if the name was already some kind of mantra—the kind that held you in awe, made you weak at the knees. "She's—"

"Oh, my God," Saeed interrupted, "I can't believe this!"

"What?" Mo said.

"Look." Saeed pointed at the text accompanying Ayaan's picture. Mo read it out aloud, slowly, as if he needed to get the full measure of every word.

> In the Name of Allah, the Most Gracious, the Most Merciful.
>
> All praise is due to Allah the Lord of the Universe, and may His peace and blessings be upon his Messenger Muhammad and those who follow his footsteps. To proceed:
>
> The Americans have been driven back in Afghanistan, in Iraq, and now we are on the march throughout all of Mesopotamia. The return of the Caliphate is nigh; the End of Days is beckoning. And we are ready. Allah has delivered Ayaan to us, and she will help us secure our prize.
>
> The apostates and crusaders have cowered before car bombs, backpack bombs. Let's see how they will react next? Ayaan is a great scientist, trained by DuPont Company, the forger of weapons of mass destruction. But now Ayaan has come Home. She is building for us a Dirty Bomb. It is time to avenge Hiroshima and Nagasaki, all the apostates' crimes against humanity.

Are they ready? Are the apostates and crusaders ready? Ayaan is asking this question. Are you ready to answer her call, follow her example?"

"Dirty Bomb?" Mo repeated. "What's that?"

"Not sure," Saeed replied, "but if it's payback for Hiroshima and Nagasaki, then it has to be big, really fucking big, something nuclear most likely."

"Really? And *she* can make it?"

"That's what it says…Damn!"

Mo looked at Ayaan's picture again. She really was hot…those piercing sapphire-blue eyes. It felt as if they were looking right through him, deep into his soul, probing his psyche, testing his mettle. Yes, he was ready to follow her example. How could he not be? He thought he'd just about follow her anywhere she'd care to lead him.

"Come on," Mo said to Saeed. "Time to get our act together. Ayaan commands us!"

"Yes, she does!" Saeed chorused. "Oh yes, I'd say she does!"

46
[24 September 2016]

Mo picked up where he'd left off. He had to think quickly, remember what the situation was, how much he still had in reserve. You never knew when the next surprise might be sprung upon you.

It was almost pitch black in the narrow alleyways, and eerily silent, except for the occasional barking dog he or one of this enemies might stir up as they crept warily along, trying to reach the exit to the next level before the other did. Mo was quite relaxed at first, but the longer it went on the more nervous he became. After half an hour, he'd be totally absorbed, lost in the pixelated immediacy of his increasingly precarious position. He never knew if he'd make it out alive, but here he was again, and still in the game. But he needed resupplying, badly, if he wished to get much farther.

He turned a corner, his back up against a wall. *Rotate left and then right this time.* He could barely see three feet ahead of him. He listened intently, desperate to hear whatever it was he couldn't see. Nothing...or, wait, what was that? He felt his foot, apparently, bump up against something. *Slowly scan down.* A box. At last! Would it be empty? Or might there be a killer scorpion, or a bomb, inside—hopefully a prize? *Click.* The lid opened. Yes! Five hundred. *Automatic update: 850.* Enough to come back again if he survived the night.

But the flash, when it came, almost made him fall off his chair. Fuck! The box had been booby-trapped. Good thing he'd still had enough points so that he'd had the option to activate his body armor as soon as he'd logged in. *Ammo check: two grenades.* Nothing else. No choice but to go for it. He heard them both whistle through the air. He'd really gotten the hang of it by now. A body popped up just ahead of him, then it broke apart, limbs and hunks of flesh flying everywhere. *Aieee!* it screamed. Yes, five thousand! *Automatic update: 5850. Congratulations! 6350 with the bonus.*

Hasta la vista, baby. Level Three now; just seven more to go.

When Mo would come back the next night, he'd start off as Regional Commander. *Regional Commander!* A Jihadi John in all but name. And he'd have enough to decapitate an enemy or two if he managed to capture them. Hold their heads up by their hair in triumph—or as near as the pixels and the wrap-around goggles would allow.

And he did capture them, again and again; and he became addicted to summary decapitation, just like Saeed had, too. Two thousand points for every scalp—*irresistible*.

"Come on, Mo, my turn now!" Saeed looked as if he was in desperate need of a fix, bug-eyed and on tenterhooks. In a way, he was. He was a regular junkie now, just like Mo…

…and just like the rookie American marine in combat training a half-a-world away. Such a drug had become an essential part of his instruction too, his skill development as an effective fighting and killing machine in the cyber-ops battlefield of the twenty-first century's Global War on Terror.

Living on-line prepared you for real combat these days, so much so that it wasn't always easy to tell the difference anymore. *On-line? Real?* What difference did it make?

And how could you tell, if it did?

(Let me clue you in—you can't, and it doesn't. I'll admit, though, even I hadn't seen this one coming—never in thirteen billion years!)

♠

[25 September 2016]

When Mo tweeted about how well he was doing, his fellow cyberspace-travelers offered up unrelenting praise and encouragement: *Burn Baby Burn!* And, *Off with their Heads!*

They were like a great flock of e-parrots fluttering around his shoulders, and constantly squawking *Kill, kill, kill!* over and over, until you couldn't resist it anymore. And when they were not tweeting, he and Saeed were in chat rooms and meeting hundreds of others just like themselves from all over the world, all dreaming of the same thing and goading each other on, a literal budding caliphate in cyberspace presaging the real one, still yet promised, to come. They couldn't get enough of it; rain-swept Rotherham, the decrepit housing estate on which they lived, Mo's grumpy old man, and the fucking police all a million miles away — at least for a treasured while, moments they increasingly were loath to let go of and that came to define them, gave them an identity and a purpose they could relish in. *Relish!* What a delicious state of being that was!

The only fly in this jihadi ointment, however, which frustrated Mo and Saeed to no end, was that after a few days the article on and especially the picture of Ayaan on *Inspire*'s website, abruptly and without explanation, disappeared. There was no follow up; no updates about her whatsoever. They wondered why, what might have happened to her and her mission. A Dirty Bomb, another *Inspire* announcement soon thereafter informed them, had eventually claimed a great victory somewhere in Kurdistan, wherever that was. But there was no word about Ayaan being connected with the episode at all; and, damn it all, where was her picture? It was as if she'd been put down a Memory Hole — even Google couldn't find her.

Still, despite this success in Kurdistan, it very much looked as if the actual End of Days had been postponed for a while. The Dirty Bomb had flattened a few buildings, taken a few dozen lives, and spewed enough radiation to panic tens of thousands to full-fledged flight; but, other than that, the Global War on Terror still seemed to be trundling on, the Great Satan and its allies responding with more air strikes and drone attacks than ever, in a once-and-for-all attempt to be rid of the jihadi cancer that was Islamic State.

In the meanwhile, though, Mo still had plenty to be getting on with, not so much to any great apocalyptic lengths it was true; but what he was about was a pretty big fucking deal for him and his brothers, nonetheless. He wondered if Saeed was ready yet. Saeed had been certainly getting off alright on the video game they played every day and all the shenanigans on the social media they gorged on, but Mo still had no idea to what extent his friend was truly infected by authentic jihadi fever, as opposed to just playing at it. But, uncertain or not, the moment of revelation had finally come.

"Saeed…" Mo said, shaking his friend on his shoulder.

Saeed was on the computer trying to catch up with Mo and reach Level Six of *Sniper Alley*, and with the headset on he couldn't hear what Mo was saying. "Fuck," was all he said, apparently oblivious to even Mo's physical presence. Saeed's body jerked awkwardly in his chair as he clumsily manipulated the joystick. "Fuck!" he hissed again.

Mo grabbed Saeed's headset and ripped it off his head.

"Ow! What the—"
"We have to talk."
"Okay, but you didn't have to—"

"All right, I'm sorry. But do you have to be such a baby?" Mo placed the headset on the computer desk.

"So what's up?" Saeed said, rubbing his ear.

Mo sat on the edge of the desk, facing Mo and looking down on him from his perch. He wore his serious, schoolmasterly expression. Saeed knew that something pretty heavy was coming. He sat back in his chair and waited for the pronouncement.

"We've been having a lot of fun over the last couple of weeks, haven't we?" Mo began.

Saeed nodded his assent: "Yeah, we have." Now that he'd stopped to briefly think about it, he realized that they had had a blast. Somehow, they'd managed to leave the wretched reality of down-trodden Rotherham behind them, at least when they'd been on the computer, and the host of new friends they'd met online had introduced them to a universe they hadn't known had existed just a few weeks ago, a universe populated by folks just like them who were doing daring things…or were at least planning to. Since Mo had been released from prison, it had been the most exhilarating time of their lives. Saeed smiled at his friend.

"Good." Mo stood up and put both of his hands on the arms of Saeed's chair. Then he leaned in close until their faces were just a few inches apart. He locked eyes with his friend's. "The fun and games are over, Saeed. It's time to get serious, time for you to honor your pledge that you owe me one — a *big* one."

Big one? How big? A hooded figure, a black flag, a bloodied knife-wielding hand, a severed… The images flashed through Saeed's mind like a rapid series of short video clips mashed together for ultimate cinematic effect, while voices bombarded him with cries of "Kill, kill, kill!" and "Allahu Akbar!"

"What are you...surely you don't mean—"

"What?" Mo asked.

Saeed gulped, then drew the tip of his forefinger slowly across his throat, all the while staring at Mo with pleading eyes. He felt sick.

Mo held Saeed's stare, giving no indication one way or the other as to whether he was indeed asking for such a "big one" as that. He replicated Saeed's throat-slashing gesture with his own, his fingernail leaving a reddened trail behind it where it had slightly indented the skin.

Saeed winced. *God, he's fucking serious!* Mo's eyes began to twinkle, his expression showing the first signs of a confirming smirk coming on. Saeed's groin began to speak to him, signal a message of alarm; he wanted to pee so badly he thought he'd wet himself before too much longer. He writhed in his seat, trying to get up.

The smirk that Saeed had anticipated took an unexpected turn and morphed into a broad grin; then it propagated a laugh that spluttered before roaring into life.

"Ha! Ha! You dumb shit." As he got up off the desk, Mo gave Saeed a playful shove. He began to pace the room, struggling to contain his mirth. "Ha! You and me—throat slashers? Do you really think we're ready for that—yet?" He turned to face Saeed again, shaking his head from side to side, as if he'd just been told the stupidest thing in the world.

Saeed sat up, and gasped: "Well, no, I didn't really—"

"We've a lot to learn before we get to be Jihadi John," Mo said. "First things first; one step at a time. No, the big one is not as big as that—but it's still plenty big for Rotherham! It's our time, Saeed. Are you ready? Are you with me?"

Saeed blinked. Big still sounded big, unnervingly so, even if it was a step or two down from cold-bloodied decapitation. "What...?

"Kathy Green, Saeed. Are you ready to give her what she deserves?"

"Deserves?"

"Yeah. We're going to fucking kidnap her!"

"We are? Then what...? What'll we do with her?"

"Oh, nothing too much. Just keep her for a while. Teach her a lesson or two, get her down off her fucking high horse, put her in her place, for once. Get her folks worried; get that old bastard of a father of hers right where we want him. Maybe we'll get him to cough up a nice ransom for her 'safe' return. How about that, Saeed? That'd make Patel's measly pay off for the iPhone seem like total chicken feed by comparison."

"But we'll never get away with it," Saeed implored.

"Oh, yes we will. I've got everything planned." Mo shook his head like an over-confident Mussolini haranguing the adoring crowds from a balcony in Rome. "What do you think I was doing all that time in the clink? Twiddling my thumbs? Jamal taught me everything we need to know. And I wasn't the only one. There's four others he also trained who'll help us. They got out on the same day I did."

"But a kidnapping..."

"Don't go fucking soft on me, like you did—well, I think you know what I'm talking about, right?" Mo glared at Saeed, laser beams of accusation searing their weak-willed target. "Besides, we've been through all this, over and over. We're doing this for Allah. We're Muslims, Saeed, downtrodden Muslims. If others of our kind like Jihadi John can fight to their martyrdoms in Syria and Iraq and Afghanistan, then surely we can do our bit here in Rotherham, small beer though it may be by comparison. It's the very absolute *least* we must do. Right? Think about all of our brothers online who have supported and placed their trust, their *belief,* in us. Think what they'll say if we fail to follow through."

Saeed felt his heart shrivel in his chest, his will sapped by the authoritative insistence in Mo's delivery. He forced a smile, doing his damnedest to cloak his trepidation. "I won't go soft on you, Mo. Never, ever again. You have my solemn promise." Tears began to well up in his eyes.

Mo embraced Saeed, enveloping him in a great big bear hug. "*Allahu Akbar,*" he breathed in his friend's ear.

Oh God, Saeed thought to himself, whether He was great or not.

♠

[26 September 2016]

"Go!" Mo commanded Saeed.

Mo pointed his arm down the narrow alleyway, and then waved his hand, indicating left. Saeed followed his instructions, dodging and weaving as he went, crouching low, his bandy legs pin-wheeling almost like a cartoon character's, a Wily Coyote who's just run over the edge of a cliff and hasn't quite realized it yet. Mo grimaced.

Saeed gave Mo the "all clear" signal. He looked so deadly serious crouched behind the row of trash cans lined up against the alleyway wall. They were getting close now, and still the old gal hadn't realized she was being stalked.

Then Saeed blew the entire operation.

Crash! The clash of galvanized steel against cobblestones, then the rumble of a dustbin on its side and trundling its way towards the back of Ma Riddle's, the neighborhood crone's, unsuspecting legs. But just before the runaway bin could take them from under her, her hearing aids finally picked up the sound of its rapid approach. With an athleticism that defied her advanced age, she somehow managed to get out of the way before the dustbin hit her. The runaway receptacle trundled harmlessly past her, until it was finally stopped in its tracks by a telephone pole.

"What do you think you're bloody well playing at?" Ma Riddle yelled. "You stupid little—" Then she recognized Saeed, standing up now and in full view, a stupid expression on his face, as if he couldn't believe what he had done.

"Get the fuck back here," Mo whispered, as loud as he dare. He was still out of the old girl's range of cataract-hindered vision. Saeed turned tail, and began to run towards him.

"Hey, stop!" Ma Riddle cried out. "Just you—" But it was too late. Mo and Saeed had already turned the corner and disappeared. "I know who you are!" *Pakis*, she hissed, *should never have let the little sods in!*

Mo and Saeed only ran fifty yards or so before they stopped.

"Okay," Mo said, already winded, "that's far enough. The old rat bag'll never catch up with us." He looked at Saeed. "What the fuck happened back there? If we're going to pull the kidnapping off, there can be no fuck-ups. Okay?"

"It wasn't my fault," Saeed complained. "It was a big fucking cat's. I must have scared it up when I went to hide behind the dustbins."

"Cat? What cat?"

Yeeow! A great furry ball suddenly leapt at them from the top of the alleyway wall, claws already fully extended and aimed right at Saeed's face.

"Shit!" Saeed yelled. "*That* fucking cat!" He swung wildly, knocking Ma Riddle's mangy old tom cat to the ground. It hit the cobbles with a sickening thud, too old and fat to do the usual feline trick of always landing on its feet. It just lay there, stunned by its fall.

"Grab it," Mo said. "Put it in the sack." Saeed picked up the inert beast and stuffed it in the hessian bag he'd brought along, an essential part of the kit they'd need on the actual night of the "Operation," as Mo liked to call it.

"What are we going to do with it?" Saeed asked.

Five thousand points. Level Four. Now you could…

"Mo? Are you alright? Mo?"

"What? Yeah, I'm fine, just fine." Mo looked at the sack in Saeed's hand. It looked heavy.

"Well…? The cat?" Saeed said.

"Oh, yeah…the cat."

Saeed wasn't quite sure he liked the look on Mo's face.

♠

Mo held Ma Riddle's tom cat by its ears, straining to keep a firm grip.

The thing looked dead, although he could tell it wasn't by the slow rise and fall of its bloated belly. Drool seeped from the beast's mouth, a foul-looking yellowish liquid. Mo looked at Saeed who was staring at him in disbelief, half daring him to go ahead and do it (that would teach the old hag!), and half fearing that he just might. Saeed very much wanted to look away, but somehow he just couldn't—the show promised to be just too titillating.

Mo brought the knife slowly to the animal's throat, stretched taut by the weight of the obese body it belonged to being suspended in midair. The merest contact should cause the skin to tear right away, he'd calculated. A nice clean cut, clean as a whistle and worthy of the sacrifice the foul beast was making in the cause of jihad.

First, a drop of blood…

…then the drop of the knife.

Finally...that of Mo.

He'd passed out.

Saeed vomited in response.

The tom cat lumbered off, hissing as best it could.

Clearly Mo had reached his jihadi limit, Saeed thankfully concluded. Maybe now he'd call the whole thing off, *Inshallah*.

47

[October 2016]

But no such luck.

Allah, apparently, wasn't willing—and neither was Mo. If anything, his commitment to the "Operation" took on a whole new level of urgency and seriousness, post-failed cat decapitation. When he'd come round from his fainting spell, Mo had been mightily mortified. Thankfully, Saeed had declined to rag him about the incident (which was never spoken of again), although he'd whined a bit about how enough was enough already, and that perhaps they might think about laying low for a while, you know, regroup as it were, think things over a bit more, just in case Ma Riddle decided to spill the beans on what they'd been up to.

But Mo had parried all Saeed's entreaties in largely dismissive silence. He'd just looked at Saeed grimly, as if to command "Shut the fuck up, will you?" And he'd foiled the otherwise compelling logic of his friend's arguments with yet another emphatic, couldn't-be-argued-with, "You owe me, Saeed—*big time.*" And so, the "Operation," such as it then was, picked up whatever steam it still had left in it, and Saeed was trailed along helplessly in the inexorable wake of its unpredictable unfolding.

Over the coming weeks Mo stalked Kathy Green, like he was some sort of cloak-and-dagger private dick or something, while his four fellow inmates from Rotherham prison prepared the basement of the derelict house he'd picked out according to his specifications.

Saeed's job was to stalk Mo, to make sure no one was tracking his leader's movements. Mo was an ex-con, after all, and still on parole. But as a petty thief, Mo was pretty low on his parole officer's humongous list of parolees, growing ever longer these days, what with the increase in crime and the draconian budget cuts brought on by the recession. So, Mo was pretty much allowed free rein to go about his jihadi business, "slipping under the radar" as some would later put it, a fish assumed to be too inconsequential to spend the time and the energy reeling in, even if you knew it was swimming about down there somewhere.

Kathy Green had no idea she was being observed; she had no reason to—this was Rotherham after all, about as far from a beach in Tunisia as you could possibly get.

After a little over three weeks, Mo had Kathy Green's schedule all mapped out. She was *so* predictable that he was certain that no further effort would show up anything different in her repertoire, no matter how long he might track her every waking move. She seemed to live her life according to a pretty regular and rather lackluster routine. He was almost bored by it all; only the promise of the expected end result of all his labors kept him going. His prized sleuth's notebook read:

> <u>Weekdays</u>: living with parents; work (where else? Dad's shop) until noonish; lunch with girlfriends, always at McDonald's on the High Street; back to work until 5; home, stays in most nights, but on Wednesday goes out for a couple of hours to the community center for Pilates class.
>
> <u>Weekends</u>: lies in on Saturday morning (bedroom curtains never open before 11); tennis in the afternoon (if not raining); pubs and nightclubbing it in the evening with same girlfriends. Sunday: home all day, if sunny and warm perhaps sunbathing in the back yard in a spaghetti-string bikini (!!!).

But, best of all, Kathy didn't appear to have a steady boyfriend, hardly any male acquaintances at all, in fact. It made him think: *Surely not...a babe like her? Then again, if she was a bit partial to members of her own "team," then maybe what she'd got coming to her was all the more fitting!* In the pubs and clubs she strutted her stuff alright, obviously enjoying to no end teasing the dozens of guys who fell over each other trying to monopolize her attentions. But none ever succeeded; she resisted all of their slobbering and their clumsy attempts at groping her, and after the last club closed on a Saturday night, Kathy *always* went home alone.

Well, not quite... Mo was close enough on every occasion to be able to claim that he was just about escorting her there, even if she was not at all aware of his stalking, lascivious presence in the shadows behind her.

"Perfect," Mo explained to Saeed at the end of his almost month-long surveillance. "We can take her just about anywhere we want between downtown and her home, and at that time of night, there shouldn't be any witnesses."

Saeed hoped to God that Mo would be right. He sounded sure enough—a bit too certain, perhaps? Oh God...

♠

[29 October 2016]

Mo looked at his watch. The evening was cold. He wished he'd worn a bigger coat, but he didn't own one. Five more minutes, thankfully, and the place would begin shutting down. He blew in his hands trying to keep them warm—he needed his fingers to be nimble, not numb. His nerves were jangling with anticipation, anxious to get started now that he, Saeed, and the others had gotten things in place and were ready to put Jamal's plan into action. The "Operation" was finally good to go, and he was more than ready to be rid of having to frequent *The Pussy Palace* any more.

That night, as always, the club's boozy stuffiness mixed with the perspiration of a swarm of frenzied dancers all gyrating like sex-starved maniacs to the throbbing, pounding music had just about driven him crazy. The sorry sinful spectacle had thoroughly disgusted him. Kathy Green, in particular, had pricked his ire, so much so that he hadn't been able to take his eyes off her. She'd been practically half-naked in an outfit designed with teasing titillation, rather than modest dress, as being its prime purpose. It had seemed as every one of her alluring bumps and curves were on deliberate, ill-concealed display. He'd almost wanted to rush across the crowded dance floor and throttle her, right there and then, but he'd known a much better moment would soon present itself, if all went according to plan. Instead, he'd pushed his way through the crowded dancehall, and had joined Saeed outside in the street. They'd taken up their position hidden in the shadows some thirty yards up the road from the club's main entrance, and had settled in, waiting for *The Pussy Palace* to finally empty out, disgorge its human refuse into the street.

"What time is it?" Saeed whispered. "Shouldn't the place be shutting down by now? I'm freezing...and I keep getting cramp in my foot. Ah!"

"Sssh!" Mo hissed. "Keep quiet, you fool." He jabbed Saeed in his ribs.

"Ow!"

"Throttle it, will you?"

"But—"

"Get back...here they come." The entrance to the *Palace* swung open violently, slamming against the iron stoppers, two mean-looking British bulldogs, meant to prevent the huge doors from hitting the brick walls to either side of them.

First came the blokes who'd failed to pick up a woman. They were truly a sorry looking bunch. Despite the promise of its name, *The Pussy Palace* perversely, so it seemed to a good many of its horny male customers, always hosted more men than women, despite the fact that the ladies usually got drinks for half-price, sometimes even for free when the owners got desperate enough to attract more of their number. But, of course, honey pots always tend to attract more bees than is often good for them, leaving a few gorged and the many feeling thoroughly cheated. These latter poor saps, the pimply "Frustrateds" as Mo thought of them, staggering from their over-indulgence in what they'd falsely hoped would be compensating booze, dejectedly made their way home alone, hands scrunched deep into their pockets and chins turned down into turned-up jacket collars. Some of them would stop momentarily to lean over the gutter or a rubbish bin before making a great noisy show of being violently sick.

Then came the few lucky "Winners," as Mo had once seen it, giggly, half-drunk girls flopping all over them and making a breast somehow available for a clumsy squeeze. Some such couples threatened to start fornicating right there in public, but just about managed to hold off, the guys frantically trying to hail a cab before the girls either thought the better of it, or, more likely Mo suspected based on his own (admittedly) limited experience, passed out.

Finally, after a pause long enough to hope that the coast was clear, came the girls who'd had a good time dancing and teasing—the "Carrots (the Bitches) Beyond Reach," one might say—but for whom enough was enough already. They'd milked the guys for all the drinks and dances they'd wanted, but they were surely going to fish in much better waters some day for someone they'd consider offering their favors to—men who weren't so desperate as to go clubbing it in Rotherham on a Saturday night, especially in a place like *The Pussy Palace*.

The Carrots (the Bitches) were Kathy Green's cohort, as Mo well knew by now.

Two women and a big bruiser of a bloke were the very last ones to come out of the club. They were engaged in conversation, but Mo and Saeed could not hear what they were saying. After a few seconds, the man went back inside, and they heard the sound of the doors being locked and bolted from within. Then the neon sign above the door went out. The two women exchanged a few more words, and then one of them set off down the street towards Mo and Saeed. As she passed under a streetlamp, Mo could see that it was Kathy Green, even though she was now wearing an overcoat and had a headscarf on. He knew her walk—he'd witnessed it a hundred times. He looked at Saeed and nodded his head, as if to say "Are you ready?" Saeed nodded back and held up a sack and a roll of duct tape. Everything was going according to plan. It was going to be child's play.

Suddenly, Mo and Saeed heard the second woman call out to Kathy, "Why don't you wait? Robbie'll be here any minute. It'll be no trouble for him to give you a lift home." Kathy Green stopped and thought for a second. Then she said: "Okay, thanks. Maybe I will tonight."

"Shit!" Mo hissed between his teeth.

Kathy walked back to the second woman, and they stood side by side on the pavement waiting for their ride, chatting and sharing a cigarette. They could have passed for identical twins, Saeed thought: same height and build, both in overcoats and headscarves. How come so modest, so nun-like, all of a sudden? Who were they trying to kid?

"What'll we do now?" he whispered to Mo, the first stirrings of panic already starting to seize him. "Where the hell did the other one come from? You said she'd be all alone for *sure*." He so much hoped that Mo was about to announce "Operation Aborted," but there was no such luck.

"Shhh! Let me think!" Mo hissed again. Jamal hadn't told him what to do if things went wrong; he'd made it all sound so easy, as they'd plotted together inside Rotherham prison. "Shit!" he said again. Maybe they'd have to call everything off, but he hated the idea of that. *Not now! Not now!* But the more he scratched his head trying to come up with a solution to their unexpected predicament, the more frustrated and anxious he became. A good nerve-wracking five minutes went by with the whole mission, his precious Operation, about to go belly up. He couldn't breathe; the clear cold night air suddenly seemed strangely suffocating, as if they'd been time-machined somehow into the depths of a dense tropical jungle, saturated with a thick layer of lung-constricting humidity. He feared that he might die, there and then, a failure yet again.

With Mo starting to gag like he was, Saeed was sure the women would detect their presence before too much longer. "Mo! What are we gonna—"

Suddenly, the second woman's voice became quite loud and much clearer, as if she was upset about something. "I can't understand it. Robbie's never this late," she complained. "I'll give him a call. Can't imagine what's keeping him."

"Oh, never mind," Mo and Saeed heard Kathy Green reply. "It's not all that far for me to walk home, and it's such a beautiful, clear night. Maybe your bloke fell asleep or something. No need to wake him up on my account. Come on, I'll walk you home first. We'll be alright. I've done it loads of times on my own with no problem. Nothing'll happen—it's only Rotherham after all. Look at it; dead as a doornail as usual!" Kathy gestured at the empty street with a dramatic sweep of her arm. There was no sign of life whatsoever.

Her companion hesitated, her cell phone open and ready for dialing. She looked up and down the street, then at the clear night sky, the Milky Way in all its twinkling glory and the Man in the Moon smiling down beneficently on them. "Okay," she said. "It is a beautiful night." Then with a playful laugh she said, "That Robbie'll get it when I get home!" She linked arms with Kathy Green and off they went.

When the two women had passed by them and gotten some thirty yards farther on down the street, Mo tugged Saeed's sleeve. After his near-asphyxiation, yet another unanticipated turn of events seemed to have revived his can-do spirits again.

"Come on," he said, "let's go."

"But there's *two* of them," Saeed cautioned.

"No matter, we're not backing out now," Mo commanded. "Two for the price of one's even better!"

"How the fuck are we going to deal with two of them? I only have one sack, and how are we going to tape both of them up with just the two of us?"

"I said 'No matter.' Now come on!"

Mo took off, like a panther on the prowl. Saeed paused just for a second, before robotically following Mo's lead, just as much afraid to be left behind as he was about engaging in an act he'd no confidence they could at all handle.

Mo and Saeed kept a good distance behind the two women until they were in the residential neighborhoods where the lighting on the streets was much less prolific than in the city center. Then they started to slowly close in on their prey.

Engrossed in their conversation, the two women had no idea that Mo and Saeed were following them. About halfway back to their neighborhood, Kathy Green and her new friend entered the public park that provided a shortcut to their homes. They disappeared into the tree-shrouded darkness. Only the weak beam of a small flashlight that Kathy had retrieved from her purse indicated where they were on the narrow pathway that cut diagonally across the grassy expanse.

"Perfect!" Mo whispered to Saeed. "Come on, this is it. *Allahu Akbar!*"

Mo began to run; Saeed followed suit, his sack at the ready. They were soon right behind the two women. The beam of the flashlight swung around and partially caught Mo in its weak glare. The women screamed and started to run. Mo almost tripped over the flashlight that one of them let fall to the ground in her panic. Despite the stumble, though, Mo soon had the slower of the women within reach. He lunged forward and grabbed her. They fell to the ground. The other woman kept on going and soon disappeared again, hollering for all she was worth for someone to help them. A straggling Saeed, running awkwardly with the opened sack in his hands, finally caught up with the tussle that was Mo and his captive rolling around on the ground.

"Bag her!" Mo ordered.

Mo had the woman's arms firmly within his grasp. She couldn't move. Saeed put his sack over her head and then taped the neck of it around her throat. Soon, she was almost suffocating and her screaming stopped. Then her body went limp — she'd passed out. Saeed taped her wrists behind her back, then her ankles too. Trussed up like safari kill, she was carried off by Mo and Saeed into the night.

"We did it!" Mo said, as they arrived at their getaway car. "We fucking did it!"

"*Inshallah,*" Saeed added, not exactly sure what it was they had in fact done. He looked at Mo, concern already beginning to etch lines in his fore-head.

"Don't go soft on me, Saeed," Mo admonished. "None of your usual softness, do you hear me? Come on, let's get this shit heap started up and get out of here!"

The boys bundled their victim into the back seat of the car, Mo sitting half on top of it in order to "keep it quiet." Saeed scrambled into the driver's seat and turned the ignition key. If a car's ignition system could feel pain, it certainly sounded as if it was having an acute case of appendicitis right then. There was an almighty screeching, but as to an engine bursting into life there was no sign.

"Pump the fucking gas!" Mo ordered from the back seat.

Saeed stomped on the accelerator, while still continuing to torture the car's electrical system. But it did the trick, and off they eventually kangaroo-hopped to their rendezvous with jihadi destiny.

The one time they'd finally gotten up the courage to nick Saeed's dad's old jalopy, Mo thought through clenched teeth, and this is what it had come to — *Keystone Cops!*

Could anything else possibly go wrong? They'd often swore that they wouldn't be seen dead in that old rust bucket, but the odds that they just might do so seemed to be rapidly shortening, lurch by gut-wrenching lurch. It was all Mo could do to not throw up.

♠

Later that night in the basement of an abandoned house in Rotherham, six young, second-generation, Pakistani-English Muslims stood in a circle around the bound and trussed body of a young white Englishwoman lying on the floor. She had a sack over her head. She was not moving.

"Well," one of the men said, "let's see our prize."

Another bent down, cut the tape, and removed the sack.

Mo flinched ever so slightly. It wasn't what he'd been expecting. It wasn't Kathy Green.

"No matter," he said, "one white bitch is as good as another, *Inshallah*."

"Oh, God," Saeed gasped, slumping back against the cellar wall.

I knew it, Mo thought, exasperatedly.

48

Barton, Chance and Carruthers
SOLICITORS AT LAW

18 August 2017

Mr. Robert Roberson
29 Saracen Lane
Rotherham
South Yorks S61 9JD

Dear Mr. Roberson:

As Ms. Jillian Dalrymple's solicitor, I have been asked to send on to you the enclosed letter from her, and to advise you on the situation with respect to your future relationship.

Ms. Dalrymple wishes to remain *incommunicado* while she seeks further medical attention, and deals with the ongoing legal matters with which she is currently engaged. Both of these issues will most likely consume several months, if not well over a year. In the meantime, and until you receive further guidance from me, it is Ms. Dalrymple's express wish that you do not try to contact her or find out her whereabouts.

We sincerely hope that you will be able to honor both Ms. Dalrymple's wishes and her legal rights as expressed in this communication. If you have any doubt about what these legal rights mean with respect to yourself, please immediately seek legal counsel, including my own, if it would assist you.

Neither Ms. Dalrymple nor I wish for you to unintentionally get on the wrong side of any legal prohibitions that may apply to your future conduct vis-à-vis Ms. Dalrymple. I apologize for my bluntness on this matter, but I hope you can appreciate my desire to make sure that both Ms. Dalrymple and, indeed, yourself, maintain unimpeachable legal standing. I am also sure that you can appreciate the difficult position Ms. Dalrymple is currently in, and that she needs maximum protection right now.

Ms. Dalrymple wishes you to know that, although she does not wish to communicate directly with you or to see you at this moment in time, she does not in any way whatsoever wish you any ill will, nor does she seek to intentionally or unnecessarily upset you. Indeed, she continues to hold you in nothing more than the highest regard.

Yours sincerely,

Caroline Carruthers LLB

Barton, Chance, and Carruthers
Solicitors at Law LLP

2 Castlegate
Sheffield S3 8LG

/enc

♠

Dear Robbie:

I'm *so*, so very sorry that it's all come down to this, but, as I told you some time ago in my last letter, there's nothing I can do about it, anymore. I'm completely spent, at the very end of my tether. In fact, it feels like it's strangling me, cutting my head off, almost. Maybe that's what it'll take eventually—if you know what I mean—some sort of decapitation, then a new head, a new mind—yeah, a fresh start as radical as that. All I can hope for now is that you'll someday, perhaps, come to fully understand where I'm at right now, how so very helpless I feel, and that *somehow* you will be able to find it in your heart to eventually forgive me. And when you do, I hope that you'll already be in a good place, having started over yourself, *however* you may want to do that.

    Don't quite know why I've just thought of it right now, or why I'm bothering to mention it. But it's the diary I wrote when I was in the cellar. I figure you must have wondered about it, what was in it. I know you must have some inkling from the two or three excerpts presented during the trial as evidence, but there was a whole lot more in it than that, as you might well imagine. I don't suppose you've actually had the chance to read it, right? No, of course not. The police must still have it under lock and key, considering it's evidence. At least, that's what Caroline, my solicitor, says. They wouldn't let you see it even if you asked!

Right? And you probably wouldn't want to, anyway. It wouldn't be the pleasantest thing you've ever read, you must know that already.

All that time down there, alone with my thoughts, my fears, my regrets. I wrote a lot of different stuff, much of it ranting, I dare say I'd think of it now. Can't remember everything of course, and I was out of it at times, delusional, confused, that sort of thing, probably saying a few things—personal stuff, mostly, I reckon—I hadn't really meant, *at all*. I bet if I or anyone else read it again now—although, believe me, I hope I never see the thing ever again, I wouldn't wish the experience on my worst enemy—we'd wonder what the fuck I'd been thinking! It was a bad time down there, Robbie—anyone would have been half out of their minds, don't you think? Not known three-quarters, perhaps more, of what they were saying.

Anyway, I was wondering, did you ever get to hear about the title I gave it, "Jihad for Dummies"? Yeah, "Jihad for Dummies"—just like you used to say, remember? I thought back then, when we'd been watching all the news about the *jihadis* and Islamic State, that you were making such a horribly sick joke, and I hadn't really appreciated it much at all. But now? Well, it's all still a sick joke, except that the joke's *real*, it's really fucking happening, and it's a thousand times sicker than your attempt at dark humor. And the joke's been very much been on me, too—that much is oh-so-fucking clear. And I'm still *not* laughing—*far* from it. I wonder now if I'll ever truly laugh again, I really do.

For the love of God, Robbie…What's been going on? What the fuck's still going on?

Can you tell me? Is it all really just dumb stuff? A comical farce? Nothing more than that?

Well, I guess that's it—that's all I have. I'm spent, just about empty.

Except to finally say, find forgiveness, Robbie, if you can. Like Jesus said, "Father, forgive them (all of us!), for they know not what they do."

I haven't always known, that's for sure—especially in that cellar, especially in this bad time for us both.

Godspeed.

Jillie

49

[4 January 2017]

The next time Jamal Shirani saw Mo Hussain again, it was in the form of a grainy black-and-white photograph of him on the front page of *The Rotherham Advertiser*.

At first, he wasn't sure that it was his former disciple; Mo's head was partially covered by a blanket that a police officer had been apparently shielding him with as he was getting out of the back of a paddy wagon on his way to court. But the flash from a reporter's camera had made Mo suddenly look up, straight at the lens, and, even though the top third of his head was still obscured by the blanket, Mo's telltale birthmark in the shape of a crescent moon on his left cheek left Jamal in little doubt as to who the prisoner was.

Mo had been caught, that much was obvious. But caught doing what, having done what? Dare he hope that Mo had succeeded? At least well enough?

Jamal could hear his heart start to race a little, thumping rapidly in his chest; his breathing became labored, cresting on his anxiety to find out what Mo had accomplished. He licked his lips, then began to read the accompanying article to the photograph.

The headline read:

Muslim Youths Terrorize Local Woman in Basement

Yes! Mo and his gang had actually done it, and he, Jamal Shirani, had been their guide, the mastermind behind their plot, their jihad against the House of the West. The debacle of Russell Square had been avenged, at least in good measure. What might be next?

Jamal turned back to the article and eagerly read on, hungry now to ascertain all the gory details, and to revel in the all the hurt, anger, and panic white Rotherham must now be feeling. Okay, so Mo had been caught and his interrogation and trial might well result in even more trouble for Jamal himself. But it was that kind of reactive rage and calls for vengeance from their victims that jihadis like Mo and he thrived on. The apostates' rantings were succor to their souls, fuel for their jihadi mettle; and the more they ranted and raved, the more the news of what Mo had done, and hopefully his, Jamal's, role in all of it too, might go viral—*would* go viral—on social media, and the more others like Mo would inevitably be recruited to The Cause. And on and on jihad would snowball like this, until the caliphate was finally built at last, bringing the House of Peace to the House of War.

Such sweet triumph! *Allahu Akbar.*

But as Jamal read on, disappointment began to rapidly set in. There were no gory details whatsoever (quite an omission for the scandal-mongering *Advertiser*, he thought). All the report said was that a young, single white woman had been kidnapped by a gang of six English Muslims of Pakistani descent. The victim—an anonymous she—had been kept prisoner in the basement of a derelict house in Rotherham for several weeks, but no specifics as to what had been done to her there, nor the domicile's address, were forthcoming. The case "was still under investigation." The article certainly strongly intimated that rather unpleasant goings on had taken place in the basement—it wasn't too hard to read between the lines—but "in order to protect the victim's privacy," no name was reported and no photograph of her provided.

As to the alleged plotters, they were identified by name, but more as primitive, subhuman Pakistani youths, being genetically inferior in some greasy, dark-skinned, exotic sort of way, than as heroic, *Übermensch* wannabes of a Mohammedan persuasion. They were depicted, by the UKIP-supporting reporter, as brutish beasts, vermin, who just didn't know any better, and who were likely to engage in acts of depravity almost as a matter of course, the result of a fundamental toxic trace element in a terribly debauched and alien culture. The boys were thugs, pure and simple, given opportunity to show their true colors by a supine, let-anybody-in, immigration policy, a shoddy defense of the much-blighted English realm in these sorry, post-imperial and EU-despoiled times.

Holy Warriors? Not the merest hint. *Jihadis?* Perhaps, but only in a very pejorative sense, wherein the capital "J" stood for "Jackasses," instead. Jamal wondered that if this was all there was to the story, whether he wanted it to go viral at all! He'd prefer to bury it, if he'd been able to; but he was helpless, still inside prison.

Even worse, it turned out, was the fact that it had been one of the plotters themselves who had gone to the police and tipped them off. Apparently, this unnamed individual, a close friend of the ringleader, Mohammed Hussain, was "cooperating fully with the authorities," according to his lawyer. *Plea bargain, no doubt,* Jamal concluded. A so-called jihadi —one of *his*, no less—turning Queen's evidence! Jamal angrily scrunched the newspaper up into a ball and threw it across the rec room.

"What's got your fucking goat all of a sudden, Shirani?" the warden on duty said, unused to seeing the usually calm and collected Jamal so irate. "Bad news, is it?"

Jamal said nothing. He just got up and shuffled back to his cell.

He slept little that night, and on the next morning he told his latest class of recruits that their sessions had had to be suspended for a while—perhaps a good while. He wasn't feeling too well.

♠

For the next week, Jamal only ventured out of his cell when the wardens forced him to or when the daily routine required him to do so. The rest of the time, he mostly lay on his bunk, seemingly in a bout of depression, his co-prisoners quickly speculated—it happened to them all, sometime or another, it was to be expected. But as to specifically why he was so morose, they hadn't much clue, and they none too much cared to find out, either.

For the first two or three days, his latest batch of acolytes did hover nervously outside his cell door waiting for him to call them back to class, but when he didn't, they soon gave up and reverted to engaging in the rather more raucous activities that was normal for most inmates. The wardens wished Jamal would come out of his funk and get his groupies back under his calming influence again. They wondered if they ought to call in the shrink to attend to him. But just then "the letter" arrived — on Friday, January 13th.

The governor himself delivered it in person, much to Jamal's surprise.

"I'm sorry this has been opened," he solemnly said. "But, as you know, we're required to. It's unfortunate…I mean…Well…here you are."

The governor offered the envelope to Jamal. Jamal saw the clean cuts where a letter opener had done its surgical work. Seeing the thin slit of an opening in the long top edge of the envelope, he already felt as if some awful revelation had already been made, had escaped before he knew it. It was a manila envelope, too, official looking. Had Mo spilled the beans, after all?

Jamal took the letter from the governor's outstretched hand, then fished out the single piece of paper from within.

9 March 2015

The Embassy of the Islamic Republic of Pakistan
34-36 Lowndes Square
London SW1X 9JN

Dear Mr. Shirani:

It is with immeasurable regret that I have to inform you that *Laila Parveen Shirani* was killed in a most unfortunate incident near her home in the village of Palosi Peshawar, Pakistan, on the afternoon of January 12, 2015.

It is understood that she was attending the wedding of Ms Hermione Pigott-Smith, the granddaughter of her former employer, Lady Judith Pigott-Smith, when the celebrations came under attack by armed fighters of Tehrik-i-Taliban Pakistan (PTT). We believe that she died instantly. Unfortunately, her body was blown up in the attack, and no remains were recovered.

I understand that you are the sole survivor among her close relatives. It appears, however, that Ms Hussein left no will and no tangible assets.

Please be rest assured that the government of the Islamic Republic of Pakistan will leave no stone unturned in bringing these terrorists to justice. The government is as incensed by their murderous brutality, as you must be in your time of grief.

Please feel free to contact me if you need any further assistance.

Sincerest condolences,

Jawad Jahkrani

Assistant Attaché

Jamal continued to stare at the letter after he'd read it for the second time. His widowed grandmother, his father's mother, was dead—murdered by, well, guys like himself. He wanted to ask the governor if the Pigott-Smiths were dead too, but quickly concluded that he probably wouldn't know. In any case, what did it matter now? He'd had no love for the Pigott-Smiths, faux-aristocratic holdovers from the old colonial administration of British India who had decided to stay on after Pakistan's independence in 1947. But his grandmother, Nanny Laila, had remained dedicated to the family long after she'd retired from being their cook for almost half-a-century. She was like a third grandmother to Hermione; the Pigott-Smiths, in her small alien world, had been as close to blood relations as one could get without actually being so. Indeed, Jamal had wondered at times as to whom Nanny Laila had loved more: Hermione or him? Had that been why, Jamal suddenly thought, he'd not gone to see her when he was in Pakistan at the training camp? He could have, but he hadn't. And now he'd never see her again.

Jamal realized he was tearing up. Of course, in the bigger scheme of things to which he and outfits like Tehrik had recently dedicated themselves, such lives were almost insignificant, pointless even, except as legitimate targets for jihad. They were lives, after all, all-too-consumed with the petty fripperies of life, all that "loving thy neighbor as thyself" crap, all that supine fawning before white Christian smugness; and, in return, all that pretense that the ex-colonial elites took their commitment to *noblesse oblige* at all seriously, hearts bursting full of *agape*, as they so pretentiously called it, and their so-called Christian charity meant to keep the downtrodden down and forever grateful. It was all so hypocritical, pathetic — so *inauthentic*.

But then, *right* then, with that letter in his shaking hands, Jamal wasn't so sure anymore. He *loved* Nanny Laila, and now she had been taken from him, *forever*. Why, for what purpose? Well, he knew what the Tehrikis would say, and before today he would have agreed with them — if it had been *somebody else's* grandmother who had been blown up for being in the wrong place at the wrong time, for consorting with the apostates. But this was *different*. They'd blown up Nanny Laila, *his* Nanny. Maybe she'd sinned, but she had loved, and loved deeply and freely, embracing all who had felt the comfort of her indiscriminate affection.

No, in the great scheme of things, her end didn't justify the means of her death at all. Her life was beyond measure by such mortals as the Tehrikis and, indeed, himself, he now realized. Only Allah could judge her...but if so, he now puzzled, why had His judgment been so harsh? Surely Allah would not want to say that Nanny Laila was, like the Americans liked to claim, just unfortunate "collateral damage," whose death was somehow justified by the Laws of War, holy or otherwise, would he?

Jamal felt incredibly empty. Everything had gone so terribly wrong. He sat on his bunk with the letter hanging loosely from his fingertips.

"Shirani?" the governor said. "Jamal, are you alright?"

Jamal slowly raised his eyes to look at the governor, but they were vacant behind the watery sheen that glassed them over.

"I'm very sorry for your loss," the governor lamented. "If you need anything, *anything* at all, just…well, you know how to get in touch with me." He hesitated for a moment, caught between the thought that he really ought to say more and the pointlessness of actually doing so. He just grunted, signaled to the warden that he was ready to leave, then stepped out of Jamal's cell and clip-clopped his way down the echoing passageway to the sanctuary of his office.

As the warden prepared to make his absence too, Jamal suddenly broke his silence. He pointed to his books. "Warden? Would you take these away? I don't think I'll be needing them anymore."

"Including this?" the warden inquired, indicating Jamal's Koran.

"Yes…that too."

♠

Jamal lapsed into despondency, maybe even clinical depression, although, if so, it was left undiagnosed and, therefore, untreated.

He refused all entreaties to see a prison psychiatrist, and when one was sent to see him anyway after five days of his stubborn resistance, Jamal just clammed up, refusing to speak or respond in any way. The shrink tried a couple more sessions, even bringing along some candy to try and tempt Jamal to open up. The psychiatrist thought at first that the chocolate might have done the trick. He believed he saw Jamal smile slightly when he saw the candy, but his apparent pleasure was merely momentary and the smile quickly dissipated, never to make a re-appearance in his presence again.

When the psychiatrist visited Jamal for what would turn out to be the last time on the last day of January, Jamal was as usual totally unresponsive. But when the doctor got up to leave in frustration, Jamal quietly retrieved a *Yorkie* bar from his pocket, still unopened.

"'Not for Girls,'" he softly said.

"Excuse me?"

Jamal picked up the chocolate bar and held it out towards the psychiatrist, so that the famous slogan was facing him. Then he raised his eyebrows and tilted his head slightly, as if to say "Don't you get it?"

But, no, the shrink didn't get it at all. And that's the way they left it between them.

♠

Still, the confection had performed *some* kind of trick for Jamal. It had made him think about Mo a great deal, as if he was almost infatuated with his former disciple.

By now, it was quite clear to Jamal that Mo had not ratted on him. But neither, evidently, had Mo's snitch of a sidekick, whoever he had been. That could have only meant, Jamal concluded, that Mo had not even told his closest associates who had been the mastermind behind their operation. Such loyalty — for that was surely what it must have been — blindsided Jamal, caught him, at first, emotionally unprepared to recognize and appreciate it.

But, soon, he found himself thinking over and over again, like a line in a song you just can't seem to get out of your head, "Mo—poor, wretched Mo." The mantra consumed him, day and night; he felt emotionally ensnared by it, like a struggling fly caught in a Venus' flytrap with no way out. But it wasn't long before he realized he'd become, rather, its willing prisoner; so much so that he didn't feel as if he was *in prison* any longer at all, despite the bars, the wardens, and the incessant rattle of keys and the clanking of locks echoing throughout the entire cell block with that sense of metallic finality they seem to possess. Paradoxically, in the pit of his despondency a seed of joy had begun to germinate in him, struggling to life. Someone, apart from his now dead Nanny Laila, *actually* respected him, so much so as to take the fall for him. Perhaps, like Nanny, Mo even…

He had to contact Mo somehow. He just had to.

♠

[Early February 2017]

It didn't prove all that difficult to establish contact with Mo, just as any number of other supposedly prohibited activities in prison was relatively easy to get done—especially if you knew who to talk to and you had the *right* kind of baksheesh readily to hand.

Beneath the impressive-looking layers of official rules and regulations, a series of decidedly unofficial networks proliferated in Rotherham prison, all meant to circumvent most, if not all, of the various strictures coming down from above. As in imperial China, "the mountains were high and the emperor—the governor—was (in essence) far away."

It took Jamal just a couple of weeks to procure the right amount of dope, tobacco, porn, and cash necessary to get the appropriate backchannel to work for him. But at least the effort required to procure such items—extra work in the prison laundry, trading what few personal items he had, and doing personal "favors" of one kind or another—and the prospect of hearing from Mo again, all got him out of his funk. The governor and his staff were much relieved by this unexpected turn of events. Maybe Jamal might be salvageable after all, they dared to hope.

Jamal's message to Mo (he had no idea where Mo was, but somehow, magically, the network did via its internet-like distributed intelligence) finally got sent. It was a simple, one sentence missive, scribbled on a small scrap of paper and handed over to the first of many couriers who would ease its passage through the complex maze that was the entire prison system's communications backchannel. Jamal waited anxiously to see what the clandestine plumbing might blow back.

But there was no blowback at all, not even the sound of a gurgling drain. Jamal anted up even more baksheesh to see if he could get his contact to find out what the problem was, if the system was backed-up somewhere and needed a bit more laxative to get it moving again.

The problem was…well, the contact couldn't say exactly. His power to divine what was going on in the system as a whole was limited to the next link in the chain up from him, and who knew how many links there were after that? Besides, it didn't pay to ask too many questions, if you knew what he meant.

Unbeknownst to both Jamal and his courier, in fact, his message had, as promised, gotten through, in a manner of speaking. But it had reached its designated destination only to immediately find its way into an unexpected "memory hole" — totally off-script.

♠

Mo was reluctant to even take the message when it arrived — on Valentine's Day, of all days.

The last thing he needed was yet another lecture from his old man; he'd had a whole lifetime's quota of them already. When he asked the bloke who delivered the message to him who it was from, the guy just shrugged his shoulders and said, grumpily, "How the fuck should I know? I just deliver this shit. Could be anybody, for all I know. Do you want the fucking thing or not? I get my due either way. Makes no sodding difference to me."

Reluctantly, Mo sat up on his bunk and took the folded scrap of paper, a wrinkled, greasy wad now that it had been infused with the skin oils of a dozen grimy hands. The courier turned to leave, then said, "Oh, by the way, mate. I'd keep a low profile in here, if I were you. You know, don't get caught somewhere where they're no wardens about. We know what you're in for. Like a fucking taste of your own medicine, would 'yer?" He bent his left arm at the elbow, then slapped his right palm onto the flexed shoulder muscle. "Whoa! It'd hurt like hell, I'd bet." Then he laughed, grinning maliciously, before winking at Mo and blowing him a kiss of farewell...*for now!*

Mo unfolded Jamal's note, and read it:

Allahumma salli ala Muhammad. Oh Allah bestow your mercy on Mohammed.
-- Forever in your debt. JS.

Debt? That was just what the judge had said, that he, Mohammed Khalid Hussein, owed a debt to society, a bill that would take him at least thirty years to pay off. How in the hell was Jamal going to pay off his debt to him?

Mo ripped Jamal's message into small pieces, mashed them together into a pellet with his spittle, and then swallowed it in one gorging go. A *Yorkie*, he said to no-one in particular, it's not for girls.

No, siree.

♠

[17 February 2017]

Jamal could barely see what he was writing. The drops of moisture blurred his vision, making his words swim like hazy jellyfish in front of his eyes. It was the hardest thing he had ever written in his life.

Dear Miss Potter,

By the time you get this, I will be out of your life forever, except, of course, for the memory of the terrible, unforgivable thing I did to your father. There's nothing I can say or do to bring him back, or to bring you some solace in your grief.

He was in the wrong place at the wrong time— as was I. Our lives for just a brief moment came together in Russell Square, a totally unplanned encounter for both of us. He was just a poor homeless guy, down on his luck; me, I was sort of homeless, too, stupidly thinking that jihadi violence would find me a welcoming resting place. At the time, it seemed like your dad might have been suffering from mental illness, but if he was, it was nothing compared to my own derangement.

There's nothing left for me to do now, except one final thing. It's wholly inadequate, even self-pitying in a sickening way—for you and me both, I'm sure.

And that's to simply say I'm sorry, so very, very sorry.

The only comfort I take with me now is the fact that through my sin you found him again. I hope that knowing where he is now might bring you some comfort.

Salaam,

Jamal Shirani

Jamal folded his letter and placed it on the small table in his cell where it would be clearly visible. He'd already stripped his bed and rigged up the sheets. He tested them one last time with a sharp tug. He propped his steel bedstead up against the wall, lengthwise, making fine final adjustments and checking all the angles. He hoped to God it would work. It was going to be a rough go whether it did or, especially, if it didn't.

What a goddamn wicked fool he'd been! Jamal Shirani, a Jihadi John? How could he ever have believed such a ridiculous thing? How had he not understood the inherent evil of what he'd been about, an iniquity that had taken his beloved Nanny Laila and, by his own hand, that wretched old boy, Potter, too? Oh, he was small beer compared to 12/25, of course, but he realized now that in measures both great and small, religiously-inspired violence was truly running amok. Would it ever end? Perhaps not: when God or Allah's name was invoked, the sky was literally the limit. He knew because he'd once known it himself — but it was doubt that seized him now.

There was just one act he was sure of, still to be done.

♠

The governor looked at Jamal Shirani's face, frozen in asphyxiating struggle.

"Untie him," he softly said, having seen enough. He turned and quickly left the cell, unable, it seemed, to be able to remain long in the dead body's unnerving presence. He had a surprisingly weak stomach for his profession, and Jamal's grotesque body posture suspended by the sheet strung up high on the bedstead was threatening to bring up his breakfast.

He was well aware, of course, that Jamal had apparently given up on his "ministering," as he liked to think of it, including, it seemed, a total abrogation of his Muslim faith. But he hadn't quite expected this. The Doc hadn't signaled anything like such a possibility at all, and the wardens had reported that although Jamal was unusually despondent, he'd hardly seemed suicidal whatsoever. His appetite had been normal, and there'd even been a certain sereneness about him, despite his unusual mood.

He might have expected, in fact, that the loss of one's religious faith might have rather freed Jamal instead of driving him to such a senseless act. Abandoning religion had certainly done so for him — his secular humanism had afforded him much more spirituality than his former dour Anglicanism had ever done. But in Jamal's case, it appeared, a loss of faith had led to useless self-destruction. He could not quite get his head around it all: fanatical religious devotion could take you to the very heights of apocalyptic passion, enough to destroy the world and bring on the so-called End of Days, but, if you subsequently lost that piety, it could equally send you to the very pit of despair itself wherein pointless annihilation—this time, self-destruction—loomed yet again. Suddenly, the self-flagellants didn't seem half so-crazy as he'd always believed.

Perhaps, the governor thought, there but for the grace of God, go I... or was it, there but for the lottery that was serendipitous genetic evolution or sociological happenstance...? Any way he looked at it, though, made his head hurt—and he had a pile of paperwork to confront that day, not the least of which had been brought about by what Jamal had decided to do to himself.

The governor picked up his pen, and sighed deeply.

Dear Mr and Mrs Shirani, he began.
I regret...

50

[15 March 2017]

He heard it from a former colleague first, with whom he still had some episodic communication, before it was later confirmed for him in the obits section of the newspaper a few weeks later. The news of Jamal Shirani's death didn't altogether shock him so much as to fill him, first, with immense relief (plus *some* shame at feeling that way), and then, shortly thereafter, with renewed alarm.

Within three days of 12/25, Imam Khalifa had gone into hiding, or at least the best effort at such he'd known how to organize — which hadn't been saying very much. Despite his theological erudition, he'd been unexpectedly spooked shitless by the drone attack on the US Capitol, thinking that, whether Allah-inspired or not, the daring strike would truly usher in something like the much feared and anticipated End of Days. He'd been fully prepared for the no holds barred "shock and awe" that the American president promised to soon unleash, in what he'd declared was going to be *the* final act in the War on Terror. But there'd been no telling just when that great act of salvation might have come, or whether it would have come soon enough to save him from the bounty hunters Khalifa had been convinced IS must have already sent to track him down by then. Every reflection he'd seen of himself had appeared to display a severed head—*his* severed head—dripping with blood. He'd become so terrified that he'd effectively abandoned his wife and children.

When he'd first feared for his own head, Imam Khalifa had hoped the government might provide him with some sort of protection program, but any such avenue of escape had been quickly nixed when he hadn't been able to get anyone he'd phoned to either pick up their receiver or to return his calls. He'd fully suspected that those from whom he was desperately soliciting help were looking at the number illuminated in their "caller ID" displays, and immediately thinking the better of it. He'd quickly realized that when push had come to shove, he'd obviously hadn't curried much of a favorable impression with his former colleagues; after all, he hadn't exactly been the greatest at turning wannabe jihadis around, and Jamal—well, he'd done himself in with zilch actionable intelligence harvested to show for it.

So, Khalifa had fled—just like that, impulsively, in a moment of sheer, gutless, terror. He wasn't exactly proud of what he'd done, he hadn't even thought about what he'd been doing all that much at the time; he'd just done it, as if on complete autopilot. And now, here he was, holed up in the attic of some old widow's rundown house in the dank nether regions of south-east London, paying a couple of hundred pounds a month for a cold room, a lukewarm shower, and one gas ring that could barely heat a kettle for tea. The damp and the near sub-freezing temperatures during the long nights, as well as the lumpy mattress that gave no quarter, were also playing havoc with his hemorrhoids. If his stalkers — he was sure he'd seen someone shady following him over the last day or two — wanted a piece of him, well they could cut those inflamed irritants out as soon as they'd like!

He looked at the tube of Preparation H on his rickety nightstand: empty. His stomach growled: empty, too. He thought of his wife and children, but, try as he might, he couldn't hold them in his thoughts for more than a few seconds. His eyes kept focusing on the tube, distracting him like it was a hypnotic neon sign. He suddenly laughed, almost demonically: that capital H suddenly spelled out "Hegira," preparing to do the Hajj. The thought of "Preparation H" as constituting one of the Five Pillars of the Faith unexpectedly amused him. But he didn't laugh for long. If his faith was now no more than a source of amusement, he knew he was truly lost. It was far too late to contemplate preparing for the Hajj, now.

Too late for Jamal, too. He had failed the boy…and he'd failed himself. His faith was as empty as that tube. *He* was as depleted as that flat thin piece of squished metal casing.

Khalifa leapt from his bed, as if he'd just gotten an electric shock. He went over to the small window that looked down onto the street. He carefully inched the filthy lace curtains back so that he see outside. It was pitch black, except for the cone of weak illumination emanating from the lone streetlamp below. Was there anyone there, perhaps one of Jamal's acolytes come to exact revenge? But there was nothing, just one of the feral cats that were rapidly taking over the crumbling, aging neighborhood, doing its nightly rounds.

Khalifa looked up at the night sky; rain clouds were scuttling across the face of the full moon as if they were in a great hurry to get somewhere important. The attic window faced north, towards the Thames and Westminster. He was struck by the halo effect the city center lights projected over the silhouetted skyline, a sea of residential rooftops stretching out before him until the skyscrapers and tower blocks took over.

He searched for the comforting dome of St. Paul's cathedral, but it was nowhere to be seen. The monstrous-looking so-called Gherkin, he suspected, must have been hiding it. The scene reminded Khalifa of the last day he'd been with Jamal in the interview room, with Jamal seated across from him, a drizzly view of the city center behind the boy's head, portending, Khalifa now realized, his gloomy future, as predictably as the English weather patterns that swept rain across the country from west to east like it was a purely mechanical process—*unstoppable*.

Where was Jamal now? he wondered. In Paradise, in Heaven—or just rotting away, six feet under?

And, what was Jamal's former gang up to these days? What thoughts consumed them, now? Did they still think of Jamal; did they care about what he'd done to himself? Some of them, he knew, were behind bars, but not all. And those who were inside no doubt had plenty of time to think—just like he, unfortunately, did.

Khalifa heard a click behind him. It made him jump. He turned around and saw the single element in his space heater quickly losing its never more than half-hearted glow. The meter had run out again. He searched for a fifty-p coin, but he had none.

He caught sight of the empty Preparation H tube, disappearing into the on-coming icy gloom. But he saw no joke there now; it wasn't a laughing matter at all, anymore.

♠

Once, his and Saeed Karlal's universes had just about rubbed shoulders.

They had come well within the "six degrees of separation," of course, that everyone seemed to prattle on about as if it really meant something; and in fact, on one occasion, they'd physically occupied interview rooms just a few yards down a long institutional-looking corridor apart from each other.

While he had been failing to get anywhere with Jamal Shirani at that moment in one room, in another, Saeed Karlal had been augmenting on his bean-spilling about what had happened back in Rotherham with the "bitch in the basement" to a counter-intelligence officer from Scotland Yard, in order to escape punishment. But Khalifa had known nothing of this almost chance meeting of their ways. He'd come to know much later about the anonymous co-conspirator who'd been "cooperating fully with the authorities," as the newspaper report had put it when a certain Mohammed Khalid Hussain and his gang had been arrested, but there had been no possible way in the world he could have connected that specific being to a certain Saeed Karlal.

And now, after that near collision, he and Saeed were thousands of miles apart, although both, in their separate ways, had been bounced to either side of the Atlantic Ocean by, in significant part, the very same event: the Big One, 12/25. But while Khalifa had imprisoned himself in a lonely, rotting garret, afraid for his life, Saeed Karlal was "free at last," pursuing the American Dream—at least he'd believed he had been.

♠

"Welcome to Dallas, son," Pastor Rich Warble had said, as Saeed had stumbled into the terminal at DFW, still druggy after his long flight from London.

Saeed had looked at the hulking figure in front of him; it had been larger than life in more ways than one. The large round eyes had beamed as if they'd just seen the Lord and Savior himself, right there in the terminal; the voice had boomed as if it had been literally God speaking, via Skype on some waiting passenger's opened laptop, from the distant heavens. Saeed had flinched as the being's massive, ring-manacled fingers had lurched forward, grasping for the top of his head. Before he'd known it, he'd been forced to his knees.

"Let us pray," Warble had chirped, looking beatifically up at the terminal ceiling as if somebody up there might have been listening, ready and waiting to receive the gratitude their munificence had been due.

Right here? Saeed had thought, while Warble had rambled on about God-knew-what. But that hadn't been all: when the pastor had boomed his last "Hallelujah!" the gaggle of folks he was with had broken into song!

What had he done?

What he'd done was this...

Miraculously, Saeed had come to America to attend university, to pursue the higher education he'd always dreamed about. And it was all going to be free: his tuition, his books, his board and lodging, even his spending money, although, as Pastor Warble had forcefully explained, the latter was going to be strictly limited, of course, so as to make sure Saeed was not tempted too much by sinful pleasures — he was a "recovering Christian," after all. Saeed had wondered about such a designation at first, but had quickly decided to let it go, for what difference could such a label amount too when the trade-off was such a great fucking free ride?

"They're going to do all this for me?" Saeed had asked, incredulous at such generosity, especially after 12/25, especially for a British Muslim they'd never met and who had only missed being convicted of "terroristic threatening" and "grievous sexual assault" by the skin of his squealing teeth. "*Who* are they again?" he'd said for the umpteenth time.

"The 'Apostles Against Apostasy,'" the president of the Rotherham Rotary Society had confirmed, tired of sounding like a broken record already. He'd been the magistrate who had agreed that Saeed, who'd received high marks for his "cooperation" with Scotland Yard, could go free for turning Queen's evidence; he'd been a do-gooder judge who'd believed in second chances, especially for poor impressionable youths having been lured into wanting to be wannabe terrorists. For a guy whose job it had been to strictly apply the law without quarter, he'd felt the stinging moral (or had it been the guilty?) weight of "He who has not sinned, let him cast the first..." all his sorry life. "'Triple-A for the Way—to the Lord,'" he'd added in a sing-song voice, parroting the Dallas-based organization's mantra.

"Sounds a bit—"

"Yes, I know, but think about it. A chance to get out of Rotherham, and start over. And if it doesn't work out, you can always come back. We've agreed to buy you a return ticket if you should ever need it. Bert Green, our Treasurer, has signed off on it."

Bert Green? Saeed had puzzled. *Kathy's dad? Fuck! God, what price a pardon, what price anonymity?*

"But why...why are they doing all this *for me*?"

"Well, they consider it's the Christian thing to do, especially in the wake of 12/25," the Rotary president had explained. "Don't ask me to clarify all the logic of it, but it seems that the triple-A folks are pacifists. They oppose all kinds of violence, including that of the American government." The president had paused, seemingly not quite believing what he'd been about to say. "To cut a long story short, it seems that they want to save you, not just from your own sins, but also from the blind rage of their very own neighbors, those Americans who'd just as soon round you and your co-religionists up and send you all to Gitmo, or to see you dead—an eye for an eye, a tooth for a tooth...a drone for a drone, if you like. I suppose, in a way, they feel sorry for you, see you, perhaps, as a kind of an 'American Adam,' youthful innocence lost in a world of corrupting sin. In any case, if you want to, you can walk out of here a free man with a free future. It's your choice, Saeed."

Saeed had been stunned. He'd never heard the word "free" used so many times—and all of them with reference to him, after all he'd done! And he'd had no idea who the hell an "American Adam" was supposed to be; but if he fit the bill (and the reward!), then bring it on, he'd play the part. His sense of residual guilt had almost tripped him up at the last moment, but it hadn't been enough, and he'd decided to walk. What difference could have staying put and facing the real moral music have made then? And if those Apostle guys, or whatever they'd called themselves, had really felt sorry for him, well, he'd rather quickly and comfortably concluded, who was he to have turned the other ungrateful, self-denying cheek?

After the hymn singing had ended, Saeed had walked right out of DFW and into the Land of the Free. And things went well for a while, *ree-all* swell, as Warble had liked to drawl it out.

Unfortunately, Saeed focused too much on the new big things in his life, like his classes and his new cute Texas girlfriends, all knocked silly and pliable by his "terrific accent" that they all "just *a*-dored." But— wouldn't you just know it?— it was a relatively little thing that got him in the end—*jaywalking!*

He was in downtown Dallas, on his way to meet Brunela, a Latina beauty whose skin tone gloriously matched the meaning of her name: "brown-skinned," although, to Saeed's admiring eye, a delicious "golden-bronze" seemed much nearer the mark. Coming down Main from the east towards El Centro College, where Brunela was a student, Saeed had a date to meet her for lunch—and she was buying! He hoped she'd soon join his unofficial harem of female admirers, a nice addition to his, as yet, exclusively Anglo set of girlfriends.

Just ahead of him, he saw a gaggle of students milling about in front of the main entrance to El Centro, late morning classes having just emptied out. Saeed was on the opposite side of the street, so he had a good view of the college's entranceway. He searched the throng for Brunela. At first, he could barely distinguish one amazingly good-looking female from another, but suddenly, there she was, waving at him, her huge smile welcoming his presence revealing two sets of pearly white teeth—like his own had once been before the endless cups of tea back in England had done their dirty work.

He waved back, and then began to jog. The sooner he'd get to Brunela, the better; too many hunky-looking *hombres* hanging around her for his taste. He took a quick look to his left out of his usual English habit, as he swiveled his body to angle it towards the curb: the traffic was going away from him, so fine, he semi-consciously thought. He took a confident leap into the road.

He heard the horn before he felt anything hit him, and straight away he'd realized his error— *Dumbshit!* he'd said to himself. *Fucking dummy!*

As he fell forward, his eyes picked out the horrified ones of Brunela, just a few yards ahead of him now. She'd dropped her books, and a hand covered her shock-stricken mouth. For a moment, Saeed felt a surging warmth rather than the searing pain he'd expected. Everything slowed down, almost to a stop, and he almost felt like he was floating. Brunela's eyes glowed sapphire-blue, and suddenly he thought of...Kathy...Kathy Green, then the myst-erious girl on *Inspire*...Ay...

And then, like folks always do when they draw their very, very last breath, he was staring straight into mine, and wondering what the fuck was going to happen next, whether there'd be an afterlife, a trip to Paradise, or just sweet FA. Poor fuck.

What had been the probabilities that he'd be done in by a road accident as opposed to being a hapless victim of the War on Terror?

Well, we all know the answer to that one, don't we—serendipity notwithstanding?

♠

If Mohammed Khalid Hussain had heard how Saeed Karlal had met his end, he might have laughed were it not for the tragic outcome. "*Jaywalking?*" he would have exclaimed. "Just like that dumbfuck. Total dufus 'til the end!" As you can see, looks like Mo's piety, such as it had ever been truly pious, soon started to wear thin after his return to Rotherham prison, bucking the trend of so many inmates finding confinement conducive to being "born again," in one way or another. But cussing's so easy to fall afoul of, isn't it? Even for me!

But Mo never learned of Saeed's unfortunate demise. He was largely *incommunicado*, as it were, at Her Majesty's pleasure, and in solitary for the foreseeable future in Rotherham prison for his own well-being—if you get my drift. Not even the convicted murderers took too kindly to rapists, especially if they were Pakis, too.

Of course, if he'd've had the wit to figure it out, he might have appreciated the brutal fact that if he could have had it, jaywalking might well have been a fine thing right then—minus the physical disagreement with a passing car, that is. But he wouldn't know that until it was far too late: that on his release thirty years later, crippling arthritis would have already confined him to a wheelchair.

Not much of a chariot for a former holy warrior, is it?

Go figure.

51
[The Void, Star Date: Alpha-Omega 7]

When the president of the United States heard the news on 12/28, he was both sickened and devastated; he even wept openly on national TV that night. (Ah, such pathos! Gets you right here, doesn't it?)

Everyone knew it had been coming, of course —I may well move in mysterious ways sometimes, but not on this one. But those who could have made *some* sort of difference to such an outcome had repeatedly refused to act (original sin notwith-standing). You couldn't, they smugly had said (and invoking my good name without *my* permission, to boot), transgress the Bible or the Constitution. Indeed, for them—especially the Second Amendment worshippers—the Bible *was* the Constitution, and vice versa, as if both tomes between them made up the double-helical structure of so-called American Exceptionalism's cultural DNA. And besides, the politicians' "open secret" about gun legislation had pragmatically demanded that they *had* to tow to this faux theological-cultural line whether they had wanted to or not, especially if not doing so meant losing significant campaign contributions from the NRA, invoking the ire of Wayne LaPierre, and besmirching the hallowed memory of Charlton "From My Cold, Dead Hands" Heston.

But *this*, apparently, is what made the Leader of the Free World *really* cry: Thirty-nine dead, eighteen critically wounded; and all of them children under the age of five, apart from the two adults who were with them at the time. The biggest such toll ever (up to that point, I ought to, sadly, add).

At the cemetery a few days later, thirty-nine teddy bears lined the entrance. Someone had sprayed red paint on them; someone, so it was said angrily, who had been trying to take Americans' God-given rights away from them, and make political hay out of the tragic loss of such innocent young lives. (Oh, the callousness of such a thing!) It was disgraceful, they'd indignantly added, getting high on their holier-than-thou rhetorical horses, just like the president's crocodile tears. What an actor, what a minstrel trickster! But it was no joke; it was tantamount to Holy War! (You'd think they might check things out with their *Supreme* Commander-in-Chief first, wouldn't you?)

The killer, when they'd finally caught him—a nerdy-looking, spotty, white kid with wispy bum-fluff standing in for what was supposed to be a full moustache and beard—had stared bug-eyed at the camera, and had smiled inanely, as if he'd been drunk, drugged, or perhaps just prematurely senile, like some sort of dumb-ass. Still, he'd had a gun, a big motherfucker of a semi-automatic, powerful enough to bring down a herd of elephants (or forty-one human beings) in less than twenty seconds. Had bought it at a gun show, just like that. No questions asked; no disqualifying secrets revealed. Crazy or not, he'd had a *right* that just couldn't be fucked with, a *freedom* to bear arms, even if it meant, perhaps, also bearing false witness. Like having added to the country's tally of 32,000 gun-related deaths a year, including 555 kids, a total far in excess of all those Americans who had been gunned down in war or at the hands of those crazy Muslim fanatics who we just really ought to have had kept out, just like The Donald had so wisely said.

Why am I telling you all this, you say?

To that I reply: Only a dumb-ass wouldn't know the answer to that, a dumb-ass who doesn't know one act of terrorism from another.

Open carry, stand your ground, the constitutional God-given right to bear an assault rifle complete with a large ammo clip; a mad moment, a flash of anger, neurons off their medication, misfiring badly; a perfect storm, and thirty-nine infants are dead—*that* enough terror for you?

♠

But in al-Adrum, the latest school shooting in America was the least of their concerns.

The new band of recruits was finally ready for jihad. And as they trundled out of the village in the back of the Toyota pick-up truck on their way to defend the caliphate, their younger brothers and sisters looked on in awe and waved them an exuberant farewell. The youngest of them, a boy no more than three years old, reached up and offered his favorite toy to his big brother leaning over the truck's tailgate.

But the loving gesture was never completed.

After the dust cleared, all that remained was a nodding donkey, splattered with blood, its crooked mouth and goofy eyes expressing a level of stupefaction quite beyond belief, as if the Great Toy Maker in the Sky (yours truly) had always meant the dumbass to look that way.

Looks like they didn't get it, either. Still, seems about par for the course.

♠

Ah, there he is! Should have known I find him there on a day like this.

It's Aaron Hoffnung—at least that's who he's been known as for just about all of his life. He's adopted, you see. His adoptive father, a former Navy Seal, rescued him on a secret mission somewhere in the Middle East when Aaron had been just a few months old. It had been a miracle, the father has later claimed on many an occasion, that Aaron hadn't been killed in the firefight like the rest of his family. *There but for the grace of God..*, he's often added, as an almost incredulous afterthought.

Indeed. It takes some believing, doesn't it?

Aaron must be in a pensive mood.

He always comes to the shore in Cannon Beach, his home town, when he's feeling like this. The almost constant strong winds here, he believes, help to sweep away the demons he thinks possess him—at least for a while. So, he's standing close to the water's edge now, letting himself be buffeted by the powerful gusts that whip up the heaving waves creeping ever closer towards him, surfing forward on the flooding tide. But he's a strong young man, at least two meters of superb athletic masculinity, so he's able to maintain his position looking out to sea. His olive-brown complexion reddens from the abrasiveness of the flying sand; his sapphire-blue eyes, straining, wince and water with the constant onslaught of Nature's fury.

What can he be looking for on a day like this? Even the surfers have taken shelter, and the local fishermen have stayed in port to mend their nets in the relative warmth of their boathouses. But scouring the vast ocean he undoubtedly is, as if he's either lost something out there, or he's hoping to find a treasure floating that he just *has* to have.

Perhaps, he's expecting a miracle of some sort. But even I can't see a goddamn thing out there, right now.

Wait a minute! He's shielding his eyes and standing on his toes. Has he seen something? Yes, what's that?

Surely not?

No, of course it's not. I knew it couldn't be. It's just another dead tree trunk washed down from the mountains, and now drifting out to sea. Enough miracles already! What does he take me for?

But he's angry now; he's kicking the sand furiously. His only bad trait, that violent streak of his; you never know when it might go off, when his life might leave the rails, and in a moment of madness, of dumbness, he might... But, other than that, he's a good kid, the kind I like to do good things for. He'll undoubtedly have a good life, for the most part; I'll try to make sure of that.

After all, what the eye doesn't see out there on the storm-tossed ocean of life, the heart cannot grieve — right?

Trouble is, as you know, I *see* everything.

But in Aaron, I see Ayaan.

It's almost music to my ears.

Made in the USA
Middletown, DE
12 June 2017